Below the Bottom Line

THE BOB STONE THRILLER SERIES

To MARILYN,
Enjoy the journey......

Eric J. Engelhardt

In Suspense Books
NEW YORK, NEW YORK

Below the Bottom Line.
Copyright © 2018 by Eric J. Engelhardt. All rights reserved.

This book may be purchased in bulk for promotional, educational or business use. For permission requests, email the publisher/author at: info@ericjengelhardt.com or call 631 495-4929

Published By: In Suspense Books (ISB)
July 3, 2018 AmazonBooks.com
July 4, 2018 Retail Book Stores globally through Ingram Spark

Cover Design by: Gus Yoo
Editing by: Holly Vossel
Book Layout ©2018 Book Design Templates

The Bob Stone Thriller Series (Book 1)
Title: Below the Bottom Line/ Eric J. Engelhardt —1st ed.
ISBN Paperback   978-1-7324021-0-2
ISBN E Book   978-1-7324021-1-9
BISAC: Fiction/Thriller

Library of Congress Control Number 2018946754

September 11, 2001

This novel honors the innocent victims and first responders who perished on that fateful day in American history known as 9/11. This story is dedicated to their families and to all those who continued to help at Ground Zero during the aftermath, who suffered from this tragic event. Additionally, this book is devoted to all those patriotic individuals who fight for our freedom and defend our country every day.

ACKNOWLEDGMENTS

For my wife, Lily, and my children, Natalie, Andrew, Ross, Alex, and my entire family, who persevered listening to my numerous readings along the way. Thank you all for being a part of my journey to complete this book and for your encouragement to follow my newfound passion.

For my parents: my father, Charles, who taught me the virtues of persistence; and my mother, Evelyn, who introduced me to the awareness that words have impact and consequences. A special dedication to my father-in-law, Arieh Korine, who passed away in June 2016 while I was writing this novel. I promised him that I would finish and publish this manuscript; he was the inspiration for one of the key characters, Ari Ahrdeni.

My thanks and appreciation to those professionals and to all my caring friends, who were willing to listen and advise me early on and throughout the writing process. Your valued feedback helped to bolster my confidence in this endeavor. Specifically, I wish to thank authors Colin Greer, Ph.D. and Susan Ducharme Hoben, who shared their knowledge with me, offered me their constructive thoughts and expressed that I had a unique story I should publish.

****

Quotes that have inspired this Author

What the caterpillar calls the end, the rest of the world calls a butterfly - Lao-tzu

The world of reality has its limits; the world of imagination is boundless – Jean Jacques Rousseau

Even if you're on the right track, you'll get run over if you just sit there – Will Rogers

****

PART ONE

CHAPTER 1

My head snapped back from the impact of the crash. I instinctively swerved to the right side of the road and was hit again from behind, much harder this time. The crunching sound of metal on metal shook me up. The air bag exploded in my face while the seatbelt squeezed my stomach until I almost threw up. A Jeep speeding diagonally across the street clipped my left front bumper, hurling my car into a 360-degree spin, until it hit a chain-link fence that absorbed the force of the collision.

No matter how hard I gasped for air, I couldn't satisfy my lungs. My heart was pounding. I tried to soothe myself with a quick pep-talk. *Just hang in there. Worst-case scenario, I'll give them all my money, my watch, or whatever the hell they want and it'll all go away.* Approaching my car were two guys wielding guns with burlap bags covering their faces, looking at me through preformed eye holes.

The first assailant shouted, "Hey tax man, get out of the car now. You'd better do exactly as you're told, if you want to live."

My pause to regain composure ended abruptly when the other attacker bellowed, "You deaf, Mr. Stone? Out of the car now!"

I was stunned they knew my name, so thoughts of a random robbery were out. My morale sank into a bottomless abyss as I now realized that I was targeted in a prearranged scheme. Following their instructions, I slowly opened the car door, pivoting to plant my left foot firmly on the ground. As my right leg followed, I cautiously shifted my stance to protect my core.

For a fleeting moment, I was amazed to see that the muscle memory of my martial arts training kicked in; I crouched down at the sight of a third assailant. He caught me off guard with a kick to my chest that put me flat on my back.

The men lifted me up to a standing position as quickly as I had hit the ground. I retaliated with a kick of my own, missing the knee of the guy who dropped me by a few inches. Out of nowhere, a fist crunched into my cheekbone . . . I was done.

While I was groggy, one of the men grabbed my jaw and pasted duct tape over my mouth. The other guys yanked my hands up over the roof of the car and taped them down wide apart. To make a final show of dominance, someone slapped the back of my head. I was now at their mercy, in a bizarre waiting game, while my mind was pondering the outcome of this attack; *these crazies went through all this trouble to capture me, so now what?*

All I could do was try to look around, so I shifted my eyes for a peripheral glance which allowed me to spot a hooded attacker positioning himself on my left. He reached into a bag and pulled out a syringe. The sight of that needle pushed me over the edge and I fought against my restraints, freeing my hands, but not before his glove covered hand moved above my shoulder. The needle was docked into my neck putting me into a state of shock.

A sudden inward thrust of foreign liquid painfully displaced my internal fluids. A moment later the needle was pulled out, allowing for some drops of blood to drip onto my shirt. My eyes crossed, then locked upwards to the middle of my forehead. Now dizzy and completely unstable, my knees buckled, dropping my dead weight to the ground.

As I lay there accepting death, I experienced a burst of visions starting with my father, the countryside lawyer, pacing in a courtroom and making his final plea to a jury. Then another vision of my mother setting up for a Fourth of July barbeque gathering, asking me to place the American flag on the front lawn—I must have been about age ten. The mental flashes moved to my wife, Laura, hugging me as the envelope she ripped open indicated that she passed the bar exam. A final vision appeared: Scrolling across my mind's eye was my laminated certificate etched in gold letters: "Robert J. Stone, Certified Public Accountant, State of New York."

These scenes ended with words spoken by a rough but fading voice, "Sweet dreams, tax man."

Darkness overcame me. Moments before everything shut down, I unexplainably thought of a strange incident which occurred a few years ago. On that fateful day, I made a flawed decision which would totally change my life forever and there could be no going back.

CHAPTER 2

There was a harmless dusting of snow on Friday December 3, 2010. The holiday season had already begun, that festive feeling was in the air. I had just wrapped up a tax audit representing a client at the Manhattan division of the Internal Revenue Service. As I reentered the street from the stuffy IRS office building, I noticed that the brisk early morning hint at winter had given way to a perfectly sunny day with a clear, bright blue sky.

Coming home on Fridays with flowers for Laura had become a tradition. While I was walking toward Penn Station to catch the train home to Long Island, I spotted a typical New York City flower store on the corner of Thirty-fourth Street and Seventh Avenue. One could not help but notice the flags billowing around the store front. A sloppy sign placed just above the doorway read "Under New Management."

What a joke, I thought. *How many times have I seen this before?*

It was typically the same owner misleading the public into believing that a new owner had taken over, when in fact, nothing at all had changed. And no doubt, it was a game to avoid paying taxes. Whatever was going on, I needed the flowers, and since I had lost a few clients recently, the interaction with a potential new client was stimulating for me. I decided to walk in and seek out a store manager or the owner. I hesitated as familiar inner random demons designed to poison my thinking popped up.

The inner voice spoke to me, saying, "You're an asshole. You screwed up after all these years and now you'll have to reinvent yourself. You're really walking into stores now to pick up clients."

I tried to shut down the negativity by reaffirming to myself that losing clients and my sudden lack of enthusiasm were just bumps in the road of life. I was thankful that I knew how to deal with it. I simply kept plugging away, vowing never to give up.

Once these thoughts faded, I decided to enter the store. I noticed the flowers presented in buckets by category and rows of assorted international oils, chocolates, sardines, and dairy products. There was a counter set up for smoothies, but that looked rather unappealing. The store lighting was dim to the point of bothering my eyes.

I noticed a guy stocking shelves to make them look full of product. His disheveled dark hair, thick eyebrows, and heavy beard were not a pretty picture. There was a noticeable scar on his left cheek. He managed to walk with an air of authority, possibly compensating for his left leg, which lagged behind him. It was easy to see that this guy had incurred plenty of injuries in his lifetime. I knew he was the owner, but he could never admit that, at least not now. It was part of the game.

I visualized flipping him my business card, followed by a pleasant exchange. The image I foresaw was a picture of a man who would smile back to me, one who would need my services. I could see myself picking up the phone in my office, and then hearing this guy asking me to come back. I projected that he was already my client.

I started my pitch. "Congratulations on the new business," I said.

I silently thought, *let the games begin*. I noticed he was cautious and refused to respond.

"My name is Bob Stone, and you?"

"Not my store, just worker," he mumbled. "What you need?" he asked.

There was no question in my mind—this guy was the owner. Paranoia was in his blood. He had to deny that it was his business. Most likely, he thought I was from the IRS or possibly from an immigration office. I sensed his fear and I suddenly felt sorry for him.

I gave him my business card and said, "Sorry to interrupt you. I specialize in accounting and tax issues for stores just like this one."

Okay, so I lied. I politely asked him to give my card to the owner. I smiled, gave him a look of confidence, bought a dozen long-stem red roses without the thorns, paid him, and left the store. I knew and he knew.

***

On Monday morning, only three days later, he called. My office phone rang.

"Hello, Bob Stone, CPA. May I help you?"

"My name Tommi. You at my store. I have you card. Come back to store. We talk, please?" the store owner asked with much humility. There was a heavy Middle Eastern accent with choppy English.

"Yes," I said. "Sure."

And there it was: The initial contact in his store last week, his positive response, and now, my chance to follow up. I smiled then mumbled to myself, *Hey, maybe I should've gone into sales years ago.*

"When would you like to meet?" I asked.

Tommi replied, "I in store all day, like prisoner."

Weird, I thought. *Why make a reference to feeling like a prisoner?* I decided to avoid the game of trying to look unavailable.

"I'll be back in your area tomorrow. How will that be for you?"

"Okay," he said. "Before twelve-thirty or after two. This my pray time."

"Fine, Tommi. See you at nine-thirty in the morning. Do you like coffee?" I asked.

"No." Tommi said abruptly.

Tommi's voice tone changed from submissive to controlling. Despite my sense that this guy was somewhat abnormal, I decided to follow through and return to his store.

The time prior to our meeting passed quickly. It was already Tuesday morning. After some coffee and toast, I took the train to Manhattan. The commute went fast, as I was eager to see how this discussion would play out. The train doors opened, and I carefully stepped off the platform. While walking up the steps to the street, I started to feel awkward and conflicted.

Once I reached the flower store, I took a deep breath, talking to myself, "What the hell, I'll keep an open mind and see how it goes."

I entered the shop cautiously, waiting for Tommi to greet me.

"Ah, come in, Mr. Stone."

I was surprised by his sudden improved English.

"Come with me, my friend," he said, his opened palm led me to the rear of the store. "My home is your home. Please sit down," he said.

I sat down at his messy table located in a disorganized back room he called his office. We were surrounded by crushed boxes and old products. The smell was offensive. Below the makeshift desk was a red carpet with intricate patterns. Clearly, it was not the usual rug. It was time to break the ice.

"Tommi, how long have you owned this store?" I asked.

He paused, gazed into my eyes, and then carefully chose the right moment to respond.

"Five yoors," he muttered.

"You called me to come back. How can I help you, Tommi?" I kept my mouth shut after asking, something I've learned over the years.

"Mr. Stone, no papers for store."

"What do you mean, no papers?" I impatiently asked.

Tommie doubled down, "No taxes, nothing."

"Do you have any letters from the IRS or NYS?"

"No. What to do now?"

"Are you set up as a corporation, Tommi?"

"No, my name only," he replied.

"Tommi, let me take a look at your business checkbook."

"No checkbook. All cash. No records."

I lost my composure. "Are you serious? What's up with you, Tommi?"

He slowly rose up from his chair, paused and said, "You tax man. You accuntint."

No matter how unpredictable his flow of speaking was at times, his humble demeanor made it difficult for me to be upset with him.

The next few minutes dragged on like the final seconds of a professional basketball game. We were locked in a tie score and I needed a time out to resolve my dilemma. *What should I do with this potential client?* An ominous feeling was in the air. I knew from experience that one client through referrals usually leads to many more of the same type of clients over time. Is this what I wanted—more retail store clients with little or no info? My professional side was against moving forward, but emotions clouded my thinking. My need for new clients took control. I was thirsty for a victory and my fragile ego needed a quick fix. I also wanted to show my wife, Laura, a rising star at the Law Firm of Combs & Walker in Manhattan, that I, too, was doing well in my profession.

This last thought pushed me over the edge. I needed to justify my decision and so, I started to convince myself why it was acceptable to work with this client. *Sure, just another business owner who needs tax help. After all, clients do have tax issues and I have the knowledge to clear them up.* In my ambivalence, I set up an escape hatch that might prevent him from working with me: I'll propose to him a huge fee. He'll say no. I'll respond with a "sorry." We'll shake hands and calmly call it a day.

I was so confused. My mind was running in six different directions. My forehead felt sweaty and my eyes began to blink intermittently. The moment had arrived for a final decision. I paused for a deep breath.

"Tommi, this is a big job and professionally, not good for me," I started. "You have no information, no checkbook, no bank statements, no invoices, no proof of sales—nothing." I went into my concluding remarks. "I will reconstruct your last five years of transactions, prepare your unfiled tax returns, and file everything for a total fee of fifteen thousand dollars."

I was waiting for him to reply with, "No way, too much money," as I had planned. I talked to him as if he understood me. I did not like playing into his poor English. Barely five seconds went by and he replied, with the confidence of an experienced businessman.

"Yes, that's fine, it's all good, Mr. Stone. When can you begin?"

I was taken aback by his sudden use of words to complete short, clear responses. My head was filled with a mixture of greed and fear. I knew in my heart that I had just entered into another world, like a child entering a dark cave for the first time.

He surprisingly added, "my real name is Ahmed, my friends call me Ammi, not Tommi."

"Okay, Ammi, or whoever you are, to get started, you must sign my standard new client letter." I was taken aback by his name game.

"Yes, I understand, you want...letter for us to work", he mouthed under his breath just loud enough for me to hear.

His broken English, his tool to deceive, automatically returned in a split second, timed perfectly. This guy Ammi was a clever man, an individual who had learned how to survive in a new land—a place far away from his prior world.

Damn, I thought. I was always concerned with trying to stay even up. Lose one client and go find another: the world of the self-employed professional. This new client was a solution to the pressure cooker. The fee was more than respectable, large enough for any CPA firm to have gladly accepted. So, yes, I accepted him and at the end of the day I remembered that a client is a client and they come and go. It was my reality, my survival, and I took ownership of my decision. The relationship was set as Ammi and I embarked on a journey born out of a mutual need to resolve each other's problems.

***

It was a difficult assignment. After a few weeks slipped by, I found a way to create something from nothing. I did not recall taking any courses back in college on creative accounting. However, I did remember being taught to spend more time developing the approach to a problem rather than diving right in.

I stepped back and took an objective look at this client's scenario. I would have to build up the figures using a common-sense approach. I had discussions with Ammi to clarify his cost of living. Turns out this guy lived off the store's annual profit to support his lifestyle, typical of most small business owners. The store expenses, such as rent, utilities, supplies, and so forth, were easy to gather. The impossible part was getting a handle on the sales figures. The best I could do was to approximate the revenues using the most applicable business ratios specific to his industry. This was as professional as I could be in this situation. I applied my skills, patience, and creativity until I was comfortable with the results.

After two weeks had elapsed, all five years of required personal and business tax returns were finalized. I lugged all my files back to the flower store in a wide brown briefcase, the dead giveaway that I was an accountant. This was the day, the moment of truth when I had to present everything to Ammi. I tried to walk him through the basics of the numbers, but he waved me off and just signed away on the documents, showing no interest for any details.

Then it was my turn. I needed to sign each tax return as the "paid preparer." My eyes intensely focused on the signature line. A pain hit the lower left side of my stomach, reminding me of an ulcer I once developed after overusing pain killers in between knee surgeries. I hesitated for the sake of a meaningless pause. At that moment, timed with precision, Ammi handed me a thick envelope.

"Here, this is for you, Stone. Count it."

I was in way too deep. Of course, he paid me in cash. He had no other way to pay, so I had no choice. This was troubling to me. As a CPA, I had no excuse whatsoever. I made it clear to Ammi that I preferred a normal business check and that either way I would have to report this payment in my records. He must be made aware that he could not hold me hostage in his world of cash activity.

I signed each tax return and shifted into the let's-make-the-client-feel-comfortable mode, sensing his helplessness.

"Don't worry, Ammi, I'll organize and mail everything out for you."

It would have taken too much effort to explain to him which tax returns should be placed into which envelope, and without question he would have screwed it up. Later that day, I mailed out all the tax returns and so, the deed was done.

The remaining issue would be Ammi's ability to pay all the various back taxes due, plus interest and penalties. Over the years, I had learned how to distance myself emotionally from various types of clients who occasionally used tax dollars to enhance their business cash flow. I realized that they always found a way to uncover the money to pay back taxes in the final hour, when the tax authorities put the hammer down. It was their way of life, their means of survival, and I learned not to feel sorry for them.

On this fateful day when I delivered the tax work to Ammi and mailed each of the past five years' tax returns to the Internal Revenue Service and to the New York State Tax Department, the Ahmed Flower Shop officially became a legitimate business.

A silent inner voice spoke to me and it would plague me for years to come. I knew that my father, the ultimate professional, the honest countryside lawyer, would have advised me not to get involved with this questionable client. The voice, possibly my father's, my own conscience, or both, harshly scolded me. *Bob, you lost your way. You compromised yourself. One day, you'll have to face the music.* This revelation would become my secret burden. I would be lugging this extra weight on my back for years to come. I learned to compensate for this flaw in my judgment by staying frozen in denial until someday—but hoping never—when I might be forced to confront the impact of my misguided decision.

CHAPTER 3

This one client, the Ahmed Flower Shop, eventually led to my office picking up more than fifty more clients all around New York City over the next five years: bagel stores, more flower shops, pizzerias, gas stations, and newsstands.

I was amazed how people from so many other countries had taken over these retail businesses. The ultimate shocker is how quietly over time even pizzerias, which were typically owned by Italians, gave way to Turkish, Pakistani, Indian, and Arabic owners. This was happening in cities throughout America.

Things had been going well for me with all these clients. As a professional, I always had mixed feelings about having allowed such a large group of these sloppy clients to be in my tax practice. They had little or no books, and no records. No matter how much I tried to change these clients, they never followed my constant requests for data. I pushed them and pushed them until I hit a brick wall. Most of these clients threatened to get another accountant the more I tried to elevate the info. The more I pushed to do better accounting and tax work, the more they got upset with me. They wanted no part of the world of accuracy. Keeping me in the dark was their way. The less I knew, the happier they were, and frankly, I could not be responsible for information of which I had no knowledge. It was the common thread that bothered me the most.

All of these retail stores were owned by foreigners who on the surface seemed to be gentle, respectful, and kind people. I would visit each store for the usual monthly ritual, even though in reality, there was not much to review. It was always the same greeting: "Ah hello, Bob. Please come in. Have some Turkish coffee. How are you and your family?" I was always made to feel wanted and important. That was their finesse, their unique style.

In November 2014, during my typical meeting at the flower store, Ammi invited me and Laura to his daughter's wedding. After four years of loyalty and cleaning up all tax issues, one by one, store by store, I suppose I had met the ultimate test of acceptance from Ammi.

The wedding ceremony was to take place on April 19, 2015, at a mosque located in Astoria, in the borough of Queens in New York.

* * *

The months prior to the wedding date passed quickly, as the day of celebrations had finally arrived. We were nervous since we had never been to a Muslim wedding before. Everything posed a question: how to dress, what gift was appropriate, how we should behave, and so on. Our better judgement was to dress nicely, but not too fancy. We decided on a beautiful vase, a more personal gift as opposed to money. The drive into Astoria in the early afternoon was nice and easy. On a side street, a parking spot opened as a car just pulled away—so far, so good. As we approached the mosque, I was in awe of the beauty of its dome. Laura and I entered the mosque. A quick scan revealed many of my tax clients were there, and of course, other guests I did not recognize. Making our way to a seat, I launched several warm handshakes, which was my way of showing respect for these clients. Then a wave of paranoia enveloped me. Sweat was slowly edging down my eyebrows, my hands were stiffening, and a nervous cough kicked in.

I turned to Laura and said, "I have to get out of here—now."

That same inner voice alerted me that I was in the middle of something wrong. We stepped outside for some fresh air. I calmed myself with a few deep breaths and then returned, just in time as the ceremony began. If we had entered seconds later, all eyes would have been locked on us. Suddenly, an official monitoring the ceremony asked us to separate, and then I noticed that the men and women were all sitting apart from one another. Stupid me, I was so focused on greeting my clients, I overlooked everything else. The man sitting to my left gave me a look of contempt as he shook his head when he noticed Laura and I sitting together amongst the men. I turned to him, shrugged my shoulders, and opened my palms as if to say "Sorry." He smiled back. I did not know this guy, but he knew I was out of my comfort zone. The ceremony began with a veil being placed over the bride and groom, followed by their recitation of a few prayers.

The man turned to me and said, "Next they bring out the wedding contract, it is called the *nikah.*"

They each repeated the word *qabul* three times. My new friend whispered to me, it meant that they "accept" each other. The nikah was then signed by husband and wife, witnessed by two others. Additional wedding vows were softly spoken, followed by the couple sharing of some food.

The man next to me said, "They each bite the sweet date next."

They plucked a date off a beige stem and shared the fruit; it was a special moment in the ceremony. The noises and clapping began, and assorted candies were thrown at them from all directions. The famous Jordan almonds, my childhood favorite, were being tossed around the room. I was dying to grab one off the floor to eat it, hoping nobody would notice, but I skipped it for fear of looking quite stupid. I shook my helpful friend's hand and thanked him for making me feel more comfortable. He replied with a smile.

The wedding festivities were set to begin in an hour from now, so Laura and I took a break and walked to a local diner. After nervously sipping a few cups of coffee, we walked back toward the mosque. Just around the corner was Ammi's house. The crowds of people were pouring in. I gathered my inner strength to join the others while pulling on Laura's hand and nudging her to follow. Once again, I had to be friendly with my clients all together, at the same time. For me, it was work, not merely attending a wedding celebration.

Laura and I meandered to the living room where we grabbed a drink of apple tea. There were two men whispering next to the picture on the wall of King Salman of Saudi Arabia. I did not know these two guys, but I listened in on their conversation, nonetheless, out of curiosity.

"America will get what it deserves, sooner than later," one man said.

The other guy responded, "This time, we must bring America to her knees."

I couldn't believe what I just heard. *This is sick*, I thought to myself. Then I figured, *Oh, it's just a couple of jerks. Just ignore it*. I dismissed it and moved around the room, hoping it was merely an isolated conversation.

I noticed Darmush, one of my more likeable tax clients. He was from Turkey and had been living in the United States for over twelve years. He owned a chain of bagel stores in all five boroughs of New York City. I admired his demeanor and his ability to be soft spoken and relaxed. His wife, Dina, was a beauty. She was the icing on the cake for me, with her long, black hair flowing down to the middle of her back. One look into her dark eyes killed me. So, given the chance to greet her and to hold her hand, even for just a few moments, was pleasant for me and hopefully, not too noticeable. After introducing Laura to Darmush and to Dina, we talked briefly about the weather.

It was obvious that there was nothing more to say. I guided Laura by her fingers into the next room, which revealed a library with stunning floor to ceiling mahogany wood bookshelves covering all four walls. I glanced at many of the books, mostly in Arabic writing.

I was surprised to see a small section of books written in English such as *War and Peace* and *The Art of War*. About one minute later, Darmush brushed past me, walking in a brisk manner. He greeted some guys in the rear corner of the library. I casually walked in that same direction with Laura until I could overhear Darmush speaking. They were all smiling, moving their hands up and down in a coordinated sequence pointing above.

Darmush's remarks concluded, *"Bismillah, Allahu Akbar."*

The group of men repeated, *"Bismillah, Allahu Akbar."*

The buzz in the room was focused on some event. I sensed it was ominous, yet I had no clue what they were referring to. There was no way I could just let it go, so I decided to confront Darmush. I felt compelled to ask him what was going on. I approached him.

"Sir Darmush," I said, typically to be cute, "I feel left out of something. I have a question for you, so let's talk privately over there in that corner next to the fireplace."

I walked without waiting for him to reply. He followed.

I gazed into his eyes and said, "Darmush, I may have heard words here today about a special event. What's going on?" I kept my mouth shut, allowing him the time he needed to reply.

As he began to respond, Darmush looked deeply into my eyes and said, "Whatever you think you may have heard here is of no concern for you. Stone, you have helped me over the years and I have grown to like you, so I can only say this: Wherever you may be during the first week of this August, stay out of Manhattan. Now for a change, you take my advice; better to go on vacation and enjoy yourself my friend."

I started to turn away mesmerized by his comments, but he continued to speak.

"You know, Bob, I have many friends: some Arabic, some Israeli, and some Christian. I love all people, but America must pay for its policies against the Arab world."

I was overwhelmed from all that I just heard. Laura and I said our goodbyes and politely left. Walking toward the car, I heard some more words, but they were not clear enough. I wasn't sure exactly what was spoken, but it sounded like, "Kill the chickens in the pen," followed by loud laugher. The two men continued talking as we walked outside towards our car. I started to turn around to hear better and to see who they were, but Laura elbowed me in the side.

Laura gritted her teeth and harshly said to me, "don't look, don't even turn around. Do not let them know that you heard them. Let's just get the hell away from this place."

We entered the car and sat silently without driving until Laura snapped at me again.

"What are you doing, get going already!"

"Sure. Of course."

Driving back home, on the Long Island Expressway, we barely had time to digest all that we just experienced. The usual slow traffic gave us more time to think. After driving for about thirty minutes, we exited the highway onto South Oyster Bay Road for Plainview, New York. We stopped at the red light located across from a gas station I've used for years. The gauge was down to half, not too low, but I figured, *why not fill up? Frankly, I was too restless to go home, so this was a welcome diversion.*

As I pulled in parallel to the gas pumps, another car abruptly entered. The front end jerked forward as the driver jammed the brakes to align the car's gas tank for a fill-up. The gas station employee came out, but abruptly turned around while no one from the other vehicle came out. I sat motionless, trying to make sense out of this weird scene. I was anticipating something, but I had no idea if I was overreacting. Maybe the other driver was drunk. Who knows?

"Well, are you meditating or are we here to fill up?" Laura sarcastically queried.

"Ah, no, I'll skip it for now." I was a mess.

My reply was aloof, which reflected the chaos in my head. I drove away, sensing that we were being set up. A few more blocks down the main road took us to the familiar right turn that led to our house. We arrived home, pulled into the driveway, parked, and remained seated in the car. I checked out the rearview mirror. I could not be sure, but I didn't think we had been followed.

We were frozen in the moment. The yellow glow from our front porch light provided a focal point upon which we stared. Laura and I turned to each other, waiting for some reaction without a word being said. There was nothing to say. No response was needed. We both knew our lives could not possibly ever be the same. It was a defining moment, and there was no turning back.

As I opened the car door, my intuition forced me to look back to the street. Was I spooked from today's events or were we really being watched? I refocused back to Laura as she approached the front door to our home. She took a tentative step into the entrance way. I heard footsteps from the street, but could not see anyone. A chill went through me. I slowly followed Laura into the doorway, yet felt compelled to turn my head to scan the front lawn, sensing that we might be in danger. I felt exposed and vulnerable.

Then I heard a familiar voice say, "Hello, Bob, long time. How are you?" It was our next-door neighbor walking his dog. I fought off my misplaced fear to force a half smile. My voice could not hide my state of mind.

I stuttered, "he-hello, Jack, next time . . . please don't sneak up on me like that." I closed with, "Good night, my friend."

He stared back at me with a confused facial expression, as if to say, *Hey, what's wrong Bob?* He continued down the block walking his dog while I was still frozen in the doorway. I was drained with the awareness that our lives were already infected with paranoia, taking over like a cancer out of control.

Laura and I embraced in the kitchen. She was breathing heavily, holding my shoulders, and burying her head into my chest while crying. She pulled back slightly and looked into my eyes.

"Bob, I see your big blue eyes are filled with fear. Your usual confident face seems worried and your eyebrows are squeezed together in tension," she remarked.

"It's going to be fine, Laura."

"Please don't just say things, Bob. Let's be honest. It's a mess. Our world has become a nightmare."

"Listen, Laura, things will settle down. I'll go back to seeing my clients. You'll see. This episode tonight will soon blow over."

It actually sounded good, but our new reality was already in motion. Our future was unclear, like a murky pond after a storm. Fear of the unknown was hovering over us.

CHAPTER 4

We sat down close to each other at the kitchen table, holding hands without eye contact. We were drained.

"Bob, I'm going upstairs to bed. Hopefully, I'll find a way to deal with this nightmare of a day. I suggest that you call it a night, get some sleep."

She slowly left the room, leaving me alone to gather my thoughts. I needed a comfort drink, but not hard liquor. I settled on basic herbal tea with a touch of milk and honey. My mind started to ponder, *How did I end up here?* I felt like running away from these clients, the stress . . . everything. *How could I ever face them again?*

Now, at age thirty-five, I had just hit the well-known fork in the road. I had become an accountant right after college. What else would I do after years and years of being pushed into this profession by my father? I was never one of those fortunate people who just knew what they wanted to be: a lawyer, a doctor, a veterinarian for the love of animals, a carpenter, or whatever. Thinking back to my college days, I was just a fun-loving guy who played lots of basketball, an above-average student for sure, and a pleasure seeker, looking for girls when the opportunity presented itself. Maybe I did not engineer my future with precision; I most likely allowed my father's push to take over. It was no surprise that I wound up taking accounting and business courses, ending up with a major in accounting during my college years.

I had later developed my own accounting and tax practice, first with doctor clients and then with these retail stores owned mostly by undocumented individuals originally from other countries. About fourteen years had evaporated already, and now, I was bored with the world of numbers and clients. I knew that I had to break out and that some sort of a significant life change was brewing.

**

The following week, after the wedding for Ammi's daughter, while glancing through *The New York Times*, I noticed a job opportunity to work for the Internal Revenue Service. I continued flipping the pages, but something compelled me to turn back. My first thought was, *Here I go again*, as the impulsive side of my brain dominated. I started to breath heavily with emotional upheaval. *I'm okay, I'll be okay.* Those feelings of breaking out of the mold and trying to figure out a new direction permeated the inner core of my mind.

I took a closer look at that IRS ad: "Unique Opportunity! International Crime Division. Immediate Job Opening." I paused and closed my eyes. Something in my brain was triggered. I had this butterfly flittering feeling that just maybe this was my chance to break loose. My gut told me to make the call. As I circled the ad, I felt the presence of someone looking over my shoulder. I slowly turned around to the right and standing there was Laura.

"Hey, what are you doing?" I asked, "When did you learn to be such a snoop?"

"Bob, why are you wasting your time looking at that stupid IRS job offer?" Laura asked.

Laura and I previously talked about my boredom and depression over the past several years and about my feelings regarding my undocumented foreign clients. I was making a very decent living, with more than fifty business clients and roughly two hundred fifty personal tax returns. The icing on the cake was being my own boss. Nevertheless, I always felt that the grass was greener on the other side. Something else was always out there for me—but what? When one has lost enthusiasm, what does it all mean?

I felt the tension building in the room. Laura and I had already been through this same conversation many times. She was a career woman, a lawyer with a strong drive and a solid direction. No doubt, she was tired of hearing about my career issues.

"Why can't you just keep going and either change or build up your tax practice again? Stop the bullshit already," she would usually say.

I was waiting for this same volley of crap to start flying any moment now. In my head, she was all over me simply because I had placed a circle over around this most likely bullshit IRS job offer in the paper. Hey, maybe she had always been right. Maybe I have ADHD and I never knew it. Or maybe it was okay to shift my life somewhat. Why not be able to give something else a shot?

Laura started to speak, and there it was: "Bob, what's your problem? I am tired of working so hard as a lawyer while here you go again looking for something else."

Over the years, I had tried a few business ideas but I never went all the way with them. Halfway was more like it. I had always found it impossible to try to develop a new business idea while holding onto the tax practice—a monkey on my back. This is what Laura was talking about. She was so tired of me trying things or thinking of trying out new endeavors and complaining about my work. She was fed up with all my pipedreams.

Truth was, our marriage was coming to a crossroads after fifteen years of ups and downs. Frankly, I would understand it if she told me right now that she wanted a divorce. I could not blame her for feeling this way. After about twenty minutes of the same old argument and my recurring thoughts, *Oh shit, she's going to divorce me or maybe we should just get separated*, the yelling ended and life went back to normal. But not this time, as Laura suddenly went into my office, and then she walked through the kitchen. The fridge door was slammed shut, with bottles clinking into each other.

"Hey, what's up, Laura?"

"In case you didn't realize it, we need milk and eggs, so I'm going to the grocery store."

This time she pounded the front door, which closed behind her.

***

I sat back down, closed my eyes and took a few breaths to let the tension flow out of my mind and body. I rose up from my brief meditation, picked up the newspaper, and called the IRS for the job offer. At the same time, a client called me, so I hung up on the IRS. The call came in on the business line.

"Bob Stone speaking, may I help you?"

It was one of my doctor clients, Josh Hartman, my worst nightmare. He just received a notice from the IRS stating that he was hit with a tax audit and he made it clear to me that he was upset.

"Josh, read the front page of the tax notice to me," I said.

They were examining his tax returns for 2012 and 2013 due to large donations and excessive business expenses claimed. I remember this clearly, as he had insisted we submit larger tax deductions for those two years to offset his high medical practice profit. Those had been two exceptional years for the doctor's practice, so he pushed the envelope to owe less taxes.

I made the usual defensive cover-my-ass notes in my tax software for each year that this client submitted his irregular figures. Also noted was that I advised the client not to be overly aggressive, and that the client had refused to accept my advice. Of course, Dr. Hartman said he did not recall me mentioning this to him. *Here we go again.*

The call ended with my familiar feelings of aggravation and resentment. This arrogant client did not listen to me and now I'll have to represent him. Then he'll give me a hard time when I charge him a fair fee. This was the shit that had driven me to the edge over the years. Again, I felt the pull of that IRS advertisement. I had to make that call—not to the IRS on behalf of Dr. Hartman, but to the IRS' International Crime Division for the job offer.

I picked up the house phone, and then hung up. *No, don't use the house phone, stupid.* I redialed with my cell phone as my fingers began tightening up. *What the hell am I doing?* My mind was playing tricks on me. One voice was saying, *Go for it!* The other voice shouting inside my head, *Be happy with what you have! Hang up!*

At this very moment, I heard a pleasant voice answer, "IRS, International Crime Division Career Office. May I help you?"

I could not speak one word. I was frantic. All I could say was, "Sorry, wrong number." I terminated the call.

I got up and left the kitchen to sit on my favorite chair in the den. I needed an outlet for my nervous energy. I decided to put on my sneakers, but I had no idea what I was going to do. I was rushing to tie the laces and they kept getting tangled the wrong way. *Calm down, Bob, calm down.*

That's it. I'll shoot some hoops in the driveway. Surprisingly, I was dribbling the ball with some hints of what I used to be, making several smooth precise shots: *swish*, another *swish*, and then another. It always amazed me how one can get right back into the game after not playing for so long.

At least an hour passed. I was sweating and feeling so free just doing something only for the fun of it. I was getting hungry and my legs were stiffening up. I remembered that's exactly how injuries develop: when you're too tired and you get sloppy. *That's it, enough,* I said to myself. My decision to stop brought me back to a quote from one of my father's favorite movies, *Magnum Force* when Clint Eastwood said, "A good man knows his limitations." I recalled how my father used to remind himself of that piece of advice, and how he tried to instill that in me. That's when I realized that I should have followed more of my father's advice years ago.

I felt alone back in the house—the silence was deafening. For no apparent reason, I strolled into my office and spotted an envelope placed on my desk. A premonition kicked in. *Could this be it? Was Laura actually going to leave me?* I opened the envelope and unfolded her note.

Bob,
Sorry, but I need to get away for a while. Goodbye for now.
Enjoy the space,
Laura.

Sinking back into my chair, I gazed into the framed photo of our wedding day. Laura just had to get away. *Get away*, she said in her note. I've been feeling the same for years, but she had the backbone to actually leave.

I was feeling strange and not understanding what I should do next. I needed to calm myself down. I found a bottle of my favorite single malt scotch, an eighteen-year-old sherry oak Macallan.

I made an attempt to sip this excellent scotch slowly, but one glass led to the next. I could not dance around this whisky. I needed to drown my self-pity with liquid therapy. As I was dozing off and feeling no pain, I used my feet to push off my sneakers. Too tired to take a shower, I melted into the couch, escaping the world around me.

CHAPTER 5

must have moved to my bed in the middle of the night, but I couldn't recall. My eyes slowly opened, but I was in no shape to face the real world. I placed a small hand towel that I usually kept behind my bed and placed it over my eyes to block out a few rays of light beaming in.

I knew I had overslept, so I checked the time on my cell phone. It was already 10:15 a.m. I'm a mess. On autopilot, I reached for the phone to call Laura. I paused. *No, don't call her yet. Just leave it alone for now.* I'll respect the space she needs.

I actually started talking to myself, as my father used to do. I recalled how Dad drove me crazy when I saw his lips moving without uttering any words. I could never understand it, but the cause of talking to oneself was being in deep focus and stressed out. This had now become clear to me. I wish I could simply turn to my father now and say, "*I get it. I understand now, Dad.*"

I had a hard time to get moving. The unused muscles from shooting hoops yesterday reminded me that I needed to get back into my workout routines. There was a time I would jog for about four miles, three times each week, and do my isometrics, mixed with some weight training as well. The other days of the week, I would focus on martial arts. Maybe one day I'd get back to all that good stuff.

I took a long, hot shower, relaxing while the hot water drained down my back. My fingertips began to shrivel, alerting me it was time to end the fun. Enough was enough. While drying off, my cell phone rang. I had to run out of the shower, dripping wet to grab the call before it stopped ringing. The caller ID revealed a toll-free telephone number, no doubt either a sales call or a solicitation from an organization. I barely got to the phone in time, answering only to hear a click on the other end. I went back to drying off and then reached for my favorite upscale but not too fancy clothes. This made me feel better about myself.

It was time to eat something, so I went for the usual one slice of toast with cream cheese, lightly spread with a bit of strawberry jam on top. I was feeling unsure of myself so for no logical reason, I decided to skip the cream cheese and smeared a thin layer of chunky peanut butter onto the toasted bread. In a plastic bottle, I blended cold water with cranberry juice to cut back on the sweetness. I really craved a cup of strong coffee, but a sense of self-control was important for me— even for the sake of feeling that I was in control of something without any real meaning. I stoically passed on the coffee.

A Monday morning appointment over at the IRS was never a good idea, but I had to deal with Dr. Hartman's tax inquiry. I left the house, walking toward my car. As I entered to sit down, my water bottle dropped and rolled down the driveway just before the car door closed. I placed my left foot down on the ground. I rose up slowly, choosing not to rush to avoid pulling a muscle, in order to grab the rapidly moving water bottle. *What a way to start a day.* I exited the car but felt compelled to take a timeout. I placed my hands spread wide apart on top of the car. A sudden sharp pain, like a needle jolted the left side of my neck.

***

I must have been dreaming for quite some time. Reality smacked me hard in the face, coupled with a cold sweat, as my dreams faded and what really happened to me became clearer. I was not in my house at all, but in some kind of detention area. I started to remember that my car was slammed into from behind, not once but twice. I was then cut off in front by another vehicle forcing me into a fence. I remember my assailants jabbing the needle into my neck, the visions of father and mother, my accepting thoughts of death, and helplessly dropping to the ground as I passed out. Yes, of course, I was kidnapped.

A sharp pain had me reaching for the exact spot on my neck where the needle had penetrated during the kidnapping. My eyes peaked open with total confusion and fear of the unknown. I scanned the room to obtain an overall picture of my surroundings. I felt like I was in some sort of laboratory: the bright overhead lights reminded me of a dentist's office; there were dull white walls; my bed was narrow; and the floor was checkered with black diamonds in between solid white squares. The only door leading into the room had a look of heavy steel; the feel was that of an isolation unit. I had no idea how many hours or days had elapsed. When I tried to sit up in the bed, I realized my arms were strapped to the sides.

"Where the hell am I, what's going on?" I yelled out.

Nobody answered. That angered me even more. A slender, reddish-blond nurse appeared.

"Calm down, you've been asleep for almost two days and I've been taking care of you."

"Really?" I asked. "Who did this to me? What's your name?"

"I'm Nurse Wendy. Sorry, I should have told you my name."

Suddenly, a well-dressed guy confidently opened the door. "Get him up and dressed. Five minutes, no more," he said and then left.

"Come on, Mr. Stone, you better get off your butt," Wendy said.

"Who was that idiot?" I asked.

"Oh, him? He's just the director of the Internal Revenue Service's International Crime Division for the entire country, no big deal," she replied sarcastically.

"What?"

"Yes, tax man, wasn't this the excitement you were looking for when you dialed that IRS number, but then hung up?"

"Oh, that call, tell me, Wendy—where the hell am I?"

She penetrated my eyes with a deeply focused look.

She paused, then replied, "We're in Langley, Virginia, and you are about to enter into a new world and a new life, my friend."

"Really? Isn't Langley the home of our famous CIA?" I asked.

"Yes, sure. We share the building with the CIA, but you are a special guest of a totally different department, Stone."

"You know what, I'm leaving here right now. This is ridiculous."

I got dressed and looked out the window. *Shit, too high to jump.* I went to the door, but two guards were at attention, holding automatic rifles. *Wow, am I that important?* I questioned myself. I tested the seriousness of the guards by running past the door and into the hallway.

"Halt, Mr. Stone," a guard shouted out.

I slowly turned to evaluate the guards. Their guns were ready and aimed at me so I immediately stopped. Resigned to accept my situation here, I walked back to the white room. Once inside, I heard footsteps closing in on me from behind, then clapping.

"Well done. Yes, bravo, tax man. Now come with me, Stone."

"Who are you?" I asked.

"I'm your guardian angel here, just relax until I'm ready to bring you up to speed on your screwed-up situation. My name is Randolph Johnson. My friends call me Randy."

"Oh, so now I'm your friend," I sarcastically replied. Randy looked aggravated.

"Listen up, Stone, it's no accident you're here in Langley, Virginia.... You should know that."

"No accident, what does that mean?"

"Stone, I suggest you remain in your room for a few minutes and ask yourself why you have been in denial for so long about those clients of yours."

I shook my head, closed the door to my room, and dropped onto the bed. I was amazed he accused me of being in denial, as this had been my more privately held concern for years. After about ten minutes, there was an impatient knock on my door, followed by an order to get moving.

"Hey, Stone, this is your guard. You have orders to get up, now!"

"Okay, sure."

The door was opened, and the guard impatiently waved me out, pointing down the hallway.

PART TWO

CHAPTER 6

was led into a plain gray room with no windows. The guards backed
off.

Randy asked me, "Ready for coffee, Bob?"

"Yeah, sure, black will do, please."

As Randy poured my coffee, I was looking for clues around the
room. I guess it was by design that there was nothing on the walls—
no carpet, nothing. I was getting nervous.

As a partial joke, I asked Randy, "Hey, are you going to torture me?"

He started to laugh, "Oh no, not here. Only joking, Stone. No, we
just need to talk. First, here's an egg and cheese sandwich. Go ahead,
eat."

"Very kind of you," I said.

I sensed it was time to break the ice.

"Randy, I'd prefer a three-egg omelet."

"Maybe next time," he responded, forcing a smile. "Okay, enough.
Let's get to it," Randy said, with a look of urgency.

I saw fear in his eyes, yet confidence in his body language.

"I agree, let's begin. So then—why the hell did you guys kidnap me
and why am I here?"

"Bob, congratulations, you asked the right question. We know that
over the years you have a developed a good number of clients, about
fifty plus business clients."

Seconds later I challenged him and said, "Isn't that what all self-
employed professionals want?"

"Of course," Randy replied. "But your clients have a common
thread."

I said nothing. Sometimes, one does not need to respond. Randy
continued on relentlessly.

"Bob, most, if not all of your clients are illegals . . . unregistered aliens, foreigners . . . use whatever label you prefer. All are living here in the States."

I chose not to respond while maintaining eye contact with him, my way of showing confidence under pressure.

"Okay, sit there and say nothing. So, here is what you're facing: You've been aiding and abetting these taxpayers and terrorists in your preparation of their fraudulent tax returns for over five years."

"Cut the shit, I did the best I could to make sense out of each client's available records."

Randy challenged me; "but there were no records, no bank statements, no nothing. More so, you legitimized these retail cash businesses with your creative figures." Then Randy added, "Stone, you've been an idiot. These store owners have been and continue to skim huge sums of unreported cash. In case you forgot, it's called 'tax evasion.' This dirty money ultimately ends up flowing overseas and I can assure you, it's not used to benefit the world."

I snapped back, "Come on! How could I have possibly been aware of all that activity?" Not allowing him time to reply, I kept going. "Nice imagination, Randy, anyway . . . how do you know all of this and if you're correct, what was the end game for this flow of money?"

"Are you living with your head in the sand, Stone?"

A few beads of sweat were forming above my eyebrows, about to roll onto my face. I said nothing trying to aggravate Randy again. I saw him getting riled up so I thought I'd better be more responsive and to speak more calmly.

"Look, Randy, I was their business accountant and I did the best I could to file reasonable tax returns for each of these clients. The information provided to me was very sketchy at best. I could not possibly have known about any unreported cash."

"That's too little, too late, tax man!" Randy snapped. "Many of your clients belong to international terror groups or home-grown cells. They set up retail stores everywhere, in our cities, our communities, anywhere they can. They report maybe fifteen to twenty percent of their sales at best. The balance goes to mosques and to other organizations in undisclosed locations. These mosques then wire the money to certain banks overseas. These 'friendly banks' are in Canada, Qatar, Istanbul. By the way, a few start-up community banks in the good old USA have been involved. These low-end smaller American banks need to show activity, so they close their eyes to accept anyone, any entity with money to deposit. Many times, large sums of money get deposited, then as soon as it clears, those same funds get transferred out. Amazing, isn't it, Stone?" Randy jabbed, as he tilted his head and gritted his teeth.

"Now you listen, to me, Randy. I have no clue what the heck you're talking about. I am ready to leave now. Thanks for your garbage breakfast."

"You're not going anywhere, tax man. No one can help you. No lawyer, no one. But, you can help yourself."

"Now what does that mean?" I asked.

"Mr. Robert Stone, bingo—you asked the right question," he sarcastically retorted.

"What are you getting at?"

"Look, you were fed up with your boring life as a typical accountant. You and I know this."

"How could you know that?" I blurted out.

"We know everything about you, Bob: Your love of basketball, your knee injury during high school, and your fading marriage with Laura."

I stood up and kicked him just under his knee. The guards behind me jumped in. I was pulled down to the ground, then whacked in the head.

"Stone, go ahead—do that again. I'll make sure you're charged with tax fraud. You'll spend the next fifteen years in jail. Got it?" Randy shouted out, with his teeth grinding at me again.

"Yea," I said right back. "Okay. Got it."

Suddenly, another guy walked into the room.

"Bob, say hi to our in-house psychologist, John Ashton," Randy said. "Ashton and I will be evaluating you over the next few days, so sit back and enjoy the ride."

"This sounds like fun," I grumbled.

"Please skip the sarcasm. Let's get started," Ashton said.

"You jerks from the IRS are all the same." I had to say that.

"Listen, Bob," said Randy. "We are not here dealing with clients, taxpayers, tax audits, and basic tax crap. So, when you say 'jerks,' get your mind off that side of the IRS. Don't you realize by now? You are in Langley, Virginia . . . the nerve center of an elite IRS division?"

"How sexy," I said. "Give me a break, Randy. I never heard about any elite IRS department like this. Tell me more."

"Okay, that's a fair request. Here we go Stone. Listen up. Shortly after the 9/11 attacks, the Patriot Act became Public Law 107-56 on October 26, 2001. I'm sure you already know that when it was signed into law, it gave our government all kinds of expanded rights to protect our homeland. Most people by now have heard of the Patriot Act, but few really understand it's meaning and intent. The official name of the act stands for 'Uniting and Strengthening America by Providing Appropriate Tools Required to Intercept and Obstruct terrorism.' One key feature was to require American citizens and resident aliens to disclose their foreign bank accounts.

"Now Stone, all you need to know is this: What wasn't public knowledge was an extra paragraph that was added into this new law at the last moment, allowing the IRS to establish a special department dedicated to uncover tax fraud and to track the illegal flow of funds moving around the world—all related to the purchase of weapons and potential acts of terrorism. These extra few words gave birth to a new internal group within the IRS called HPAT 21, or Homeland Protection Anti-Terror. We dedicated this unit to all who perished in the September 11, 2001, attacks with the number 21. You're an accountant—add up 9, then 11, and 01. That's the 21. Along the way, we expanded our reach and capabilities. Over the years, we were not so effective, but now we do what we have to do to win. Understand, Stone?"

"That's interesting. So, in plain English, "what does that mean, 'we do what we have to do?'

"Let me handle this one," Ashton blurted out. "Simply this," Ashton added, "It means we developed specialized tactics needed to get the job done. This includes torture, entrapment, surveillance, espionage, and murder if need be—you name it. Okay, so there you have it. This is not bullshit, this is not the spin zone. America is at war all over the world and we are losing. Frankly, we're desperate. Just when we thought the Taliban and Al Qaeda were minimized or eliminated, now we're facing ISIS, other extremist groups, and more acts of terror here at home."

I was totally taken aback, so all I could say was, "Alright, Ashton, thanks for the info."

It was hard to comprehend that it had come down to this: A secretive unit within the good old IRS, a stealth killing machine capable of almost anything.

"Somehow, Stone," Randy explained, "You're right in the middle of all this insanity with your undocumented clients."

Where are these guys going with all this talk? It had been three hours already and I was fed up with this nonsense. So I probed. "Listen, people, I hear you and I've been patient, but I do have one question."

"Make it a good one, tax man," Randy curtly replied.

"Of course, it's simple," I said. "You owe me an explanation. So, Randy, of all the tax preparers in the good old USA, why me? Why was I the lucky one you kidnapped and brought into this damn command center?"

"Fair question, Stone. Now we need to shift gears and get back to the IRS you are familiar with. On September 11, 2011, the tenth anniversary of the 9/11 disaster, the commissioner of the IRS at that time, Daniel B. Jenkins, came up with a mandate. The focus shifted to developing a software program designed to cross-check tax preparers and their clients. Sure, other tax guys got on our hit list and they were pursued, but you—believe me when I tell you, Stone, it did not take long before your name hit the radar. Your name and tax preparer identification number were immediately referred over to us here at HPAT 21. Come on, out your fifty or so business clients, every single one of those bagel stores, gas stations, flower shops, newsstands, and pizzerias—all are owned by undocumented illegal aliens, foreigners, or whatever the hell you want to call them, and they're all still here on expired visas."

I stood up and responded, "I've had enough. What do you want from me? Exactly why am I here?"

"I'll take it from here, Randy," Ashton said. "Stone, we need you to join us in this fight. The future of our country depends on individuals like you who are willing to stand up and do whatever it takes. America is in trouble. We are clearly losing the battle. We must turn the tide immediately."

"How many times do I have to ask you guys the same question?" I demanded. "What do you expect from me?"

"Bob," Ashton replied. "If you are mentally and physically fit, if you meet our standards, then this is what you'll need to do—"

"Go on, let me hear more."

Ashton continued, "After about one week of intensive training, you will go back to your clients as if everything is normal. You will continue to make your monthly visits to each client. You must figure out a way to get more personal with them. There are specific clients who we have been tracking for the last three years. They have clear ties to terrorist organizations. You will need to take these client relationships to a much deeper level. You must gain their trust—way beyond being their tax advisor. Things do change rapidly around here, so this is our plan for you right now. Understood?" he asked.

I chose not to reply directly. "Excuse me guys, but are you absolutely sure that I have clients dealing in terrorist activities? How do you know which clients have been involved?"

I was trying to smoke out a few answers. Feelings of embarrassment were closing in on me. It was impossible to hide. I am sure it was coming through in the tone of my voice, so I began to talk less.

Now Randy jumped back in on the discussion, "I can tell you this, think about Ahmed Abdul with his three flower shops; Darmush Khan with his ten gas stations; and Mohammed Ali Sababa with his five bagel stores. These eighteen retail stores in New York City are barely scratching the surface, but they are your worst client nightmares. They have connections to terrorist groups. Listen to me, Stone. As Ashton said, HPAT 21 has been tracking the movement of money from these clients for the last three years. You would be blown away to know the huge sums of cash that have been moving around. There are unreported movements of cash from your client's businesses into bank accounts of mosques, charities and other entities. These nonprofit entities wire money to banks around the world. We have relationships with some of these banks. We know these bank accounts are in the names of certain Iranian, Saudi, and Afghan warlords and more recently, ISIS leaders. It's a fact that when ISIS kidnaps journalists, the ransom money first goes to mosque bank accounts in Qatar, and then the funds start moving all around the globe. That's when things get scary. I know, Stone, it's too much info overload. Sorry, but once I get started, my brain keeps racing and I get carried away."

"Okay, Randy," I said. "I understand."

I was badly shaken up, but keeping my composure was important. I was always able to shore up confidence when I needed it the most. Everyone has a gift in life and this was mine. *Stay strong, control my face and voice, and just remain positive.* My father had taught me this at a young age when I used to go to court with him. Dad was an amazing lawyer. I would sit in the seats and just admire my father as he would shake off whatever the opposing lawyers threw at him. He had unbelievable composure. I suppose it rubbed off on me. This resolve gave me the inner strength to control myself as Randy continued to lecture me about my clients.

I needed some personal time, so I calmly said, "Hey guys, how about giving me some time to absorb all of your comments? You must know this whole thing is not so easy for me. Maybe we can take a break. Is that alright?"

"Sure," Randy said. "But when we resume, it will be just you and Ashton talking. I'm out of here for now. Bob Stone, you have been compromised—big time."

"Okay," I said wearily. "Give me a break, I need to chill out now."

"How much time do you need to freshen up?"

"Give me an hour," I said. "I need to close my eyes and absorb everything. Know what I mean?"

"Sure," Ashton replied gently. "You should be alert, anyway, when we resume. See you back here in exactly one hour."

"Thanks, Sir John the Psych," I cutely said, making sure he caught my smile.

"Let's stick with Ashton, going forward," he said.

I just waved my right hand in the air in acknowledgment as I was escorted out of the room.

CHAPTER 7

The guards led me back to my bedroom. I was confused and dazed, so I decided to close my eyes and allow my mind to travel to wherever it wanted to go. I used to do this while walking in the neighborhood after arguing with Laura. I always found it amazing to see just where my brain would take me. Would I go to negative or positive thoughts? Would I be fearful or strong? Would my thoughts be random or logical? One thing was for sure, I always took great pride in taking a lemon and turning it into lemonade. But this time, I would have to somehow dig deep for the inner strength that I now needed. As I closed my eyes, I commanded my brain to be tough. *Be strong, somehow everything will work out for the best.*

Suddenly, I heard the door opening, which interrupted my thoughts. While opening one eye, I saw Wendy. And now she closed the door very slowly, looking back at me. Before I could get one word out, she sat down next to me in bed. She sensed that I was troubled.

"Bob," she asked, "What do you want right now?"

"Just give me some space," I replied. "I need to think things through." I wasn't nasty, just honest.

She kissed me on my forehead and then said, "I want to be your friend, Bob. You're in a real bad situation and I know your wife, Laura, left you."

Realizing that my whole life was everyone's business here, I didn't bother to ask her how she knew that.

I simply said, "Thanks."

I sensed that I was constantly being tested. My responses were being analyzed in various situations. *Yeah, that's it. I'm being evaluated.* I also felt that Wendy wanted to get closer to me. The question was—why? My instincts took over.

"Wendy, tell me, are you really a nurse?"

"Well, to be upfront with you, Bob," Wendy said. "No, I am not. Sorry I had to bullshit you."

"So, what do you really do here?"

"I am supposed to evaluate you, Bob."

"Evaluate what?"

"Let's talk later. You get some rest."

She walked away and for the first time, I noticed her gait, her curves, her hair draping down past her curvy behind.

Here I am checking her out and I haven't even called Laura. The pace at this Langley Virginia Command Center has been intense! It's time for me to try to contact my wife, ex-wife, friend, or whatever. I went to grab my cell phone out from my coat pocket. No doubt they had already searched through my contacts, texts, emails, and so forth. The battery was dead. *So much for reaching Laura.*

I shouted out for Wendy, "Hey, do you have a phone charger?"

No answer. Louder this time, I shouted and repeated the request.

"Hey, calm down, *amigo!*" Wendy said. "What's up?" she blurted out.

"Any chance you can bring to me a cell phone charger right now?" I asked.

"Be right back, Bob."

"Thanks, sweetie," I said, trying to befriend her.

She came back quickly, leaned over my bed, plugged an end of the charger into my cell phone, and then reached over me for the wall outlet. As she did, I said, "Well, hello there," in a deep flirty voice, and then laughed.

"Hey, Bob Stone," Wendy answered back. "Okay, so you're handsome, confident, and I do like your wavy black hair and blue eyes, your nice white teeth, and your swagger . . . but let's calm down."

"Wendy, you are a real cutie," I said. "I appreciate your honesty."

"Great, now keep your paws off me," she said.

I guess I was too slow to pull hands off her hip, so within about three seconds, her right hand grabbed my left wrist. She pulled it down and swiftly turned it hard until I was in acute pain. I had no choice but to turn in the direction she was pulling my hand in order to relieve the sharp pain she inflicted.

As she released me, I asked, "What was that?"

"Oh, not much," Wendy explained. "Just a wristlock I learned years ago in martial arts. This little maneuver saved my ass many times while I was—"

"While you were what?"

"Never mind," she whispered below her breath, her face looking the other way.

I now realized that Wendy was a well-trained fighter. Who knows what she had really been involved in? I knew she was not a white-collar exec working at a desk from nine to five, nor a nurse, for that matter.

"Wendy," I said. "If that's your real name—"

"Yes!" Wendy was quick to confirm.

"Let's cut the crap," I continued. "We can be friends, but I need your honesty. Maybe I can somehow help you."

I was now turning the table to evaluate her response. They were all playing mind games—so I decided to join in the fun.

"Listen," I said. "I have to go back to talk with Ashton in about fifteen minutes."

"Okay, so what?" she flippantly asked.

"Well, we have a few minutes to talk about you," I replied. "Wendy, I am going to guess you are recently divorced, about thirty-eight, no kids, and pissed off at men. How am I doing with my evaluation of you?" I sarcastically asked.

"Screw you, tax man," she replied. "Have fun with the doc, I'm out of here."

Apparently, I had hit some of her emotional hot buttons. I noticed that my cell phone picked up just enough of a charge, so I called Laura. No service.

"Damn it!" I exclaimed. "Is no contact with the outside world part of my incarceration?"

Wendy shrugged her shoulders without any reply.

"Do me a favor, please?" I requested. "Get me the doctor and tell him no meeting until I can get a call out to my wife."

"Okay, Bob," Wendy said. "Let's see what I can do for you."

"Thanks, sweetie," I said again, attempting to soften up the friction between us.

***

Dr. Ashton entered my bedroom authoritatively.

"Sorry, Stone, we cannot yet allow you to make any outside calls. Not just yet. Security issues, I'm sure you understand."

"Ah, okay," I said. "But I need to call my wife—or ex-wife. As you know, I'm having marital issues."

"Yes," said Ashton. "I know all about your rocky marriage. Go ahead, use my cell phone to call your wife. Here, Stone, just take it."

"Thanks so much, Ashton," I said appreciatively. "You're actually a decent guy."

I smiled at him to let him know I valued his act of kindness. I needed someone in my corner in this place, so I figured why not befriend him.

As he left the room to offer me some privacy, I called Laura. I could not get through. I tried again and it went immediately to her voicemail. That concerned me quite a bit. I was about to call out for Ashton to come back for his phone. Instead, I started to check his text messages. Wrong thing to do, but nothing is out of the question now. "All is fair in love and war." Wendy had stepped out so I kept going.

The first text he had received was from Randy two hours ago. He asked the psych if I had broken down yet.

"Any new info from Bob Stone so far?"

"No, not yet," Ashton texted back.

"Any feedback from Wendy yet about Stone?"

"Nothing solid yet," Ashton had replied.

The last text from Randy was a long one;

"Ashton, you are the psychologist. Relax him, get to know him. I don't care how the hell you do it. We need to know if this guy will help *us or fuck us up in the end. Hypnotize him if you need to. I don't give a damn, just do your job. Things are moving too fast, Ashton. No more time to waste here."*

Ashton replied: *"No worries, sir. I'll hypnotize Stone ASAP later today."*

Oh my God, these guys were crazy. I called Laura one more time. Her voicemail now said that her phone had been disconnected. This was very alarming. *Did she change her cell phone to avoid me or is she in some sort of trouble?* Things had just taken a turn for the worse.

At that moment, Ashton knocked on my door and peeked in.

"Bob," Ashton very politely said, "It's time we talked. And I want my cell phone back now. Let's get this interview over with."

"Sure," I said, "Give me two minutes to pee, wash up, and I'll meet you right away." I flipped him his cell phone.

As he left my room, he passed Wendy, who was standing just by the doorway. She gave me a wink as she also walked out. *Now what,* I asked myself. I need to understand what these guys are trying to figure out.

Getting myself mentally prepared for an interrogation, I developed a plan: I'll rope the psych into believing that I'm either easy to hypnotize or very willing to be open with him about my feelings. If he takes the bait, I can analyze the nature of his questions. Then I will know what they're looking for. My next session with Ashton should be interesting. I'll make use of all the times I watched that game show *Jeopardy*. You know, "What is a blue lagoon?"

CHAPTER 8

The same guards led me back to the gray conference room. This time, I addressed the doctor before he could speak.

"Hey," I said. "Why can't we do this in a more pleasant environment? I need a room with windows, some air flow, some feeling, some colors, a carpet. ... Come on, I'm not a terrorist."

"Okay," Ashton said. "That's a fair request, tax man. Follow me."

We took an elevator up to the tenth floor. As we walked onto the landing, I saw that Wendy was waiting for us.

"Over here, gentlemen," Wendy said.

I had no idea why she was wearing such a hot dress, but she had my attention. Wendy pointed to a room then she spoke.

"Over to the right, conference room D."

I followed Ashton inside. There were large windows, a round desk, artwork of scenes from the American Revolution, and the names of all the presidents listed on a plaque on the far wall. The navy blue wall-to-wall carpet softened the room. The American flag was draped on the opposite wall. As I sat down and took a deep breath, I turned and saw Wendy walking in. I was a bit surprised by this.

"Ashton?" I asked. "Are you talking with me one-on-one, or is Wendy here acting as a witness?"

The psychologist was surprised that I picked up on that point from the get go.

"Well, tax man," Ashton said. "You are right. I need to make sure you don't leave here telling someone that I sexually assaulted you during our discussion." He laughed with an unnatural chuckle. "In all seriousness, though, I do need someone here to document what we are about to talk about. Bob, I also have to inform you that we have another visitor joining us and he will be here in about five minutes."

"Oh," I simply said, leaving the doc a choice to continue talking or not.

He then said, "FBI Southeast Regional Director, Franklin Conway, is about to arrive."

Blown away by this development, I chose not to respond. I did catch a glance from Wendy—I sensed that she was trying silently to communicate with me.

In walked an obviously tough-looking red-haired dude. He was well-dressed, looking dapper in a power suit with an American flag pin on his lapel.

"So, you are the famous, or should I say infamous, Robert Stone, CPA," he said to me. "I've been watching your every move for the last two years. How nice to finally meet you."

"Right back at you," I said. "What should I call you—Franklin, Mr. Conway, or what?"

"Oh, let's keep it informal since we'll be working closely together, so call me Frank. Listen, I'm here for a quick meet-and-greet. I'll leave you all alone now. See you tomorrow morning, Bob, 9:00 a.m. sharp— right here."

"Hey sure, Frank," I said as I stood up and reached to shake his hand.

Frank didn't extend his hand back out to me.

"I'll shake your hand when and if you pass the evil test," Frank said. "Then we'll know if we can truly count on you."

He had a firm look in his eyes and his jaw tightened. More games, no doubt a show of force to keep me off guard. I figured by now it was time for the psychologist to get into my head.

Out of nervousness, I said, "Okay, let's talk, the show must begin."

I first smiled over to Wendy, then eyeballed the doc, my interrogator, my hypnotist.

Ashton began by clearing his throat. "And now I need you to relax. We're here to work together, so there is nothing for you to be worried about."

So far, it's all lies, I thought, but I repeated, "Work together, sure."

"To help you to relax," Ashton continued. "Move your eyes upward and visualize a dot in the middle of your forehead. Hold that for four seconds. Take a deep breath, hold it for three seconds, and then exhale slowly over two seconds."

I did as he instructed.

"Good, and now Bob, let's repeat these steps two more times."

I felt a wave roll through my body, moving from my ankles up to my head. I caught myself letting go under his influence. I had to hang on. I started to think about Laura, how and where she might be now. I thought back to our decision not to have children. I regretted that. Then my mind drifted to my love of basketball and of my time when I learned martial arts during those great college days and after. I focused on some of karate moves to avoid going under—I hated the feeling of losing control.

"So, Bob Stone," Ashton continued. "It's time for a few questions. Is that alright with you?"

"Yes, that's fine, go ahead."

All my efforts to divert my mind were temporary. This interrogator was a pro, real slick. Yes, he was a deceptive bastard.

"And how do you feel right now?" Ashton queried.

I knew where he was going with this, trying to get inside my head, to hypnotize me, just as Randy had told him to in that text message. *Okay, I'll play his game.*

"I'm feeling fine."

"Good," Ashton replied. "I'm happy to hear that and now, I have a few questions for you. Bob, where were you born?"

"Brooklyn, New York."

"Did you have a happy childhood?"

What a stupid question. "Yes, I did."

"Did your parents have a good marriage? Did they get along well?"

"Yes, they were very much in love."

"Do you have any siblings, Bob?"

"No, I was an only child."

"Do you know why your parents did not have any more children?"

"I am not really sure, but my mother did have a few miscarriages." I was getting pissed off with his questions.

"Bob, was it easy for you to make friends as a child?"

I did not answer. I wanted to bother him, hoping to worry him that he lost his control over me.

"Bob, did you hear me?" Ashton tried again.

I said nothing.

"Okay," Ashton mumbled, obviously aggravated. "Tell me about your old friend, Larry Grayson?"

Holy shit, how did he come up with that name? Larry G. and I were close friends at the American University in Washington, D.C.

"Have you maintained your relationship with this friend?" Ashton pressed.

"No, we have lost contact for the past fifteen years," I mumbled.

"Why do you think you have not stayed in touch with your other friend Arnie?" Ashton asked.

"I'm not sure," I said.

Ashton had hit one of my tender spots. I regretted not maintaining that relationship. I never quite understood how one can became so close with someone and then so far apart. He was getting inside my head.

Ashton started up again. "Bob, do you see a pattern with your friendships and now with your wife, Laura?"

Asshole! I thought to myself. "What do you mean by that?" I asked.

He was hitting a hot button and he knew it. The prick was trying to crack me.

"Bob, do you have a hard time with relationships?" he asked.

"Not sure," I replied.

Truth was, maybe he was onto something.

"Bob, I am wondering about your ability to be a loyal person," Ashton remarked. "Are you a loyal person, Bob?"

"Yes, I am," I said. "I have never cheated on my wife. I have always been a friend that can be counted on."

"Bob, do you feel loyal to America?" Ashton asked.

Ah, so here it was: the key question.

"Absolutely," I said. "I love America. I feel privileged to live in America. I love my country."

"Bob, why do you feel this way?" Ashton pressed further.

"I have always felt lucky to live here," I explained. "I have always told my clients that it's okay to pay your share of taxes, that we live in a great country, and that paying taxes means you're doing well."

"Bob, let's talk about your parents, shall we?"

What the hell for? I thought.

"Were your parents patriotic toward America?" Ashton continued.

"Yes, my parents always hung the American flag for the Fourth of July. My father served in the Vietnam War."

"Where were your parents born, Bob?"

"In Brooklyn."

"Is Stone your real last name?" Ashton asked.

I was shocked. *Did he know that much about my family history,* I wondered.

"Well no, not really," I replied.

"What does 'not really' mean? Please tell me more, Bob."

I didn't see the harm, so I continued. "My father's parents came from Germany in the year 1919. They went through Ellis Island."

"Yes, go on," Ashton encouraged.

"I was told as a young boy that when my grandfather was interviewed going through the immigration process, they asked him, 'What is your name?' He answered his correct surname, Sohn. The interviewer wrote down Stone, stamped a form, and then told him to move on to the medical area. And that was that. Sohn became Stone."

"Bob, thank you for that story. Now tell me, were your grandparents Jewish?"

I hesitated to respond. *What's this about? What a jerk,* I said to myself.

He pushed me a bit more, "Bob, can you hear me?"

"Yes, yes I can."

"Okay, let's move on. Did your grandparents escape from Germany after the First World War?"

"Yes, this is what I was told."

"Do you know why they had to escape?"

"I recall that the Germans blamed the Jews for everything that went wrong in that war. They had to leave."

"Thank you, Bob. Oh, and Bob, how about your mother's parents? Where were they from?"

"They were from Minsk, Russia."

"And what happened to them?"

"My grandmother left Russia and met my grandfather in a camp for dislocated people. Then, they came to America to start a new life free from religious persecution."

"When did they arrive to America?"

"I believe in 1921, not exactly sure."

"You are doing fine, Bob Stone. Please tell me, what did your parents do to earn a living?"

"My father was a lawyer and my mother, a nurse."

"Thank you. You should be proud of your hardworking parents."

I said nothing, hoping he would lose his patience again.

"Bob, before I wake you up, I want you to do your best to remember your karate moves. You will need to rely on your martial arts skills now. This may save your life as you help us to protect the homeland. Bob, do you understand me?"

"Yes," I replied with conviction.

"Oh yes, Bob, one more thing: You may have to kill to protect our country. Have you ever killed a man?"

My hands were shaking. I said, "No." *I was close to killing this asshole of a psychologist, however,* I thought to myself.

"Do you feel you could kill someone if you had to?"

"I don't know what you mean." I was looking for extra time to think.

"To protect your own life, your wife, or your country—could you kill?"

I could not respond. I looked for some saliva to swallow and found none, but tried to swallow anyway. I clenched my teeth, causing pain in my jaw. The sockets just below each ear went into a spasm.

"Are you alright?" Ashton asked, concerned.

"Sure," I replied.

"Should I repeat my question?"

I needed time. "Yes, please repeat," My eyes were blinking rapidly.

"I need you to listen carefully now." Ashton said. "You must allow yourself to do whatever it takes to save the American people, to protect our way of life. Our country needs you. Can we count on you to do this, Bob Stone?"

"Do what?" I asked to gain some time to think.

There was a pause. I sensed I may have frustrated Ashton.

"Okay," Ashton continued. "Again, I'll ask you: Bob Stone, could you kill someone in order to protect America, our homeland, our way of life, and our freedom?"

I served up a passive "Yes."

He pressed me, "Yes what?"

"Yes, I could kill if I had to."

"You said yes," He prompted me, "If you had to do what?"

I had no more wiggle room. I caved in.

"Yes, I could kill to protect America and our way of life."

I actually felt comfortable with my response. Yes, I did feel that I could kill if I had to save our country, our people, and our freedom.

"Well done", Ashton said, obviously pleased. "Now repeat these words: I could torture to save America."

I remained silent. This was a tough one. Somehow, I saw killing and torture as two different elements of evil.

He started again, "Bob, please say it."

I was stuck, yet I knew I had to get past this part. I also needed him to think that he did, in fact, fully hypnotize me. I went with it.

"Yes, I could kill and torture someone to save America."

"Very good. You'll need to be much more focused, more alert. You have to sharpen your memory. Do you understand me?"

"Yes, I do. More focused, more alert, and better memory," I threw in for good measure.

"The country you love so much will be depending on you. Robert J. Stone, can we count on you to remain loyal to America?"

"Yes, of course," I replied.

Truth is, in some way, this guy had actually gotten into my head.

"We are almost finished, Bob. Right after I count down from five to one, you will abide by and follow through with all my commands. You will feel great, refreshed, and more confident. Are you ready Bob?"

"Yes, I am."

"Here we go: five, four, three, two, one . . . and wake up."

My eyes popped open. I did feel refreshed and at peace with my-self.

"Bob, it's me, how are you?" Wendy asked.

"Great, relaxed," I said. "I'm fine, Wendy. Actually, I'm ready to eat."

They both laughed.

"What's so funny?" I asked.

"We're happy to see that you have an appetite, that's all," Ashton replied.

"How long was I out or under?"

"Oh, about two hours," Wendy replied.

"Well, how did I do?" I asked. "Did I put on a good performance? Was I nasty or what?"

"Bob, seriously, you were amazing," Ashton remarked. "And I can tell you that we all have our emotional baggage, but you spoke from your heart. You have a good aura about you."

"Thanks for the nice comments," I said. "I'm starving, let's eat before I get cranky and you change your mind about me and my good aura."

We all stood up and left the room.

CHAPTER 9

Ashton departed, then Wendy led me down to the lower level, where we grabbed some junk food from the vending machines. On the way back up to my bedroom, I noticed a serious look on Wendy's face.

"Bob, there's an important meeting tonight. It's going to be a working dinner. Something is going on and it's big. Things are moving fast and I'm very worried."

"Okay, Wendy, so tell me what's up?"

"I can't say any more. See you at 8:00 p.m. on the sixth floor. The guards will escort you to the door marked 'Secure Conference Room.'"

"Sure, Wendy."

The stress level was building around here—it was in the air.

"Oh, Wendy," I continued. "By the way, how do you know all these things?"

She smirked and replied, "I'm your partner in international espionage, tax man. We'll be working together. By the way, Stone, you'll be meeting with a key player in our HPAT 21 unit tonight. He's the head honcho, the guy who calls the shots. His name is William Levine, a twenty-five-year career IRS man from the Criminal Tax Division. After 9/11, he requested a transfer over to HPAT 21. Anyway, he's a dedicated man, a true patriot, and a great guy."

"Thanks for the heads up, Wendy."

As soon as I entered my bedroom, I dropped my pants, changed into a polo shirt, removed my socks, and hopped into bed. I needed to catch some news, so I switched on the TV. Breaking news popped up on Fox News. A homeland terror alert was just raised to the max. However, no one knew why. *I suppose I'll learn more at dinner,* I figured. As I was dozing off, there was a nervous knock on my door.

"Yeah, yeah," I curtly shouted out. "Who's there?"

"It's Wendy, Bob. They just moved dinner back to 6:45 p.m. Everyone seems crazy."

"Give me a break, I need some down time."

"Yeah, right," Wendy said flippantly.

"Okay, okay. See you in twenty minutes, Wendy."

"Just meet me at the elevator," she demanded."

Compelled to hear more news, I hit the remote and lied down to catch a few more minutes of rest. Local news was interrupted with a special announcement: A former national security advisor to former President George W. Bush had become an advisor to Fox news. This advisor was being questioned by the anchorman about the president's speech scheduled to be on national television later tonight.

"The president is going to make a live statement at 8:00 p.m. tonight, at which time he will issue a warning about global terrorism," the advisor stated. "The White House will be issuing an alert regarding a new trend in acts of terror threatening the homeland. The anticipated warnings will be regarding American ambassadors around the world at increased risk of being kidnapped and held for ransom by ISIS. In other developments, the U.S. Department of Homeland Security's website may have been hacked and a series of simultaneous attacks on historical buildings may be in the planning stages. The president may also comment on the consolidation of various terror groups that have previously been competing with one another. These groups may now be forging alliances."

Now I understood why everyone around here had been on edge. I closed my eyes, as it was quite depressing.

***

So here we were, up in the sixth floor Secure Conference Room. Randy and Ashton must have arrived early. They were seated and nibbling on a few bread sticks. As soon as Wendy and I walked in together and sat down, Randy stood up, placed his right-hand palm over his heart, and started the Pledge of Allegiance. At that moment, we all stood up and joined in. Wendy elbowed me to put my hand over my heart. I was so surprised, I had forgotten. I think the last time I did this was back in high school, maybe earlier.

Then Randy spoke as he sat down, "At eight o'clock tonight, the president is going to be live on national television. The pres' will say that the U.S. Department of Homeland Security Command Center has picked up much higher than normal internet traffic, indicating a series of possible terror attacks at various locations throughout Europe and in America. As a precautionary measure. The president will issue a worldwide terror alert advising all Americans to leave certain countries on the USA terror list. The president may announce that ISIS, Al Qaeda, and the Boko Haram have joined forces to wage war against the West."

It was then that I noticed an empty seat. A confident, stocky guy with brown hair wrapped into a man bun approached the table.

"Hi, I'm Bill Levine," he said. "Most people just call me Levine." He made the rounds of shaking hands and then said, "I suppose you're the tax man, Bob Stone?"

"For better or worse," I said. "Yes, that's me, Mr. Levine."

"Well then, Stone, I'm your immediate supervisor and the caretaker of your life," Levine replied.

"That's quite a responsibility, isn't it, Mr. Levine?"

"All part of the job here at HPAT 21," Levine said. "By the way, you're not a good listener, Stone. I just said most people call me Levine."

I ignored his remark. Levine continued.

"Okay, people, here's what I know: A few months ago, the IRS initiated the International Data Exchange System. It's called IDES. This department now has international agreements with over one hundred and fifty governments around the world to track the movement of money to terrorists. HPAT 21 recently uncovered that there is a huge account at the Royal Bank of Toronto with hundreds of millions of dollars in it. IDES has spotted a sudden drop in one of the banks' nonprofit foreign accounts. The account dropped by at least $50 million overnight; that could be enough to buy a dirty backpack nuclear device, maybe an airplane, or whatever else can be found in the black market. It's scary, people."

"Levine, in what name is that account?" I asked.

"It's a well-known mosque in Toronto, the Al Zarqah Jahmal Mosque. Nobody has a clue where that money was transferred to. We're thinking that maybe these funds went to an extremist group in Yemen, or maybe to another group in Syria. But it's all guess work right now. This is fresh info, but it's getting staler by the minute. Only you guys know about this. Not even the president is aware of this flow of funds issue."

I became a bit disoriented. Stress, no doubt. My mind took me back in time. I remembered my letter to the editor of *The New York Times* that I had submitted a few years ago. It appeared in the "New York Today" section. I had emailed the editor and it was published the following week. I couldn't believe it.

I was fed up with all the anti-American acts of terror. They had hit our Middle Eastern embassies and then hacked into our government databases. The lone wolf attacks had started. I had to do something, say something. I had seen the writing on the wall. How the hell can the United States afford to fight wars and chase terrorists around the world and at the same time, protect the homeland inside? That's when I had come up with my idea. John F. Kennedy once said, "Ask not what your country can do for you—ask what you can do for your country." That had stuck with me forever. So, I came up with an idea that every American should pay $5 to the IRS from their income tax returns in order to defend the homeland. Yes, some form of a war tax.

I've always loved history and then I remembered It was Abraham Lincoln who initiated the first federal income tax by signing the Revenue Act in 1861 to help pay for the Civil War. Since he is on the five-dollar bill, I figured, *Why not ask every American to donate the same five dollars to fund the war on terrorism?* People from all walks of life, colleagues, and friends praised me for months about this idea. Then the excitement of my idea phased out abruptly. Suddenly, Levine jumped all over me.

"Stone, hello? Are you alright? I'm talking to you!"

"Hey, sorry. I was just thinking about something else," I replied apologetically.

Randy verbally slammed me, demanding that I stay focused.

"Jerk ass!" Randy exclaimed. "Lose your focus and lose your life. That's my last warning to you, tax man. You mess up, we all lose."

I stood up, eyed him, and said with a grin, "You need to calm down. Now, let me buy you a drink."

I was joking, as there was no bar here and we all laughed. I tried to lighten it up. The key was always to throw in a smile. Break the tension.

"Chill out, Mr. Randy," I said.

Everyone nervously smirked.

Levine took over, "Look, Bob, I was one of your greatest fans five years ago after I spotted your editorial in the New York Times. You were brilliant suggesting that Americans donate five dollars each to help our government pay for the war against terrorism."

"What, you actually spotted my editorial?"

"Of course, Bob," Levine complimented. "And I thought it was genius. I really admired you for that. That's one of several reasons why we need you. We believe in you, but you must get on the same page with us. By the way, you don't have much of a choice. You do know the dilemma you're in here, don't you?"

I paused then responded, "Sure, I get it."

CHAPTER 10

A surfeit of food was waiting on the counter at the far end of the conference room. A self-serve buffet was in the works. I sat alongside Wendy, Ashton, Frank, and Randy around a long table with Levine at the head. There were three televisions. Levine hit the remote to check out the news. One of those cooking shows was on. After a few moments, it was interrupted, just as the judges were about to "chop" someone. A local news reporter was talking in a low tone, saying that the president was walking to the podium. The president began earlier than expected. The president began his presentation.

"Good evening, my fellow Americans. I promise to be brief. Over the past few years, our homeland and our allies have been under attack by extreme terror groups around the world. Times are different, and the world is changing rapidly. We now face a coordinated effort by ISIS, Al Qaeda in the Arab Peninsula, Boko Haram, and other splinter groups working together against the Western world. I am announcing a global alert to all Americans living and traveling abroad. You must immediately leave the countries on the published U.S. Foreign Terrorist Organizations list. I now welcome to the podium our director of the Department of Homeland Security."

"Good evening, and thank you, Mr. President. Today, I have raised the homeland threat level to the maximum. This is due to substantially increased internet chatter and other information that points to actions most likely in process by extremists, as the president just mentioned. My counter parts at the FBI and the CIA are working in a coordinated manner to manage these terror threats. Back to you, Mr. President."

The president concluded, "To our journalists seated before me, I say respectfully that I cannot take your questions at this time. We are implementing numerous steps to protect all Americans using our assets at home and abroad. We do ask you all to be alert, observe those around you without prejudice, and if you do see something, say something. Good night, and may God bless the United States of America."

Randy started in immediately after the president's speech ended.

"Same garbage. The most influential leader of the free world without a plan. Damn it!"

Ashton told Randy to calm down. Frank muttered, "Bullshit," as he shook his head in disgust. It was then Levine's turn.

"The real plan is at this table."

I found the nerve to get a word out. "So, let's hear it. What's the plan, Stan? Just kidding, Levine."

He looked at me with a phony grin, then continued. "Do you remember the only thing that nailed Al Capone, the mafia king pin, was by proving tax evasion?" Levine reminded us. "And that's where you come into the picture, Stone."

"Interesting point, Levine," I confirmed.

"So, tax man...that's going to be your job."

Staring at Levine, I sank back into my chair. My urge to snap back got ahold of me.

"Hey, Levine," I said. "Do I look like Eliot Ness from *The Untouchables*?"

"Stone, follow the FOF and we will defeat them," Levine replied.

"What is FOF?" I queried.

"You should know that by now," Levine replied. "Come on, it's the 'flow of funds.' See, you're not focusing. That's why you need additional training, Stone. We have protocols around here and you'll need to learn fast."

"Speaking of training, we start tomorrow at 8:00 a.m. sharp," said Randy. "Stone, you and Wendy will be working together on this case. You will need to be brought up to speed on espionage, money trails, and other fun stuff. Go to the fifth floor and wait in the lobby. Be there at 8:00 a.m. sharp."

Everyone else called it a night. Wendy and I hung around for a decaf cappuccino from the buffet. This was a good time to talk with my new friend, Wendy. For lack of not knowing what to say next, I made some silly toast to good times.

"So, what's the story of your life?" I asked her.

She looked at me, hesitated, and then said, "I don't have the patience for that crap right now. Let's just say that I'm divorced, no kids, and I love to travel. Let's start with that. Good night, Stone."

She jerked the chair around, stood up, and walked out with an attitude.

"Hey, are you okay?" I asked.

"Sorry, I'm burned out. I need to get some sleep and, frankly, I'm worried about the enemies all around us. The world as we once knew it, is falling apart."

I was going to say, "No worries, it will be all right." However, in this new world of extremism, beheadings, and worldwide acts of terror, that comforting motherly philosophy didn't make sense anymore. There was no sugar coating this new reality. I called it a night and followed her out of the conference room, walking toward the elevator. There were two guards watching over me in the lobby. They seemed more relaxed around me now. Anyway, I saluted them as they led me into the elevator. As the elevator stopped on my floor, the doors opened up to another two guards.

One of the guards said, "Good night, Mr. Stone."

I saluted and thanked them for watching over me. By now, Wendy was out of sight, but not out of my mind. It was a draining day in this crazy command center. I was so much more tired than I realized. I opened the door to my room, looking forward to some peace and quiet. Wendy was lying in my bed wearing a cute red flannel shirt and matching pajama pants.

"What the heck are you doing here?" I asked.

"Bob, just get comfortable," Wendy said gently. "Nothing's going to happen between us. We need to talk."

"Wendy, I think you should call it a night. I'm dead."

I sat on the chair and tried to relax. A few minutes elapsed without us talking, so I moved over and sat next to her in bed. I had no agenda. I was glad for the silence.

It all caught up with me as soon as I rested my head on the pillow. I suddenly realized just how wiped out I was. So much had happened to me and so fast. The last few days had zapped my energy. I was done and dozing off while Wendy cuddled next to me.

As I was drifting off, she said, "Well, so much for talking."

I took a quick look at her cute face. She had a few freckles on her cheeks and manicured eyebrows hovering over her green eyes. Her appealing lips turned me on, especially when she smiled.

"Good night, sweetie," I said sleepily.

Then I smiled with a touch of lust, too tired to get anything started. I thought about how Laura could be doing. I would try to call her again in the morning before the training session.

CHAPTER 11

I t seemed like three minutes slipped by, but it was three hours later when I awoke and sat up abruptly, my tee-shirt totally drenched in sweat. My forehead and the back of my neck were sopping.

My thoughts led to a flashback to that day in April when Laura and I attended the wedding of Ammi's daughter in Astoria, Queens.

Darmush had said right to my face, "America must pay for its policies against the Arab world. Wherever you may be during the first week of this August, stay out of Manhattan. Go on vacation, my friend."

Yet somehow, I had never taken his words seriously. I wasn't sure what was going on, so I closed my eyes again to try and sleep it off. My head had barely touched back on the pillow. *No, no* I thought to myself.

I mumbled, "Stay out of Manhattan that week."

"Hey, Bob," Wendy said softly. "Are you talking to me? What's up? You just said something."

"Yes," I replied. "I mean, no." I was a mess. "I must be having a nightmare."

Wendy rolled over, tugged the covers around her and fell back asleep. I swung my legs to the side of the bed and went to the bathroom. After this usual late-night pee ritual, I noticed my face in the mirror while washing my hands. *What a sight*, I looked like crap, with bags under my eyes and pale-looking cheeks. I splashed some cold water on my face to cool me down.

It was tough to go back to sleep, but I had to, especially with another full day tomorrow. After walking around the room for a few minutes, I realized that if some of my clients were, in fact, connected to terrorist groups, as Randy had informed me they were, I might unknowingly have critical information to pass on.

Okay, enough. I went back to bed, careful not to wake up Wendy again. I left the bathroom light on, leaving the door ajar to allow for some light. I finally made it back to my bed without smacking into anything. As I slid under the covers, I realized Wendy was no longer wearing any clothes. *Oh my God, this is crazy.* I hesitated for a few seconds. I lost any sense of self control as my hands glided down her sleek back, then lower to the top of her butt. *Such smooth skin…* I gently kissed her ear, then her shoulder and my lips touched the back of her neck as I continued down and all the while, she was in and out of sleep.

"Hey, are you okay?" I asked.

She barely responded.

"Hey," I tried again. "Wendy, are you awake?"

She said nothing, but a moment later she turned over and edged up to kiss my lips. Her hands slowly caressed my upper chest. Her breasts were firm and perky. We were both losing control. I could not help but notice how she arched her back as she turned to move over my body.

"Wow," I said to her. "It's been a long time."

"Me too," Wendy mumbled under her breath. "Don't worry, I'm alright. It's all good. Ya know … birth control."

"Are you sure? We should not do this without protection," I said.

"I take birth control pills. I'm good, no worries," Wendy said.

I wanted her and I needed her closeness. I was in another zone, free and loaded with excitement. All I wanted to do was to please her. I turned her on her back, pushed her hands up over her head, and then gently pinned them down. The touch of my lips got her nipples firm. Instinctively, I moved my face down to her hips, reversing my body so she could reciprocate. I had to take charge, it was my nature and I sensed she was ready for me.

Wendy's body was firm, strong, and curvaceous. Her fragrance pulled me into a frenzy. I sensed she was letting go, unwrapping herself with wild jerking motions, moans, and groans. I was in between trying to control myself while allowing myself to let go. I continued to kiss and lick her as she pulled me further into our journey. We collapsed onto one another.

The next few hours afterward were spent cuddling and feeling the warmth of our spooned bodies, with occasional sleep in between.

"Bob, what were you saying last night?" Wendy asked at some point. "You were half asleep, scared, trembling. . . . Did you know that?"

"Sure, I was terrified."

Then I described to her the conversation I had remembered earlier that night with Darmush at the wedding.

"Let's get you debriefed on this info fast, Bob," she said, her tone suddenly turning serious. "I need to call all the guys from dinner last night and set up a security conference."

"Absolutely," I said.

"This is solid information, Bob. It's a huge thing. Bob, get your head together on this. Rethink what you were told, who told you, and who else was in that room. What other conversations did you hear that day? Did your wife, Laura, pick up on any other comments? Bob, any and all words can be critical. Take some time right now. Close your eyes and think. I'm leaving to shower and get dressed in my room. Let's meet in the fifth-floor lobby at 8:45."

"Okay," I said.

"See you in one hour," Wendy said, putting on her pajamas to leave. "Meantime, I'll make the calls and set up that meeting."

"Oh, Wendy, listen, I need to try Laura's cell again."

"Not right now, *amigo*," she said.

Wendy turned swiftly and shut the door behind her. I shook my head and hit the shower, unsure of what to make about our intimate moments together. There was no time to think about that anyway, I had to focus back to that day in April and try to dig up more helpful details from my memory.

CHAPTER **12**

I just stepped out of the shower and wrapped a towel around me when I heard the door of my room open abruptly. Before I could ask who was there, I heard Wendy's voice call out from the other side of the closed bathroom door.

"Bob, I have to call my contacts over at the Department of Homeland Security, meantime, you need to hurry up and get ready for your training day. Check out the closet over there. You'll find sweatpants, sneakers, sandals, and a martial arts uniform. You know the drill: get dressed, go up to the tenth floor, and wait outside the elevators for your instructor."

"Listen, Wendy," I said urgently. "I've already told you, I need to reach out to Laura. I have a bad feeling and I need to know where she is and if she is okay."

"Don't you worry, we'll need to bring Laura in for questioning anyway."

"Wait, so what the hell does that mean?" I demanded.

"The burden is now on us to find your wife. She may have overheard something you did not pick up on that night at Ahmed's house. Get the point?"

"You guys can't just call Laura without preparing her for everything that I've been through over the past several days."

"Bob, we don't have time for bullshit." Wendy said impatiently. "Someone in our system will reach out to her and explain just enough without overloading her with too much info, okay? We will do our best not to shock her."

"Do me a favor? I think John Ashton, the psych man, may be the gentlest one to contact Laura. Do that one favor for me, please, Wendy, Okay?"

"Amigo," she said playfully. "I will absolutely do my best to honor your request. Meantime, let's get this show on the road. I'll make the calls and arrangements to bring in Laura. You go upstairs for the training sessions and Stone, don't be late."

"Got it, thanks," I said. "Oh, and Wendy? Last night was—"

"Bob, drop the subject," she said, interrupting me. "It was… what it was."

"What the hell does that mean?" I asked.

"See you later, tax man," she replied.

And off she went to another day of homeland security issues and who knows what else. I opened the double door closet. Everything was there: a white martial arts uniform with a black belt, and a USA red, white, and blue sweatband tucked in between the uniform. I was ready in two minutes. I slipped on the sandals and exited my room, closing the door behind me.

About halfway past my room to the elevators, I noticed one armed guard. As I walked past him, he nodded his head at me with a smile. I returned the nod.

The elevator to the tenth floor was quick, but I managed to collect my thoughts. *How could Laura possibly understand what this is all about?* She will be in shock, but as a lawyer, Laura will hopefully find a way to be logical amidst the chaos. It was out of my control now and since the safety of our homeland now came first, I had to trust that Laura would ultimately be fine.

As the elevator doors opened, I was greeted with a bow by my trainer: a lean, bald man with a bright wide smile. He, too, was dressed in a martial arts uniform: black belt, tenth degree. I bowed back to him while keeping my eyes focused on his core. My past training began to resurface. Focus on the core to avoid being tricked by sudden movements.

"Good morning, tax man," he said. "I'm your trainer and most likely the one who will end up saving your life someday. My name is Claude Olsen."

Claude then extended his hand toward me for an amiable hand-shake. I responded accordingly. He pulled my hand toward him and snapped me with a gentle frontal kick just above my knee. I had a gut feeling that something like this was about to happen. I forgot to trust my instincts. It was time to be more street smart and sharpen my skills. To avoid injuries, I purposely fell flat on my butt and stayed down.

"Hey, dude," Claude said casually. "Be alert, my friend. Follow me. We have a shitload of work to do."

He extended his hand to help me up off the floor. This time, I thought twice.

"Nice try, but no way, Claude, get away from me."

He laughed hard and said, "Much better, I would've put you right back on the floor."

"Screw you, trainer," I said with a smile.

"So, here we are," Claude said, gesturing around the room. "We have the usual mats, exercise equipment, and a whole bunch of other toys for fighting practice. Okay, Bob, I'm gonna leave you alone for the next fifteen minutes so you can stretch out. We need to avoid injuries. Make sure you stretch out your quads. We'll be working on kicks and bringing you up to speed with some other moves."

"No problem, Claude."

"See you in a few, Stone and do take the stretching seriously," Claude said as he left.

I took his advice and stretched out carefully. He was right, it was always very important to stretch out before playing any sport and es-pecially in preparation for martial arts training. Claude walked back in shortly after.

"Now let's walk through our katas nice and slowly together," Claude began.

"Okay," I said. "But I'm a bit rusty."

"Don't worry about it," Claude reassured. "Just get started and do your best."

After four or five moves, my adrenaline started to flow. Out of no-where, a feeling of confidence took over, as if a voice in my mind commanded me. One by one, the moves I had spent so many years learning came back to me.

"Time's up, Stone," Claude said at last. "Let's go to the mats. We do not have time for all the bowing and finer martial arts traditional stuff. It's my job to elevate your skills—quickly. Now we move into kill-or-be-killed drills."

"Isn't there anything in between?" I asked politely.

"Yes, but not for you, and not for the situations you'll be dealing with. You need to integrate street fighting skills into your existing skills. Bob, let's review your roundhouse kicks."

We started to spar a bit and before I could blink, his kick landed one inch away from my forehead. I didn't even see it coming.

As I regained composure, Claude chuckled and said, "Now, Bob, you try it."

I was moving around the mat trying to confuse him. I saw my spot and I faked a strike with my fist, instead launching a roundhouse kick to his lower back.

"Nice move, Bob, where did you learn that one?"

"At a dojo in Brooklyn," I replied.

"Try that again," Claude said.

So, I faked a roundhouse kick to fool him, but instead swung a frontal knee blow to his side. He easily blocked my attempt using two hands, one crisscrossed over the other. He then flung me backward— an amazing counter move.

We continued to practice kicks and hand-to-hand combat moves for the next two hours. He was a great trainer, teaching me how to generate more power into my kicks and hand strikes.

"Bob, it's now time to move into more dangerous tactics," Claude said. "Are you ready?"

"Sure, I'm ready and interested."

"Bob, take this knife and lunge for my throat. Don't worry, I'll be fine. Come on, go ahead…do it in slow motion."

As I began to slowly initiate a knife attack, he stepped aside and grabbed my forearm. This took my energy and redirected it to his advantage. As he pulled my arm into his direction, he went through the motion of a gentle blow to my throat, and then he stopped.

"Bob, do you see what I just did?"

"Yes, sure."

"And now for the finale," Claude continued. "I will now destroy the vision in your right eye using your own energy coming at me. In a real attack, I would have ripped the eyeball right out of your eye socket."

"Give me a break, Claude... Are you serious?"

"Damn right I'm serious and you better be, too. This street-fighting shit is mean. The goal is to severely hurt or kill within the first three seconds of contact. Let's take a break... go get some water."

***

Over the next three hours, we practiced all sorts of moves: a frontal blow to the heart, a knee shot to the kidneys, a finger-spear strike next to the ear, an elbow to the side of the head, rapid takedowns by sweeping the feet of your attacker and much more.

"Claude, what do you call these moves?"

"It's a combination of Israeli Krav Maga and Karate," he replied. "Okay, Stone, moving on. Let's focus on getting out of trouble when your attacker has a gun. Take this pistol and point it at me. No bullets, it's okay."

I did as he instructed. In a split second, he grabbed the gun out of my hand and swept me to the ground.

"Your turn," he said. "Let's reverse."

I didn't have the speed for this, but I got the idea. After four attempts, I finally figured it out. I smoothly ripped the pistol out of Claude's hand, while at the same time, I stepped inside his space, and then came through with my right elbow to his face.

"Nice move, Bob," he said "You're a fast learner."

"Thank you, sir," I said.

Next, Claude set up a scenario on how to handle being confronted when sitting in a car.

"You're sitting in the driver's seat, someone gets into the car on the passenger side, while you are stopped at a red light."

This was the most difficult of all situations he addressed thus far. With incredible speed, I had to learn how to deflect a pistol and simultaneously break the attacker's wrist. Claude showed me how to pull the attacker deeper into the car to close off his space. Next was a move to choke off his breathing with a three-finger grab onto his Adam's apple. Claude simulated this, so he spared me the pain. It was truly amazing stuff. I had forgotten how much I really loved this world of offense and defense as an art form.

I realized that Claude was absolutely right; these were the self-defense tactics that might end up saving my life. These moves were so dangerous that I could easily kill someone looking to pick a fight with me over nothing, like road rage or whatever. This was a fact I had to respect.

Finally, Claude ended our session.

"Bob, you were great today, you really surprised me. I wish we had more time to practice together. I've heard that serious acts of terror are brewing and they may be triggered sooner than we think, so let's wrap it up here. Head back to your bedroom, take a shower, and rest."

"Thanks, Claude," I said with respect as I bowed to him.

Wendy was waiting in the hallway. We went down to my room and I dropped onto the bed.

"Bob, you were fabulous in there today," she said.

"What—how could you know that?"

"Come on, I watched the whole training session through the window on the side wall while I made my calls."

"There was no window there," I said.

"Oh, yes there was, anyway, it's now 4:00 p.m. and I need to update you on Laura's status."

As I started to ask, Wendy cut me off and said, "Relax, shower up, and meet me in forty-five minutes."

"Where?"

"At the elevators by your room," she replied. "Go take a break, Bob. You deserve it."

CHAPTER **13**

had no patience to wait. I took a two-minute shower, got dressed, and went to Wendy's room. I knocked rapidly.

"Hey, who's that?" she called out.

"It's me, Bob," I said. "Open the door."

"Ooh, what's with the edginess, just hold on for a moment, *amigo*."

She opened the door wearing a shirt but no pants. I started to turn away, having no patience for games despite my attraction for her. I was exhausted from training and concerned about Laura.

"Come on," I said with frustration. "Please get dressed and tell me about Laura. Did someone contact her yet?"

"I really don't know,"

"What's happening, Wendy?" I demanded. "You know this is difficult for me."

"Okay, so here it is," she said. "I did talk with Ashton. After all, he will be the one who debriefs Laura. Problem is that right now, our guys in the street cannot find her."

"What? With all of the power you guys have at your fingertips, you're telling me that they cannot find my wife! Where have they looked?"

"Your house, obviously. We had two cars stationed near your house hoping she might stop by. Laura never did show up."

"Okay, where else?"

"Another patrol car went to Laura's mother's house in Westbury. Nothing. And another car went to her sister's house in Huntington. Nothing. We're all trying, Bob. Let's meet with Levine. He texted me an hour ago and needs to talk with us."

"Yeah, about what?"

"Bob, I'm not a mind reader."

Wendy pulled up her tight black pants, then popped her feet into knee-high boots and off we went.

"Very stylish," I said.

"Why not?" she asked. "And see these pointy boots? They're my weapons. How do you like that?"

Then she let loose a roundhouse kick in the hallway. I nervously laughed. Actually, I knew she was serious—dead serious.

"Real cute," I said. "So, where are we going to now?" I asked, as we stepped into the elevator.

"Second floor to a secure area. Let's see what Levine has to say."

"Hey, Wendy, I know how to read people. Something is wrong, so what's up? Tell me right now."

I paused and hit the red emergency button to stop the elevator in between floors, waiting for an answer.

"Hey, cut the crap, Bob, we'll find out what's going on in about three minutes."

"Are you telling me you have no idea what's been happening with Laura?"

"Hello, like I already said, no, I absolutely do not."

"Wendy, I just don't believe you, you're holding back something, aren't you?"

She ignored me. Then snapped again.

"You know what, Stone? You really disappoint me. Just how nasty do you think I am? I know your wife recently left you. I know you're going through a weird time and contrary to what you think, I do have a heart. Do you understand me? So, if I had some concrete information, I would give it to you. Now get off my back, unlock the damn elevator, and let's get to our meeting."

I pushed the button again, allowed the doors to open. I was taking out my frustrations on her. At that moment, I knew I should talk to her. *Tell her, stupid, tell her...* and so I did....

"Hey, Wendy, I'm sorry. I shouldn't be taking it out on you."

"Yeah, yeah," she said. "Sure, tax man."

"Just give me a break," I requested.

"Alright, no problem, I'll give you some slack."

We got off the elevator onto the secure floor and walked four rooms down on the left. Wendy knocked on the door. We waited for a minute, but it seemed like an hour. I was bracing myself for some shocker news that would shake me up.

Levine opened the door slowly. He clearly had a troubled look on his face. He avoided eye contact with me.

"Hey, super spies, come in," Levine said.

"Levine, how come you didn't call me 'tax man' this time?" I asked. Everyone else around here loves to say that."

"I guess this was my way of welcoming you officially into the world of global terrorism and espionage," he replied.

"Oh, thanks, so, now I'm officially a graduate of the IRS Spy College. That's pretty fast."

"Okay, 'tax man' —feel better now?" Levine asked sarcastically.

"No, not really."

"Anyway, it's time I update you both on what's been going on," Levine smoothly shifted.

"Hold on a moment," Wendy said. "Bob senses that Laura is in possible danger."

Levine replied, "Look, here is my thought: Bob, who do you know at Laura's office? Anyone you've met over the past few years at the law office where Laura worked—a secretary, an associate, or someone she might confide in?"

I stood up and paced around the room. Then it hit me.

"Yes, there was this guy, Ray Jackson, who does legal research for her. When I used to call to Laura, he'd pick up if she was busy. I'd joke around with him by calling him 'Ray Jay.'

"Great, let's get a secure line for Bob right now," Levine said to Wendy. "This could be a break, let's get on it and see what, if anything, this guy knows."

Wendy got up abruptly. Then Levine turned back to me.

"Okay, Stone?"

"I'm ready, let's do it."

Wendy came back with a portable phone. I dialed the law office.

"Hello, Combs and Walker, may I help you?"

"is Ray Jackson available?"

"One moment, please."

"Thanks."

"Who is calling, please?"

On the spot, I invented a name and went with, "Oh, it's Robert Schafer, a client."

Realizing I was quick on my feet with the fictitious client name, Levine smiled and whispered, "Quick thinking, Bob," as Wendy gave me a glance of approval with her thumbs up. A few moments passed before another voice came on the line.

"Hello, Ray Jackson here,"

"Is this the famous 'Ray Jay?'" I asked jokingly.

"Hey, the only dude to ever call me that is Bob Stone. How are you? What's up?"

"Hey, Ray Jay, long time. How are you, the wife, kids, girlfriend, whatever?"

"It's all good," Ray said as he laughed off my girlfriend joke. "Why complain, right?"

"Right, who wants to hear it anyway?"

"So, Stone, why are you calling me?"

"Listen, Ray, I need your help."

Silence lingered on the other end.

"Can we talk in confidence, Ray?"

"What's this about?" he asked, sensing my urgency. "If it involves Laura, I want to help. I've known her for about eight years, she's a great lady."

"Thanks so much. Ray. I cannot tell you much, but I sense that Laura may be in some sort of danger."

"Really, why?"

"We had a bad argument last week. She bolted out of the house. I figured she left to blow off some steam. Well, I underestimated her angst...she took off, left me, and that's the story. I have not been able to reach her since the day she walked out. Ray, things have been happening that I cannot talk about, but I need to know where she might be. If you know where Laura is, I need to know. There is no time to waste."

"She made me swear not to reveal her whereabouts. Now you're putting me between a rock and a hard place."

"Ray, please."

"Stone, I understand that she asked the law firm to use up her sick days and overtime hours early. She told me that she needed to chill, to rethink her life. She was not in a good place."

"Ray, I made some mistakes along the way and, like most guys, I'll end up being the asshole and I'll face up to that crap. Now, I'm talking about something way above and beyond marital stuff. Laura's life may be in danger. Where is she, Ray?"

"You never heard it from me, got it?"

"Sure, of course, Ray."

"Laura rented a place on Fire Island."

"Really, which part?"

"Ocean Beach. She told me that it was only two cottages away from the beach."

"Ray Jay, you're the man. When did she go there?"

"I believe about five days ago. Bob, keep me out of this, we never even talked, okay. I'm not asking you, I'm telling you."

"No worries, Ray. You're out of this, we never even talked."

"Good luck, Bob. Hey, keep me in the loop. You never know how I might be able to help out."

"You are a good soul. Thanks again, Ray Jay."

"Okay, see ya, Bob."

Wendy kicked me just below my knee to grab my attention.

"Her cell phone, stupid," she whispered. "Ask for her new cell number."

"Wait, Ray, what's her new cell phone number?"

"Come on, Bob, you're killing me."

I said nothing and waited in silence until he broke. After a long fifteen seconds, he started to cave.

"Bob, that's the ultimate invasion of anyone's privacy."

"No, no, Ray, not at all. I can always say I did a cell phone search."

"Laura is no dummy, come on."

I stayed silent again.

"Bob, let me call you back on my cell."

"No good, Ray, I can't do that."

"Bob, are you in some kind of trouble over there?"

"No, but I cannot be reached where I am at right now. I'll explain it to you another time."

"Now you sound weird," Ray said cautiously. "Did the CIA recruit you?" he asked with a nervous laugh.

"You're getting warm, but no cigar. Ray, I'll call your cell right back. Anyway, as you said, I may need your help one day, so let me have it."

"Okay. Call me right back, Bob."

Two seconds later, I called back and Ray gave me Laura's new cell number. We said our goodbyes again. I felt a firm pat on my back. Looking off to my side, it was Levine.

"Great job, Stone," he said.

"Thanks." I spoke out loud to myself, "I suppose after she walked out on me, Laura felt the need to get away from everything."

Yeah, that's it and I get it. I shook my head and a tear found its way out of my eye. This was all my fault. My mind drifted back to when I turned thirty-five. I was impatient and restless. I was comfortable years ago, but I made myself unhappy. Does anyone truly love what they do? Maybe I could have found a way to not love what I was doing, but also to not hate what I was doing. My mind was so far away from Levine and Wendy right now—a bad time to do soul searching.

Just then, Wendy yelled at me and said, "Bob, where are you? What's up?"

"Oh, sorry guys," I said apologetically. "I was thinking about my life, that's all." I laughed out loud. "I need a break," I said. "Ten minutes, please."

I went outside and sat down on one of the hard-wood benches in the hallway. My brain was locked in the past. I recalled that I had this need to change my world just for the sake of change. I remembered that at the time, I felt like I had to break out of a boring career. I was afraid of living my life the wrong way. But Laura was always right. She had told me to stay the course, to keep my bread and butter—those doctor and dentist clients. She even suggested that I get into forensic accounting, pursue being an expert witness, or whatever I had to do just to keep my clients. She always said that I could reinvent myself. I didn't even give her ideas a chance. If only I could have just controlled my lousy attitude at that time. If I could go back to the comfortable, boring life I once had . . . I would kill for that. I had screwed up my career, my marriage, and my life. *Why?* I was simply an impulsive ass-hole.

Now what? Now what? Now what?! I shook my head and took a deep breath to shrug it off. I had to snap out of this. All I can do now is to make a difference in this sick world. I must improve myself, my life, and what I stand for. I had to turn this lemon into lemonade. All I had left now was my self-respect. I stood up slowly, took another deep breath, exhaled, and then another. I stretched my hands high up to the ceiling and then touched the floor with my fingers, repeating this sequence five times.

I walked back into the room and smiled to make myself feel better. I then apologized.

"Let's continue, sorry guys."

"Okay, Bob," Levine said, "Listen. We need to bring Laura in here. With all due respect, we need to debrief Laura as we would debrief anyone else who may have key information. Anything, a word, a phrase, or even a subtle remark that she may have overheard at your client's wedding reception after the ceremony in the mosque that day. If Laura heard something that got past you, it may end up being vital to protect the homeland. Bob, you cannot possibly disagree with this, understand, are you with me on this?"

"I'm fine," I said. "But I don't want to shock Laura. I asked Wendy to see if Ashton, my psych friend, could be the one to reach out to my wife first. He's not my most favorite guy, but he may be the gentlest of all you crazies."

"We already talked about this Stone; it's already been set up, guys," Wendy said with a bit of an attitude.

It was so easy to spot her irritation when her lips tightened up.

"I have access to a helicopter out of New York Harbor," Levine said. "I'll order a crew of four guys—no—make that five to set up surveillance on Laura. At the right time, she will be escorted off Fire Island. We can't risk losing her, not even for another day. Too much is going on. Bob, you don't even know the half of it yet. Here's my promise to you: We'll put two guys close to her Fire Island cottage. Now that you have her new cell number, I'll have Ashton call her first to break the ice."

"Perfect, I appreciate that, Levine."

"Hey, that's the only nice thing you've said to me so far, tax man," Levine said. "Anyway, thanks for the compliment, Stone. Ashton will make the call in about thirty minutes."

I was relieved, but still nervous. I saw Levine pick up his cell phone. He started to text, and then he showed me after sending it. It just said, *Laura & Hardy, do it.* The response came right back, *TBD in ten min.*

"Laura and Hardy—what's that?" I asked.

"Code name for bringing your wife in," Levine replied. "Kind of stupid, right? Ya know, the famous Laurel and Hardy comedy duo."

"No, kind of cute," I said as I shrugged my shoulders and twisted my hands out, as if to say, *Yeah—it's kind of silly.*

***

His ten minutes became thirty. I was nervously coughing and pacing around the room when Levine's cell sounded.

"Bob," he said. "Ashton is texting me now."

As Levine focused on his cell phone, I saw his eyebrows edging up.

"Hey, what's going on?" I asked.

Wendy put her hands out silently, telling me to calm down. I imitated her, flipping my hands down to the ground, telling her to leave me alone.

Levine put his phone down and said, "Bob, contact was made with Laura. Ashton filled her in on a few key points. For good measure, Ashton threw in that you miss her very much, that we have been holding you here in our Langley Virginia Command Center for various reasons. Although confused, she seemed to take it in stride. Your Laura has really good composure."

"Why do you say that?" I asked Levine.

"Ashton told me that after he mentioned that she might have access to information that could save American lives, she remained calm. She was more pissed off that somehow her new cell number was given out. Ashton handled that very well."

"Oh, and how?" I asked.

"He just shrugged it off by saying, We have our ways, Laura, nobody gave it out.'"

"Wow, nicely done!"

"Bob," Levine continued. "Now that Laura's ready, I'm sending my five guys to Fire Island right now by helicopter."

"I need a moment to absorb this, too much, too fast. *This is crazy. There was no time to absorb anything. We simply cannot lose her.*

"Oh, and Bob," Levine added, ignoring my request, "You should know that your house has been under surveillance by others."

"What!"

"Yeah, we spotted them when we were looking for Laura at your home," Levine explained.

"Are you sure?" I asked, while wondering, *who is them?*

"Absolutely positive, Bob. It's time to get your wife. It's time, and it's a damn good thing we brought you in off the streets. We all knew your time was up, Stone. You were in trouble and you had no idea."

"Okay, let's do it," I said. "Yes, get Laura, just do it. Thanks, Levine. Thanks."

I got off my chair and left the room with Wendy. I felt like I was in a hospital waiting for the results of a surgical procedure. Levine called us back in with the wave of his hand.

"The chopper just left for Fire Island. Our guys will be there in twenty minutes. After learning you've been followed by others, we deployed a whole team of HPAT 21 trained forces for additional security. We've also notified the New York Harbor Coast Guard for safe measure. I'll be receiving live reports on my laptop. Let's just wait it out. Wendy, do you mind bringing us some coffee?"

"Hey, Levine," Wendy said sharply. "Give me a break—get one of your grunts in training to bring it up here. I'm not your waitress."

"Sorry, I didn't mean it that way."

"Bullshit," she snapped back at Levine.

"Okay, Okay, bad idea," Levine humbly responded.

He called out and had one of the guards bring up coffees and donuts. Then, the shit hit the fan.

"Our HPAT 21 team is dressed in casual clothing, beach hats, and whatever else to avoid making a scene," Levine remarked. "They're armed with pistols, silencers attached and carrying knives, as well. They also have the exact same needles that we used to bring you in here, Stone."

"Very impressive," I said. "But what's going on?"

"Just a few minutes ago, our team began closing in on the cottage and reported that Laura was walking very closely with two other guys. They seem to be walking in the direction of the ferry. Yes, a report came in. They are waiting on line to board the ferry."

"Shit, so what's up next Levine?"

"Only good thing is, there are about thirty people ahead of them," Levine said. "A zoomed-in shot from security cameras revealed that Laura is being held by her wrists, with one guy on her left side and one on her right. No cuffs, just a very tight grip from each of her captors. Come over here, Bob, you can see her on this monitor."

"That's her, definitely Laura. And I can tell you she is scared, I know her face. She is scared despite her stoic look. What's that behind her lower back?"

"Let's find out," Levine said, focusing in for a clearer visual. "It's a knife. It's a damn knife. Okay, stay calm, our team knows what to do."

"What's the plan, Levine?" asked Wendy.

"The guy on the left will get bumped into and simultaneously injected with a needle. Within three seconds, he will be unconscious. The man to Laura's other side will be distracted and asked if he knows what time it is, while they edge up behind Laura to grab the knife discreetly. Quiet now. This is happening in ten seconds."

"Ten seconds to rumble, everyone," Levine commanded into his cell phone.

He counted down to coordinate the HPAT 21 team near the ferry. Another plain-clothed person was slowly moving in on Laura's left side.

Levine followed my concerned gaze and explained, "Stone, that's one of ours; they will need to hold the attacker upright after being injected to avoid drawing attention and prevent other people from getting scared. Can't create a scene over there."

I then noticed the two others on Laura's right side to hold the much larger assailant upright. Another HPAT guy moved in to nail him with a syringe.

Levine counted down again out loud to the HPAT 21 team, signaling the go ahead, "Five, four, three, two, and one. Go."

I couldn't swallow, I couldn't move. My eyes were on Levine's monitor, watching live. Wendy was grabbing my hand. Now she was digging her nails into my skin. My hands were sweaty. It's happening. The HPAT 21 team was working in harmony. I could not see any needles, but both guys next to Laura went limp. They were held up by the others as planned. Each injected assailant was walked over to a nearby bench discreetly. Simultaneously, one of ours gently grabbed the knife away and another escorted Laura in the opposite direction, away from the ferry area. All of this was done in a split second, with perfect timing and unnoticed by the ferry crowd.

I took a deep breath, stood up, and then went to the bathroom. I hit the urinal, washed my hands and face, and looked at myself in the mirror. I had no energy to start talking to myself. Anyway, I had no time to get into any mental crap now. I had to keep the demons out of my head. I just looked at my unshaven face and laughed. Why, I don't know. Maybe it was nervous laughter. One thing for sure, I would be seeing Laura in a few hours. That was my next challenge. *Thank God, she is safe now.*

Levine came into the bathroom. He patted me on the back and said, "Are you okay, Bob?"

I managed to squeak out, "Yeah, yeah. I'm okay. Frankly, Levine, I thought you were more of a traditional IRS guy?"

"Wrong. I told you, I run an elite, highly-trained anti-terror unit of the IRS. As part of HPAT 21, we protect the homeland, Bob. I guess you did not take me seriously when I mentioned this to you the first time."

"You're right. And Levine, you were amazing in there. Thank you."

"No problem, tax man, no problem."

We went back to the secure room. Wendy was waiting there.

"Now what, guys?" she asked.

"Laura will need to be checked out medically for any issues," Levine replied. "Who knows what those two assholes may have done to her. Let's hope for the best."

"By the way, she'll need clothes from the Fire Island cottage," I added.

"Oh yeah, of course," Levine replied. "Our team already walked her back to the cottage, gave her time to pack, and off they went back to the chopper."

"Aren't they taking her first to Bellevue Hospital in Manhattan?" Wendy asked.

"Yes, correct," Levine answered. "She'll be kept there overnight for observation."

Just as I started to open my mouth to ask, "What about security?" Levine said, "Bob, don't worry. Three guys from homeland security will be at her door all night. It will be fine. You know what? Looks like Laura will get here tomorrow by lunchtime."

"Amazing, thanks, Levine," I commented.

"Stop thanking me already. Enough." Levine smiled and said, "Let's get out of this building for a real dinner tonight. We're going to a nice restaurant. It's 4:35 p.m. now... how about we meet in the first-floor lobby at 6:15 p.m.? Now we can all take a well-deserved rest. I will connect with Ashton, he should be with us."

"Absolutely, sounds good to me," I said.

"Same here," Wendy added.

We walked out, drained and relieved in securing Laura, but pretty nervous about what insanity was waiting for us in this crazy world. I walked Wendy to her room. She held my hand and kept holding on.

"See you later. Thanks for . . . errr . . . your moral support today," I said.

She smiled and closed her door. I was halfway down the hallway when she cracked open her door and blurted out, "Bob, you are a good man."

"Why do you say that?" I inched back toward her room.

"You really care about your wife. I envy you. Maybe you can make things right with Laura."

"Nice idea, but I have no clue how to do that."

"Take it one day at a time, one day at a time."

CHAPTER 14

I needed to close my eyes and let go. Tired but not sleepy, my brain was like a shooting star, moving in haphazard directions. It hurt to close my eyes. I was so focused on Laura's rescue that I had forgotten to ask Levine about the two assholes who tried to kidnap her at the Fire Island Ferry. *How stupid.*

Too impatient to let it go, I went to Wendy's room. I was about to knock but was actually afraid she would open the door with no clothes on. I had to avoid being in that position again. So, I knocked, and then walked down the hall. She opened her door with a slight delay and then she poked her head just outside the door.

"It's you," she said. "What's up?"

"Hey, I can't sleep, I'm a mess."

"Okay, then come into my room, we can just talk."

"No, no, what the hell happened to those two jerks?"

"I believe they were detained."

"What does that mean?"

"They are being held for questioning. Standard crap, you know."

"No, I don't know."

"Okay, Bob, let's see Levine right now, I'd rather not guess."

"Let's see if Levine will be in the same secure room from earlier today. Let's go now."

"Give me five minutes. Hold on, Bob."

"Sure, but come on, move it."

She didn't bother to answer my last remark. We took the usual elevator down and without knocking, we entered the room. Levine was still there doing some paperwork.

"Hey," Levine shouted. "Did you forget how to knock first? And why are you guys back in here? You should be getting some rest!"

"I was trying to," I explained. "But no way, that's not in the cards right now for me."

"Well, what's up, Bob, sounds like your brain is fried."

"Sort of," I replied curtly. "So, what did our HPAT 21 team do with those two guys who were holding my wife?"

"We didn't get into that, did we?" Levine pondered.

"No, we did not."

"My oversight Stone, Levine admitted.

"Those two assailants were checked from head to toe. No IDs were found on them. Their fingerprints showed nothing. No cell phones were found. Surprisingly smart. They must be undocumented aliens, but we're not yet sure from what country. Not a damn thing, nothing."

"Have they recovered yet from the injections?" I asked.

"Much too soon, no way," Levine replied.

"Okay, Levine, please listen to me. Can you somehow implant a tracking device on these guys?"

"We can do just about anything, Stone. The answer is, yes, of course."

"Then just do that and let them go free. Where are they now, still on Fire Island?"

"Yes," Levine answered.

"Leave them on the beach with enough money for the ferry."

"Where are you going with this Bob?" Levine queried.

"Say hi to your reinvented tax man, now, a street smart spy guy! This is my transformation, like a caterpillar morphing into a butterfly."

Levine and Wendy looked at each other and nodded their heads, as if to say, *quite impressive*.

I continued on, "Anyway, we must know who sent those two guys to grab Laura, right? So, let's track them back to their source. Let them go free. Then, we'll figure it out in twenty-four to forty-eight hours. Trust me," I added to reassure them.

"I agree with you, Bob, but it's not so easy," Levine replied.

"Nothing is easy these days." It was a pretty good line.

"Hello," Wendy interjected. "What about protocol, rules, all kinds of crap to deal with?"

"I'll need to jump through hoops to set them free," said Levine. "Let's see what I can get done right now—I need to make some calls, starting with Randy Johnson. If he is with us, we'll have a much better probability of making it happen. Why don't you both stay here for a few minutes? I'll call Randy now. Then, Bob, it will be your time to step up. You will present your idea to Randy. You'll need to speak with conviction. From this point going forward, you must understand that it's all a game of confidence."

"No problem, I know this is the only way to go."

Levine picked up the secure line and started talking to Randy. Then he handed me the phone.

"Here, take the phone, tax man."

"Hello, Randy, this is Stone here," I paused.

"What's up Stone? I hear you want to take the lead on those two characters who grabbed your wife. What's on your mind?"

"Thanks, we have absolutely nothing to go on. No info, no prints, no IDs, not a damn thing on those two low lives. We need to let them free and track them back to their source. We need to place a tracking device in their shoes or in their damn skin, whatever."

"That's up to the technical people," Randy explained. "Right now, I understand they are still out from the injections, just lying on the beach far away from vacationers."

"Perfect. Make sure they each have enough cash for the ferry. Let them find a way to reconnect with their people."

"I promise that in about two days, we'll be able to find the source."

"Normally, I would tell you to back off, but you have just elevated yourself. I'll make it happen, and agree to play it out. Thanks, Bob. Good thinking."

"Thank you, Randy," I said.

"Just take a break, Bob," Randy reiterated. We all know what kind of a tense day you just experienced. Leave the rest to me for now. I assure you, it will be done."

"Levine, I'm out of here, but please, keep me in the loop."

"Stone, no need to say that. See you at dinner. Let's meet in the first-floor lobby in one hour. I'll update you then."

"Great, later." Wendy and I exited.

I was wiped. We headed back to our floor. I sensed that we needed each other's moral support. It was in the air.

"Wendy, let's chill out in my room, talk, whatever," I was being sincere and not looking for anything sexual.

"Let's skip it. I need to rest. Ya know Bob, I'm a bit down. I'd rather be alone right now. Maybe we can talk after dinner or another time?"

"I understand, sorry you feel that way."

I left Wendy, realizing that although she had a tough exterior, she too was human. I headed toward my room thinking, *how self-focused I had been, not even thinking for a moment about Wendy's feelings.* As I entered my room, I crashed down into my bed and thought that I more than likely had also been ignoring Laura's feelings for a long time. In an unexpected way, this place here in Langley Virginia had become my personal mental health rehab center. I chuckled with that thought while drifting into an easy sleep.

***

The sudden knocking on my door was a shock to my system. It seemed that an hour had passed when only one minute had gone by.

Wendy yelled from the hallway, "You're late, stupid, come on."

Shit, I had to force myself out of bed immediately. I threw on whatever clothes I saw scattered around the room and splashed some cologne onto my cheeks. All was done in two minutes flat. I opened the door to greet Wendy.

"Hey, you smell pretty good, but look like crap," Wendy said, mocking me. "First of all, shut your pants zipper."

I smiled as I looked down.

"Then, go back and put on a sports jacket," she ordered.

I headed back in my room to change. I came out and she gave me her seal of approval with a look, followed by a thumbs-up.

"Much better, let's boogie."

I followed her to the elevators.

"Levine is waiting in the lobby, Randy is joining us. He will meet us at the restaurant. Randy is always late, pain in the butt."

The elevator doors closed behind us, and down we went. We met up with Levine and he gave me a pat on my back.

"Bob, the deed was done. No time to cut and stitch, no tracking device under the skin. Better yet. We have a new device: a patch so tiny that it's impossible to notice it, right behind the neck. It latches into the skin's surface and won't wash away in the shower. Already been tested."

"Amazing, I said for good measure."

"Let's take a break from this crap and enjoy a nice Italian dinner.

It's a family style restaurant just a few miles away. You'll love the food, Levine assured."

We entered a car waiting curbside for us. As we pulled away, I noticed two more cars following us...I kept turning around to get a better look.

"Bob, no worries, the two cars behind us are HPAT 21 security detail," Levine explained. "Don't be concerned."

"That's reassuring."

"Here's a little trivia. . . . Since we don't have access to the normal secret service guys, we work with many of my former employees who were previously with the regular IRS Crime Unit. These guys made the crossover into the arena of anti-terror. Those who requested to be transferred were assigned over here to HPAT 21."

"I appreciate the history. Thanks.

I noticed that Wendy was zoning out, staring out the car window.

To snap her out of it, I said, "Hey, keep it down. Why are you so quiet?" I asked.

She laughed and said, "Frankly, I'm worried Stone."

Levine intervened saying, "Listen, let's just enjoy ourselves, I know there's so much going on. It will all be good—keep the faith!"

Wendy replied, "You know, I needed that, Levine! Thanks!"

"Look, there's our restaurant straight ahead," Levine said, pointing. "Let's go, I am starving!" I couldn't help noticing the colorful sign, Mama's Trattoria, as our car pulled up to the restaurant. After Levine exited, I held Wendy's hand and led her out from the car. Two guards followed us into the restaurant. Two other guards remained outside the front door. As we were entering the restaurant, a well-groomed man smiled and asked us to follow him inside. He led us to a table set up in a back room. Looked like Levine was a regular from the warm greeting he received.

Ashton was already waiting at the table and greeted each of us. The owner came right to our table and embraced Levine with one of those feel-good, man-to-man hugs. No menus were needed, just round after round of great food.

After we devoured the appetizers, Randy stumbled in and breathlessly said, "Sorry I'm late, lady and gents."

"What happened, Randy?" Levine commented.

"I'm starving," Randy snapped. "Let me dig into this first, then we can talk."

Randy devoured a few apps, then asked the waiter to bring two house wine bottles, one cab, the other a merlot. After his first half glass was gulped, Randy took a deep breath and looked around the table anxiously. I noticed that Wendy and Levine reached for the cab. I was too much on edge to bother with wine right now.

"Come on, Randy," I said. "You seem to have something to say, so let's hear it."

"Okay, here we go. We decided to leave four of our guys at the beach to see what would happen next. The chopper was moved to another part of Fire Island. Since we had no time to wait for their recovery, I gave the order to inject each guy with a chemical to wake them up. About two hours later, the two dudes slowly got moving, then walked behind a large rock about thirty feet away. They picked up a bag, pulled out their cell phones, and made a call."

"Then what?" Wendy asked impatiently.

"We traced the call to another cell phone in the New York area. Not yet sure of the exact location or who they may have talked with."

"What about our two unidentifiable dudes?" I queried.

"Twenty minutes after their cell call, a small speed boat picked then up near the ferry. Off they went and now we wait, *amigos*." He gestured with his glass to me and said, "To your quick thinking and smart idea, Stone."

I then poured the merlot into my wine goblet halfway up. I stood up as something came over me. I gently moved my glass in a few small circles, placed my nose over the top of the glass to check the aroma, and enjoyed a healthy sip. I began to speak from the heart.

"To HPAT 21," I said. I must have hit a hot button.

They all stood up and repeated, "Here, here! To HPAT 21."

A few minutes later, an array of family-style platters was brought over by two waiters carrying enticing food with a heavy garlic fragrance. It was a tossup: Should I stare at the food to appreciate the presentation or dig in and eat like a pig? It didn't take long to decide. After being stuck in that command center for a few days, which felt more like weeks, I lost my self-control. We all stopped talking and just feasted; we ate and ate, and then ate some more. The waiters brought more food as we knocked off the earlier plates. This kept going until Levine finally spoke to the owner.

"*Grazie mille* . . . but enough."

The busboys cleaned up the mess and the crumbs were delicately scraped off the table. Randy asked the head waiter to hold off on desserts. Then, about fifteen minutes later, various sweets appeared.

"Is this our last meal?" I asked. "This is crazy."

"No, no," Levine replied. "Just a well-deserved treat, my way of apologizing to you for the rough manner in which you were brought here to Langley. I wasn't happy with the way we had to bring you in here, but we had no choice. You had to be extracted for your own safety and for national security reasons. Stone, you were already being compromised."

"Ah, I get it...No problem. It's no big deal, guys. I thought you ruined my life, but now I see you may have actually saved my life. I find it all hard to believe. So, now that you saved my ass, how about replacing my lost income somehow? You know, my tax practice and my career can never be the same, right?"

No one responded, but I had planted the seed. I let it go for the moment.

As the coffees and Sambuca shots were being poured, it happened: Randy and Levine each received the same group text. They both practically dropped their coffee cups. Levine passed his phone to Wendy, while Randy gave me his cell to read it: *The Eagle has landed. It's a mosque in Astoria, Queens.*

We all looked up at one another . . . there was nothing to say. The connection was made and for better or worse, the link to my clients was now unquestionable. I started to think about why Laura was a target. It made no sense to me that my wife was in harm's way due to my clients.

Wendy then said what I was thinking. "Something else has to be going on with Laura. Obviously, it's something she has no idea about. This is what we need to find out. Bob, what kind of law firm does Laura work for? What do they specialize in? And what cases had Laura been working on lately?"

With that, Levine immediately agreed with Wendy. Randy nodded his head.

"I don't really know, Wendy but If I had to make an educated guess, I would say that Laura worked on deals."

"What type of deals?" Wendy asked. "That's too general. Think, Bob."

"Well, a few years ago she started out handling landlord/tenant matters, leases, things of that nature. She was bored with that after one year and asked the partners for their permission to work on more interesting cases. Over time, the senior partners threw real estate deals to her."

"Tell us more?" Wendy asked.

"Why don't we get Laura on the phone for this?" I asked. "I don't have anything else . . . Something must have happened at her office. She's too much of a hardworking, driven career person to ask for time off like that, even with our argument."

"Come on, Bob," Wendy jumped at me. "Think, think. Sip your coffee, relax, and think it through."

I took her advice. Wendy was being professional, not nasty or sarcastic. I sensed her genuine concern.

"Guys, I need two minutes outside."

"Sure," Levine said. "Take a break, Bob."

We all stood up, stretched, and took a much-needed time out. I grabbed a mint and then walked outside. Two HPAT 21 guards followed me.

"Sorry, Mr. Stone, we are here to protect you."

"Thanks, guys, I understand."

As I continued to stroll outside in the parking lot, I was trying hard to think about Laura's work. Over the years, we both chose to avoid talking about our professional issues at home. But I was usually the one complaining about my clients, while Laura chose to leave her work issues at the office, I suppose respecting the attorney-client privilege. Somehow, I always needed to vent, while she had the restraint not to bring the office crap home with her.

I needed to walk. I had a unique way of walking and thinking by not directing my mind on what to think about. This usually allowed my brain to release some untapped lost information. As I approached the restaurant's front door, somehow it hit me that in the past year Laura was working on the sale of a few very large Manhattan properties, the names and locations were never mentioned. I immediately returned to the table and mentioned this to everyone. Wendy, in particular, seemed to be locked in on it.

"Guys, I want to take the lead on Laura." Wendy insisted.

They all gave her the nod. She looked my way to make sure I agreed. I nodded followed by a thumbs up.

"Of course, I'll need to be introduced to Laura, so we can talk calmly," Wendy said, turning to Ashton. "How about it, Ashton? Maybe you can make the segue for me. You could be the one to contact Laura and mention my name as her liaison to us here at HPAT 21."

"Sure, however, I can help, I'll do it."

I felt a bit weird about Wendy dealing with my wife. Then I decided to put the homeland before my self-interests.

"Okay by me," I said. "Let's do what we have to do."

Levine and Randy looked at each other.

Randy turned and said, "Wendy, it's your baby. Ashton, you call Stone's wife. You have my TOR to move forward on this immediately."

"Excuse me, what's 'TOR'?" I asked.

"Oh, just some new jargon, it means transfer of responsibility."

"Well, well, how cool," Wendy said, shaking her head and smirking.

Ashton became assertive as he urgently said, "Guys we don't have time to waste. It's not my normal approach to debrief anyone long distance, however we're hitting a critical point. How do you feel about me calling Laura now? Randy, Levine, Wendy . . . what are your thoughts?"

They all shrugged their shoulders as if to say, *we don't know.*

"This is your decision, Ashton," Levine said. "You're the relationship guy, our in-house psychologist."

"Then, Bob, if it's okay with you, let's keep Laura where she is in New York and avoid complicating things or risking her safety by transporting her. I'd like to talk with her right now."

"Fine," I said. "Go for it...maybe I can say a quick hi to her first."

"No Stone," Wendy said and rose up placing her two hands on the table. "I've got the lead on this, remember? Ashton, please call Laura, then make the transition to me, directly."

"I agree," Randy replied and added, "This one is for you, Wendy."

Ashton got up, grabbed Randy's secure cell phone, and began walking to the other room.

"Give me a few minutes, then it's all yours, Wendy," he said. "Come with me now so I can hand off the phone to you at the right time."

"Excellent, Wendy confirmed.

"You guys chill out here. Have ten more cups of coffee—whatever it takes," Ashton said.

I decided to go and listen in on the phone call to Laura. As I entered the room, Ashton and Wendy gave me a look of aggravation.

Before they could say a word, I said, "Guys, I'm here with you on this. I won't say a word, but I have to be with you."

Their silence was passive permission, so I stayed. Ashton called Laura. He told her that someone else on our team needed to go over a few things with her. He said that he was now going to ask his colleague, Wendy Gilmore, to talk with her.

Ashton then said to Laura, "Don't be concerned, everything is totally fine. My colleague Wendy can be trusted. She just had a few additional points to review with you. Thank you again, Laura."

Laura must have said "No problem" or "Sure" because Ashton passed the phone to Wendy without hesitation. Wendy then introduced herself.

She paused and said, "Hold on, Laura. One moment please."

She put the phone on mute and turned to me and Ashton.

"Guys, I cannot do this with both of you over my shoulder. Leave now," Wendy demanded.

So off we went back to our table. After about thirty minutes, Wendy returned. The waiter brought more coffee, more bottles of Limoncello and Sambuca, and a few more cookies.

"So?" I asked. "Talk to us, Wendy."

She took a deep breath, before replying, "I asked Laura about that night when you both went to the wedding of your client's daughter in Astoria, Queens. I asked her to think back to what she overheard during the cocktail hour in the living room. Laura told me about that remark, 'America must pay for its policies against the Arab world.' Laura also told me that she recalled being surprised to have heard a mixture of Arabic and English spoken among the guests, most of whom were obviously foreigners. She told me about how you were both in shock on the way home that night. Laura also recalled that she may have heard some people who said something like, 'Kill the chickens in the pen.' She confirmed that she did hear this remark a few times. Each time she heard it, a few guys were laughing. It was a sinister, very weird laughter, she remembered. I did ask Laura about her job, however, she reacted in a defensive manner."

"What does that mean?" Ashton asked.

"I wasn't sure, but Laura suddenly had cut off the conversation," Wendy replied. "Laura did say that she was too drained to get into her work life right now. Her tone and pitch became irregular and anxious. She was obviously affected with the subject of her work at the law firm. I backed off at that point and simply let her know that if she could think of anything else, we would appreciate a call right away. I also told Laura she could call me directly. Oh, and Bob, she did say that she misses you. Your wife did seem concerned about your well-being. No bullshit."

Levine stood up and paced around the dinner table. He had a work in progress going on in his mind. He began thinking out loud using us as a sounding board, as he continued moving to and fro, hands coupled behind his back, in deep focus.

He finally blurted out, "Stone, we need a strategy to make one of your key terrorist clients really uncomfortable. Listen to me now. I need to get the audit division of the Manhattan IRS tax office to step in."

"What does that mean?"

Levine finally ended his moving about, looked up to us, and spoke, as if he just had an epiphany. "Here's my plan. I'll contact my people at the IRS in Manhattan. On the basis of national security, I'll authorize them to issue a tax examination letter to your client Darmush Khan. He's your client who owns the ten gas stations, right?"

"Yes, good memory."

"You'll obviously have to represent Darmush for a 2012 and 2013 personal and business tax audit. This asshole client of yours will need you now more than ever before. Believe me—he will be calling you in no time. He'll be shitting in his pants. My IRS guys will make sure that your client will end up owing at least $500,000, not including interest and penalties. In fact, I'll have the IRS auditors expand the audit back to 2010 to 2011 based upon tax fraud. Stone, you know we can go back six years when it comes to tax fraud."

"Sure, of course I know that."

"At some point during the audit process, your Darmush will have to come to the IRS office in Manhattan for a friendly sit down," Levine explained. "That's when Randy and I will show up to give your client some extra attention. Bob, can you handle this?"

I took my time to respond, needing a pause to absorb the implications of Levine's phony IRS tax audit scheme. *Pretty ingenious,* I thought to myself. I knew this would be totally awkward, maybe even dangerous, but I had no choice.

"I've been through enough tax audits during my career. What's another one right?"

Randy just let out a smile, he then clapped his hands in laughter.

"Hey guys," I added. "It's funny—I never went into a tax audit knowing the outcome in advance."

Levine laughed so hard he almost spit out his last gulp of Sambuca.

"Well, tax man," Wendy said. "There's a first time for everything."

"You guys can really do this?" I asked.

Levine stopped pacing and replied, "Bob, don't ask me that question anymore, it insults me."

"Yeah, yeah, I know, this is an 'elite' IRS group' . . . I get it."

No one bothered to respond to my yada yada routine. Wendy suggested that we call it a night. She wrapped up saying,

"Tomorrow, I'll get back to Laura about the recent law firm deals she had been working on."

We all headed out to the cars waiting for us. Levine handled the dinner bill and we drove back. The guards dropped us all off at the lobby of the Langley Virginia Command Center, my "prepaid vacation resort."

Levine stopped and asked, "Are we all on the same page, people?"

Wendy and I nodded silently to confirm.

"Randy, are you backing me up on my IRS plan?"

Randy shook Levine's hand and said, "Go for it."

Ashton offered his advice, "Wendy, you need to shadow Laura. Gain her trust, get to know her. Then learn about her job or whatever else she may be aware of. I'm still unsure, maybe she needs to be here."

Randy jumped back in. "Let's stop with the flip-flopping on Laura. Here's the deal: It's been a while, so I'll put in a call to Frank Conway over at the FBI. We'll keep Laura in New York and get her into a totally different place to live temporarily. She'll have round-the-clock security."

I patted Randy on his shoulder with appreciation.

Randy wrapped up, "Late tomorrow morning Wendy and Bob will fly to New York. You'll both be taken to the airport by HPAT 21 security guards, undercover of course. Once you guys land at JFK Airport, Wendy will be escorted to the hospital and connect with Laura. Then you'll take her to the new place. I'll get the location to you ASAP. Bob, you go back to your house in Plainview and wait for further instructions. Of course, Bob, you'll have HPAT 21 security guards." Randy turned to Levine. "You know what, Levine? After we button up a few things, you'll get on a flight to New York, too. You will be escorted to the Manhattan division of the IRS to initiate that tax audit in person. Ask your assistant to book a nice hotel room for you. Keep it near the IRS building." He paused and added, "Any questions, people?"

No one replied.

"Good, then I'm out of here. I'm tired, drained, and we need to get a jump on these plans."

He rose and then gave a nod of his head with a wink directed at me. I felt that I needed to say something but had nothing to contribute. I decided not to force any words.

"Yeah," Levine said. "Let's meet on floor six at 8:45 a.m. for breakfast."

We called it a night. Wendy went to her room and I collapsed into the bed in my room. It took me about six seconds to fall asleep.

CHAPTER **15**

Although I had fallen asleep easily, I still woke up in the middle of the night. I had been twisting and turning most of the night thinking about Laura and trying to understand what she might be thinking. I also had Levine on my mind with his wild IRS plan. No question, I was nervous about it. I was being thrown right in the middle of an illegal tax scheme by a secret unit of the IRS.

At the same time, I was thinking about Wendy down the hall. I had just played out some scenes in my mind with her. I was a prisoner of her feisty personality and the twinkle in her eyes. She knew she got to me from day one. My overthinking wore me out and I dozed off again.

I woke up early, at 6:15 allowing for enough time to get organized, pack my limited clothes, and get ready for further instructions. As I eased off the bed, I heard two knocks and a voice.

"Bob, it's me, Wendy. Can I come in?"

"Wendy," I said, opening the door to greet her. "What's up?"

I couldn't imagine why she would knock on my door so early unless something was wrong. I opened it. She looked into my eyes and walked right in without saying a word.

"Okay, what's up, Wendy?"

"Listen, Bob, we're going back to New York and you will be super busy, under pressure, and dealing with your wife. We won't have any more private time. So here I am. I want to be with you."

"I was just about to take a shower."

"Perfect, let's take a shower together."

I was too weak. Nothing was said as we dropped our clothes to the floor, went into the shower, hugged, and started to soap each other. The water was hot and the steam was rising. After fifteen minutes, I still couldn't wash away the stress.

"It's time to get going," I said, interrupting the moment. "Wendy, we have a full day ahead of us. Let's wrap it up."

"Yeah, you're right, Sir Bob Stone. Can you hand me one of those large towels over there?"

"Oh, sure."

"Okay, I'm going to hustle out of here and head back to my room. I'll see you in forty-five minutes on the sixth floor."

"Right, that's what Levine said last night. Wendy, thanks for being here, it was nice."

She smiled and left. So I packed quickly, got dressed, and hustled over to the sixth floor. Two minutes later, Wendy showed up and Levine followed into the room.

"Come on, people. Let's inhale some breakfast and talk."

"Fine with me," I said.

I was hungry from the early morning stimulation. Each of us grabbed our coffees and a Danish pastry before sitting down at a table toward the side of the room. Levine sipped his cup and distributed our airline tickets. It was from the Norfolk International Airport to John F. Kennedy International, taking off at 1:30 p.m. this afternoon and arriving at three. We basically had time to eat, talk, and get going. As we were saying our goodbyes, Levine stopped me and Wendy.

"Oh, sorry, before I let you both go, there is one thing you each need to do. I should say—that we need to do *to* you."

Wendy gave it away as she said, "I know the drill. Bob, they have to implant a tracking device into the back of your neck, just like they did to those thugs on Fire Island. You won't even feel it, but just in case either one of us is abducted, we can usually be found pretty quickly."

"Thanks for that, Wendy, you made my job easier," Levine said.

"Hey, this is like a reality TV show," I said. "You guys are serious, aren't you?"

"Hey, tax man, you should know by now, nothing here is even remotely close to being a joke." Levine starting in with a pep talk. "Stone, you're about to embark on a journey that will take you deep into the world of badass people and evil schemes. Shit happens and it's beyond dangerous. You'll need to be careful. Remember, Stone, kill before you get killed and do what you have to do to protect our homeland and our people." Levine then turned to Wendy. "Please give our tax man and me a few minutes alone."

She looked surprised, and then left the room without a word.

"Bob, Frank Conway will be here in five minutes. He wants to look you in the eye and give you a final talk. He is a powerful man in the FBI. No doubt he may end up saving your life down the road. He also needs to witness your sworn oath to protect the homeland. Let's take a two-minute break. Stay here. Chill."

I felt scared—real scared. A feeling came over me. I was totally overwhelmed. I began to understand how serious this all was. I was entering a bad dream with terrorists, money moving globally, and maybe even murder. I took a few deep breaths. A strong tap hit my shoulder, I was startled. I turned around to see Levine and Frank standing in front of me.

"It's just me. Hello again, Stone," Frank said.

He was a powerful man and no dummy. I stood up, shook his hand and said nothing. I was sure to make eye contact. I waited for him to sit down first.

"Okay, so here we are," Frank continued on. "Stone, do you fully understand what you are about to get into?"

"Yes, to the best of my ability, I answered while contemplating... *but how can I possibly comprehend it all?*"

I must have mumbled a bit too loud; he seemed put off by my question.

I had to say something as a follow up, "I'm not at all trying to be sarcastic, just honest."

"I appreciate that," Levine said, cutting into the back and forth. "Frank, I already walked our tax man here through some situations he may expect going forward. You know, like killing someone, breaking into an office, getting closer to his clients, rubbing shoulders with terrorists, and so on."

I started to talk, but Levine cut me off, putting his hand up. I shut up.

"You know, Stone," Frank interrupted. "You'll need to drop in on a few banks overseas. We already told you about the FOF. You know, tracking the 'flow of funds' from mosques and other supposed non-profit accounts to and from banks and to wherever that leads you to?"

"Yeah, I recall that."

"Good. It's time to swear under oath, your loyalty to our homeland. Are you ready?"

"Yeah, sure."

"Levine, you take over and I'll witness."

"Bob, put one hand on this bible and the other over your heart," Levine commanded me. "Repeat after me: I, Robert J. Stone, fully understand and accept all responsibilities in acceptance of working with the Homeland Protection Anti-Terror 21 Unit and promise, under oath, to remain loyal and to always act in the best interests of the United States of America. I will accept all assignments, even if they involve possible torture and killing of terrorists. I will never reveal any actions, nor divulge any information to anyone else, not even to my family, in this capacity. He continued....

"I understand that HPAT 21 is a specialized department within the IRS, established under the Patriot Act to do whatever it takes to defend America to thwart the actions of those who wish to destroy the homeland. I accept this work and all the conditions mentioned above. In exchange, the U.S. Department of Justice agrees to waive any and all charges of aiding and abetting terrorists and other clients by you, as a licensed CPA, over the past five years in the preparation of fraudulent tax returns, whether intentional or not. Finally, I pledge my allegiance to the United States of America. I understand it is my duty to protect our constitution, our citizens, and the homeland."

I repeated word for word, all along. I was mesmerized. Levine and Frank had their eyes fixed on mine. There was no turning back now.

PART THREE

CHAPTER 16

After I pledged my life away to HPAT 21, Wendy was called back in the room. Frank signed the pledge form on the table and I countersigned it. We were done.

"Ah, you just did the Homeland Pledge?" Wendy asked.

"Yeah, I did."

"It's quite a vow, isn't it? I took the oath four years ago. I've been with HPAT 21 ever since. I love what I do. What else do we want in life? Do something good, help our country, and do what we believe in. Isn't that better than cranking out tax returns?"

I was frozen in thought for a moment.

"You know what, you're right, Wendy. I've been looking for something for so long. I found my purpose in life, right here under my damn nose. Thank you. Thank you all."

Frank and Levine shook my hand, then Wendy's. Levine wished us good luck.

"You don't need luck," Frank said, "You need to be smart, and smarter than the other side. Bob, you've got what it takes. Remember, we need you."

Frank left first, smiling. The rest of us went down to the first floor.

"Guys, I'll wait here until your guards arrive. Go finalize your packing," Levine suggested.

"Okay...Yes, sir," I threw in with a salute to be cute.

"Cut the crap, Stone."

I just smiled. I went back to my room and hit the bed for five minutes, my clothes and personal items were already packed. I started to think back to high school, remembering the infamous yearbook. During those days, I was deemed "Most Likely to Be a Professional." Who could possibly believe that I would end up being an HPAT 21 agent? I laughed out loud thinking about this turn of events in my life. I could not stop laughing until I heard knocking at my door.

"Bob, it's Levine. Open up."

"I'm coming, wait a minute."

I was hoping he did not hear me laugh. If he did, he might think I was crazy.

"What's up?"

"I almost forgot. Bob, you see this little round tab? This is the tracking device we talked about. Turn around so I can snap it into the back your neck. You'll feel a little prick. It's no big deal," he said.

I turned around and let him do the deed. It was a little more painful than expected, but really nothing at all.

"You'll get used to this by the time you arrive in New York. It's flesh tone, so nobody will notice it. You should thank me...this little device may save your life."

"Thanks for continuously trying to scare the hell out of me. Now, Levine, be a good guy and get out of my room. Give me some privacy. Before you walked in, I was laughing like crazy about my past and my future, so give me my space."

"Okay," that's all he said. I must have been caught off guard. Suddenly, he added, "sure, no problem Stone... Keep laughing at yourself."

He had to get the last word in, so I let him have it.

***

It was now 10:45 a.m. We had to leave here by 11:00 to allow enough time to check in at the airport, then board without rushing. I gathered my bag and knocked on Wendy's door. No answer. She must have left already. I continued down the hallway to the elevator, got in, and then out to the main floor. Levine was sipping his coffee. Wendy was sitting down. Everything was calm.

Two HPAT 21 guards came in through the lobby entrance and said, "All clear, Mr. Levine."

"Fine with me, get going everyone."

That was it—time to get out of this command center.

"Catch you both in Manhattan tomorrow," Levine called to us as he began walking away. "And be ready for another great dinner."

I gave him my salute and we were off. The ride to the airport was twenty minutes with mild traffic, but no big deal. Our personal guards escorted us inside the terminal. We went through the normal airport security stops. An HPAT 21 guard accompanied us on board.

"Hey, what's your name?" I asked him.

"James, sir."

"Cut the 'sir' stuff, just call me Bob, Bob Stone."

Wendy imitated me, "I'm Wendy, Wendy Gilmore. Thanks for watching over us, James."

"My pleasure. Hopefully you won't even need me, but I'm assigned to you anyway."

"Let's go grab some junk," Wendy said.

While in the candy, newspapers, and magazine shop, I couldn't help noticing the caption on the front page of the *Wall Street Journal*: "Cyber-attack brings down major U.S. banks, Wall Street takes a dive." I started to read the article. *Shit, it was a terrorist-related cyber-attack. This time it was through the internet*—a different approach.

"Hey, Wendy, take a look at this," I said.

"Wow. Wendy read a few lines. "Hundreds of millions of dollars were stolen from three major banks yesterday. Looks like it could have been Russian or North Korean computer hacks."

"Wendy, who the hell knows who did that, I wondered, maybe it was ISIS, they're internet savvy."

With that rude awakening to financial terrorism, we had to start boarding. The flight was pretty empty. We had extra seats to spread out allowing for Wendy to be in the next aisle, while James was between us. *Good opportunity to meditate.*

"Seatbelts fastened please. We're getting ready for takeoff," a voice announced over the speaker.

The flight attendant went through the usual script of emergency exits, oxygen masks, and so on, before the plane thrusted into a smooth takeoff and up we went. We were soon flying over the clouds in mere minutes. The sun was shining. I grabbed some Junior Mints out of my bag and popped a few. James was constantly glancing over, doing his guardian thing. Wendy's eyes were closed. A flight attendant came by.

"Would you like a drink, sir?"

"Oh no, I'm good," I replied. "Actually, how about a blend of cranberry juice, ice, and some water? Thanks."

I allowed myself to relax, controlling my breathing and letting my brain go. I was thinking of how my parents would view my life—my new life, my new world. My father was an American patriot, proud of his years as a marine. He would be proud. My mother would probably think I messed up somehow, getting into all this danger.

I dozed off but it seemed like no time went by as we landed at the JFK Airport early. We only took carry-ons, so there was no need to wait for luggage. *Pain in the butt, this airport. Too much walking.* At last we made it outside and hit the brisk New York air. James received a call.

He turned to us and said, "Follow me to that car over there. It's an HPAT 21 escort."

"Okay, we're in your hands, James," I said.

Probably by design, we were picked up by an average-looking black Jeep. We piled into the car.

"Hello, my friends," the driver said. "I'm Jason, you can call me Jay."

The usual greetings were exchanged. James sat in the front seat next to Jay. James turned around with two large envelopes in hand.

"Here, these are for you both."

"What's this?" Wendy and I asked simultaneously.

"I don't know, it's sealed," James replied. "I was told to give these to each of you just after we landed in New York. Let's just call it, 'Package X' for now. If I had to make an educated guess, consider it your instructions," he said with a smile, showing a few spacey teeth. "Oh and Mr. Stone, here is your cell phone. You had thirty-nine texts and sixty-four calls over the past eight days or so. It's fully charged now."

"Nice invasion of my privacy." I snatched my cell phone from his hand.

"Hey guys, where are we going now?" Wendy asked.

I was so caught up in the package and my cell phone, I didn't think to ask.

"We are going to your hotel, Wendy," James answered. "You will be dropped at the Holiday Inn, Midtown Manhattan."

"I will be watching over you," James said. "We will be there in a few minutes. Just check in, head to your room, chill, and open your 'Package X,'" James said, and then turned to me. "Bob, before you can go home, Jay will take you to connect with your wife at Bellevue Hospital. She is waiting to be checked out. Frank and Levine agreed that it was time you both reconnected. Laura is waiting for you."

James then held up Jay's ID and showed it to us both.

"Jay isn't just your driver; he is your protector and your confidant as well. Here is Jay's HPAT 21 badge. No worries. In fact, here is my badge as well," said James as he extended his hand to show us.

"Bob, after you have talked with your wife for about one hour, she will be escorted to a safe location," James continued. "Not sure where just yet, but you and Wendy will be updated on her whereabouts. Jay will then bring you back to your home to settle in, review your client's mail that we have been holding for you, have a shot of your favorite scotch, and open up your envelope, I meant your Package X."

James and Jay snickered, then repeated, yeah, package X."

"Real cute guys," I said. "Right, 'Package X.' So, I'm now in a movie, like *Mission Impossible*. Skip Bob Stone, just call me Phelps. I can be flexible."

We all laughed hard and loud.

"Hey, Mr. Phelps, I didn't know you had a sense of humor," Jay said. "I thought all tax guys were boring as hell."

"Not this one," Wendy said.

"Not me, now let's get to the Holiday Inn already.

James calmed me down a bit, "Right, Bob, we do have a time frame here, people, but it's only three blocks away."

Jay sharply drove the Jeep into the unloading zone near the hotel entrance. James quickly hopped out to open Wendy's door. She turned to me.

"Bob, my cell is now in your contact list. Stay in touch."

"Come on, you guys," James said, rushing her along. "You'll be seeing enough of each other."

"Okay, let's go." Walking away toward the lobby, she threw out a wave without turning around.

I admire her... I thought, as I watched her walk away.

"Okay, Jay," James said. "Take Mr. Stone to his lovely wife."

"Yes, sir," Jay answered.

James stayed behind at the hotel to guard Wendy. Jay pulled away and we were on our way to the hospital.

***

"Hey, Jay, you seem like a nice guy—smiling and polite," I said, trying to make small talk. "Where did you get that from?"

"Don't know really. I think I just decided a long time ago to be nice and polite at all times. You know, good karma. Thanks for the compliment, Mr. Stone."

"No, it's Bob, let's cut the formal stuff."

"Yes, sir."

"Hello?" I said sarcastically. "Did you hear me, Jay?"

"It's automatic, sorry. I got it now, Bob."

"You know, Jay, I'm starving. Those short flights never offer a decent snack. Do you think we can get a sandwich on the way?"

"Tell you what, save it for the hospital. We can grab something there. Not too much longer, Bob, we're almost there."

He swung around and took a sharp right turn into the Bellevue Hospital parking lot. Jay got out first to open my door.

"Let's go," he said. "I know the deal about your wife. HPAT 21 told me everything."

"Okay, thanks for telling me that."

"Yeah, in HPAT 21, there are no secrets," he said. "Over there is a café. Let's grab some lunch."

Music to my ears. We were getting along great. He seemed like a good guy, down to earth, no spin zone. I appreciated that.

"Oh, Bob, here is some spending money Levine asked James to give you."

Jay put a sealed envelope in my hand. The outside was marked "$1,500 for Stone."

He smiled and said, "Enjoy the spending money and the reading of Package X."

"Alright, Jay, actually, I could get into a good spy thriller novel."

"I admire your sense of humor, Bob."

"Well, when we lose our ability to laugh, even at one's self, we're in trouble."

"You are so right," Jay replied. "We should catch a laugh over dinner some time.

I gave Jay a wink and then I suggested that I'd need to clear the choice of restaurants with Levine. That guy loves Italian.

"Wow, we must be starving," I said. "Here we are dreaming about dinner. Let's start with a quick lunch."

"Yeah," Jay agreed.

We arrived at the café on the first floor of the hospital. I was more hungry than tired, so I went for the Signature Farmhouse Omelet, a whole wheat bagel and coffee. Jay had the Avocado BLT sandwich with a Diet Coke.

"So, Jay, starting more small talk and stalling. I obviously wasn't ready to face Laura yet. "Where are you from?"

"Upstate New York, just outside New Paltz."

"How did you end up doing this?"

"Long story, Bob. Another time."

"Okay, let's just eat quickly then. What floor is my wife on?"

"Let's ask at the front desk. Meantime Bob, come on, finish your food. You'll need time to talk with her. She will be getting discharged soon."

"I guess I'm in avoidance mode. Thanks, Jay."

But this reunion with Laura needed to be done. Laura and I had to clear the air. I was determined not to argue with her. I ate about half my plate and then pushed it aside. I guess I was too nervous to eat after all. I almost felt like throwing up, I had to control myself.

"Let's go," Jay said.

"Wait, I need to close my eyes for two minutes to calm down and to think."

What does one say to his wife when her husband screws up the marriage after ten years? I must have said this out loud unknowingly because Jay answered.

"All you have to do is to be real, be yourself, and it will all fall into place. Now close your eyes for another two minutes and think about being totally honest with Laura. Then stand up and let's go."

I was silent and then stood up. I looked at Jay and he stood up. We gave each other a smile.

"You will be great, Bob."

"How do you know?" I asked for an extra round of reassurance.

"My wife left me five years ago. Great wife. I learned my lessons too late, but I was thankful for her decision to remain friends. Today, she is my best friend. It's love, but a different form of love. It's real. So, Bob, just be real with Laura. Talk from your heart. That's your goal."

"Thanks, Jay, You're a good man."

CHAPTER **17**

W e dumped our food in the bins, left the café and walked to the elevator. There was a slight delay, but the elevator doors finally opened up. Seven, maybe eight, people were coming out. My eyes were focused on the floor as my nerves took over. Then I looked up and noticed Laura stepping out of the elevator with two guards. She was the last one to exit out. Our eyes merged. We both froze as the elevator doors closed behind her. After a mutual hesitation, we gave each other a tentative hug. I leaned back for some eye contact and followed with a kiss to her cheek. Laura backed off and put her hands on my shoulders.

"Laura, I was just coming up to see you before you got discharged. How are you? You look great, all things considered."

"Well, I obviously had a difficult week and a half. Then I was scared to death at Fire Island, but I got through it."

"Did those two guys hurt you?"

"How did you know there were two guys, Bob?" Laura asked.

"We saw the whole thing in real time, Laura. I was worried beyond your imagination, but I knew the plan. You were in good hands."

She pressed on. "What are you talking about? How did you see all that?"

"Long story. Later I'll tell you more, promise."

"All I wanted was a few days to myself," Laura said. "So I went to Fire Island. It was crazy. I wasn't hurt but I was scared—damn scared. Those guys did put quite a squeeze on my wrists. The team who rescued me was amazing."

"Yeah, I know. The way they executed with perfect timing, injecting each guy with a syringe. It was truly a work of art. By the way, this is exactly what they did to me. That's how they kidnapped me and brought me to the Langley Virginia Command Center for interrogation."

"That's what happened to you?"

"Yeah, I didn't just go on vacation."

Then I turned to her two guards and to Jay.

"You know what, do you guys mind if Laura and I go back to the café? We need to sit in a private corner and talk for a little while."

"Yeah, sure," Jay replied. "But we need to stay close by."

"Okay with you, Laura?" I asked her.

"Yes, sure."

Jay pulled the two guards aside for a moment. He whispered into their ears. They waved us on toward the café.

"Go ahead, you two," Jay said. "We'll be at that corner table over there keeping an eye on you."

"Thanks," Jay.

Jay smiled back at me silently telling me to follow his advice.

"Laura, let's go to that table down there. Please sit down, let me get you a drink. Coffee?"

"Yes, a little skim milk and half a Splenda." She thought I had forgotten, but I did not.

"Anything to eat?" I prodded.

"I already had lunch, but I'll have one of those Danish pastries for now," she replied.

"I'll be right back."

I grabbed two coffees and a Danish to share and rejoined her.

"Listen, I need to get a few things off of my chest. First, I want you to know that I have always loved you and respected you Laura. I am so sorry that over the years I had lost control of my emotions. I now realize that I've been self-centered, always thinking of myself, dwelling on my problems and clients, while you built your law career. Somehow during that time, I lost my focus. For all of this, I'm really sorry." A few tears dropped out of my eyes as I spoke—real tears.

"You know, Bob, I always knew you had some emotional baggage," We all have that shit. But you just let it get to you. I always told you to hold on to your doctor and dental clients as a base. You grew too impatient too quickly. I just don't understand what happened to you, Bob."

"You were right, you were always right. But, I need to open up to you about something. A few years back when I was giving up and losing clients, you were a rising star in your law firm. I was beginning to feel that I had to hold up my end of the financial side in our marriage. That was when I buckled and started to accept all kinds of garbage tax work. The fees for these clients with tax problems were great, but deep down I knew that these undocumented business owners were somehow going to come back to haunt me in the future."

"Right," she agreed. "And here you are today, Bob—totally fucked up. And you know what? That's why I walked out of the house recently."

"I understand … I really don't blame you. In fact, I blame myself. Laura, I want you to know that I love you. I want you to be happy more than anything else."

"That's very sweet of you, Bob."

"Is it too little, too late, Laura?"

"Listen, I know you're a good man at the end of the day. You took a detour in life. You know what happens when you bend an index card? It's never quite the same again. There's always a crease in the middle, and you know what—that's what happened to me. I'm done. I am burned out, Bob. I'll tell you what, though, we can be friends and we don't have to get divorced right away either. Maybe I can love you as a friend. That's it for now and I really do wish you well."

"I can love you as a friend, too and hopefully, as a very close friend, Laura."

We both edged into the middle of the small table and kissed each other.

"Bob, aren't we both overlooking something pretty huge? Why the hell were those two weirdos trying to kidnap me? What the heck is really going on? Ashton and Wendy seemed to give me only a part of the whole story."

"No idea, it's crazy,"

"I've been thinking about it all, of course," she said. "It's nuts. Maybe one of your weird clients sent those two guys after me in Fire Island? What do you think of that theory, Bob?"

"No way, they need me too much to keep them out of their tax troubles. They would have no interest in you. No connection to you. Wendy Gilmore will be debriefing you about your law firm activities. Maybe there's something you overlooked at work. Some deal you were working on, something you may have stumbled over, some detail in one of your client's cases, whatever. Laura, tell me more about what your role has been at the law firm lately, especially over the past few months. I know you can't say much due to ethical reasons, but anything you can think of, would be helpful in figuring out this mess."

"Okay. Well, you know that I was trying to move ahead in the firm. I pushed the partners to allow me to do more than just handling leases. That bored the hell out of me. They knew I was talented and thorough. To avoid losing me to another law firm, they started putting me on small real estate deals. They loved my work, so they assigned me to larger deals."

"What kind of deals?"

"Foreign buyers with big money looking to acquire New York real estate. It's been all over the news. Foreigners had been throwing huge sums of money at sellers to snatch up well known New York City buildings. I was working on buys, sells, and swaps of some well-known Manhattan buildings. The money involved was huge, however I remembered sensing that some of those deals made no economic sense."

"What makes you say that?"

"Economic reality," Laura replied.

"What's that?"

"I'll explain. There came a time a few months after I went from those leases into medium-sized property transactions, and then to larger buys and sells of Manhattan properties. It does not take a genius to understand that for example, the sale of an abandoned warehouse worth, say seven-hundred and fifty thousand dollars, makes no sense to be sold for three million-seven-hundred-and-fifty thousand. It seemed like the law firm became a factory, representing foreigner investors from the Middle East, Asia, and Europe. The deals came fast and furious from some rainmaker, some key player acting as 'of counsel' to the firm. I had the suspicion that these investors were possibly being concealed in limited liability companies."

"Well, hindsight is twenty/twenty. I can say the same about my client choices over the last few years. No sense in dwelling on what we can't change. Let's move on. When you requested time off to chill at Fire Island, did the firm have any issues or suspicions? You never took time off at Combs and Walker prior to this."

"Here's the bottom line, Bob. I asked the office manager for a day off so I could have a long weekend at Fire Island. Next thing I knew, I was told to take three weeks off. I was shocked. They said I accumulated too many unused vacation days. It was weird to me because I was right in the middle of a huge deal. That's when I decided to rent a place in Fire Island. Funny thing was, they had me working sixty-five hours a week on that one hot deal. Remember all those late nights I had? It was the talk around the office. Then they pulled me off it. Of course, I was mad as hell. At the same time, I was too upset about our argument to also fight at work. It's difficult to fight two wars simultaneously."

"Keep going, Laura, you're doing great, but we need details, details." As I watched her try to compose herself, I had a better thought. "Wait, let's wrap up so you can save any further information for Wendy," I said. "I don't want to step on her toes. It's her role to talk with you in greater detail about the law firm. She's got years of experience with this sort of thing."

I guess now was the right time to spill the beans. The Homeland Pledge didn't apply here, since Laura was already involved in this mess. It was time she learned everything.

"Those guys who kidnapped me were from a special group within the IRS. They call the unit, HPAT 21. I'm not sure what you already learned from talking with Ashton and Wendy, but the gist is that they focus on homeland protection and terrorism. They gave me a choice—more like an ultimatum. I either help them, or they would charge me with aiding and abetting fraudulent tax returns. They told me they had proof that several of my clients are terrorists. It ended up that those two guys who grabbed you were tracked back to the same mosque in Astoria, Queens. Remember, that's where the wedding of Ammi's daughter was located. Fair to say that I really fucked up by dealing with these small businesses owned by undocumented immigrants. I chose not to listen to my gut feelings about that first client, the flower shop. I compromised myself, yes, I was in denial all these years. Long story short, I am now a life member of HPAT 21."

"So, they entrapped you?"

"Call it what you want. I had no choice and It's crazy, Laura. I actually love this whole new meaningful world I've been thrown into."

"What? You really are one crazy dude."

"Maybe," I agreed. "But for the first time in my life, I'm doing things with a purpose, things that I believe in. Protecting our homeland and saving lives worldwide. Somehow, I don't dwell on my life like I used to." I smiled than reflected; *I was amazed and proud of what I had just told her.*

"What do they expect you to do?" she asked.

"Get closer to a few key clients, try to learn what I can about money in motion from one bank to another, figure out where the money ends up, maybe even uncover the purchase of lethal weapons."

"And you love this, you could easily be killed!"

"I know, Laura, but I won't go down easy. I'm ready to do what I have to do for our country. I'm done creating figures on tax returns for clients. That's my old life as Robert J. Stone, the tax man. Now it's Robert J. Stone, the rookie spy guy. Technically, I'm an employee at the IRS. But Laura, this is not the IRS that you and I and the rest of America know. This is a secret unit set up under the Patriot Act after 9/11."

"Bob, it's your life, and I wish you well. I guess you must have called about that IRS International Crime Division job after I decided to leave you. So, you got the excitement you wanted and unfortunately, much more."

"Yeah, it's been enough stimulation to kill a horse."

We both laughed so hard that our eyes got watery.

"Time out, we need a reality check. What the hell should I do about my job, my career as an attorney?"

"That's way over my head," I said. "I'm still new at all of this. Talk with Wendy. She'll have to check in with our supervisors to brainstorm a plan. Then, you'll be told what to do next. Laura, there is something going down at Combs and Walker. Be careful."

I looked up, sensing we might be at the end of our allotted one-hour talk. I turned to look for Jay. He waved back and motioned for us to follow him down the hallway back to the lobby.

"One minute," I mouthed, using my finger.

We both stood up to leave. I hugged her and said, "I'm so sorry, but this is the new journey of my life now. I'll always love you. You really do look great, by the way."

"Yeah, it's called weight loss through stress," she sarcastically replied.

"Whatever you need at any time, I'll be there for you. I promise."

I kissed her cheek as I would kiss my sister. We both left the café and started to part ways, but both of us turned back for a look.

"Bob, be careful, you don't have to be a damn hero."

"Everything will be fine, I reassured her. Meantime, start thinking about the firm, the huge deal you were pulled away from, and whatever else you can remember. Wendy will need your help and as much information as possible. You may be into something way over your head, but we are all going to be there to help you."

"Absolutely," she said.

"Let's get going, Jay, whispering to him, I'm totally drained."

"Yes, sir—I mean, Bob. It's time we brought you home."

Laura and I waved goodbye to each other. I hesitated for a moment as I watched the two guards escort her away.

***

"Jay, I followed your advice. It was amazing. I was honest, sincere, and totally up front with her. Well, I was mostly up front with her, I paused, thinking of Wendy. Some things are better left unsaid at this point to avoid unnecessary pain. Anyway, thank you, my friend."

"No need to thank me, Bob," Jay replied. "Hey, we help each other. That's the name of the game."

"Right you are, Jay. The good karma thing, it works."

"Bob, are you ready to head back to your home?" Jay asked as we drove down the road leading to the expressway.

"Sure,"

"Okay then, we'll be there in about forty-five minutes," he said. "You chill out and leave the driving to me."

My cell phone buzzed with a text from Levine, stating that he had just arrived in New York, followed by his instructions:

Go home, take some time to review the envelope James gave to you. Call me when you're done reviewing Package X. Dinner back in Manhattan at 8:00 p.m.

Another message:

It's a great place called Baba Ghanoush off Broadway near Church St. and Chambers St. See you there.

"Yes, see you later,"

I texted back.

CHAPTER 18

The ride back made me recall how we felt the night we drove home after the wedding back in April. It was a feeling I will never forget. We both knew our lives could never be the same as we pulled into the driveway on that fateful evening. And here I was once again, pulling into the driveway of our home in Plainview, Long Island; only this time, our fate was validated. Our lives had already entered a strange new world and there was no turning back.

"Hey, Bob," Jay called out as we pulled into the driveway.

"Yeah, what's up Jay?"

"Where have you been, in some far-off island on a vacation?" he joked.

"Oh no, just thinking about a few things, that's all, Jay."

"Okay, but stay alert, my friend," he warned.

"Yeah, right you are."

As we left the car, Jay waved his large hand at another car just as it pulled up across the street.

"Hey, who's that?" I would have been nervous if Jay hadn't waved.

"Bob, these guys are backup HPAT guards," he explained. "You are an important dude. Don't you know that yet?"

"I guess so."

We entered through the front door.

"Bob, me first," Jay warned. "Hold on."

"Okay."

I waited impatiently at the front entrance. Two minutes later, Jay waved for me to come in.

"It's all clear," he said.

I immediately saw that there were no file cabinets in my home office.

"Where are all my client files?" I asked angrily. "Jay, what the hell is going on here?"

"Settle down, Bob. Your friends at HPAT 21 seized all—and I mean all of your files. They are stored at a facility near the Manhattan Holiday Inn where Wendy is staying."

"The assholes could have at least swept up the damn dust," I said, looking around.

"Come on, give it a break, Bob, anyway, I was asked to tell you that Wendy's assistant back in Langley will be handling your client calls. Also, this is a good time to open that package of yours. I can't tell you more because I don't know anything else."

"Good idea, Jay. Sorry, I have no bone to pick with you."

I walked around the house for about ten minutes first while Jay waited patiently for me to settle in. Then I dropped into my favorite lounge chair. It was time to open up my Package X.

"Jay, please hand that to me," I asked, motioning at the oversized envelope next to him on the table.

He threw it across the room with a perfect landing.

"What was that?" I asked. "Football or baseball, huh, Jay?"

"Actually, my game was basketball, long story. Maybe tomorrow I will tell you about my days in the NBA."

I laughed out loud. I figured he was kidding around with me.

"Really, no joke," he insisted. "No joke, tax man. Whatever, now you need to focus. It's Package X time."

I opened the folder. It had printouts from each HPAT 21 staff member whom I had dealt with so far. Levine's file had a series of well-thought-out instructions for my next steps. Just then, Wendy texted me as I started to read further into Levine's notes. *Did you see your Package X yet, Bob?*

I replied quickly with, *I just opened it up. Why, what's up?*

Looks like you'll be on the road soon, Bob, she texted back.

I'll soon find out, and with that reply, I turned back to the package and started to flip through the papers.

Wow, it's time for the real thing... Levine was instructing me to get on a flight to Toronto in two days. I was to meet with the branch manager and the compliance officer at the Royal Bank of Toronto.

Levine's notes were specific:

Do whatever it takes to track the flow of funds from that nonprofit foreign account with the huge drop in balance. Find out more specifically exactly where those funds had been wired to. Wherever the money went, go there. Wendy will stay here to work with Laura and oversee the screening of your tax client's calls coming in to her assistant. Meantime, the IRS in Manhattan will send out a formal tax audit letter to Darmush Khan as planned. End of day one, you are to contact me from Toronto after the bank closes. We'll recap your findings. Then decide on the next step.
Good luck,
Stone.

Ashton's recap was marked "Internal Memo":

Subject: Robert J. Stone
Personality Evaluation (Traits listed on a 1–10 scale, with 10 showing highest tendency of trait):

Self-Centered: 8.0
Confidence: 8.5
Communication Skills: 7.5
Self-Control: 7.5
Judgment: 7.5–8.0 (Depends on Stress Level)
Alertness: 7.75–8.0
Cooperative: 7.5
Patriotic: 9–9.5
Overall Ability to Connect: 8.5
Learning Skills & Speed: 9

Ashton wrapped up with a personal note to me:

"Thank you, Bob, for putting up with me. I wish you well. I feel I have learned much about you. You're in a tough spot, but I am sure things will work out in the end. You are a very patriotic American. We all want to thank you."

I saw an official-looking letter from Frank. He confirmed that I had met all the requirements to become an official member of HPAT 21. I found my badge enclosed with the paperwork. It was official. The final sheet in the package included a sentence from Levine:

"Stone, you are on your own. If you are captured, neither the White House, nor the Department of Homeland Security, nor HPAT 21 can help you."

I suddenly felt totally alone. *How can I go through with all this?* I asked myself. *For the love of country,* I mumbled and laughed.

Then Jay asked, "You talking to me?"

"Ah, no, not at all."

"We need to get back to Manhattan for that dinner. It's 5:30 p.m. already, Bob. The traffic will take us a while."

"I actually wondered why we went all the way back here only to return back to the city? Jay shrugged his shoulders. I need a quick shower."

Mr. Stone, you need to make it a three-minute military shower," Jay said. "Please hurry up."

***

We were back in the Jeep in no time. As I took a deep breath, Levine called me.

"Hey what the hell," I greeted him. "You actually moved all my client files?"

"We had no choice," Levine answered back then continued on... "If you bolt on us, we have proof of your aiding and abetting —or let's just say, highly questionable tax returns. Anyway, better for you.

Remember, your home has been under surveillance for the past few months. We don't yet know exactly who or why. Enough, let's have a great dinner. Wendy and James will be with your wife. Wendy needs time to learn much more from Laura about her work in the law firm. So, it's a 'boy's night out' tonight."

"Okay, no problem, Levine, that's never a bad idea."

"Good, see you in about one hour. Ten-four."

"That's really cool, Levine," I said sarcastically. "Yeah, ten-four, out," I imitated him then hung up.

Jay cracked up laughing and said, "You two guys are like Laurel and Hardy."

I smiled to Jay as I said, "Then what are me and you, Jay?"

"Abbott and Costello."

"Alright, sounds good."

"Hey, Bob, we're going to a very authentic Middle Eastern restaurant. The place will be filled with foreigners and tourists who know great food. That Levine, he knows how to pick great places to eat."

"Okay, Jay. So we have something to look forward to."

"Absolutely."

"Jay, wake me up when we get there."

"Yes, boss, enjoy the peace and quiet while you can."

""Thanks, you're the man," I said.

I heard him let out a polite chuckle.

The bumps along the highway initially bothered me, but I chose to ignore them, actually allowing the uneven paving to rock me into a well needed respite.

"OK, here we are—time to open your eyes," Jay barked out to me.

"Yeah, OK, Yeah," I mumbled back to him. "Ya know, you can be a pain in my butt sometimes. Why are you so loud, Jay? I'm just a few feet away from you."

Ignoring me, he pulled into a parking spot across the street from the restaurant.

CHAPTER 19

We all sat down at a private table in the far corner with a clear view of the whole restaurant. This place was a trendy hot spot. What a scene, just as people were leaving, more people kept coming in.

I turned to Levine, "Hey, the food here must be phenomenal! Look at this crowd!"

"Wait and see for yourself, you're going to love this place."

The waitress showed up and asked for our drink orders. The beer menu had a great selection of beers from Turkey, Israel, Belgium, and on and on. As the beers were served, we made our usual toast to HPAT 21. I barely swallowed my first sip of Efes Pilsner beer when a text from Wendy came in.

"Hey, Levine," I said. "Wendy and Laura have been talking all afternoon and they are drained. They want to get together with us later."

"Okay, Levine said. Call Wendy and invite them both here for dinner."

"Great idea. Wait, hold on. Wendy responded to my text about dinner. They just finished eating at a restaurant in the Midtown area."

"Why don't you suggest that they meet us here for some of the best desserts on the planet...the baklava is to die for."

"There you go again, Levine, in love with your food. You must be a great cook. You definitely know what you're doing when it comes to restaurants."

"Actually, I'm just an above average cook, who appreciates great food."

Hey guys," Jay chimed in. "Let's just eat already, I'm hungry *amigos*."

"Jay, first things first," I said. "You're in the wrong part of the world with that word, amigos. In a place like this, as I've learned from my clients that it's either *chaver* in Hebrew or *sadiq* in Arabic."

Jay sarcastically replied, "Oh, thanks for that info."

Levine took a gulp of his Israeli Maccabee beer and almost choked as he laughed.

"So, you think there are no Spanish-speaking people here, is that it?" he asked me. Then he turned to Jay, "let's just skip it."

"Here's the deal," I said. "Wendy, Laura, and James are going to meet us here in about an hour for desserts. Let's get the dinner orders in, so the timing will work out."

"Right, Bob," Levine agreed.

"I like hearing you say I'm right, Levine," I joked. "My wife would rarely say that to me."

"Well, I'm not your wife. I'm just dying to eat the hummus, the baba ghanoush, the homemade falafel, skewers of beef kebabs, and the chicken over rice dish. Oh, and the rice here is perfection."

"Levine, control yourself."

"Okay, I'm hitting the bathroom. You guys order the dinner now."

"Okay, go ahead, Bob," commented Jay as the waiter came over.

After we ordered, I nodded back to Jay, as if to say, "can't wait to eat."

"What a crowd! Mostly foreigners clearly looking like they're from Turkey, Israel, or a variety of other Arabic countries. The food really must be fantastic here. It's like when Chinese people go to their favorite Chinese restaurant. You can be sure you'll get quality authentic food. And now, I'm acting just like Levine, he definitely rubs off on me."

Levine came back from the bathroom. Our appetizers started to come out quickly and all at once—it was overwhelming.

"Lucky me," Levine said. "Timing is everything. The apps look amazing, guys. Let's dig in."

It was a feeding frenzy.

"You guys are a bunch of beasts," I said. "Calm down, people."

"Bob, if you snooze, you lose," Jay teased.

"You take your time and be calm," Levine said. "I'm going for the food, tax man."

"Right, Levine."

"Let's talk later," Jay mumbled in a state of food nirvana.

"Okay, dudes," I said. "If you can't fight 'em, you join 'em. Crazy so far—amazing starters! Levine was so right. Guys, I have had my share of Middle Eastern food around Manhattan with my clients over the years, but this is one of the best places."

"Does that surprise you, Bob?" Levine asked. "Come on, really? Wait till you try the main dishes."

"Okay," I said with a full mouth.

"By the way, I'm always looking and working," Levine said. "It's my years of experience. Don't ever think I am stuffing my face and I have my head in the sand."

"What's up, why are you suddenly talking like that, did some spice hit your brain? Baba ghanoush overload?"

"No, just look at those two guys to the far right at the other end of the room."

"I am trying to enjoy my food, as I looked over. So, what's up with them?"

"They seem weird to me, I can't put my finger on it. They also appear to be self-conscious. You know, when someone has that on-edge, insecure look about them. Well, that's what I sense. Finish your appetizers and take a spin Bob. Do not look overly interested, okay? Just be cool."

"Of course, no big deal."

I grabbed the last sip of my beer and dipped a pita into the hummus. Then I stood up as if to stretch before taking a calm walk around the restaurant, trying to act like I was looking for the bathrooms. I could not help notice the beautiful waitresses, some looked Israeli while others looked Turkish. This was like taking a walk down testosterone lane.

At last I spotted the two guys Levine mentioned. I actually decided to slightly bump into the elbow of the guy with his back facing me.

"Oops, so sorry," I said apologetically.

He turned his head around slowly and looked up at me. He said nothing, but I flicked his shoulder, implying that I dirtied his shirt.

"Hey sorry," I apologized again. It's real crowded in here. Can I buy you a beer?"

He looked at me again, staring this time and still said nothing. *Time to keep walking I guess. I knew when it was the right moment to stop.*

"Enjoy your food, *sadiq*," I said and waved my hand, "Goodbye."

I had broken the language barrier, so the guy finally smiled.

"Okay, okay, *sadiq*," he said.

I headed to the bathroom and waited before returning to Jay and Levine at our table.

"You know, Levine, I'm not sure, but they did seem to be very guarded. Borderline nervous."

"What the hell did you say to them? I told you to be cool about it."

"Ah, nothing much. I decided to gently bump into the one guy's elbow to get a reaction. He said nothing until I said 'goodbye' and called him friend in Turkish.

"Nice," Levine said. "Nice touch."

"Then he said back to me, 'Okay, okay, *sadiq*.' Levine, let's relax and eat. The ladies will be here in about forty minutes for dessert."

I saw Levine text someone, but he apparently did not want to be public about it. He turned to his side with the cell phone.

"Anything you want me and Jay to know?" I asked. "What is the text about?"

Levine said, "Nothing."

"Come on," I pushed. "What's up?"

Levine moved his head in to the middle of the table and spoke in a hushed tone.

"I put in a call for back up."

"For what?"

"Don't ask me because I'm not sure yet."

The waitress finally brought over the entrees.

"Okay, Levine," I said. "I am new at this homeland HPAT 21 stuff."

BELOW THE BOTTOM LINE • 151

"Now, it's time to really enjoy," Levine said with a look of food rage. "Dig in, guys. Let's talk in about ten minutes."

We not so graciously dealt with three family-style platters of the best food I'd ever tasted: kebabs, grilled onions, and heaps of chicken and rice with slivered almonds and raisins. We ordered more beers.

"What a food fest," Jay said in disbelief. We started to laugh as we overate, each taking a deep breath, and then going back for more food.

"Guys, I'm done. Anymore, I'll explode," I said, then added, "How can I possibly protect our homeland if I overeat like this?"

Levine and Jay gave me a look, they both leaned back and laughed.

"Well said, tax man, putting down his fork.

"Thanks, Levine," I replied.

"But of course, you'll join us for those desserts, right?"

There was only one answer. I said nothing, but smiled, thinking, *Okay, sure*.

"Hey, take a look and see what the wind blew in. There's James, Laura, and Wendy."

I knew it would be awkward, but I went to greet them anyway. I gave Laura a hug and a double handshake to Wendy. A host pulled another table adjacent to ours and they sat down to join us.

"Levine, you take charge of the desserts," I suggested.

"Fine with me," Wendy said.

"Is that okay, everyone?" Levine asked.

We all gave a nod of the head in agreement. Levine called over the waitress, gave her the order, and then requested for her to go around and ask who was having coffee.

"Oh yeah," I added. "Try the Turkish coffee. It's the best."

Ten minutes later an amazing display of delicacies, including walnut baklava, a tray of mamoul cookies and wardeh pistachio were placed in the middle of the table.

"Levine, you really meant it," Jay said, drooling. "To die for and you were right."

James, Laura and Wendy let out oohs and ahs at the sight of the unique mélange of desserts—they were in heaven, we all were in a stupor. Jay and I were sipping the strong coffee and tasting pieces of the sweet treats. Levine sat back and savored every bite. Laura and Wendy were quiet, almost detached.

"Hey, are you all enjoying the sweet stuff?" I asked to break the ice.

"It's all delish, Bob. I wish we had dinner here," Wendy said.

"Agreed," Laura sniped. "We went to a local diner. Good, but not like this."

"Sorry it worked out this way, Laura," I said.

Laura then stood up to excuse herself to the bathroom. Wendy joined in and walked with her. James trailed behind them. *James, the great protector* was the thought that came to my mind.

The restaurant started to thin out, allowing for those hanging around to be more noticeable. The waitress stopped by and asked us for refills and if we wanted anything else. Levine wrapped it up and asked for the check while he impatiently placed his credit card into her hand.

"You in a rush this time, Mr. Levine?" the server asked.

"No, but ah—" he didn't bother to complete the sentence. That was out of his character. He was bothered. Troubled. I could not put my finger on it. On her way back, I noticed Laura moving toward our table first, with James and Wendy lagging behind. Suddenly, Laura's face turned pale. Her hands were shaking as she sat down. She started to mumble to herself, I'd never seen her behave like this before. She made me quite nervous, I didn't know what to think.

I texted Wendy from across the table to ask, *What's up with Laura?* Wendy leaned next to Laura and whispered something. Then Laura put her head down and coupled her hands over her face. Trouble was amongst us—but what?

"Hey, Levine," I whispered to break the tension. "How do you spell 'trouble'?"

It was a stupid remark, but it just came out of my mouth.

"Why?" Levine asked.

"Just look at Wendy and Laura," I replied.

Levine and Wendy abruptly stood up to talk in the corner behind my back. I overheard Wendy talking to Levine.

"It's the two assholes from Fire Island and our Laura is freaking out," Wendy said.

Levine then leaned over to fill me in. Shockingly, the two men I had approached were the guys who had tried to kidnap Laura. I felt a rage swarming over me, but I had to remain calm. Maybe this was my first test as an HPAT 21 agent. I knew that I could not make a public scene here. I also knew that just in case those guys had backup, I could not be linked to what was about to happen. I had bigger things to deal with in Toronto. I also needed to get back to my clients as the Bob Stone they knew, their tax man.

"Levine—" I said.

"What!" he cut me off. "Bob, I called for backup. Remember? I have five armed HPAT 21 guys outside in two cars. This place is surrounded by our guys. They are waiting for my signal. I always trust my gut. Those guys were out of sync, and I absolutely knew it—always trust your gut Stone."

"So, what do you suggest now?

"Okay, Bob . . . you need to take a step back from this shit. You have much bigger fish to fry. Package X, right Bob?"

"Yeah," I snapped, frustrated. "You want me to just go to sleep and curl up in my damn bed as if they didn't try to grab Laura back in Fire Island."

"Listen to me, Stone, we have access to a basement in a building near Avenue A and Eighth Street, otherwise known as Saint Mark's Place. My guys will do what it takes to nail those two assholes. Then they will have a 'vacation' in our little hideaway basement until they tell us what we need to know. You can join in on the fun before you leave for your trip. It's time that we all get out of here calmly."

We started to get up from the table and say our goodbyes.

"James, go outside and stay with Bob, Laura, and Wendy," Levine instructed. "Jay, come with me to the entrance."

Just as we left the restaurant, I turned around and noticed the two dudes also leaving, just outside from the door. I told Levine. He held up his cell phone flashlight as he walked away with Jay. This must have been the signal Levine mentioned. We must have created a scene despite our discretion, as several people entering and exiting the restaurant started to look at Levine's cell phone flickering. The two guys walked about a half block south and then all hell broke loose. Five backup HPAT 21 agents surrounded them. They released a smoke bomb allowing their taser guns to finish the job. The two guys didn't have a chance. Both collapsed in seconds. They were handcuffed and pushed into one of the cars . . . off they went.

As we loaded into our car, James jumped into the drivers' seat.

Levine texted me: *Stay with your wife for now, she needs you. I'll let you know when to take the next step. Now, it's time for some fun in the basement. Talk later.*

"Okay, of course."

***

We drove with a sense that something more ominous might occur. I sat up front in the passenger seat next to James. Wendy and Laura rode in the back, each looking out their own respective windows. Finally, the silence was broken.

"Excuse me, but it's time to get moving, and I mean right now," James said while he was nervously looking into the rearview mirror, then to the side, and back again into the rearview.

"James, what's wrong? Why do you keep looking back and forth into the car mirrors? Are we alright?"

"A car has been right behind us for a few blocks, we're definitely being followed," James explained.

"Don't jump to conclusions. Let's not get spooked—It's way too soon to know that," I suggested, trying to calm him down.

"After twelve years with HPAT, you know when you're being followed," James replied. "Just let me do my thing. It may be a bit bumpy."

James took a few sharp right turns, then two sharp lefts before hitting a red light. By now we were in a quiet area near a dead-end street. I turned to check behind us. A car rapidly approached from the rear, jammed its brakes, and then maneuvered itself to our left side.

As James lowered his window, Wendy yelled, "No don't!"

The window in the car parallel to us was already lowered. It all happened so fast. I ducked down when the oversized pistol became visible. James took a bullet in his head. His body slumped against my left shoulder. He was a goner. I raised his right shoulder and ducked down further to block my head from another bullet. Blood was splattered everywhere—all over the windshield, my face, and my shirt. I glanced behind me hoping to see that Wendy was hunched over Laura, protecting her, somehow trying to calm her down.

Meanwhile, the gear was in neutral, allowing the car to roll forward, inching its way onto the dead-end street, where a few bodegas and retail stores had already closed for the night. I shoved James' upper torso away from me, just enough for me to turn the ignition key off. The car jerked to a sudden stop into a perfect location for a killing.

There was no time to think as two guys approached the car, yelling, "Out! Get out now!"

I had to collect myself and go with the flow to bide time. *Look for an opening,* I thought. My brain was racing, seeking an answer. *Were they going to just shoot us like James? No, they wanted something. Maybe it's Laura that they want. So then, they'll probably blow us all away. We are of no value to them if they capture her.*

We had no time left, it was do or die. I turned to see that Laura had passed out. Wendy and I were looking at each other. We each knew what we had to do and it had to be fast. As one guy walked to my side of the car, I knew he was going to put a bullet in my head, too. A scene was developing around us. People were hiding in various spots at a distance, but kept looking at what was about to unfold in fear.

"Move!" one man yelled at me. "Get into car over there."

"Yes, just don't hurt anyone else, please."

Wendy asked the other guy to be calm. She said that he could take her money, making believe it was a robbery.

"Shut up," he said to her, yanking her out of our car.

"Hey, Wendy," I said gently. "Let's count to three." She nodded.

I had a flashback to my training with Claude back at the Langley Virginia Command Center. We had gone over almost this exact scenario.

He had said, "The goal is to hurt or kill within the first three seconds of contact."

More than three seconds were just lost as I calmly stepped out of our car. I was about to lower my head to get in to their vehicle, making the movement believable. That's when I counted: one, two, and three. I deflected the man's gun hand and simultaneously broke his wrist as I whacked it down over my knee. Then I speared his right eye, trying to yank his eyeball out of its socket. I barely missed his eyeball, but did enough damage. He fell in the street, screaming and moaning while covering his face with both hands.

Meanwhile, Wendy was handling the other guy with the poise of a well-trained fighter. Before he could say a word or react, she said, "Go ahead, shoot me, asshole."

She grabbed his gun, slapped it away, and put him into a wrist hold behind his back. The guy dropped to the ground in agony, clearly from a broken wrist. For good measure, she kicked him in the head with her pointed boots. Blood began to drip out from his ear. Both guys were rendered useless. We immediately ran to help Laura out of the car.

I heard a buzzing noise overhead. It was a drone hovering about thirty feet above. Moments later, two HPAT 21 cars came by to clean up the scene. Levine texted me as we watched: *Nice. very nice moves, tax man. . . . Wendy, you were amazing. We saw it all. You and Wendy are off to a great start. Too bad about James. He was a great guy and a dedicated agent.*

I didn't even respond. My hands were shaking too much. Maybe this was all part of the job for the others by now, but I had just witnessed my first murder and it shook me more than I wanted to admit. Laura had awoken but was unable to speak.

***

We were all taken back to Wendy's hotel by an HPAT 21 Jeep. Two guards accompanied us up to her room.

Round two at trying to figure out why they wanted to grab Laura, I texted Levine. *Why her?*

He replied, *Get some sleep and watch over your wife. Tomorrow is another day. You will be coming to interrogate our two guests.*

I felt a tap on my shoulder.

"Bob, Laura is really shaken up," Wendy said. "She must calm down. Someone needs to get a pill to relax her. She has to sleep this whole thing off, otherwise she won't be able to focus on helping us to figure things out and that's critical."

"You're absolutely right."

I texted Levine asking him to send someone to the nearest twenty-four-hour drug store for an herbal sleep aid. We weren't about to go anywhere now.

I brought Laura a bottle of cold water and gave her a hug.

"Hey, it will all be fine. Those two guys are now being held by HPAT not too far from here. It's all okay for now, Laura."

"What about James?" she asked. "He's dead. Not a chance."

"Why the hell he lowered his window, I have no idea," said Wendy.

"A bad call, he simply froze then panicked. . . . Who knows, I could have done the same damn thing," I added.

Then Wendy helped me peal Laura off the couch, moving her to the back bathroom to help her take a shower. I went to the other bathroom to wash the blood off my face and to take my shirt off. *Shit, I have nothing else to wear.* I texted Levine: *I need an undershirt, some boxers, and a scotch. We all need to clean off our bloody shoes or try to get us all new shoes.*

Levine quickly texted back, *"No problem."*

About forty-five minutes later, one of the guards heard the door knock as someone called from the other side, "HPAT 21."

"Okay, HPAT 21," said the guard, cautiously opening the door. A bag was handed to him. It contained an herbal sleeping supplement, a bottle of Macallan twelve-year-old scotch, a new pack of undershirts, and some funky-looking briefs (possibly a Levine joke), three pair of shoes, and clothing for each of us. Toothbrushes and toothpaste were at the bottom.

I sent out a final text to Levine: *Great service and great scotch, my friend.*

He responded with a joke: Chaver *or* sadiq? *At this point, I'll go with* amigo. *The other languages are too complicated.*

The day was over and somehow, we had survived it. I collapsed on the couch. The two fingers on my right hand hurt from my attempt at ripping out the guy's eye. I was drained. My eyes closed as I saw Laura come out of the bathroom in a robe with Wendy helping her. Somehow, I forced my right eye halfway open.

"Did the shower help?" I asked Laura.

"Much better now," she replied.

I reached down and handed her the herbal sleeping aid from the bag.

"Thanks, Bob."

She took the bottle of pills from my hand and headed into the other room".

You get some rest now."

"Night, Bob," Wendy said as she got ready for bed.

"Good night, Wendy."

With that, I dozed off thinking about James. I saw his smile in my mind—and that's exactly how I'll choose to remember my pal.

CHAPTER **20**

I woke up slowly to tapping on my shoulder.

"It's time to get going, Bob, come on," Wendy said.

I was so damn groggy. As I opened my eyes, Wendy was hovering over me. Laura was still sleeping in the other bedroom.

"How did you sleep?"

"Not bad, Wendy, actually, it's one of those cushy couches, quite comfortable."

I swung around slowly and paused. At the edge of the couch, my two fingers throbbed again as I pushed up to stand. *I must have really bruised these little weapons last night.* Wendy overheard me talking to myself. I always hated bruised knuckles from playing basketball, paper cuts from tax returns, and other stupid annoying things like these.

"Now you sound like a tax man again," she said. "The old you."

"Let's be nice, Wendy."

"Have you heard from anyone yet?" she asked.

"Not since Levine's texts last night, no...but we should check in with him. What about some coffee first?"

"No thanks, Bob," she said. "You go shower and I'll get one of the guards to bring you up a cup and something to munch on."

"Thanks, you're a good lady," I said. "Oh, please make it a large black coffee—hot. Sorry to be picky, but the last thing I want now is lukewarm coffee."

Wendy gave me one of her looks that could kill out of the corner of her eye. Then her usual hand in the air move to brush me off. Wendy Gilmore, what a character.

I let the shower heat up and stopped in to take a look at Laura. She was still sleeping well. As I turned to back out of the room, I heard her mumble. She started to say things in her sleep.

"No, no, I want to." She paused. "I want to stay on this deal," she continued.

"What deal?" I asked softly.

After a delay, she answered. "I can do this," she muttered. "Why are you pushing me out?"

"Which deal, Laura?" I asked her. "Which client?"

"I remember it as a child. My mom and dad took me there. I remember!" she said.

She sat up abruptly with her eyes still closed, and then fell back down. I noticed tears falling down her cheeks. *How strange,* I thought, *I wonder what she remembered.*

***

Wow, I really need that shower already! I thought to myself. I decided to take a long, hot one and enjoy the moment without stress. The hot water was rushing down my back and the steam felt great. As I wrapped up, I did a few stretches reaching my hands to my toes, took a deep breath, and at last, called it quits.

Shit. I forgot a towel, I realized.

Then I heard Wendy call from the bedroom, "Here's your large black hot coffee, Bob."

"Great, but I need a towel," I yelled. "Can you throw one in here, please?"

"Better yet, I'll bring it in just for you," she said with sarcasm.

"Come on, just fling it to me," I laughed, peeking out from behind the shower curtain.

She walked into the bathroom smiling, and then she flung the towel at me with a wink.

"Thanks, but I need to be alone."

"No problem," she said. "Don't flatter yourself. Your wife is in the next room."

"Wendy, see if Laura is still sleeping?" I asked as I dried off.

"She is," Wendy replied. "What's the big deal?"

"I went in a few minutes ago to check on her," I explained. "She was having a weird dream, talking out loud, saying stuff about her job. How far did you get with her about her law firm deals?"

"She was not ready to get into those things yet," Wendy said. "Seemed like we needed to break the ice some more, so I dropped it. Why do you ask?"

"In her sleep, she said, 'Don't take me off this deal.' And something about remembering a place as a child. Must be a building deal her law firm was involved in and that location had a huge impact on her when she was a kid. Just a guess for now. Wendy, we need this information. Levine will want me to deal with those two jerks from last night at the restaurant. While I do that, can you work with Laura on this? Try to get her to remember more from her dream?"

"All I can do is try, Bob."

"No, you have to find a way," I urged. "You know this could be huge, Wendy."

"Of course, I'll give it my best effort."

With that, we heard a knock at the door.

"Open up, it's me, John Ashton."

The guard let Ashton in and Wendy greeted him while I got dressed. Then I joined them in the main bedroom with the couch. Wendy went to check in on Laura and wake her up.

"What are you doing here?" I asked him.

"I was told to get here right away," Ashton explained. "We need Laura to talk."

The psych gave me a smile and a sincere hug, so I went with it.

"I heard you guys were up and running," Ashton commented.

"I'm not sure what that means, but right after dinner, we were almost killed," I replied.

Wendy came out of the other bedroom with Laura.

"Hello," Ashton said. "You must be Laura Stone. Nice to meet you in person."

"I'm sorry, but who are you?"

Wendy took the lead and replied, "This is Dr. Ashton from our initial phone call. He is sort of like our HPAT 21 on call counselor, available as needed."

"Oh, how nice. How much do you charge? I could use your help," Laura sarcastically remarked and chuckled.

We all laughed with her.

"Hey, why don't we all do a group session?" I chimed in.

"Very funny, Bob," Ashton said.

Suddenly a text from Levine came through on my cell.

"Apparently I have to go to the 'basement,' right now," I said. "I have a meeting, or whatever you call it, and I need to move it."

"You mean a 'debriefing session'?" Ashton suggested. "Don't eat too much for breakfast before you get there, Bob. You may not be able to keep the food down."

"Hey, what's that supposed to mean?" I snapped. He knew how to trigger my emotions.

"Just take it one step at a time, Stone," he replied. "You'll get used to the basement. It takes time, that's all."

"Come on, don't say things and then just drop it."

"Look, Bob," Ashton said. "You and whoever else over at the basement will have to do whatever it takes to get those guys to talk. Do you understand me?"

"Yes, but—" I protested.

Ashton interrupted me by walking over and whispering into my ear. I suppose he didn't want the others to hear.

"Let's step out of the room for a minute," he whispered.

I knocked on the inside door of the hotel room. An HPAT 21 guard opened the door, and two other guards were also outside near the elevator.

"Ashton, what am I getting into over there?" I asked.

"Look, if they talk, it's all good," Ashton said. "If they do not, those guys will have to be hurt, tortured, and beaten until they tell us something really useful."

"Is that it, no more details?" I pressed.

"Why are you pressuring me?" Ashton asked. "Go there and you'll see for yourself. But I can tell you this: We have a 'doctor' near the basement who helps us at times. Dr. Singhdal is a retired dentist who brings all his tools with him. Over the years, he earned a nickname; we call him Dr.Sing and why, because he always and I mean always, makes his victims sing. Now get the hell out of here and go do something for our country, tax man. I need to deal with your wife now. Oh, and if I have to hypnotize her, do I have your permission?"

We gave each other a weird look.

"You better ask Laura that question, not me."

I poked my head back into the hotel room and said, "See ya, ladies. Laura, you're in good hands, please relax and do your best."

***

I turned to the two guards and one of them asked, "Mr. Stone, are you ready to take on the next challenge in this crazy adventure."

"I don't know how to answer that, where are you taking me, to the basement?"

"Yes, sir, Mr. Stone," one guard replied. "Both of us are escorting you. It's not too far. Please, let's go now. We're a bit behind schedule already."

One guard got into the elevator first. The other stayed behind me.

"What are your names?" I asked.

"I'm Carl," one said.

"Stu," said the other.

"Okay, Carl and Stu, I'm in your hands."

"There are two more guards outside," Stu said.

"Wait. Who will be watching Laura, Wendy, and Ashton?" I asked.

"Oh, don't worry, Mr. Stone," Stu reassured. "These two new guards here are giving us a shift break. They are going upstairs now."

"There should not have been any gap in security!" I exclaimed. "Let's all go back upstairs. Then we can come down again with cleared heads."

I had to do this. We all went back up to check the room. Ashton was talking with Laura already, and Wendy was just listening as she sat next to her for support.

"Why are you here again?" Laura asked.

"Nothing, Laura," I said. "Just introducing you to your new guards. Guys, say hi."

"Hello everyone," one of the new guards said. "I'm Bill."

"And my name is Roger," said the other.

"We are your replacement security guards," Bill said. "We are here to do whatever it takes to protect you. And if you need some food or whatever, just let us know."

"Thanks, guys," said Ashton. "And Stone, see you later today."

"Sounds good."

I headed back down to the lobby with Carl and Stu, then hopped into another Jeep. It was a nice day, mild with sunny clear skies. Another reminder of 9/11 for me, also a picture-perfect day. *How could anyone forget? And now look at what I'm doing with my life!* That shit could not be allowed to happen again in our homeland or anywhere else around the world. All I could do now was put my best foot forward and do the right thing.

"Mr. Stone?" Stu prompted. "Mr. Stone, your phone has been receiving texts."

I had been in my own world.

"Thanks, Stu, it's Levine. He said to hurry up and that they need us over there."

Okay on the way, I responded. After gliding past a string of green lights, we finally caught a red. I had a flashback to James being shot. Just then, a car pulled next to Stu and I had a reaction.

I ducked and shouted, "Keep the window shut!"

The other car pulled away. Stu pulled over and turned to me.

"Are you alright, sir?" he asked.

I ignored his question and told him to keep driving. The truth was that I was not okay. My forehead had droplets of sweat and my neck was stiff from tension. A few deep breaths helped me to shrug it off, but not completely.

We finally seemed to be close. Stu took a sharp left onto St. Mark's Place, and then drove straight a few blocks to Avenue A. He found a parking spot fast in a section just off the avenue, away from the hustle and bustle. The guards walked me about a half block down to a brownstone. We went around the back and into a doorway partially covered with vines. There were six steps down to the hidden entrance.

Stu knocked and then said, "HPAT S-21."

"What's the 'S' for?" I asked.

"Oh, that's just for my name," he replied.

The door did not open yet, but a voice let out from behind it.

"Confirm again," the voice commanded.

Stu replied, "HPAT 21, S-21."

The door was opened, Levine appeared.

"Come on in, tax man," he replied. "It's a great day, isn't it?"

"Yeah, just like 9/11," I answered back. "Clear as hell with blue skies. A perfect day for a Jihad attack."

Everyone nervously laughed at that. I sensed that maybe I was a bit out of line.

"Sorry, guys," I said. "Every time I see a day like this, I can't help but think back to 9/11 when I dropped my wife off at the train station in Long Island early that morning. She was making her usual commute to Manhattan, but this time she forgot her cell phone. When I screamed out the car window to let her know she left her cell phone in the car as the train was coming, she just waved it off. I looked up to the sky and it was perfectly clear. I remembered thinking, *What a day for a terror attack.* It was just like today."

"And your wife, what happened to her that day?" Levine asked.

"Well, when flight eleven crashed into the North Tower of the World Trade Center, I obviously could not reach her. She planned on going downtown before work that day. She would sometimes go down to the mall at the World Trade Center to check out the stores, buy perfume, or just to clear her head before heading to the office. I was terribly worried about her and almost threw up, my stomach in knots thinking she was gone. I could not reach her for hours. She finally called my cell."

"How?" asked Levine.

"A good guy let her call me from his cell phone. She got off the train in Queens and took a taxi home."

"Wow, at least she wasn't hurt," Levine said.

"Yes, we were very lucky that day."

A voice interrupted my thoughts.

"Anyway, Stone, it's time for a tour. Welcome to our basement."

The voice sounded familiar. I turned to my left—it was Frank from the FBI, who had just walked in.

"I hear great things about you lately, tax man," Frank continued. "You and your partner, Wendy, both deserve medals for blowing off the attackers last night. You have our respect, well-earned."

"Thank you, sir, that means a lot to me."

"Hey, Levine, take the tax man around for a quick tour," Frank ordered. Levine looked at me as if some ugly scene was about to unfold.

"Follow me, Stone."

In turn, the guards followed me as Levine led the way.

"Levine, how many rooms are there?" I asked, looking around.

"Four rooms, we have rooms for interviews over there," he said, pointing. "You'll be there in a few minutes. There's also a holding room for sleep. Let's walk down here," he said as he gestured for us to follow him down a hallway. "Pretty basic, like a mini prison down here," he continued. "There's a back office where we can watch the debriefings, do paperwork, eat, or deal with calls. This back room is around and behind the interview room so that we can observe and listen through the one-way glass window."

"Hah, just like on TV," I commented. "You know, like *Law and Order*." I couldn't resist.

"Very cute, Bob. Finally, there's another holding room down the hallway for other situations. Oh, we call it the situation room," Levine said with a smirk. "It's a very simple layout, Bob."

"So, 'other situations' meaning what—torture?"

"That really depends on each scenario. That's why our friend Frank is here. He is also our liaison to the CIA, remember? So when it comes to other tactics needed to gain information, he's our go-to guy for authorization."

"Understood."

I was starting to get edgy down here in this hell hole.

"Bob, I can see you're having a reaction, just take it easy. This basement has served us well. We've obtained more life-saving intel from terrorists in this hell hole down here than you could imagine."

"That's good enough for me, Levine. Thanks for putting things back into perspective for me."

He touched my shoulder and gazed into my eyes, as if to say, *You'll be fine.* I took notice of how he kept his hand on me, though. It seemed to be a bit too long, but I let it slide.

"Let's go talk with our two prisoners, are you ready," Levine said.

"Damn right, I'm ready. These assholes tried to hurt my wife not once, but twice."

Levine eyeballed two more HPAT 21 guards who would accompany us to the interview room. One guard opened the door and made the initial step in.

"Prisoner is under control," another guard confirmed.

We walked in. I saw a food tray on top of a narrow table. The prisoner had barely eaten any of his breakfast. His hands were cuffed to his chair on each side. This was the guy I had bumped into at the restaurant.

"Where's the other guy?" I asked.

"We need to keep them apart, he's in his own holding cell."

"So we focus on this guy first?" I asked.

"Yes, nothing to read into, let's simply start with this one. Let's get started. Bob, look and learn as I interact with terrorist number one. Stay here, but don't talk to him, not yet. I have to get Frank in here and our interpreter, Jamil."

Levine stepped out and I stared at the prisoner's face. I saw a hard life filled with misery and anger. Scars and marks overtook his facial expressions. His face told a story. Levine returned with Frank who began to read from a pre- printed sheet of paper.

"My name is Franklin Conway. I am with the United States FBI. I am informing you that we assert our right to hold and to question you as to your intentions against our homeland. If you refuse to respond, we will have no choice but to take alternative measures. As an agent of the U.S. government I have the authority to apply other methods against you in order to protect our citizens from potential acts of terrorism. Do you hear me? Do you Understand me?"

The guy did not respond and continued to look down at the floor.

"Thanks, Frank," Levine said. "Let me get started."

"Go ahead, meantime, Jamil and Dr. Singh are on their way. Hold on, I have an emergency text coming in."

"What's up, Frank?" Levine asked.

He held out his hand, as if to tell Levine to stop talking. Frank's face could not hide his anger. *Now what?* I thought. *Seems like every day, there is so much intense situations to deal with.*

"Here we go again, people," Frank uttered.

"Well, what's up?" Levine asked.

"Let's take a break and go to the back office," Frank replied.

***

We all stepped out to the hallway and headed into the back office, where we were able to watch the streaming news on the television that hung just under the ceiling on the far corner of the room. Jane Oliver, a well-known news anchor, was covering a story on CNN. Oliver began her report—

"A plane took off fifteen minutes ago from LaGuardia Airport to Boston Logan International Airport. At twenty-five thousand feet, the aircraft shifted off its flight path and is now flying at an unusually low altitude closing in on the George Washington Bridge. U.S. fighter jets immediately scrambled and tried to intercept the airplane, but there was no response. It was a shuttle from New York to Boston with ninety-eight people aboard."

Frank abruptly left the basement and Levine dropped into a chair. At this moment, I had visions of this American landmark being destroyed, cars crashing into the waters below, causing the deaths of so many innocent victims.

Oliver introduced four security experts, one from Homeland Security, the Transportation Security Administration (TSA), the FBI, and a contact from the Department of Defense. No one had much to offer at this point, just more of the same old speculations. I knew whatever information the network had, we must have a leg up on them.

Levine turned to me and said in a low voice, "We need help from the Israelis."

"What does that mean?" I asked.

"Very few people know this, Bob, as a payback for American military forces partnering up and supporting the development of the Iron Dome Weapon System, which blocked hundreds of missiles and saved thousands of Israelis over the last ten years, the Israelis developed for us something quite unique."

"So, tell me more?" I queried. I was anxiously waiting to hear more from Levine.

"We all know the Israelis are so damn smart. Okay, here it is: It's called 'Remote Access Flight Control.' Pretty much means what it says. The software enables us to lock onto any aircraft displaying unexplained, irregular changes in flight patterns and redirect it within seconds."

"Incredible."

"Yeah, and this is what we need right now," Levine replied.

Another news flash came through.

"I cannot believe what I'm seeing," Jane Oliver exclaimed. "The Boston shuttle was about to ram into the bridge, then it somehow turned away. It's now heading to Newark Liberty International Airport in New Jersey."

Levine turned to me and said, "That was no coincidence. Somehow, the Israeli software was implemented, and the damn thing must've worked!"

The news continued on with Oliver reporting, "The plane was escorted down and landed safely. But now, there will tragically be a hostage situation."

"This crap never ends," I said.

"I know, I know," Levine agreed.

We were both angry as we walked back toward the interrogation room. Dr.Sing was waiting for us outside the door, seemingly observing the prisoner. He was a gentle-looking skinny man, possibly of Middle Eastern descent, I couldn't be sure. He was carrying an old-fashioned doctor's black leather bag.

"Good day, Mr. Levine," he said.

"Hello, Dr. Sing," Levine said, obviously shortening his name out of familiarity. Have a seat, doctor and thanks for coming over so fast."

"No trouble whatsoever. I love my work."

Levine followed up, "Say hello to Bob Stone, one of our newest HPAT 21 operatives."

The doctor looked me over, studying me in a strange manner.

"Hello to you, Mr. Stone. And why am I here today, gentlemen?" Dr. Sing asked.

Levine responded, "It's the usual, you're on call. If we need you, we'll let you know in about fifteen minutes."

The doctor nodded his head and said, "I am ready to do whatever is needed to gain the information you require from them."

It struck me how weird this doctor's demeanor was—his very slow verbal responses, coupled with deliberately sluggish movements. A careful methodical man moving at the pace of a slug.

We finally reentered the interrogation room with the guards behind us and two guards still waiting with the prisoner. Levine walked in with a bottle of water he'd been sipping and gave another bottle to the prisoner. He asked the guard to release his right hand to drink.

Then Levine began.

"What's your name?" Levine asked.

No answer.

"Where are you from?"

No response.

"Who do you work for?"

Nothing. Levine glanced at me, visibly pissed off.

"How did you get into America?"

No answer.

"What do you want with Laura Stone?"

The guy cracked a slight smile but said nothing. I slowly rose up off my chair. I was boiling over in anger. I walked over to him, Levine stepped back.

"Go ahead, Stone, it's your turn."

"You fucking asshole!" I shouted. "What do you want with my wife?"

No response. I asked him again. He turned away. I lost it. I stepped a bit past him and smacked the side of his head with my right elbow. He moaned as his head drooped over to the side.

"You tried to hurt my wife. Why?"

The guy just would not open up to us.

Levine said, "This is typical. I'll give it another nine minutes before we ask Dr. Sing to step in. We have to give him a chance. Let's bring in the interpreter." Levine touched a buzzer. Moments later, in walks a well- dressed Middle Eastern man in a sports jacket. He was Jamil.

"Jamil was listening in from the outside room," Levine explained. "He is going to ask the same questions translated into Arabic. Let's step back and let him do his thing."

After about seven minutes of questioning, there was zero progress.

"This is one stubborn dude," Levine commented. "Stone, come with me."

We left the room. Levine whispered into a guard's ear on the way out. The guard then entered the room with the others and stood near the door. We watched from the back room, through the window. The prisoner could not see us.

The guard was a thick, rough-around-the-edges man. He cuffed the prisoner's hand back to the chair and moved behind him. The guard wrapped his large arms around the prisoner's neck in a semi tight choke hold while the other two stood ready to pounce. Jamil placed his lips close to the prisoner's ear and whispered a few Arabic words.

I tapped Levine's shoulder and asked, "Hey, what did the interpreter just say?"

"This is the moment where I have to decide on bringing in the doctor based on the prisoner's willingness to talk. My educated guess is that he gave the prisoner a final warning to either talk now or we would torture, maybe even kill him. This is Jamil's standard message."

Jamil pulled away and rose up, clearly upset. He exited the room and gave Levine a look, a signal to elevate the process. The guard stopped the choke hold to avoid brain damage from lack of oxygen. Everyone left the room to regroup.

The prisoner was taken away and the other prisoner was brought in. The same interview process took place, with this prisoner also showing absolutely no willingness to talk. Both guys chose to remain dead silent. After the second interview had been concluded, we all took a break. I had to get outside.

"Come on, Levine," I said. "Let's get out of here for some fresh air. I have to get out of this hell hole."

I knew the real insanity was yet to begin with Dr. Sing's methods. The situation room must be next.

Stu guarded us as we walked to the street and paced around. A text came through on Levine's phone. By now, I could easily recognize how Levine would react when an important message came in. This time, a tear flowed down his cheek as he read the message. I said nothing. I waited for him to speak. It was a long gap, a nasty silence. When he finally broke the silence, he called me Bob. I had not yet figured out why or when he switched from the different names of Stone, Bob, or tax man, but I sensed I was about to learn.

Levine showed me the text as he said, "That Boston shuttle plane was blown up by the hijackers. Everyone is dead. The crew, eighty-two

people, including fourteen children. No group has yet to claim responsibility."

I sensed Levine needed a wakeup call. He was uncharacteristically
distraught. I've yet to see him at a total loss of words, as he was in this
moment.

"Levine, hey, it's time to get back the basement. One of those guys
must talk. Otherwise, a whole lot more than eighty-two people are going to be killed. So, let's put things into perspective and get back to
work."

Levine looked at me intensely and said, "I see that you just elevated
yourself. I didn't realize how rapidly you could become a changed man.
I'm impressed with your ability to remain calm and collected."

I chose not to respond and walked back inside with him, Stu trailed
behind us. I was nervous wondering if I could handle what was about
to unfold back in the basement. *Torture and poise don't go together*.

"Hello," Dr. Sing

I called out to him observing that he was still waiting and watching
outside the interrogation room again. "Are you hungry?"

"No, I'm fine, had a late breakfast," Dr. Sing replied. "If you guys
need me, it's time. Otherwise, I'm calling it a day."

"No, no, get started," Levine replied. "Just do your thing."

Two guards again followed the dentist into the interrogation room.
Levine and I tailed behind. The two prisoners remained in separate
rooms. Jamil rejoined us, visibly shaken. He knew what was about to
take place and clearly, he didn't wish to interpret the final warning to
each prisoner.

He turned to Levine and asked, "Do we have to do this?"

"I'd rather not...do what you can, Jamil. We'll give it one last shot.
All of us except you and one guard will leave the room. You talk with
these guys again and describe to them the pain they will experience if
they don't talk. Take five minutes on each guy. That's it."

We walked out with little hope. These guys were totally unwilling
to cooperate. Jamil pleaded with the prisoners and appealed for them
to work with us. His Arabic was amazing. I heard the word *sadiq* several

times. I was sure he was telling them something like, "We do not wish to harm you, but we cannot allow our people to be killed."

The prisoner responded. No one but Jamil understood what was being said. Jamil nodded his head as if to say, *I understand*. He rose from his chair and gave one last look back to the prisoner.

When Jamil came out of the room back to us, he said, "How sad. The guy feels that we have been killing and abusing his people for decades."

"Who exactly did he mean by 'we'?" Levine asked.

"The prisoner was not specific," Jamil replied.

Levine turned to Dr. Sing. They exchanged some eye contact and without a word, the next phase was set in motion. The guards moved one of the prisoners into the situation room. Levine and I slowly followed while Stu remained just outside the door.

The slender doctor entered the room, every step he took towards the table was measured. He opened up his black bag on the small table that one of the guards had previously brought into the room, pushing the uneaten breakfast remnants off it. He neatly laid out various instruments, some recognizable, some not. A dental drill, an extension cord, steel tooth scrapers, a mini saw used to get in between teeth, a small hammer, and a tiny eyeglass screwdriver. He then took out thick, long nails from the side pocket on his case. Finally, the guards brought in a thick, narrow, wooden table. Dr. Sing asked Jamil to stay and translate as he progressed.

"Looking at Jamil, the doctor said, the prisoner needs to know what is about to happen. I will begin in two minutes…If we cannot get him to talk, we must apply other methods using different tools."

Levine told the guard to place the prisoner's right hand on the wood slab and hold it down firmly. Dr.Sing reached for one of the long nails— a nail that could be used to pierce a three-inch wood slab. He grabbed the small hammer.

"Hey, aren't you a dentist?" I asked. "Why all of these other tools?"

He did not look at me nor answer me. The dentist then completely changed his persona.

"I am here for fucking results," Dr. Sing snapped. "Do not ask me stupid questions." He was enraged.

I backed off. Dr. Sing placed the nail over the prisoner's hand and started to hammer away. Surprisingly, the prisoner was in another world—not a sound. Dr. Sing hammered more and more. Then the screaming started, the blood was shooting out with each hammering, spraying all over the dentist's shirt. Jamil held up his hand and Dr. Sing stopped. The prisoner was given another chance to talk. Still no answers. Dr. Sing finished hammering the nail deep into the hand. The prisoner was now incoherent and screaming in Arabic.

Dr. Sing turned to us and said, "That was a good start." He smiled.

"Great," I said sarcastically. "So, what's next?"

Dr. Sing asked Jamil to repeat his words to the prisoner. He then raised his eyes slowly and tilted his head to respond to me.

"I practiced dentistry for thirty years, but I always wanted to be an eye doctor," Dr. Sing replied. "This is my opportunity to learn. Strap his head in."

A guard wrapped a wide leather belt around the prisoner's head, somehow weaving it around and securing it to the chair.

Dr. Sing announced, "Whoever wants to leave, leave now."

"Thank you," I turned to walk out but, I suddenly froze in my steps. I needed to see this jerk get what was coming to him.

Dr. Sing picked up the hooked steel tooth scraper and moved in slowly into the prisoner's eye. Jamil pleaded with the prisoner for him to respond. The captive man was shaking and screaming, trying to get up from the chair. Dr. Sing inserted the dental scraper into his right eye and started to poke around. The prisoner passed out.

"Shit!" Dr. Sing yelled. He stood up and said, "Throw water in his face. I can't be here all fucking day."

One of the guards filled a bucket with cold water from the basin in the corner of the room, and then dumped it over the prisoner's head. He came to and spat at Dr. Sing's face.

"Guard, place the other hand over the wooden block."

Another nail was hammered into his other hand. More screaming, more blood. It was getting crazy.

Jamil appealed to the prisoner frantically, this time in Jamil spoke without thinking, in English. Jamil was badly shaken up

"Tell us," Jamil urged. "Who are you? Who sent you? Why did you try to kidnap that woman?"

The prisoner answered, "I no talk." He was breaking down. At least he said something.

"We can protect you and your family," Levine said. "Even get you back to your country. We need your help. You can trust me."

He made eye contact with the prisoner, who still said nothing more.

Dr. Sing and Levine gave each other another look. The dentist reached for his drill and an extension cord.

"Get your Arabic ready, Mr. Jamil, tell this guy, "Open sesame." Obviously, a bad joke.

"Open your mouth," Jamil repeated.

The guard had put gloves on and pulled open the prisoner's mouth. The drill was positioned onto his tongue and started to twist and churn. The gagging reflex was ugly.

Dr Sing went deeper and said, "Oh yes, please tell me if anything hurts."

A flashback to his days as a real dentist, I imagined.

Dr. Sing told Jamil to repeat his words, "Tell the prisoner that if he still refuses to talk, I will cut off his tongue with my saw." He held up the jagged-edged mini saw for effect.

The prisoner looked at Dr. Sing and bobbed his head up and down, then left to right, as tears rolled down his cheeks. He caved in. Dr. Sing immediately stopped his work.

Jamil then asked in Arabic, *"Hal 'ant jahz?"*

The prisoner gagged and moved his head up and down again. Apparently, he was ready to talk.

"Well done, Dr. Sing," Levine said. "Another day at the office, huh? You were splendid today."

"Thank you so much."

We all left the room. A medic came in to free up the prisoner's hands and clean the wounds.

Just before Dr. Sing left us, he said, "You see, nothing was done to the eye or to the tongue, but the intimidation worked. At the end of the day, perception is reality."

Nothing more was said. Jamil spent the next thirty minutes talking with the prisoner. I was dying to hear what was learned. We were pacing nervously outside the situation room. At last, the door opened, and Jamil walked toward us. He sat down with a clipboard, papers, and scribbles. This was the moment of truth.

"The two prisoners were from Yemen," Jamil began. "They somehow entered Canada through connections with a mosque in Toronto. They trained there for over four months. To avoid the border, they took a ferry from a small town in Toronto and slipped into the United States They then went to stay at the mosque in Astoria, Queens. It was there that they met Darmush Khan and other anti-American extremists.

"A higher up, whose name they do not know, showed them a photo of Laura Stone. They were told to follow her. That's when they took a ferry to Fire Island the day she went there. They were instructed to capture her but did not know why. They were to bring your wife back to the mosque in Astoria. He did tell me that the man who ordered them to capture Laura was a well-dressed man once referred to as 'the Lawyer.' The prisoner's name, by the way is Nori al Tabach. The other guy is Kaleb Mansouri. I was given a description of the Lawyer and I was able to sketch out a rough picture."

Jamil turned the clipboard toward us and said, "Here, check it out."

"Amazing job, Jamil," I said, patting him on the back. "You're an interpreter *and* an artist?"

"Yes, that why I get paid the big bucks," Jamil joked.

Levine also complimented him, "Great job, Jamil, thank you. Now, call it a day. In fact, let's all call it a day. Bob, let's catch up with Ashton, Laura, and Wendy. Oh, and we have to show Laura Jamil's sketch. With any luck, maybe she'll recognize our latest person of interest."

***

We left the basement and I got into the Jeep with Levine. Stu and Carl were up front. A security detail of guards followed closely behind us. On the way to the hotel, Levine told Stu to pull over.

"Bob, it's almost two o'clock and I am starving, call Wendy and ask if they want sandwiches. See that crappy-looking deli over there? Best sandwiches, the brisket is great."

I called Wendy. She sounded happy that we were bringing lunch. I continued to talk to her.

"Listen, Wendy, we had a breakthrough here. We'll see you all in about fifteen minutes with some info and lunch."

Stu stayed with us while a guard from the other car went to the deli and returned carrying a large bag loaded with sandwiches, sodas, and side dishes. We began driving back to the Holiday Inn.

"How much did you pay Dr. Sing for his work back there?"

"Not important," Levine replied. "But if it really means something to you, he gets a thousand dollars, let's call it a consulting fee."

My tax man brain kicked in, I naturally asked, "How do you pay him?"

"You damn accountant." He put his arm around me and whispered, "Cash."

"You're a damn hypocrite. You work for a division of the IRS and you pay this maniac who specializes in torture with cash. He pays no tax on what you, the IRS, pay him?"

"What can I say, Stone. what the hell would you expect, we should issue him a tax form, you know a 1099, and we'll call it 'consulting services'...give it a break, will you. That's the way it is in the world of terrorism—it's the dark side of money and it flows everywhere. You have no idea how much cash we spread around the globe, and even locally right here. I suggest we drop this subject."

The Jeep pulled up at the hotel. We got out with the huge bag of food, walked through the lobby, and took the elevator upstairs to the room. We knocked three times, followed by me saying, "HPAT 21," allowing the inside guard to open the door.

Wendy greeted us, "Hello, people. So, what's the good news?"

"You know what," I said. "Let's make this a working lunch. I have a flight tonight to Toronto." I was feeling very much on edge with the ugly torture scene in the basement and I was not looking forward to the conversation we were about to begin.

CHAPTER **21**

There was a moment of silence in the room. I reflected on the torture and its results—my first experience in the "basement." Ashton was right, good thing I didn't eat too much before I witnessed Dr. Sing's methods. I might not have been able to keep any food down.

"I'm starving," Wendy said.

"Hey, everyone, grab your grub, let's get started here, Levine said."

"So, how did you all get along while I was over at the basement?" I asked.

"It was just great," Wendy said, slightly sarcastic.

I could sense the slight undercurrent of nervousness in the room.

"Laura, would you like to talk?" Ashton asked.

"Sure, thanks. I appreciate that. Dr. Ashton, you somehow got me to rethink my last two months at the law firm. A group of foreign investors was aggressively looking to buy Manhattan properties."

"What do you recall about this group of investors?" I asked.

"Not much, we knew that it was set up as a Delaware limited liability corporation. Ya know, in Delaware the names making up the LLC entity don't have to be published. There is a huge cushion of privacy by forming a Delaware-based company."

"Okay, so far, no big deal," Levine said. "That's a common tactic."

I nodded my head in agreement.

"Last year, this group acquired a large hotel on Forty-ninth Street near the United Nations Plaza," Laura said.

"Okay good," I said. "What about the deal you were working on that—"

"Let me finish," she said, cutting me off. "At first, this group expressed an interest in buying the Empire State Building. That's what triggered my childhood memories. My parents took me all the way up to the top when I was twelve years old. We were visiting the city. It was one of my best memories as a child. I remembered how my mother and father were so together at that time and how connected our family was as a whole, including me and my younger sister. The vacation ended, and we went back to my childhood home in Maryland. A week later, the unthinkable happened."

Laura paused and cleared her throat, no one said a word.

"Someone knocked on our front door just after our first dinner back home. My father opened the door without asking who was there. He was always so trusting and carefree. Sure, open the damn front door. Don't even ask, 'Who is it?' So stupid! In walks this bad-ass guy with a knife. He tells my dad, 'Give me your watch and all your cash or I'll kill ya.' Dad was a pretty tough guy, but not as strong as he used to be. He refused to give the asshole anything. He shouted, 'Get the hell out of here before I call the cops!' The robber stabbed my father in his stomach two times. He collapsed and died at the hospital that night. Our family was ruined." With this last sentence, she took a few deep breaths, started to cry, turned and left the room.

"Why don't we all take a break here?" I suggested.

"Yes, I agree, Ashton said.

About five minutes later, I got up to check on Laura. She was in the bed, laying on her back, her hands resting on her stomach. She looked so peaceful. I gave her a kiss on the top of her head, unintentionally causing her eyes to pop open, so I began to talk to her.

"I understand now, you never told me any of that Laura. You only mentioned to me that your father died when you were twelve years old."

"I'm sorry, I feel so stupid. What the hell am I doing here anyway?"

"Look, I want to be here for you and help you through this, but I'll be in Toronto tomorrow. I just have to go."

"Really, Toronto, what for?"

"My orders are to talk with the manager at the Royal Bank of Toronto. I have orders to follow the flow of funds. Levine believes it involves a scheme of planned terrorist acts against the homeland. Many countries have gotten involved in the fight against terrorism. Our allies keep us informed about unusual money transfers around the world. I have to figure out what's going on with this huge nonprofit account in Canada and uncover why and to where these large sums of money were recently transferred to. I leave tonight. In fact, it's time for me to pack up and get to the airport in about two hours.

"Laura, please. Let's get back into the other room. Please, try hard to tell us anything more, anything at all. There is no right or wrong here. You may say something that could make a difference. Ultimately, you can save lives."

With that, Laura got up and we walked back together.

"Let's all take a breath," Ashton said. "Go ahead, Laura."

"Right, so, back to that deal. Either the price was way too high or the sellers decided to back off, I didn't know for sure, but that deal to acquire the Empire State Building fell apart."

"What was the name of the investment company?" Levine asked.

"The Shirango Group, LLC. It's based in Luxembourg, When the law firm gave me the Empire State Building deal and it went south, I was upset. I had a feeling that the rug was pulled out from under me. I emotionally associated that building to the loss of my father. I can thank Dr. Ashton for that wisdom. Meantime, the managing partner of Combs and Walker, Arman Danelli, asked me to come to his office about two months ago. He told me that the firm has another deal pending and they wanted me to work on it. He complimented me on my attention to detail and told me that this one was not so exciting. It was not a flashy landmark Manhattan property, but a deal is a deal. He gave me a thick file to review labeled 'The Narico Group, LLC' and asked me to get started the next day."

Laura looked drained, so I prompted her to keep going to avoid gaps in her thoughts.

"The Narico Group put out an indication of interest to buy two ad-jacent warehouses on the corner of Eleventh Avenue and West Six-teenth Street. Arman gave me an additional file and at that time, he suggested that I start reviewing the files that night. I was taken aback by such urgency. Oh yes, and they wanted me to form another Delaware LLC. The name of this entity was Eleven-Sixteen Properties LLC. Stupid name, if you ask me."

"So, what's the big deal here?" Levine asked.

"I have no clue, you guys made a big deal over all this crap, not me." She abruptly rose up from her chair. "Hold on! Why the hell would a bunch of foreign investors want to buy two crappy old warehouses with building violations?" Laura continued and wondered out loud while pacing. "Actually, I remember now that there were enough problems to block the purchase. That's what Arman wanted me to check out: environmental problems, ink spills from printing presses over the years, and health code violations."

"Great job, Laura," Wendy commented. She got out of her chair and added, "You have to go back to work, act like everything is normal, and show the law firm your renewed enthusiasm to work. Yes Laura, go to the law office tomorrow and show them your burning desire to be that rising star of a lawyer you've been over the years. Get back in the groove so you can help us. You can do it."

"By the way, Laura," Levine interjected. "Look at this sketch. Do you recognize this man?"

She hesitated upon looking at Jamil's sketch. She finally said, "Looks familiar, but I just can't connect the dots."

"We learned earlier that this guy regularly pops in at the mosque in Astoria," Levine explained. "He is known as 'the Lawyer.' We don't know his name, just his nickname. The one guy we debriefed thought he might actually be a lawyer. He's always well-dressed and plays the part. He is probably an advisor to the mosque."

"Sorry, Mr. Levine," Laura said. "I still can't place the man in the sketch, but he does have a familiar look to me. Right now, my mind has a lot of blank spaces. It has to be stress, I know this man, but, whatever."

I checked my cell for the time, sensing that I had become so involved that I was out of touch with my schedule.

"That's it for me, I need to get ready for the airport."

"Bob, it's all set," Levine said. "I have an HPAT 21 car taking you to LaGuardia Airport. They will be here in forty-five minutes."

"Oh, and I forgot to tell you," Wendy added. "You have about twenty-eight phone calls from your clients. My assistant returned every call except for Darmush Khan's. I know how he's a key figure, so we decided not to return his call. That's one for you to handle"

"Great work, I appreciate it. You and your assistant are efficient. What did you instruct the assistant to say to my clients?"

"That you've been away taking educational courses."

"That's it?" I asked.

"Yeah, and that you'll be seeing them in a few weeks," she added.

"Perfect."

Wendy patted me on the back, smiled and said, "My pleasure, tax man."

"What did Darmush want? And did he leave a specific message?"

"My assistant told me that he was checking in with you regarding a tax question."

"Levine, did your IRS contacts send Darmush that phony tax audit examination letter yet?"

"No, of course not, that will take time to get approved. I'll need two weeks. Right now, you need to get on that flight and focus on your visit to the bank in Toronto."

"I know, follow the flow of funds."

"That's it, Stone."

Everyone else left the hotel room, leaving me, Laura, and Wendy behind with the guards posted outside.

"I'm dead tired and need a rest," Laura blurted out.

"Yeah, me too. Come on, Laura, let's rest in the other bedroom for a while," Wendy agreed.

I waved my hand to them and lied down on the couch. Realizing that I was getting deeper and deeper into this HPAT 21 thing, I decided to call Levine before he drove too far away.

"Hey, aren't you supposed to give me a weapon, some James Bond toys? Something?"

"How would you get past airport security?" Levine asked. "You have your brain, your karate moves, and now the krav maga skills. Claude taught you well. Plus, you have the tracking device in your neck. Oh yeah—and your instincts."

"I think you're a bit crazy."

"One step at a time, trust me, Stone. You don't need to be a super hero. Just play the accountant-tax man routine for now, follow the money and you'll be fine."

"Why don't you make up your mind?" I asked, sort of sniping at him.

"Huh, what are you talking about?"

"What do you want to call me going forward? Bob? Stone? Tax man?

"Hey, what's up, tax—"

I cut him short, "I guess that's your answer then: 'tax man.'"

"Don't be so edgy, Bob, all will be good. There is no simple answer to what we should call you. Funny, it seems to change with the situation."

We both laughed off the tension.

"Don't forget to take good care of Laura, she needs your protection. The calmer she is, the more she will remember."

"We've got your lovely wife covered. You have my word on that. Have a nice flight. Check in with me tomorrow by two p.m. I may need to advise you before the bank closes. Remember, they are our allies. They want to help us."

"Okay then, goodbye for now."

I gathered my wallet, passport, and some cash, finished packing and rested on the couch while waiting for the HPAT 21 car.

Twenty minutes later, I jumped up to a knock on the door. I said my goodbyes to Wendy and Laura. Two new guards greeted me and flashed their HPAT 21 badges. We all went downstairs to the Jeep, which was doubled-parked outside the lobby door. The other two guards, Carl and Stu, stayed behind with Wendy and Laura.

It hit me that I was approaching the next level in this journey. Frankly, I was both nervous and eager to accomplish something. I hadn't had this feeling in years: a sense of purpose and being part of something so much more important than my own needs. At the same time, fear of the unknown was building and taunting me.

PART FOUR

CHAPTER **22**

The HPAT 21 guards dropped me off at LaGuardia Airport's Air Canada terminal. One of them stayed with me, maintaining a distance of no more than five to ten feet away. Good thing I packed light with one small bag over my shoulder, an easy check-in process. For a tax guy who had become a homeland spy guy overnight, I somehow felt relaxed.

With an hour to spare, I went through the usual security check-in rituals pretty smoothly. The biggest pain in the ass was taking off my shoes. After getting past the security area, I noticed the usual magazine store and café shop. It was only yesterday that I had left Langley, Virginia, and gone back to New York. Now I was leaving for Toronto. *What a fast pace! Oh well, it should be an interesting trip.* I needed a diversion. I didn't have the patience to start eyeballing magazines and browsing articles, so I went to get coffee. *Ah, over there, Dunkin' Donuts.* If I could only go there and not get a donut with my coffee—that was always the hard part. I was checking out the menu's combo options when I heard a voice.

"How can I help you, sir?"

I paused, "Make it a large iced coffee, skim milk, shot of vanilla with half a Splenda, please."

"Yes, sir," the barista replied.

"I hate that 'yes, sir' crap," I said jokingly "Makes me feel old. Don't forget a lid and some napkins, please. If you call me 'sir,' then I'll call you 'young man,'" I said with a smile.

I was in one of those moods, a good karma mood. Be good to the world around you, make people you connect with feel good, and maybe it will come back to you. It was probably a self-serving thought or wishful thinking. Maybe I was more nervous about this trip than I realized. I sat down by Air Canada in Terminal B. While sipping my coffee, I came up with a great thought: The only way for me to look at this trip was to make believe I was going to see a client—period. *Yeah, that's right.* I was merely going to meet with a client, the branch manager at the Royal Bank of Toronto. I had to trick my mind into thinking that I was about to do what I've been doing for years: a CPA dealing with individuals and businesses.

Just then, an announcement came through over the loud speakers, "Thirty minutes to board, thirty minutes to board."

I closed my eyes for a few minutes. When I reentered reality and opened my eyes, two seats away was an attractive lady wearing red high heels. *Can't miss a nice woman in red high heels,* I thought. She made the first move to talk.

"Hi, my name is Evelyn, Evelyn Carter. And you?" she asked, extending her hand to shake mine.

"I'm Bob, Bob Stone," I replied, emulating her style of introductions and shaking her hand.

"So, here we are in New York waiting to board a flight to Toronto," she continued, making small talk. "What brings you to Canada, Bob?"

"Funny, I just didn't know to say, but somehow found a way to respond.

"I'm a tax advisor and my client in Toronto needs some help. And you, Evelyn? What's your story?"

"I'm going back home after a New York City vacation."

"Sounds great," hope you had a good time. I suppose you live in Toronto?"

"Yes, I do. Oops, I think it's time to board the flight, Bob."

I spotted my guard walking away. He turned back and gave me a look to reassure me, as if to say, *you're alone now, but things will be fine.*

We checked in, boarded the plane, took our seats, and settled in. I rose up to place my briefcase into the overhead bins, but then realized I'd better keep it near me on the floor.

Evelyn was coincidentally sitting in the aisle seat to my left within talking range. I decided not to push any conversation. In fact, I just felt like being quiet.

The standard preflight announcements were made, and we were up in the air within ten minutes. It was a perfect day to fly, not a cloud in the sky.

Evelyn glanced over toward me a couple of times, and I let out a smile with minimal eye contact.

Uncontrollably, I asked, "So, tell me more about you, Evelyn Carter."

"Well, for starters, I work in downtown Toronto with the Canadian Bankers Association."

"That sounds interesting, how long have worked there?"

"About six years. There are good and bad days, but overall, it's a pretty good job. I handle the association's public relations, switching her focus to the approaching drink cart. Hey, Bob, what would you like to drink? It's on me."

"Oh no, please allow me."

"Give me a break, Bob. I'm a divorced self-made career woman. Don't feel threatened. So, what's your choice, beer, bourbon, or scotch?"

"Now, how did you know I like bourbon and scotch?"

"Woman's intuition, whatever."

"Okay then, first round's on you. Maker's Mark with one ice cube and if they don't have Maker's Mark, they won't have Basil Hayden, so I guess I'll go with whatever Bourbon they have. And you, what are you drinking?"

"I'm just going to have a good ol' Molson Canadian Lager."

"Of course, of course.

No doubt there was something in the air. A friendly connection, or perhaps a bit more. The flight attendant came back with our drinks. We clinked our glasses.

"So, Bob, your turn, now tell me about your client."

I hesitated then keeping it vague by design I said, "Nothing much to talk about, just boring tax stuff." I added, "Actually, I'm auditing a Toronto-based bank. Don't even ask me which bank. I cannot tell you."

"Sounds rather mysterious, if you ask me," Evelyn said. "What's the big deal? A bank is a bank."

"Yes, but in this case, it's just not something I can discuss."

"Okay, Bob Stone, or is it James Bond?"

We started laughing and I thought, *If she only knew.*

"Okay, let's go with James Bond. Anyway, sorry but I need a break. I have to review a few files before landing."

"I get it," she said.

"I'll tell you what, though, let's exchange cards now. Maybe we can talk more over the next day or two, possibly meet for lunch?"

"Nice idea. Let's see."

We exchanged cards and smiles. I took advantage of the rest of the flight to relax and reviewed my Package X notes to refresh my brain. At last, we landed at Toronto's Pearson International Airport. I walked with Evelyn to pull her luggage off the rotating conveyor belt. We spotted the airport exit and strolled outside. As we parted ways, a gust of wind swept her jet black, wavy hair behind her ears, revealing her sharp jaw line and making her high cheekbones more prominent. She had a special appeal, no doubt about that. We then shook hands with focused eye contact, as if we just made a toast to something special.

Outside the terminal, I flagged down a taxi and off I went to downtown Toronto.

"Take me to the Hilton Garden Inn, please."

"Yes, sir."

"Thanks, and skip the 'sir.' How long is the ride to the hotel?"

"At this time of day, you'll be there in twenty minutes."

"Okay, so for the next twenty minutes, it's okay to call me Bob. What's your name?"

"Jabar. My friends call me Jaab."

"Interesting name. Where are you from, Jaab?"

"Originally, from Indonesia."

"I've done my fair share of traveling, but I've never been to Indonesia. How many years are you in the Canada?"

"It's already been five years. I lived in New York for four years, and then moved up here to Toronto. I love both countries."

"Nice to hear that, Jaab."

"Oh yeah, and the asshole terrorists who want to destroy our beautiful way of life, fuck them," he volunteered, with a tinge of disgust.

"That is music to my ears, Jaab. Hey, I may need your help over the next two days. Can I have your number? Maybe a pick-up and drop-off around town?"

"Sure, Bob. Here is my card. Call me as needed. I'll be your on-call, go-to guy."

"Perfect, thanks."

"Here's your hotel. Good evening to you."

"Thanks, Jaab," I said as I flipped him a great tip, sensing he just might be helpful to me later.

***

Check in was quick, the keys to my hotel room were given to me. *Pretty classy hotel.* It had bird cages in the lobby and marble floors with area rugs of deep purple and green. I entered my room, dropped my small bag, and jumped on the bed. The remote was to my right, an invitation to turn on the TV. I had no patience to hear the typical world events, so I went to a non-news channel.

A text came in from Levine: Just a quick note. *Your tracking device is working well. Rest up at the hotel and good luck tomorrow at the bank.* I texted back: *Thanks, Levine.*

I had to focus on the meeting that was set up for tomorrow. I checked through the rest of Levine's notes from Package X. The branch manager's name was Scott McCann. The hotel was within walking distance from the bank. My head flooded with questions. *What will I ask him? What will I end up looking at? How should I approach this guy?*

Levine's notes informed me that over one hundred countries coop-erate with the U.S. regarding the unusual flow of funds globally. I sup-pose this Scott McCann and I should be on the same page, then. I'll just assume that we're working together to protect our homeland and Can-ada's as well. This approach could only be a good thing.

With that, I set my cell phone alarm for 7:30 a.m. I began to doze off when I realized that I should check in with Laura. My brain went into overdrive. *But why?* I questioned myself. Even though we're still married, it's a friendship now and not the usual married couple rela-tionship anymore. I should not be feeling any guilt. On the other hand, *If I feel it, maybe there's a reason.* So, I called, and Laura picked up.

"Hey, Laura. How's it going?"

"We are fine here, Bob and you? How was your flight?"

"All good. Quick flight. Resting in the hotel now. Oh, it's interesting that I met this cab driver from Indonesia who hates terrorists. Great guy, who knows, maybe he'll drive me around here. I'm getting my brain set for the bank meeting tomorrow morning. Not exactly sure what I'm walking into."

"I understand. Well, you know what you need to do after all your years as a sharp tax man."

"Good thought, thanks. Are you with Wendy? Are the HPAT guards with you?"

"Yes, and yes."

"Okay then, I'll be in touch, good night."

"Good night, Bob and be careful."

"Will do."

It was a brief call, but it relaxed me and it was the right move to-ward a friendship with Laura. My head rolled to the side and my eye-lids closed.

The morning arrived fast. I woke up before my alarm to bright sun-light beaming in through the windows. I stretched in bed and pulled my knees back to my chest five times to get me started. Off the bed, I did a few hands-to-the-floor stretches before doing pushups, deep knee bends, and hands-to-ceiling motions. I practiced a few slow karate moves to help me focus: frontal kicks; blocking a punch to my chest; and finally, walking away from another pretend enemy with a sudden reverse kick to his invisible head. I was done and pleased with myself that I recalled these moves.

Next, I took a hot shower without rushing. I felt great and ready to get into the flow-of-funds game at the Royal Bank of Toronto. I got dressed and headed out to catch the all-inclusive continental break-fast. I was too hungry to sit down and went right for the starters: juice, coffee, and cereal. With my tray and briefcase, I grabbed the first avail-able table in the rear, not to be bothered by anyone.

That was when I saw her entering the restaurant: It was Evelyn Carter. I was amazed, yet curious. I stood up and waved her over. She wore a wide-rimmed orange hat, a long skirt, but no red high heels this time. She came toward my table. I noticed her poise and correct pos-ture, and her overall demeanor. *What a well put together woman. Take it easy, just be friendly, nothing more.*

She extended her hand and said, "Well hello, Mr. Bond."

"Hello, Ms. Money Penny. What brings you here, Evelyn? Aren't you recovering from your vacation?"

"Oh, I'm just attending a seminar here today," she said dismissively. "Listen, there is something I need to tell you."

"Okay, so go ahead. Let me guess. You really work for the Canadian FBI?" As soon as I spoke, I wondered where that remark came from. It was understandable that I'd grown suspicious of everyone around me, but I didn't need to sarcastically grill every person who was nice to me.

"Nice try, you were close but no cigar. Bob, listen to me."

"Well, I'm listening—"

"I'm an HPAT 21 agent, just like you. Levine assigned me a support role on this Toronto bank mission."

"So, you're not really with the Canadian Bankers Association, are you?"

"No, but it sounded good, didn't it?"

"Yeah, and I thought that was too good to be true. I'm not exactly an idiot, Evelyn."

"I can tell you this—I did enjoy the flight with you, you're an interesting man."

"Well, I'm also a hungry man. Why don't we get something to eat? Then we can talk more. Hurry up, I need to get to the bank in about thirty minutes."

As she walked away, I admired her gait. She was even curvier than I thought. *Stop it,* I thought. I rushed to eat my cereal and juice. By now, the coffee was cold. I got up to refill the cup and picked up some of the watery eggs and an unappealing cold English muffin on my way back. Evelyn brushed past me with a plate of her own.

"You know, Bob, I've been around all kinds of people in my thirty-five years and I want to give you a compliment."

"Go ahead, I love compliments."

She smirked and said, "You seem to be very comfortable with yourself. You can tell when someone is in sync—you know, at ease in their own skin."

"Now that's a true compliment, thanks."

"How did you get there?" she asked.

"I'm not sure but it may have something to do with finding one's mission in life. I then refocused the discussion. "We need to eat and get going. So, when I am at the bank meeting with Mr. McCann, where will you be?"

"That, according to Levine, is up to you."

"By the way, mind showing me your HPAT 21 badge?"

She took it out, looking insulted, but it was the right thing to do; I should have asked sooner.

"Okay, thanks. You can get that aggravated look off your face now."

"You know damn well I had to see it. Wait one minute."

I stepped away to call Levine.

"It's me, Stone."

"You seem angry."

"What the hell is your problem, Levine?" I demanded. "You should have told me about Evelyn."

"Bob, you need to trust me and the way I work. Don't ever bitch about having backup, especially a beautiful lady like Evelyn."

"I'm not so sure about that."

"Whatever. Just don't get into a fist fight with her. She can kick your ass in less than ten seconds. She'll be your guard, your partner, and your... whatever you need her to be in the line of duty, I mean."

"Oh, really?"

"Yes, really."

"Alright, enough bull shit. What am I supposed to do with her when I'm with Scott McCann at the bank? I need to decide and get over there in ten minutes. You planted her here, so what do you say, Levine?"

"Take her with you. She has a talent for creating a great distraction. She will end up helping you in some way, you'll see. She's been with HPAT 21 for eight years, one of our best."

"Okay, I hear you. Thanks."

He was convincing, and I had no choice anyway. I headed back to the table and sat down across from Evelyn.

"So, Bob. Are you okay now? Can we move forward?"

"Sure, but don't throw any karate moves on me. It's too early in the morning for that stuff. Levine told me all about you."

"So, I'm going with you to the bank?"

"Of course, just play along with my approach, okay?"

"Bob, this is your baby, but I'm going to jump in as needed," she asserted.

"I can't argue with that and your proven experience. Sounds good."

***

We walked out of the hotel and down a few blocks. The Royal Bank of Toronto came into our view. It was a historical structure with its tall, thick columns in front and detailed carvings above the roofline. I took a deep breath and walked in with Evelyn, who paced herself a few feet behind me. As we entered, a young man approached us.

"How may I help you?" the greeter asked.

"I am here for a meeting with the branch manager, Mr. McCann."

"One moment, please. You are mister—?"

"Bob Stone, the tax consultant from New York."

"Thank you, sir. One moment please."

The young man came back with, "I'm sorry, but Mr. McCann is on a conference call. He will be with you shortly."

"Okay, that's fine."

After fifteen minutes, I started to lose my patience and began to pace.

Evelyn whispered close to me, "take it easy."

Her breath founds its way into my ear and got me excited. Anyway, I exhaled and turned to her, then sat back and decided to chill. After another ten minutes, Scott McCann walked into the lobby to meet us.

"Hello, I'm so sorry for the wait. You must be Mr. Stone. And your guest?"

"Evelyn Carter, my colleague."

"Hello, Ms. Carter."

"And hello to you, Mr. McCann."

I felt like being snippy, so I said, "Thank you for your delayed, but warm welcome." Nevertheless, I smiled.

"Follow me to my office, please."

"Please, please, sit down," he continued once we had entered. "Now that we have more privacy would you mind presenting your HPAT 21 badges, one can never be too careful these days. Surely you understand?"

We nodded and showed him our Identification.

"Excellent! So, how can I help you?"

"Let me turn things around for a moment, first, call me Bob, and may I call you Scott. Is that alright?"

"Sure, we are all friends here."

"Good, I hope we're on the same page, Scott. Our world is under constant threats from extreme terrorist groups, we need to help one another."

"You're absolutely right, Bob"

"America has cooperative banking relationships with over one hundred countries, including Canada, regarding questionable bank accounts, flow of funds, and unexplainable transactions. That's not a question, it's a fact."

"Of course, that's correct." Scott agreed.

"As you know, we are here to today to investigate a nonprofit account at this branch."

"Ah, you must be referring to the mosque account."

"Absolutely."

"Yes, quite troubling. The account balance recently went down dramatically lower, suddenly and without any explanation.

"Yes Scott, and we need to review that account with your blessing: the history, the authorized signers, other recent transactions, money in-money out, etcetera. Are we together on this, do we have your bank's authorization and cooperation?"

"Certainly, let's get you started. Go down the hall to the last room on the left. I'll give you the computer access codes. Go ahead, I'll see you in a moment."

"Excuse me, Scott," Evelyn interrupted. "Where is the bathroom?"

"It's the other way, closer to the lobby."

"Bob, I'll meet you in a minute," she said to me, with a look I couldn't understand.

We walked out of his office and I headed to the left while Evelyn turned to the right for the bathroom. As I walked down the hall, I looked back over my shoulder and saw Evelyn inconspicuously place a device into her left ear as though she was flipping her hair before she headed back toward Scott's now closed office door. *What the hell hopefully she knows what she is doing, but Scott is on our side, so I had no clue what she was up to.* I waved her back over, but she ignored me. Scott's door was mostly glass, so I was concerned he may have seen her insert the device despite her discretion. I walked back toward Evelyn, as Scott opened his door. It was terrible timing.

"Are you guys okay?" Scott asked.

Evelyn turned to her side, allowing her dark hair to hide the earpiece.

"Oh sure," I said, ""We hesitated not feeling comfortable without you accompanying us, Scott. Please, walk us back there. We don't want to invade your space, ya know, we are in your 'yard' now," I added.

"The yard" was an expression I remembered hearing from one of my father's Canadian law clients many years ago. I figured I'd throw it out to break the ice.

Scott smiled and said,"It's my yard, but you are my welcome guests."

He led us to the room and turned on the computer. He wrote down a few letters and numbers on a sticky note.

Scott spoke softly. "Turn away please so I can enter the bank's password to get you into the system."

"Perfect. Thanks, Scott."

And with that, he left us alone. Evelyn waited with me for a few minutes before speaking up.

"Bob, he needs to be distracted. Trust me."

"Okay, I agree. So, go ahead. I'm going to make a prediction."

"Yeah? What's that?"

"You'll see. All computers will miraculously go down in five minutes. Go ahead, Evelyn, do whatever it takes to sidetrack Scott."

"Okay, handing me another device. Here's the earpiece so you can listen in. You may even enjoy it. If I need you, I'll give you a cue. Just listen in, please."

"Sure, will do," I reassured her as she left the room.

I started to poke around, but it didn't take long. My experienced eye knew what to look for. *Ah, here it is, the Al Zarqah Jamal Nonprofit Mosque Account.* As I scoured over documents, I heard Evelyn start talking to Scott in the other room. The earpiece was not that clear, but good enough. It was hard to focus on sound bites while reviewing banking activity. She was doing a great job of getting him off track so far.

"Mr. McCann, please don't mind me popping in on you like this. "That accounting stuff Bob is doing bores the hell out of me. I'd much rather be here talking with you. Is that okay?"

"My office is always open to a sweet lady like you."

"Thank you, Mr. McCann."

"Let's start off by calling me Scott."

"That's nice, may I be upfront with you, Scott?"

"Certainly."

"Well, here's my story. I've been divorced for four years. It's been lonely—a long time already, know what I mean? And you're quite the handsome man. My friend in the other room might be there for some time. May I come closer to you, Scott?"

I couldn't believe what she was saying to him, how she was being so forward with him. I was over here looking at bank transfers while she's been hitting on this guy. I was actually starting to get excited. But I couldn't let myself get distracted. I needed to get this done before something weird happened. My hunch that there would be some kind of "accidental" interference might limit the time I would have to figure out the flow of funds. Just as my focus deepened, I started hearing a more intimate exchange of words. My ear was on fire.

"Hey, Scott, what would you prefer? I can take my clothes off right now or I can take your clothes off. Either way, I promise you, we will have fun together—even if it's only for a few minutes. It's not a bad way to start the day," Evelyn said.

There was a pause. I heard nothing. And then it appeared—the huge transfer I was hoping to find. It was a $300 million transfer into an account at the International Bank of Turkey dated May 31, 2015. Now I need to ask Scott who approved this, and who requested this transfer on the other side. I printed out the proof of transfer documents and grabbed them off the printer behind me.

Evelyn started talking again, "Scott, that's a bit too much for my first time in your office. There will be time for so much more when I come back or if we meet for dinner sometime soon."

I figured that was my cue to bail her out. I gave them one minute, and then knocked on the door.

"Hello, it's me, can I come in?"

"Yes, just a minute. One moment please," Scott replied.

I left the earpiece in and heard the poor guy ask, "What happened, Evelyn?"

"Bad timing, I guess, next time, my dear Scott."

"Okay, no problem," Scott replied and then called out to me, "Bob, come on in."

I slowly opened the door and Evelyn gave me a smile that spoke volumes. Before I could get a word out, Scott said, "I have just been alerted that our computer system went down. So sorry, but I must deal with this matter urgently."

"Oh really? What a surprise," I said. I decided not to question him about the transfer and played along with his bullshit. "Wow, too bad, I barely had a chance to get into that account. I'll tell you what, Scott, maybe you can help me save an additional day or two here. What can you tell me about that account?"

"Mr. Stone—ah, sorry, but there is a fine line between our efforts to cooperate with one another in the name of national security and breaking the rules of privacy. I know you are with the HPAT 21 division from the States, so I will try my best to help you without breaching my responsibilities. There has been a lot of money going in and out of that account for the past three years. I have seen withdrawals here and there, maybe once or twice a year. The amounts withdrawn typically range from one to about five million dollars. The transfer we informed your Department of Homeland Security about this time was much higher." Scott's face became pale before he finished his last statement . . . his lips tightened—something just affected him. He continued talking, "Maybe in the area of forty to fifty million dollars. I haven't looked at it in quite a while, but that's my best guesstimate."

"I see, Scott. Are you sure it wasn't a much larger amount?"

"No, absolutely not."

"Since I can't get back into the computer now, where did this transfer go to?"

"The transfers from this account usually get wired out to either a bank in Qatar, or at other times to a bank in Kuwait."

"This is important, so I need to ask you. Do you know who has been requesting these transfers and who has been approving these transfers from your bank?"

"I can't tell you much more, but I can leave you with this: My supervisor usually signs off on the larger wire transfers. I know you'll ask, so his name is Hassam Al Boudeh Kandallah. He has been a key player in this bank for about twelve years. On the other side of the equation, I don't know who has been requesting these transfers from overseas. Sorry about that one, Bob, I wish I could help you both out more on this. And now, I must call it a day. Where are you both headed to now? Lunch or dinner would be my pleasure if you have time."

"Oh no, thank you anyway, Scott. We have things to look into, and reports to fill out. You know the drill. How about a raincheck?"

"Anytime, anytime, oh and by the way, Evelyn, I want to thank you for keeping me company while Bob was doing his research. You are quite an interesting lady. And if Bob cannot make it for that next lunch, then it would be my pleasure to take you to one of the most exquisite restaurants in downtown Toronto."

"Scott, you are too kind and let me tell you, you're a gentleman. I appreciate the offer and thank you for allowing me to bother you today." Evelyn's smile melted both of us.

***

We left the bank and started walking back toward the hotel. I hesitated and reached for the earpiece I had placed in my pocket.

"Evelyn, did you leave the base for this listening device in Scott's office?"

"Absolutely, it's flat so I just slipped it under the lip of his desk. I could've left it in his underwear, if you know what I mean."

We both tapped each other a high-five in the air, laughing hysterically.

"So here, take this from me, handing Evelyn my earpiece. "You're in charge of listening in. Tell me what's going on right now. Pop this baby in your ear and let's walk to the nearest quiet place for some lunch."

"Okay, Bob, great idea."

She grabbed my left elbow as we started to walk.

"Scott is already on the phone. Apparently, his supervisor, Kandallah, is screaming at him. Not sure why, but Scott keeps apologizing. Ah, here it is—he just said, 'Mr. K, please. I shut all the computers down right away as soon as I could. I had to give the guy a chance to get into the room to do something. Otherwise it would've looked too obvious. Please calm down, Mr. Kandallah. I can assure you, Bob Stone saw nothing, and I told him very little. We talked for five minutes or less and he had to leave. Thank you, sir. Thank you, and please don't worry. Goodbye.'"

"That's great work, Evelyn. I'm going to text Levine and have them do a background check on this."

I sent the text out, along with a few comments about my progress.

"Come on, let's go. I'm starving."

"Same here, me too."

We sat down at a local pub. The menus were handed to us quickly.

"Evelyn, check out the burger combos. Burgers with a fried egg on top, mushrooms, cheese, relish, olives—"

"I see, it's amazing."

The waitress came by and asked, "Are you folks ready to order?"

"I'll have the Cobb salad, no onions please. Light Italian dressing."

"And you, sir?"

"The T Burger, medium to well. Please toast the bun, whole wheat, if you have it. Thank you, your name is?"

"Oh, I'm Jenni."

"Okay then. Thanks, Jenni."

"What's with the name thing?" Evelyn asked after Jenni walked away to put in our orders.

"That's just me, wherever I go, whomever I meet, I always get the name."

"Why?"

"I like to use a person's name, it's more personal. And if something happens, if I leave something behind or whatever, I can always call back and say, 'I was at your restaurant yesterday. Jenni was the waitress.' Get the idea?"

"Yeah, but you're crazy."

I smiled then said, "You don't need to understand me. Hey, here's Levine's reply," I began reading it out loud: "I ran a check on Kandallah. He was born in Iran, a U.S. citizen since nineteen-ninety-two, graduated from the McGill University School of Business in nineteen-ninety-seven. He was questioned by the FBI for possible terror links in late nineteen-ninety-five during college. Nothing showed up, so they stopped watching him. He also has a master's degree in finance from the University of Toronto in nineteen-ninety-nine. He's been employed with the Royal Bank of Toronto since two thousand. If you have what you need, be careful and get back to New York ASAP."

I thanked Levine for the information and looked up at Evelyn after sending the text. She was nervous, drinking her first sip of water without thinking. She started coughing as she swallowed.

"I have a bad feeling about all this," she choked out. "We need to eat, make decisions, and take a flight back to New York immediately."

"Right, Evelyn," I reiterated as the food arrived. "We're on the same page, so let's eat quickly and head back to the hotel. This burger must be over six inches high. Insane!"

"Everything okay here?" Jenni asked, checking on us.

"Yes, Jenni, I'll have a Diet Coke with lemon." The waitress asked Evelyn if she also wanted a drink.

"No, the water is fine."

"Jenni, here is my credit card, just bring my drink and run the card. We're in a rush."

"Yes, sir," Jenni replied, looking at us with surprise and picking up on our edginess.

Suddenly, the pub became very crowded. The line was out the door. We finished up and slipped through the crowd, walking down the street toward the hotel a few more blocks away. Suddenly, Evelyn slowed her pace and grabbed my arm.

"Bob, do you see what I see?" Evelyn asked.

"What, what, Evelyn?"

"Those two guys over there, they're from the bank. I saw them when I went to the bathroom as you went to the other room to look into those transfers."

"You sense we're being followed?"

"Not sure, but I do think so."

"Okay, let's cross the street and then stop. We'll kiss and act like tourists, or whatever. We can go into that gift shop or we can just go for the kiss on the street. Which will it be, Evelyn?"

"Don't put that on me, you can make that decision."

There was a break in the traffic, so we hurried to the other side. We pretended to window shop near a few stores, and then I turned to her. We both went for the kiss, it was natural and easy. I actually enjoyed the feeling of my lips pressing onto hers and I was in no rush, either. The guys were opposite us now, but still across the street.

"Evelyn, just follow me."

We walked passed the hotel, then turned around. Apparently, they called it off.

"Seems like I was just spooked, Bob."

"No problem, better safe than sorry. And look, my darling, we broke the ice with that kiss, didn't we?"

I smiled, but Evelyn did not, nor did she reply. In just a few minutes, we were back at the hotel—I offered her to rest with me in the bedroom. It was a draining day, so we set our cell phone alarms for one hour and dozed off. She chose to crash down onto the couch. I curled onto the queen-sized bed in the other room. While trying to get comfortable, I realized something was bothering me, but I couldn't put my finger on it. I sat up on the edge of the bed. My mind was blank. I started to pace around the room, waiting for an answer to surface. I sat down on the bed again and scanned the room. *That's it, my brief-case. . . . Where is my briefcase?*

I panicked and went to Evelyn. "Hey, wake up, wake up."

She was in a deep sleep, but I had to wake her. I jarred her shoulder a few times.

"Can you hear me ...did you see my briefcase?"

"Take it easy, I have no clue what you're talking about."

"My briefcase, it's not so damn complicated?" I started frantically searching the room.

"I don't know Bob, I have no idea. Wait, this may not be good. You left the hotel with it this morning, and then took it to the bank. You probably placed it under the desk by the computer when you started reviewing the account transfers. And you did not have it at lunch."

"Oh my god, Evelyn. Whatever it takes, we have to go back there and get my briefcase."

"Sure, do exactly what Levine told you *not* to do. We're supposed to get out of here, get to the airport, and head back to New York. Now you're telling me that you want to go back to that bank?"

"I have no choice. In addition to the printout of the account transfers, I had other papers and instructions from Levine inside the briefcase. There's no way around it, we absolutely must go back, and I mean *right now* before the bank closes. Let's go and while we walk, we'll think of a plan."

"Hold on, let's first pack up."

"Okay, you're right," I replied. "Then I'll make a call first to the taxi driver who took me here. Great guy, his name is Jaab."

"Great, his name is Jaab. Big deal, Bob, who cares?"

"Let me finish. He said he would help me out anytime, that he would be happy to be available for me. I'm calling him right now."

I pulled out Jaab's card and called the number. It rang twice before he answered.

"Hello, hello is this Jaab?"

"Yes, this is Jaab. How can I help you?"

"This is Bob Stone, you dropped me off yesterday at the Hilton. I'm the guy from New York. Do you remember what we talked about?"

"Yes, of course, we discussed terrorism, how's it going, Sir?"

"That's right, now I'm in a huge rush. Can you swing by here right away, say in five minutes?"

"Sure, where are you now?"

"I'm at the hotel where you had driven me to."

"Yes, I can do that for you."

"Jaab, I need to tell you something. Do you recall what you said to me about terrorists trying to destroy our freedom, our lives?"

"Yes, sir, I also recall that. I said it and I meant every word."

"Well, I'm with my friend and we may be in danger. Are you okay with this, my friend?"

"Bob, there is a rear entrance to that hotel. I will be there for you in exactly five minutes."

"You're the best, bless you my friend. See you here and please, no delays, Jaab."

"It's done, no worries."

"Evelyn, we've got maybe ten minutes to pack, get organized, go down, and check out."

"I'm good with that."

"Okay, so let's get moving. I have next to nothing to pack up, so I'll meet you downstairs by the rear entrance. Meantime, while you finish up, I'll check out."

"Sounds like a plan," she confirmed back to me.

"Okay, see you in a few minutes, Evelyn."

I took the elevator down. Thank goodness there was no one in line at the front desk. I paid the hotel bill and walked toward the rear exit. I was feeling hyper, maybe I was overreacting, but Evelyn was taking longer than I expected. My sense of urgency was in high gear. Taken over by my instincts, I went back in and hit the elevator button to go back upstairs, but it was either stuck or intentionally jammed. I ran up the stairway to the third floor.

As the door came into view, I was struck by the silence in the stair-well. I tried to catch a glimpse of the hallway through the diamond shaped glass piece in the door. My fear became reality. There were three people walking down the hall. One guy had Evelyn in a wrist hold, the other guy had a gun. I hesitated briefly to collect my thoughts, yet I had only seconds to react.

As soon as the guys turned the corner in the hallway, I opened the door to avoid being noticed. I decided to use my jacket as a weapon, so I took it off and quietly approached them from behind. I knew what I had to do. The only question was, which of the two guys should I deal with first? My choice became clear. I approached the gunman, increas-ing my pace until there was a gap of, tops, three feet between us. Wrapping my jacket over his head, I then whacked his gun hand down and turned his neck hard to the left until I heard a crack. I tripped him over my foot and let him fall to the floor. A split second after he went down, the other guy holding Evelyn turned to me. He was totally caught off guard with my sudden attack.

Evelyn dropped to the floor, sweeping her legs against the assail-ant's ankles, forcing him down to all fours on his knees. Evelyn knew exactly what she was doing. She used the bottom of her open hand and she gave him a direct blow hard to his nose with a precise upward motion. She may have killed the unsuspecting guy. We both ran back to the hallway door down the stairway.

Jaab was outside by the rear entrance. We were lucky, the timing was amazing.

"We have to get to the bank before it closes. Jaab, get us to the Royal Bank of Toronto as fast as you can."

"No problem. I am familiar with the bank. Do you want the front or the rear entrance?"

"Good thought. The rear entrance is closer to the room where I left my briefcase. Yes, the rear entrance, Jaab."

I noticed Evelyn putting the earpiece back in as we approached the rear parking lot.

"Bob, Bob, there's an argument in Scott McCann's office. It sounds real bad. Let's get in and out of that bank—and I mean now."

I started to get out of the car, but she stopped me.

"Wait, take the earpiece. You'd better listen to this."

I listened carefully.

"Please, Mr. Kandallah, please. I did my best for you."

"You screwed up, Scott. There is no room for that, you put us in jeopardy, and you must realize that you know too much. It's over for you."

"Go ahead, fire me if you have to. I don't care anymore."

"Oh, Scott, that should be the least of your worries. It's over. Your life is finished. You can make this easy or difficult. It's all up to you."

"What the hell are you talking about? I've known you for years. Why would you do this to me, Mr. Kandallah?"

"Because there are things going on that are much more important than you or me. So here, take this drink and in less than three minutes, you'll be at peace with yourself, Scott."

"And if I don't?"

"We will cut your throat and make it look like a robbery."

I heard enough.

"Evelyn, they're going to kill this guy. Maybe we can do something. If we can save Scott and bring him back to the States, he could be useful to us. That's it, I'm going in. Sorry, but I need you to play the role of the distracter once again. Go outside, walk around to the front door. Make a scene in the lobby, be an angry customer, just do your thing."

"You're a crazy fool, Stone, putting all of us in harm's way like this."

"Isn't that what it's all about? HPAT 21, putting ourselves at risk to save the homeland? So, cut the shit and help me out here."

She reluctantly exited the car and walked around to the front entrance.

"Please wait here, Jaab," I requested.

He nodded, and I got out. I walked past the rear door and waited in the hallway to hear Evelyn create a disturbance. A long minute went by before the scene began. She was yelling and screaming about some bank error and bad service. That was my moment to act. The automatic door opened as I approached, and I rushed in straight back to Scott's office unnoticed. As I was about to turn a corner, I spotted two guys leaving Scott's office. One was a well-dressed executive type, possibly Kandallah. I wasn't sure if they had left anyone behind with Scott. It was time for me to engage. I gently pushed his office door open with my foot just in case I had to defend myself. Scott was sitting at his desk with a rugged-looking hitman type by his side. I walked in with a calm, but authoritative approach, not knowing what I'd do or say.

"Excuse me, the problem up front is really bad and they need your help right now. A crazy customer is out of control. They want you, the big guy in the lobby. I will stay with Scott here."

"Yes, sir," the man replied.

It was like a hot knife going through butter. The guy just walked out the door.

"Scott, no time for questions. Come with me right now."

We bolted out of the room and then went to grab my briefcase where I had left it this morning. Same spot, still there, just as Evelyn figured.

I picked it up and rushed out pushing Scott ahead of me "Come on, move it Scott, we have to hurry, move it, get to the car waiting just outside by the rear exit. I'm right behind you."

We got inside the car.

"Where do we get Evelyn?" Jaab asked.

I figured she would be leaving the bank from the front lobby door by now. We drove around to the street, but Evelyn was nowhere to be seen. We waited another two minutes. It was nervous out there. She finally appeared, saw us, and started to walk down the street. *Very smart move.* We followed her about two blocks, as she approached, I opened the door, allowing her to dive into the vehicle head first at the next red light. We headed to the main highway toward the airport. It was quiet for a while before I broke the ice.

"Scott, are you a single guy?"

"Yes, Bob."

214 • ERIC J. ENGELHARDT

"Good, no family to deal with. That makes things much smoother. Well, if you stay in Canada, you're a dead man. I can get you settled in the States and you would be protected under our IRS HPAT 21 department, clearing the way for your resident alien status. You would work for us under a new identity. You have about three minutes to decide. If it's a yes, we need your passport now."

"I have no choice. Of course, it's a yes. Thank you all for saving my life back there."

"Where do you live? You'll need your passport for the airport."

"My house is on the way, about fifteen minutes from here. It's in my bedroom closet, I can grab it in two minutes."

"Perfect, let's go before your friends at the bank get there first."

"Come on, let's move it."

"Yes, Bob."

"Address?" Jaab asked.

"It's five-twenty-five Bluebird Lane, coming up in about ten minutes now," Scott answered. "It's a rental apartment complex."

"I know it, been there many times," said Jaab.

My text alert sounded. It was Wendy: *I know your situation. Next flight for you and Evelyn is from Toronto to NY in one hour.* I replied with a text that said, *We're under pressure here. Need you to book an additional ticket. It's for a new friend who needs our help. His name is Scott McCann.* I had Scott enter his information needed for the flight ticket and sent it to Wendy.

Wendy confirmed, *Okay, will do Bob.*

Scott's apartment was all clear. He went in and came out in five minutes with a carry-on bag. I felt bad for him. His whole life was in that little bag.

"Scott, there's no room for screw ups. Passport?"

"Yes, got it."

"Good. You know why we went back to the bank?"

"No, I was shocked but happy to see you again."

"I left my briefcase in the computer room this morning. My stupidity and Evelyn's quick wit saved your life, along with our getaway driver here. That's why I want to make sure you have the passport. There is no time to come back here, Scott."

"Look, here it is," Scott said, showing me his passport.

I nodded and turned to Jaab to say, "Let's get to the airport, please step on it."

"It's only ten minutes away," Jaab informed us.

I reclined with a momentary calm before I was hit with another text message from Wendy. *Pain in my butt, always something.* Her text said: *Airport not safe. No go. Plan B—Drive to Buffalo, NY.*

She must be joking. *How can I ask Jaab to do this?* I had already pushed him to the limit, but I had no choice.

"Jaab, do you have your passport with you?"

"Surely not. Why, Bob?"

"I have just been informed that the airport is too dangerous, we cannot go there."

"Now what?" Evelyn asked.

"I need Jaab to drive us to Buffalo, New York, from there, we either take a flight to New York City or drive all the way back." I turned to Jaab, "we need you now, more than ever. Are you in?"

"Yes, I am with you. I have to get my passport to cross over into New York."

"Is that a definite yes?"

"It's a yes. From the moment we first talked, I knew you were a special man. I want to work with you, Bob, and I'm also ready to get back to the States. I want to be a part of something special."

"Jaab, I will take care of all your needs. You and Scott will be introduced to my colleagues. In my world, we call ourselves HPAT 21."

"What's that?"

"It stands for Homeland Protection Anti-Terror."

"What's the 21 about?

"That's in honor of our 9/11, I'll tell you more another time. How far from here do you live?"

"About twenty minutes south, on the way toward Buffalo."

"Okay, let's do it, Jaab. Any loose ends to tie up?"

"My family is in Indonesia. I am a very hardworking man. I send most of my earned money to my wife, kids, and parents back home."

"That's admirable. Okay, you'll need to quickly grab the necessities from your place. Then we must pick up our pace. You and Scott can settle your affairs later. Are we getting close?"

"Not yet, please be patient, it's only two more miles from here."

We arrived in another few minutes. Tripping as he left the car, Jaab was in and out fast with his possessions all in a large laundry bag. The scenery blurred as we quickly sped away.

A new text came in, from Levine this time. *No time for driving to Buffalo. You'll need to fly to Istanbul ASAP, but first, you're needed in Long Island first. Too much going on. Drive thirty minutes east, then go to a private airport. There will be a farm about two miles from the airport. All arrangements done and cleared for landing at Republic Airport in Farmingdale, NY. Please confirm.*

"Understood."

"Here we go again," I said, exasperated. I informed them of the change in plans. "Jaab, are you familiar with a farm about two miles from here with a nearby private airport?"

"I know of it, yes, it's a tiny private airport just past a farm."

"Great, let's move it. I want to thank all of you so much for being flexible and cooperative."

"We're a good team, Bob," Jaab said.

"And thank you all for saving my life," Scott added.

"Know what? We really are a good team," Evelyn reiterated.

"Okay, people, I love the compliments, but it's time to get to the next leg of our journey. Let's relax and enjoy the ride while we can."

CHAPTER 23

After twenty minutes, we passed by Nature Hill Farms along a winding road that wrapped around to the left. The airport appeared quickly, a few miles later just as Levine had said. We were greeted by two guys wearing black caps and matching sleeveless yellow-trimmed jackets. Noise from the private plane's jet engines made it difficult to hear them talking to us.

"Which one of you is Bob Stone?"

I stepped forward, "That's me," I responded.

For a split second I got paranoid. A trap? A setup? In seconds, I may have to switch into kill or be-killed mode.

"Mr. Stone, please show us your HPAT 21 badge.

I reached into my pocket and flashed it.

"Thank you. I suppose you are Evelyn Carter?" he asked her.

She nodded her head.

"Badge please."

Evelyn flashed hers as well.

"Okay, people," the guy continued. "This has to be done fast. Stone, bring your group over there and get into that Gulfstream G-one hundred beauty. The door is unlocked. You'll be where you need to be so fast, you won't believe it. By the way, your boss, what's his name, Levine? —he knows what the hell he's doing. He asked for that jet over there."

I nodded my head to agree and asked, "By the way, who is our pilot?"

"It's me," he replied. "I'm Smith Richards. Sorry, I should have been more personal. My copilot here is Kenny Jenkins."

Jaab whispered to me, "What about my taxi?"

"Don't worry, Jaab," I reassured him. "Smith, may we keep my friend's car here for the duration of our trip?"

He did not respond. *I wonder if this is his way of asking for money?*

"Here, take this hundred-dollar bill," I said, pulling it from my wallet. Are we okay now?"

"Sure, that's fine, Stone," Smith replied.

"Thanks, we'll be in touch."

"Sounds like it could be a while?" Smith asked, hinting at more.

"Got it, here, take another hundred, but that's all I have now. Keep an eye on this taxi and we will show our appreciation at the right time."

"Okay, Stone, will do."

I turned to thank him with some eye contact and a smile. Just before we took off, Wendy texted me. *When you land, you will be met by three guards. Two black Jeeps will be close to the landing strip. They will bring you all to an undisclosed location in Long Island. Your Canadian nightmare is over. Please confirm.*

"Understood. Great work."

The sky was clear, maybe too clear. *Stop that,* I said to myself. But that's how I had felt ever since 9/11. It was the same perfectly clear sky that day and continued to haunt me. There was absolutely no talking among us. I was and surely each of us were thankful for our escape, and no doubt quietly assessing the future.

Liftoff was swift. The jet was flying smooth as silk. Jaab and Scott were uneasy. Frankly, I was a bit queasy, not being used to this intense speed in such a small aircraft. The jet was so fast, yet so quiet. I felt frozen in time within a protective chamber. My mind entered a split zone, in which I felt both inner peace and many worries about Laura, the homeland, and the world. *Funny, I didn't even consider my own* life *hanging in the balance.* It was clear now that I had become a changed man and I felt so proud of this new me.

It depressed me to know that so many innocent people would be killed by terrorists. Each terrorist group had their own set of extreme beliefs and their justifications to kill. They had lost their hope and direction in life, those who chose hatred and murder to fulfill their goals.

I paused to think about how the world desperately needed leaders from the peaceful side of all religious groups to denounce murder and stand up for change through nonviolent venues.

Suddenly, the jet adjusted to a slower speed. My ears were affected by the change in pressure. A few minutes later, Smith announced that we'd be landing soon. The small airport became visible, followed by a sudden jolt from the landing. It brought me back to reality, pulling me away from my thoughts. The pilot grabbed his handheld speaker.

"Please remain seated until we receive security clearance to move closer to the airport's buffer checkpoint," Smith requested.

A text from Levine came through: *Your tracking device is amazing. I see that you just landed. How was the flight in that beauty of a jet that I arranged for you?*

"*Smooth as silk. Thanks for the Gulfstream, Levine. The ride of my life.*"

"*Thought you would like it, only way to travel.*"

"*What's up now?*" I texted back.

It must've been too much discussion to explain in writing because Levine immediately called me, I answered promptly. "When Smith confirms, you'll head out with the others in the Jeeps waiting for you, just as Wendy reported."

Levine, I want to check my house."

"No way, too dangerous," Levine insisted. "An HPAT 21 drone has been hovering over there 24/7 for the past ten days. Talk later about that. You're going to a house in Westbury, Long Island. Chill out there for the night. Plenty of beds for everyone."

"Okay, Levine."

"Anything for you, tax man," Levine replied. "That reminds me, you must contact your clients... Wendy will update you tomorrow morning. Welcome back to the next leg of your journey. Istanbul is your next stop."

"No downtime and never a dull moment, eh, Levine?" I commented jokingly.

"You spent too much time in Canada, Bob, what's with the 'eh crap?"

"You should know that wherever I travel to, I grab a few choice words and local phrases," I replied.

"Whatever. Get some solid sleep Stone, you'll need it."

Smith received security clearance and moved the jet over to the checkpoint. He turned and waved his hand to get us moving. I took the lead, everyone followed as we headed toward the two black Jeeps approaching the plane. They stopped about twenty feet away. The driver from the first Jeep opened his door and came to greet me. He saved me the trouble of asking by showing me his HPAT 21 badge.

"Mr. Stone, we are in a rush. Please hurry up. My name is Roger." He patted me on the back while introducing himself.

We made it to Westbury within twenty minutes. Roger drove to a house two blocks off the main road. We were all escorted inside.

"Mr. Stone, three guards will be here overnight to watch over you all," Roger said. "No one is allowed to leave the house whatsoever, on strict orders from Levine."

"Okay, understood, Roger."

"Thank you, sir," Roger replied. "There are three bathrooms, each with plenty of towels. Why don't you folks do what you have to do, and we will bring back some dinner for you guys in about an hour. It's now 4:30 p.m. See you at around six o'clock with food. Hope Italian is okay?"

"Perfect, Roger," I said.

Roger left us and headed out.

I turned to Evelyn and said, "Hey, ladies first. Why don't you take the first shower and you can rest up in that bedroom over there."

"Thank you for being so thoughtful," Evelyn replied. "Frankly, I have no idea what the hell we're doing in the middle of nowhere in Long Island, New York. But it beats being chased around in Canada."

"I totally agree with you, so let's enjoy the down time here."

"Sure, Bob, sure," she said.

Scott and Jaab dozed off on the two couches in front of the fireplace. After an hour or so, Roger entered the front door with a burst of aromas from the Italian food. We ate dinner fast, since we were starving, and the food was better than expected.

I was edgy. It was time to speak to Wendy about Laura's progress with the law firm and get an update about my tax clients. It was early in the evening, yet I was feeling the need to wind down after a difficult day and that intensely fast flight back to Long Island. Just before I dozed off, I called Laura. She was in good spirits and that relieved some of my concerns.

I then texted Wendy to say that we had to meet the next morning to discuss her progress with Laura and whatever else was going on. She agreed, then finalized her text by saying: *Get some sleep, you'll need it. It's going to be a busy day tomorrow, tax man.*

"You're not scaring me, Wendy. Every day has been crazy."

Levine then sent me a text: *You're booked on a night flight to Istanbul, day after tomorrow. FFOM to International Bank of Turkey.*

There he goes again. I replied, *Yes, yes FFOM . . . Follow Flow of Money. Of course.* I faded as my eyelids uncontrollably closed.

***

After our dangerously slim escape from Canada, we all slept like babies. Upon waking up, showers were a must for those that had dozed off, so we took turns taking brief showers to avoid running out of hot water. Meantime, muffins and coffee were brought in by one of the guards. We finished up our light breakfast and headed out.

The drive to Manhattan at 10:00 a.m. on a Wednesday avoided the early morning traffic. We were taken to an apartment building on Second Avenue near East Eighteenth Street. It was a sticky, overcast day with a slight breeze. We were escorted to the second floor by two guards and allowed in after an HPAT 21 clearance signal was confirmed. Waiting inside were Randy, Ashton, Laura, Wendy, and

Levine—a full house. My initial thought was that something important was going on

"Hi, everyone," I said. "Say hello to my new HPAT 21 friends, Jaab and Scott."

Levine approached them to shake their hands. Laura smiled and patted me on my back, in essence saying, *I'm proud of you.*

"Welcome back," Wendy added.

My psych friend, Ashton, interjected, "You and Evelyn have been through so much in a very short time. We should talk. I'll keep it brief. Oh, and no hypnosis this time, Stone."

"Thanks, psych, I'd appreciate that."

Evelyn replied, "Sure, I could use a talk and some mental health tips. Thanks, Mr. Ashton."

Levine interjected, "Bob, you and Evelyn were very impressive at the bank in Toronto. I want to congratulate both of you for your bravery."

Thanks, Mr. Levine," Evelyn said graciously. "Nice compliment, It was quite scary for a moment there."

"I was kept informed all along about the problems you all had in Toronto," Laura added, "I had no idea you could be so brave, Bob."

"I had no idea either, but sometimes, one has to step up."

Just then, there was a knock at the door.

"That must be our FBI Director, Frank Conway," Levine said to our new HPAT 21 members.

Frank was allowed in after the usual HPAT 21 confirmation. I remembered at the Langley Virginia Command Center what a take-charge kind of man he was as he stepped into the room authoritatively.

"Hello, everyone, hello, Scott. Hi there, Jaab. I heard all about you both. Our various departments including the U.S. Department of Homeland Security, the FBI, and of course, our IRS HPAT 21 team all thank you for your service in Toronto and welcome you to our team."

"Thank you for your kind words," Jaab said.

"And I'm extremely grateful for the efforts to save my life," Scott said, rising from his seat. "Now, it's my turn, eh. I am ready to return the favor."

"Thank you for saving me some work," Frank said to me and Evelyn before he wrapped up with, "So now that we're past the intros and the compliments, I'm turning it over to Levine." Frank received a text, took a quick look and ignored it.

"Okay, Jaab and Scott," Levine started. "Frank and his team will escort you both to our debriefing command center in Langley, Virginia. There he will make sure you're properly evaluated and trained quickly. Then new IDs and passports will be issued for you. Ashton, you need to talk with Bob and Evelyn—no marathons, keep it short. As you know, Bob and Wendy must deal with his tax client issues and calls. Wendy, please check in with your assistant and get details on those client calls. We then need to discuss Laura and the law firm. Guys, it's getting late in the game and we must connect the dots sooner rather than later."

"Well said, Levine!" Frank exclaimed, looking at his phone again. "Listen up, people, bad money is moving rapidly around the world and we must figure out what's going on."

Frank departed with Scott and Jaab trailing behind him, heading off to become HPAT 21 agents.

Levine seemed nervous or impatient, maybe both. But whatever it was, urgency was in the air.

"Tell you what, Ashton," Levine continued. "Do your thing, but ladies first. So, give Evelyn time first, then have a talk with Bob. I'll need to talk with Wendy, Evelyn, and Bob together as soon as possible."

"Okay, that's fine."

"Great," Levine replied. "So, you guys can go to the other room and get started."

"Okay, Ashton, let's get started," Evelyn said. "Where shall we talk?"

"Over there in that room," he pointed.

"As for me, I'm ready to talk, but I'm not in the mood for too much self-analysis."

"It'll be brief as promised, Bob," Ashton replied.

Evelyn came out of the back room after barely ten minutes.

I walked in after her and sat down, inhaling deeply.

"How do you feel today, Stone?" Ashton began.

He was already aggravating me. A perfect pain in the ass, with his open-ended questions designed to get me talking.

"I'm fine."

"That's it?" Ashton asked.

I knew my short answer would irritate him.

"Yes, really, I'm okay."

"Well, Bob, you've been through so much since you left the command center, I'm here to help you. You know that, right?"

"Yes, I know and you're right," I said in agreement. "It's been hell, I was almost killed or kidnapped two times. So sure, it's been stressful."

"Of course," Ashton acknowledged. "All in all, you seem to be under control, your eyes are not blinking rapidly, and I do not see signs of excessive stress."

"I have my issues."

"Oh?" Ashton said.

Another trick response from our HPAT 21 on-call psychologist. But it worked and prompted me to talk more.

"Sure, my head is filled with all kinds of thoughts . . . about Laura and how I ruined my marriage with my bad choices years ago, the homeland, my tax clients, sorry, I should say my terrorist clients—and oh yeah, the whole world. Then there's my life, other than all these things, I'm just fine."

"That's a tough combination, Bob," Ashton said understandably. "Maybe try to break it down into manageable pieces."

"Good idea."

"May I suggest you talk with Laura first, then Wendy?" Ashton said. "Touch base with some of your clients. That will take the edge off."

"I agree."

"Then let's focus on Istanbul," Ashton continued

"You know, Ashton, you're damn good at what you do," I admitted.

Ashton was surprised. "Ya know, Stone, we all need that positive reinforcement—even me. So, thanks." He stood up to shake my hand and said, "Stone, you ought to know something. All of us here at HPAT 21 are amazed by your instincts, your bravery, and your overall drive."

I was speechless.

"We're done here," Ashton concluded briefly, as promised.

I got up to leave the room, anxious to hear more from everyone else. Something was going on, it was in the air. I felt as if there was an underworld of evil percolating, something *below the bottom line* was in progress. My apprehension didn't go unnoticed.

"Go, go ahead, Stone," Ashton encouraged. "You can leave already. I need to make some notes anyway."

As I left the room, I realized how huge this apartment was. For Manhattan, it was amazing: two bedrooms, two bathrooms, an office area, a den, and a small office. Laura walked passed me, apparently to talk with Ashton for mental soothing. It was only then I noticed that Laura had cut her hair short. No makeup. Somehow, she had a tougher look than I could ever recall. I didn't like it. It didn't seem right for me to comment, so I kept my observations to myself. Levine gestured for me to come over to join him and Wendy.

"Hey, Wendy, it's been a while," I said to her.

"Yeah, right. You okay, Bob?"

"Oh yeah, I'm good. Just ask Ashton." I smiled sarcastically. "Thanks for getting us out of Toronto. You were fantastic."

"That's what we do, Stone," Wendy replied. "Let's move on now, shall we?"

"Sure, I'm all ears," I said.

She turned to grab my attention more and said, "You may need to call about fourteen of your clients. My assistant already called most of them. According to my bullshit, you've been out of town on a tax matter. They loved it, must have sounded impressive. I was told that most calls were trivial. Darmush Khan, on the other hand, seemed really up-set."

Levine laughed out loud. *I knew what that meant.*

I turned to Levine and he said, "Yes, tax man, the deed was done."

"You mean you had the Manhattan IRS division send him that tax phony tax audit letter already?"

"Damn right. We had no more time to waste. It went out a few days ago. Now this Darmush is, to say the least, a bit nervous." Levine turned to Wendy and asked, "What was the voice message Darmush left?"

Wendy recalled, "My assistant handling Bob's calls told me Dar-mush said something like, 'Stone, why IRS letter? Why me?' Darmush then called back to leave another choppy message, 'Stone, IRS 2012 Tax Audeet.'"

"That's sounds like Darmush Khan alright."

"You need to call him back before we break for lunch," Wendy said. "Tell him you will call the IRS today and not to worry. Relax him."

"Give it a break, I think I know what to say."

"Of course," Levine replied. "Wendy, finish updating Bob."

"Hold on guys, time out," I said. "First give me a few minutes to call Darmush. I walked a few feet away from the room, called him, and left a voice message. "Okay, that's done and off my mind," I said reenter-ing the room. "I told him not to worry, and that it's probably a standard tax audit, but that he needed to email or fax the IRS letter to my office. I told him he was in good hands and we'll talk tomorrow."

We resumed our discussion and Wendy filled me in on my other clients. After fifteen minutes, we concluded.

"So then, Wendy, we are done with my tax clients for now, right?"

"Yes," she replied.

"By the way, your assistant is doing a great job. I could have used her over the years."

"Sure, but that's history now."

"Absolutely and now about Laura, What's up? What did you find out about the law firm?"

"Okay, we all agreed that she had to get back in the groove at the law firm," Wendy began. "Laura made a surprise visit to the office as if nothing happened. She made the rounds, saying hello to everyone from the receptionist to her research assistant and finally, she stopped in to talk with the office manager, Janet Ford, a huge Laura fan. Janet suggested that Laura spend a few hours in her office, making believe Laura had work to do. Then Janet said that she needed to talk with Laura over lunch."

Holding the palm of my hand up, I asked, "Why isn't Laura here to tell me this?"

"It's all very upsetting to her," Wendy replied. "She needs to talk with Ashton. Laura will be back here in a few minutes to tell you the rest."

"Why don't you just keep going while Laura is still with Ashton?" I impatiently asked.

"Okay," Wendy continued. "So, Laura meets Janet for lunch and tells her that part of her job is to review the office's phone bills for abusive employee and partner long-distance calls. Janet also logs the telephone time, so bookkeeping can include phone time in client invoices."

Wendy trailed off as Laura reentered the room and approached us, leaving Ashton to his notes again. *I had a gut feeling this was going to get ugly.*

"Perfect timing," Wendy said. "Laura, join us here. We're talking about your lunch with Janet Ford and the phone calls."

"Oh, yes, that crap." Laura shrugged her shoulders and took over the conversation. "During our lunch, Janet started to cry. Her hands were shaking. I had to calm her down. She said she didn't know who to turn to. I reassured her and said, 'I am with you, Janet, I'm with you.'"

"What else did Janet say?" I asked.

Half my brain was on Istanbul tomorrow, the other on this conversation. I was starting to feel the stress hit the back of my neck.

"Chill, Bob," Laura said.

I let that pass.

"Janet told me that over the past few months, numerous calls have been coming in from all over: Teheran, Iran, Damascus, Syria, and even Hiroshima, Japan," Laura continued. "All the calls came in on one line. The firm has a rainmaker, you know, a guy with contacts who brings in a ton of business. His name is Omar Korbachi. He is called 'Of Counsel' to the firm." Laura paused for some water, and then continued. "In a nutshell, this guy is a retired lawyer, but still uses his contacts around the world to refer clients and deals to Combs and Walker. All those international calls came in from Korbachi."

Levine politely interrupted, "This Korbachi is a dual citizen of the U.S. and Turkey. Bob, we need you to meet with this guy. It's critical to somehow uncover what he's up to. We know that Korbachi went to Istanbul yesterday. Ari Ahrdeni may be able to help connect you with Korbachi." Levine looked to Wendy and said, "You're back up now."

I interrupted, "Hold on, who is this Ari Ahrdeni?"

"I'll explain that to you in a few, Bob," Wendy replied.

Evelyn had been taking it all in from the couch opposite a blank TV. Suddenly, she came alive. "Let me guess, this Omar Korbachi knows the asshole in Toronto, Kandallah?"

Wendy was blown away, responding, "Yes, in fact they both graduated college in the same year from the same university. They have been colleagues and friends for years. Evelyn, you are amazing, how did you figure that one?"

"Over time I have learned to trust my instincts."

"It's a slow process, people, but we're beginning to put this puzzle together," Levine commented. "And you, Stone, talk to us about those bank transfers?"

"Sure, in a nutshell, large transfers went from Toronto to Istanbul. But where is the money flowing to next and why? This, I do not know. Maybe it's time to have Frank and the FBI penetrate the law firm, since Kandallah and Omar Korbachi are linked."

"Good thinking, tax man," Levine commented and added, "and that's why you need to go to Istanbul tomorrow night. You need to—"

I cut him off, "I know, Levine, I need to follow the money trail. Excuse me, the 'flow of funds' as you love to say, from the Royal Bank of Toronto to the International Bank of Turkey."

Levine smiled. Wendy started to pace around the room.

I saw she needed to talk, so I said, "Go ahead, Wendy, nothing can shock me at this point. What's up?"

"Well," Wendy started, but she paused. "It's no big deal since we all work here together, but it's time you knew."

"What's up? Just spit it out."

"Ok, here we go. I'm an Israeli Mossad agent working jointly with the U.S. Department of Homeland Security and obviously with HPAT 21. I am also telling you this because I have Middle Eastern contacts. I know of a weapons middleman who you will meet in Istanbul. *That's* who Ari Ahrdeni is, it's his international alias. His real name is Arieh Korine. He is a special man, who was once high on the list to become a member of Knesset, the Israeli national legislature, years ago. Long story, but he decided to join the Mossad, the national intelligence agency of Israel. Ahrdeni plays all sides in the world of weapon's deals. He understands what goes on below the bottom line in the world of terrorism, like black money and tax evasion using various currencies to fund large weapons deals. He may be able to help you to uncover what's going on."

"I understand. This Ahrdeni guy seems like a real pro," I said.

"And by the way, Stone, my real name is Aviva Geelmor. But let's stick with Wendy."

I was speechless and impressed. My eyebrows reached high, I was truly taken aback.

"Okay, let's wrap up," Levine said. "So, Stone, you will be going to JFK with Evelyn tomorrow night. You guys worked well together in Toronto, let's stay with what works."

Evelyn and I looked at each other, then I caught a glimpse of Laura and Wendy smiling at one another while holding hands. It seemed to me that they were connecting in more ways than one. Levine shook my hand and patted me on the back, zeroing in on my eyes for attention.

"Bob, be careful. You can absolutely rely on Wendy's contact, Ari Ahrdeni. He will be your guide, your lifeline. Keep it simple. As I told you before your trip to Toronto, focus on the flow of money and you'll be going in the right direction."

"So, Istanbul is the next leg of my journey," I was talking to myself, but the words came through.

"Think of all the great food you'll eat," Levine said.

"Again, with your food."

He grinned, walking toward the front door saying, "Oh yeah, later today, HPAT 21 tech support will check all your implanted tracking devices."

Evelyn bobbed her head and stood up to shake Levine's hand.

"Almost forgot," Levine said, while holding her hand. "Good news, people. All of you will be given a special gift tomorrow."

Evelyn replied, "Ooh, I love gifts."

"It's a new HPAT 21 pen," Levine said, holding one up.

"How amazing, a lousy pen. Wow thanks," Wendy said sarcastically.

Levine countered her offensive tone, "This is no ordinary pen, people. It's a combination laser taser gun and it cannot be detected during airport security. A new antiterrorist tool fresh out of our weapons lab. Tomorrow morning, these LT pens will be handed out to each of you. You'll all be picked up at eight-thirty a.m. and brought to the 'basement' for a quick shooting lesson. Guys, this new toy could save your lives. See you all mañana."

Levine left us alone, which allowed me a moment to reflect. *Less than two weeks ago, I was leading a boring existence as a tax advisor in Long Island looking for a more exciting life. Be careful what you wish for,* they say. *What a life changer this has been.* I began to laugh, shaking my head in disbelief while pondering, *Maybe one day I'll write a book about all this insanity.*

CHAPTER **24**

I t was an intense afternoon after Levine left. We rehashed Laura's conversation with Janet Ford at the law firm and discussed the upcoming trip to Istanbul. I collapsed on the couch in the den. Wendy and Laura dozed off in the back room. Evelyn slumped into a large leather chair tilted all the way back.

A simultaneous text came through on my cell phone and Evelyn's: *Check your emails for Istanbul flight info. E-tickets as follows: Turkish Airlines, flight TA242. Leaving JFK tomorrow at 6:40 p.m. Flight time: nine hours and fifty minutes. Staying at Pera Palace Hotel Jumeirah just off Taksim Square. One room, double beds. Booked under the pseudonyms of Savemoor and Carver.*

I was nervous as hell. The last trip to Toronto was real scary, but at least it was near the good ol' USA. Now we're taking a ten-hour flight to a foreign country. I'm an IRS agent with HPAT 21, an under-the-radar stealth unit established to fight terrorism. This Istanbul campaign will be dangerous. I was nervous enough that I almost picked up the phone to call Ashton, but I just couldn't do that. Fear of the unknown, that's it. I needed more detail. I had to stay in control.

I repeated some positive thoughts to reassure myself: *I can do this, it will be alright. What do these two guys, Omar Korbachi, the big shot deal maker and Ari Ahrdeni, Wendy's weapon contact, look like? How and where would we meet? How would I figure out how to peel the onion away from Korbachi and his network? What monsters and potential acts of terrorism could all this lead to?*

This last thought gave me a feeling of purpose. That's right, I'm in this to save lives, to make a difference. About a hundred pounds just lopped off my head. So that's it, tomorrow morning, I'll need time to gather detail from Wendy and Levine. I bolstered my confidence, realizing that the more information made available to me, the calmer I would be. Then I dozed off.

***

The morning arrived with the sunlight slipping through the sides of the window treatments. After fifteen minutes, we gathered in the den just off the kitchen. One of the outside guards tapped on the door. I returned the knock and awaited his confirmation that he was HPAT 21. Once the guard responded and the HPAT signal was returned, our inside guard opened the door.

"Orders from Levine," one of the guards said. "Time is tight, we need to leave now and head over to the 'basement.'"

The mood was edgy, we all felt tentative. The need for someone to step up was obvious. This time it would be me. A leader was needed.

"Come on, everyone, let's move our butts. We'll eat soon, I promise."

I smiled and picked up my pace, as an example for the rest.

"Come on, people, let's move it. It's going to be fun. Ya know, learning to use an LT gun embedded inside a little pen. Crazy, right?"

Evelyn looked at me as if I was an idiot. We started driving in the usual black Jeep down to East Seventh Street, then turned on Avenue A. On the way, I texted Levine to be ready with more detail and photos of Ahrdeni and Korbachi. *Oh yeah, and we need some food now, otherwise it's gonna be a real nervous meeting.*

Okay, no problem, Stone, Levine agreed.

He arrived shortly after with coffee, donuts, and muffins spread out on an unappealing wooden table.

"Go ahead, people," Levine said. "I'll talk while you eat and sip coffee."

"Thanks, I said on behalf of everyone. we're a hungry bunch and, frankly, a bit nervous today."

"Understood," Levine said in an aloof manner. He was preoccupied and launching into presentation mode as he said, "Here we go, Stone,

Wendy, Evelyn, and Laura. Let's give a warm welcome to the man who has developed this new weapon, the man whose invention may save your ass when you least expect it."

"Come on, Levine, cut the drama, I remarked."

Levine kept on and said, "Now, this man who we call 'the Professor' is an MIT graduate engineer with a master's degree, class of nineteen-eighty-seven. He has been with the Department of Homeland Security since the day after 9/11. Alright, I'm done. Please say hi to James Callahan, aka, the Professor."

"Thank you, Mr. Levine, I'll be brief. I know you have flights and deadlines. Come with me to the other room, down the hall over there." The professor spoke in a choppy manner.

We followed the Professor four doors down into a well-lit long and narrow room.

Trying to ease the tension, I said, "Must have been a bowling alley."

Everyone ignored me. At the far end, there were four manikins, one next to the other.

"What's going on here?" I asked.

"Mr. Stone, please, the Professor said, his lips forming together indicative of his displeasure.

"Sorry, Professor."

Sensitive guy, I thought.

He handed out a pen to each one of us and said with urgency, "Don't click the pen yet. These pens are deactivated now, so don't worry. They were not designed to kill, but rather seriously injure an aggressor and stop one in his or her tracks." Just like that, he snapped two of his fingers together to emphasize his point with a crisp noise. "Allow me to lead by example."

This weapons guru was like a kid doing show-and-tell at elementary school. He was about 5'9" and overweight by about thirty pounds with a burley black beard and a ponytail. Actually, he was sloppy-looking. My guess, he was roughly forty-five to fifty years old.

The Professor took control again, "Okay, everyone, move over to the right side and stay behind me." He then crouched down. "You must

234 • ERIC J. ENGELHARDT

first activate the pen by tapping the bottom on a hard surface two times, then you press the top button once. Another click will trigger a laser shot strong enough to put down a pit bull. Oh yeah, my friends, this laser can also mess up a helicopter and its pilot. Click the pen a third time and you will release an electric Taser shot so strong it can drop an antelope in seconds."

"Okay, Professor, that's truly amazing. How many shots does each pen have?" I asked.

"It is limited, but it's the best we have now—only two rounds," he answered. "In six months, the new pen will have five shots."

"Let's give it a try," Levine suggested. "Go ahead, Professor."

"Yes, of course, sorry." The Professor laughed with a weird snorting sound. "Sorry people, I got lost with my new toy."

The proud inventor crouched down again and activated the pen. Click number two let out a laser beam that put a hole into the manikin's arm. The next click released a sparkling electric stream into the chest cavity of the same manikin. The force and effect were shocking. The manikin flipped up, almost touching the eight-foot ceiling, then crashed down to the floor with the blink of an eye. Each of us took turns with our LT pens. First me, then Wendy, then Evelyn, and finally Laura—yes, even Laura. The feeling of power was addictive.

I had to double check on what Levine had said, "And these crazy pens will not be spotted at the airports?"

"Good question, Stone," replied the Professor. "And the answer is absolutely not. There's a carbon seal around the guts of the pen. But you must remember to deactivate the pen when you are finished each time. Like I said, just tap the bottom of the pen twice on any hard, flat object."

Levine took over and said, "Okay thanks, Professor. Please keep doing your weapons research. We need you and your talents."

Leaving, The Professor put an unmarked black baseball cap on his head, awkwardly saluted us and wished us good fortune.

"Okay, people. Now listen up," Levine said. He had something up his sleeve. "Here are new passports for you, Stone, and you, Carter.

Open them up. Stone, say your new travel name so we can all hear you."

I looked at him with a smirk and said, "It's Robert Savemoor."

"Good, Stone," Levine said. "That's a reminder to keep you focused on your purpose at HPAT, which is clearly to 'save more people.'"

"How cute, Levine," I said. "Actually, I love it."

"I thought you would," he replied. "Evelyn?"

"Yes, Mr. Levine," she responded." "Ah, my passport reads, 'Evelyn Carver.'"

Levine said, "Nothing sentimental here. Just remember, 'carve up' the enemy before they rip you apart."

"Thanks for relaxing me, Mr. Levine," Evelyn replied sarcastically.

Wendy and Laura were laughing so hard, they suddenly had to pee and departed for the bathrooms. Nervous laughter, no doubt. I couldn't help myself laughing too, so I turned around to regain my composure, burying my face into both my hands. Evelyn was just standing there staring at the manikins. Levine suggested that we take a five-minute break. He knew he had lost control.

We resumed after a few moments with Levine saying, "We need just a bit more time and the fun and games here are over." He took out a file folder.

"Photos, Levine?" I asked.

"Yes, of course, Stone."

As Wendy came back with Laura from the bathrooms, she took over the conversation.

"Bob, this guy is my contact, Ari Ahrdeni, who I was telling you about," she said, pointing at one of the photos of a slender guy with a well-trimmed black beard sprinkled with a few grey clusters. "He'll be wearing a solid, dark-green scarf around his neck and round, black-rimmed sunglasses. On his right ear, you'll see an earring in the shape of a star. You can't miss him. He will be waiting for you inside the south entrance of the Grand Bazaar market in Istanbul at the first Turkish booth on the immediate right. The store sells apricots, pistachios, and stuff from around the world.

"He will approach you and say the words, 'Try the large pistachios, they are fresh.' You must respond with, 'Thanks, my friend. I am here for the apricots.' He will respond with, 'My friends call me, Ari.' You respond with, 'I am Bob.' He will scratch his left shoulder, then shake your hand and give you, Evelyn, a two-handed shake.

"Next, Ahrdeni will ask you to follow him for a cup of Turkish coffee. Join him and feel free to ask him whatever you want . . . confide about Korbachi and other players. Make it clear that his help and a plan are needed."

"I got it," I said. "What about Omar Korbachi? What the hell does he look like?"

"Here is a recent FBI photo of Korbachi," Wendy replied, sliding another photo in front of me.

Laura eagerly said, flipping the picture toward her. "I saw him once at the firm, about five months ago. It's a good photo."

"Let me see the photo again," I said.

I stared at the photo, memorizing Korbachi's appearance. He was a chunky, well-dressed man about the age of sixty, height about 5'10." He had a jagged indentation or scar on his right cheek, just below his eye and a black handlebar mustache with a totally bald head. He had a black mole on his left cheek.

"Good memory, Laura," Wendy said, turning to me and Evelyn. "Back to me. Taksim Square is the most well-known spot in Istanbul, famous for protests throughout history. You'll see stores and dozens of restaurants with döner foods, you know, the lamb meat rotating as they slice it from top to bottom. The Grand Bazaar is past Taksim Square near the Galata Bridge. You'll figure it out. You guys will love Istanbul. I've been there a few times myself. And no question whatsoever, you can lean on Ahrdeni, he is an incredible resource with valuable info."

"Thanks, Wendy, so, it's okay if I mention your name to Ahrdeni?"

"Sure, but he would know me by my nickname, Veev, short for Aviva," she replied.

"Okay good to know," I said sarcastically, showing aggravation for me needing to ask the question. "By the way, how did you go from Aviva to Wendy?" I asked.

"Bob, you'll never believe it, but since there is no direct translation of my Hebrew name to English, I simply went with Wendy because when I was a child, I looked very much like the girl from Wendy's hamburgers."

"Don't Israeli women tend to have dark hair?" I posed.

"Sure, but I'm the exception. My sister got the black hair from my mother, and I picked up the reddish-blond hair from my father, who had blond hair and blue eyes. He was from eastern Europe."

"Interesting, thanks for sharing that with me."

"Okay, kids, enough nonsense," Levine said impatiently. He quickly moved the conversation to other details. "Here are a few credit cards issued obviously with your pseudo names and the equivalent of nine thousand euros each for tips, bribes, and whatever. Okay, good day and good luck. This Istanbul campaign is critical. I can smell it, we're getting closer, the puzzle is coming together."

Levine started to walk away. He then pivoted back to us, paused, and spoke. "Friends, listen up: All of us here at HPAT have total confidence in you. Each one of you was carefully selected for this campaign based upon your background and unique skill set. You know your purpose. Be smart, be careful. Think clearly, make your decisions, and then act accordingly. May God bless and keep you safe."

Levine stood up to give us handshakes. "Oh," he added, "Slight change of plans. Your guards were instructed to bring your luggage to the Jeep before you arrived here this morning. You are being taken right now to an apartment on Third Avenue and Twelfth Street. Go there and rest for a few hours. Your guards will bring lunch and an early dinner in before you all head out to your assignments. No need to go out and waste time. Evelyn and Bob, you need to think about various aspects of this campaign. Call me later if any questions arise."

"Yes, yes, Levine," I said.

"Will do," replied Evelyn.

We left the basement, hopped into the black Jeeps and were escorted to the Manhattan apartment. It was just past noon.

***

It's amazing how time can move so fast. As the time approached 4:00 p.m., I decided to review the contents of my one small bag to make sure our newly created passports and the laser Taser pens were inside. I was all set when Evelyn was ready to head out. It took us about forty-five minutes to get to JFK Airport.

I felt that Evelyn and I were on our own until some guy stopped to ask me if I knew where the bathrooms were. He whispered to me that he would be keeping an eye on us at the airport until we boarded the plane. I recalled Levine's lecture from the other day, how HPAT 21 could not rescue us if we fell into the wrong hands overseas. My worry right now was getting past security without alarms going off and successfully carrying our LT pen weapons. Despite the Professor's reassurances, I was still doubtful. We got in line and started the security process.

"Evelyn," I said in a hushed tone, noticing her apprehension. "Let's trust the Professor. He did say the pens have a wrap-around carbon cover. Let's be calm." I was speaking more to reassure myself than her.

"Okay," she said, her response sounding weak.

I went first to instill some confidence in her.

A young airport security guard, looking new in his job, was announcing, "Belt and shoes off, watch, coins in your pockets, all metal objects in the bin, cell phones, etcetera." As I approached the front of the line, he asked me, "Pockets empty?"

This asshole had the word *troublemaker* written on his forehead. There was nothing nice about him. His self-important smirk was obvious and exactly what we did not need.

"Ah, yes," I replied. "I just have a pen in my right pocket, sorry."

"Didn't you hear me, all pockets empty?" he said curtly.

"Sorry, my friend. Actually, this pen was a special gift to both me and to my colleague behind me on line. We have both been with the same company for twenty-five years and we were just awarded these pens as a gift."

The guard tapped my pen on the table, looking for my reaction.

"Please don't do that. I just told you, it's a special gift."

The guard eyed me for my reaction.

"Must be very special," he said. "I love pens myself. Is it a fine point or what?"

I was a breath away from whispering to this guy that we were with HPAT 21, a specialized secret crime unit of the IRS, so back off—but Evelyn did what she does best and put the guy in his place confidently.

"Okay, give it a break already," Evelyn said. "Do you see those thirty people behind us? It's enough already. A pen is a pen, cut the nonsense. Keep harassing us over pens and I'll have your supervisor over here right away."

About five people waiting behind Evelyn started to complain. The guard was pointing the pen just below my throat. He had his right finger on top of the pen and was about to give it a click. He called it quits and flipped it into the bin. I calmly grabbed the pen and tapped it twice on the metal counter top to be sure it was deactivated. If that guard tapped the pen twice, I could have been killed. The Professor was clever to set it up for two taps and one click to activate.

By now, my hands were sweaty, and my neck had tensed up. The airport security guard directed me away with his hand motion. Then Evelyn followed. This took me back to Toronto as I recalled how fantastic Evelyn was as a diversion in the bank. She's truly amazing, stepping up just at the right time and Levine was right—we did work well together.

Drained, we went directly to our terminal and relaxed. The scene reminded me of the terminal at La Guardia Airport for my recent trip to Canada. I closed my eyes and imagined Evelyn a few seats away, appearing with those classic red high heels. It was recent, but it seemed so long ago. I had to remind her.

I turned and said, "Hey, Evelyn, where are your famous red high heels?"

She turned to catch my attention, smiled, then said nothing and closed her eyes. I would have killed to get into her mind at that moment. My fleeting comment faded, as my head was filling up with the various aspects of this delicate Istanbul campaign. The boarding announcements came through on the speakers. The lines approaching the ramp moved smoothly.

"Hey, Stone, the first drink is on me," Evelyn smiled as if to say, *Remember?*

"Sure, sounds familiar, Evelyn. The Toronto trip, right?"

"Of course, and you'll have that bourbon with one ice cube."

"Perfect," I said. "And you're going to have a Turkish beer this time, Efes Pilsner right, not your usual Molson Canadian Lager?"

"Exactly, no Canadian beer on this trip, that would be ridiculous," Evelyn replied.

PART FIVE

CHAPTER 25

The flight was calm, with a few old and unappealing movies, so we dozed off. The hours passed as our drinks kicked in. The pre-landing announcements were spoken in three different languages. The descent onto the tarmac went smoothly and disembarking the airplane was easy—our passports were stamped after the usual customs process.

We exited the airport to find taxis lined up waiting to catch travelers. Within thirty-five minutes, we were dropped off at the hotel close to Taksim Square. It was midday. The sun was bright, and the heat was difficult. We did not have the luxury of extra time to relax. We needed to get focused, grab a bite to eat, and meet Ari Ahrdeni at the Grand Bazaar at 2:45 p.m. sharp.

We changed into more appropriate, loose-fitting clothes, avoiding conspicuous bright colors so as not to be too noticeable. Evelyn tucked her hair up into a gray scarf, revealing her facial features. I loved her look, but I caught myself. *Stop, just think about Ahrdeni, don't be a jerk.*

We took the elevator from the fourth floor down to the lobby. I had a moment to absorb the beauty of this hotel: amazing chandeliers; domed glass windows in the ceiling; intricate deep red carpets placed over wooden floors; fine, detailed woodwork and archways; antique lamps and plush furniture.

"Come on, Bob," Evelyn said. "Let's get going."

"Sorry, I got wrapped up in this unbelievable lobby."

"I see it, but I'm starving, and we need to be on time."

"Okay, you're right."

The revolving door led us out of the hotel directly into the massive crowds of locals and tourists. A fifteen-minute walk brought us to the heart of Taksim Square. The scene was frenetic, people were bumping into one another, moving to and fro like swarms of sardines.

We went to the first restaurant in sight, Cafe Duram. The sign read: "Istanbul's Oldest Restaurant." We went right in to quickly satisfy our hunger, trying the Turkish coffee to help fight off the jet lag, and ordering some typical local dishes, and of course, a sweet dessert. The doner lamb kebabs with rice and grilled veggies arrived quickly and were spectacular. The strong, dark coffee was served with our rose water-flavored, creamy dessert. It was a perfect combination.

Then we were off and heading up a hill near the bridge and down toward the Grand Bazaar. We walked slowly, since it was only 2:30 p.m., giving us fifteen minutes to spare. For a moment, I stupidly felt like a tourist on vacation.

That feeling passed quickly. A blast was heard behind us, followed by screams and smoke rising into the sky. The explosion seemed to have been near the area where we just had lunch. As the police cars and sirens moved in, my gut instincts directed me to pull Evelyn toward the Grand Bazaar—fast. A few minutes elapsed. We went to the south entrance as Wendy had instructed, then stopped. By now, we were precisely on time.

Evelyn said, "Hey, check out those huge jars of nuts and fruits. I've never seen anything like it. This must be the booth, it's in the far right corner, as they told us."

Off to my left, I heard a voice, "Excuse me, but you should try the large pistachios, they are fresh."

I turned and saw Ari Ahrdeni standing there, exactly as Wendy described him. He was exactly as I had seen him in the photo and wearing a solid, dark green scarf and black-rimmed sunglasses.

"Thanks, my friend," I replied. "I am here for the apricots."

"My friends call me Ari."

"I am Bob."

"How about some Turkish coffee?" Ari asked.

I nodded my head.

"Follow me."

This was it, the start of our Istanbul journey. I gently reached for Evelyn's hand.

"Let's go with it," I said.

"Sure, let's move on," she agreed.

We kept up with Ari as he led us out to the western doorway, exiting the Grand Bazaar. We walked down the street, took a left, and then walked down a hill to the boats resting on the Bosporus Strait, a waterway separating Asian Turkey from European Turkey.

"Come on, let's hop on one of these boats and talk while you see the sights," Ari said.

"Nice idea, Mr. Ahrdeni," I said.

It was mid-afternoon, a time of day when the boats were more crowded than earlier. This was my chance—I had to connect with him.

"Mr. Ahrdeni," I said.

"It's Ari, please."

"Thanks, Ari. I've heard wonderful things about you from Wendy—sorry I mean Aviva, or Veev." I was embarrassed by my screwup, so I added, "Or however you prefer to call her. I just learned her real name; it's confusing, forgive me." *Stupid me, I'm already screwing this up.* "Anyway, Ari, you are highly respected. I understand you are a pro, and I'd like to learn from you. Somehow, I feel as if I already know you, Ari. We need your help and your resources, we need to strategize with you."

"I'm honored and I too feel that I already know you, Mr. Tax Man, now a U.S. Department of Homeland Security—or is it, an HPAT 21 special agent? That's an amazing change-of-life event. One day you can tell me how that happened, but for now, I'm here to assist you both and my colleagues back in America."

"Ah, you know my nickname and much more," I replied. "That's good. We are now familiar with one another's background. Now, please say hello to my colleague, Evelyn."

Evelyn extended her hand with grace. Ari's face could not hide that he absorbed her presence, and a visible jolt of small adrenalin hit him.

246 • ERIC J. ENGELHARDT

I decided to be humble, to let him know we were confused and in need of his help.

"Ari, I honestly don't know where to begin, but I can say this for sure: We need your help, your knowledge, and your guidance."

"Stone, it sounds to me that you just figured out where and how to begin. Give yourself more credit, *chaver.*"

I recognized *chaver* as the Hebrew word for friend and I responded, "*Todá rabá,* thank you."

He smiled, apparently touched by my use of his language. Then he nodded his head with focused eye contact, as if to silently say, w*e are all comrades.*

"Ari, we have been on the money trail recently. Huge blocks of money have been flowing from a mosque account in New York to the Royal Bank of Toronto, and then to the International Bank of Turkey, right here in Istanbul. Something unusual is in progress, whatever is going on, it must be stopped."

"How much money has been transferred from that bank in Toronto to the International Bank of Turkey?" Ari asked.

"There was approximately three hundred million U.S. dollars moved already—and I mean very recently over the past few months."

"Ari, what do you say? Can you help us?" Evelyn asked.

"Stone, I get it that you are following the money, but I know the key players around the world when it comes to the use of that money to buy weapons. I'm sorry to inform you, but that kind of money can be for any number of things, including a nuclear backpack, a missing airplane, chemical weapons, maybe even germs as well. I suspect the last two would come from Syria and for sure, those would be the never-to-be-found weapons of mass destruction that moved from Iraq into Syria at the start of the Second Gulf War. If these people are not stopped, if any of what I just mentioned is actually developing, your 9/11 attack will look like a tiny episode in American history."

Evelyn grew quiet, absorbing every word. My darkest fears were taking shape as Ari was talking.

"Enough," I said. "Where are we going with all this? Ari, come on, tell me something positive."

"Listen, my American *chaverim*, here is my plan: I am good friends with the supervisor at the International Bank of Turkey down the street. I will introduce you to him tomorrow morning. This is delicate, I cannot put him in a position to lose his job, yet we need his coopera-tion. Next, one of the three major weapons buyers around here is Win-throp Carmichael; he's British. One can never be sure, but I believe we can rule him out. The next contact is Vladimir Mosgov, obviously a Rus-sian, and they are never predictable. Finally, there are two guys who work together. They are both originally from Yemen, names are Kor-bachi and Kandallah. They operate under the business name, K and K Exports, LLC."

Evelyn stood abruptly in place in an automatic response from hear-ing those names.

I said, "Ari, we are almost finished here. You've narrowed it down. Kandallah is a supervisor at the Royal Bank of Toronto and he almost killed us."

"This is all moving so fast," Ari said. "You should know, this guy Kor-bachi will work any deal. He has a taste for bringing foreign money into New York for purchasers who need to bury their black-market money into legitimate Manhattan properties. Korbachi is smart, but his greed will mess him up some day. You see, Korbachi takes a finder's fee of six to eight percent on every deal."

"To be sure, Ari, do you know where this K and K Exports, LLC is located?" Evelyn asked.

"No, not really," Ari answered. "But I've heard that they may be based out of Astoria, Queens."

"That's it. I've heard enough, Ari, you just nailed it. Your friend and my colleague Aviva, sorry Veev, or as we know her, Wendy Gilmore was so right about you."

"Veev has more names than you think," Ari said. "She's an amazing lady."

"Yes, absolutely," I agreed. As my thoughts turned into strategies, I said, "Let me talk, people. Plan A is Ari' baby."

"We should arrive to the bank at ten a.m. tomorrow. This will give me just enough time to personally stop in to say hello and talk man-to-man with my old friend, Ismael Najeer, the bank supervisor. Then I will come out to the lobby to bring you both into his office. I know this man, he will give you max fifteen minutes and you'll have to wrap it up."

"Now for plan B," I said. "Tell me, Ari, if this makes sense to you?"

"Go ahead, Stone."

"You call Korbachi. Tell him that you have a client with a huge block of American dollars, money that needs to be made legitimate. Tell him it's about four hundred mil if he asks. Next, he needs to know that about half will be used to buy serious weapons—don't tell him why just yet. Then he needs to know that the other half must be earmarked to buy a historical landmark in Manhattan."

Ari nodded, indicating he fully understood my ideas, and then answered, "Stone, that's damn good. You have more than a numbers background. Are you sure you are new at this game?"

I gagged bit on my coffee and moved to stand near Evelyn, who was bobbing back and forth, trying to hold in her laughter. I barely got it out saying, "Yeah, something like that. Let's just say they call me, tax man, however, I've come a long way in a short time. I'd like to believe I am much more than only a tax man. Anyway, back to plan B. Ari, can you set up a meeting with Korbachi? Are you comfortable with this approach?"

"It's not so simple but it does sound like a typical start of a deal that a guy like him could find appealing. So yes, it could work, he just might take the bait. Just be aware that a meeting with a guy like this is no joke. There will be bodyguards, any mistakes and we'll all be executed. Just play the part correctly. Act serious, be confident as hell, believe in your story, and the wheels will be in motion."

"Great, Ari, it's good to know we are on the same page."

"To play the game, you will need to open up an account at the International Bank of Turkey some point after we meet the bank supervisor. Then you will need it to look real, in case Korbachi checks you out. And you better have your people wire the four hundred million right away into your new account at this bank, preferably into an entity such as EB Partners, LLC."

"Ari, great name," I said. "How did you—"

He cut me off, "Just keep it simple. It's Evelyn and Bob, right? So, EB is not rocket science."

"Perfect," Evelyn said and smiled while shaking Ari's hand.

Once again, Ari was more than receptive, holding her hand for just a few extra seconds, as he studied her slender fingers ending into her pink nails. The boat pulled ashore and we followed the others out. I extended my hand to Ari and shook his hand firmly. He gave me a hug and then a pat on my back.

Evelyn waved goodbye and said, "we thank you so much."

"You're welcome, now you need to go down that way, take a right, and then a left up the hill. Walk through Taksim Square, then head two blocks to your left and you will be back at your hotel. I prefer not to be seen walking with you for obvious reasons. Meet me at the bank tomorrow morning at nine-fifty a.m. sharp. Precision is the key, trust me. And order dinner in tonight from room service, it's possible you are being watched."

"You are our trusted advisor, Ari," I said.

He and I exchanged longer than usual eye contact, he then said, "Hey, friends, this is very serious, you are about to meet the worst of the worst, the most dangerous people on the planet. Relax tonight, don't fight the jet lag. All of us better be alert going forward."

We exchanged cell phone numbers and began to walk away.

"See you tomorrow at the bank, and do call me tonight should any questions come up," Ari insisted.

We started our nervous, twenty-minute walk back to the hotel.

I sensed that the mystery of the missing money in motion would be unraveling sooner than later. All the while, I was consumed with worry

250 ERIC J. ENGELHARDT

as my mind began to dwell on the consequences of so many opportunities for disaster to take place anywhere and at any time. To avoid the anxiety, I shifted my focus on the task at hand, the crucial meeting tomorrow morning;

Tomorrow would be revealing. We had to find a way to make that meeting go well. I tried not to over think but it seems that an American disaster was looming over us. Ari's words while on the boat ride were scary, indicative of a potential event of epic proportions. Ari mentioned a dirty bomb or nuclear backpack, missing airplanes, chemical agents, or germs. I could not imagine the results of these weapons of mass destruction. At all costs, even my life, this had to be prevented. My instincts told me that time was running out and that millions of lives in our homeland were hanging in the balance.

CHAPTER 26

T he walk back to our hotel was necessary. The sun was edging down while a breeze made its presence known. Walking gave us time to digest the strategies discussed. There was a mysterious feel about Istanbul, something unexplainable in the air, an undercurrent of danger.

A text came in from Wendy, *Darmush was picked up at JFK airport with a one-way ticket to Turkey. HPAT 21 agents escorted him to the basement for interrogation.* I realized that he must have been scared to death by Levine's fake IRS tax audit letter. I texted back, *Copy that—* I had always wanted to say that. *Oh yeah, we met Ari. Amazing man.*

She texted back, *I told you, he's a great resource, great friend, and great guy.*

Absolutely right, Wendy. He's setting up two meetings, one tomorrow morning at the bank, and the other meeting is not yet firmed up. There's a sense of danger around here, can't explain. Tell Levine things are moving fast, need his help. Details to follow.

"Okay."

Two minutes later, Levine texted me, *Hey, what's up?*

I lost my patience with all the texting, so I called and filled Levine in. "Briefly, tomorrow morning Ari takes us to the bank to meet Ismael Najeer, the bank supervisor. Then Ari will try to set up a meeting with Korbachi, me, and Evelyn to do a fake weapons deal with him. Need four hundred mil transferred tomorrow morning to open an account at the International Bank of Turkey. The account name is to be EB Partners, LLC. Text me the wire instructions ASAP."

"That's a huge request, we will definitely need approval on this one, Stone," Levine replied.

"It's urgent, Ari says we must look like serious players, otherwise we're dead meat. By the way, how is Laura?"

"She's good, you stay focused on Istanbul."

"Okay. Right, Levine, last point, it may be time for the FBI to jump in regarding the law firm and Korbachi."

"FBI is already positioned," Levine quickly replied. "They're coordinating all details with Frank."

"If we don't get killed and Korbachi is as greedy as Ari claims he is, we'll see how the money trail unfolds. Still trying to figure out the intended purpose of the money transfer from Toronto to the Istanbul bank. The closer we get to uncovering what's going on, the more stressful it becomes."

"Keep moving forward," Levine reassured. "Stay smart, alert, and careful."

We hung up as Evelyn approached me.

"Bob, you look troubled, what are you thinking?"

"I can't put my finger on it, Evelyn, something is missing. Money moving from New York to Canada and then to a bank in Turkey. Some crazy elaborate scheme is in progress. I'm a financial man, and so much movement of large funds seems to me like it's a sophisticated cover-up for a major event. It smells of terrorism, but some different, a new twist on acts of terrorism. Yeah, something strange is unfolding, Evelyn."

"But what?"

"That's what is killing me," I confessed.

She tried to relax me and said, "Okay, enough for now. Let's take an hour to doze off, and then maybe it will hit you."

"Yeah, you're right, it's been a long day already."

The TV remote was a few inches away from me. It was a perfect time to catch some international news—always so much more interesting for me to listen to the BBC News with their European perspective. I used my feet to push off my shoes and leaned back into the bed. The news was reaching the end of a segment, approaching 5:00 p.m. Turkey time.

"Today we conclude with our special report, 'Germ and Chemical Weapons, Out of Control,'" said a well-respected British journalist, Charles Danforth. He wrapped it up with, "Chemical weapons have been moving around the Middle East over the last two decades, mostly stockpiled by Syria, who inherited them from Iraq years ago. The critical question for today is, where are all the sealed canisters of germs and bacteria around the world? They've been out of sight, but not out of our minds."

At that moment, my instincts took over and I remembered Ari mentioning germs as a possible weapon. I figured that Korbachi could be a major player in the dealing of germs and other bacterial substances used for targeted acts of terrorism.

"The whereabouts of these substances is unknown," Danforth continued. "Putting massive populations at risk around the global."

The report concluded... I looked to Evelyn for some response.

"Have you been listening?"

"No, I dozed off, what's up?"

"You slept through this amazing report? Well, that's it, I believe in my gut we're down to Korbachi selling some form of bacterial weapons, but for what and to be used where, damn it? I was just watching the end of this BBC report that summarized the unknown whereabouts of chemical weapons, and then the journalist warned about the total lack of global awareness as to who controls germ and bacterial substances. Now, I can't wait to meet Mr. Korbachi and his friends—the sooner the better."

"Okay, in due time," Evelyn reassured me.

"What do you say we order up some dinner, what are you in the mood for?"

"You really think I know what to eat around here?"

"Well, when in Rome, eat as the Romans do. Maybe we should text Levine and ask him?"

We both laughed.

"Okay," I said. "I'll call room service and put in an order for some basic Turkish food and a couple of sweet things."

There was a heavy mood in the room, a feeling of self-doubt, and a sense that we may not solve the puzzle in time to prevent a massacre. It was disturbing shifting from confidence then sinking into self-doubt.

A text then came in from Ari, *Tom. Morn. confirmed. Lobby at Intl. Bank Turkey, 9:50 a.m. exact. Remember, the bank supervisor is Ismael Najeer. He and I are friends. I will do most of the talking. When I feel you need to talk, I'll turn to you and put my two fingers on my chin. Confirm?*

Yes, understood. We're having dinner in as you suggested. See you tom. morn. No worries, we'll be on time.

The knock on the hotel door was followed by a male voice saying, "Merhaba, hello, it's your food service." We were beyond hungry so that food delivery was a timed perfectly. That was a welcome announcement. The young boy who wheeled in the food wagon was wearing a multicolored purple cap with beads hanging down. I handed him five euro.

He smiled from ear to ear and said, "Thank you, mister."

He paused and stared for a moment as he struggled to say,

"Injoy yoor deener."

The boy left, as the door closed behind him. Clearly, the young man was nervous, or he was simply bashful. I followed him out into the hallway, but he was already gone. As I reentered the room, Evelyn removed the large dome cover off the first dish.

"Bob, come here now! Read this!"

A note was taped to the underside of the cover: *Americans, save your lives, leave Istanbul now.* We just sat down, remained silent trying to preserve our poise then gave each other a look. I decided to text Ari to call me right away. A moment later he called.

"Listen, Ari, we took your advice and ordered up dinner."

"So, what's up?" he replied impatiently.

"A note was dropped off with the food."

"Read it to me?"

'Americans, save your lives, leave Istanbul now.' Any suggestions, Ari?"

I put him on speaker so that Evelyn could hear as well.

"First, do not eat any of the food, good chance it's been poisoned, next, you need to get the hell away from that hotel. Take all your things and leave but do not check out. Let's meet in Taksim Square just off Mis Sk. Street at a restaurant called Zübeyir Ocakbaşı. Go inside, grab any table, just be calm and I'll see you soon."

I was barely able to say thanks, he hung up so quickly and then I became distracted by the next BBC report. Organizing my clothing and odds and ends was easy since I had packed lightly. Evelyn had more stuff, so a few extra minutes were needed. The broadcast started a new segment about the history of how the USA and Japan became enemies during the late 1930s up to the conclusion of World War Two in September 1945. It was fascinating to learn how the Japanese invaded Laos, Cambodia, and Vietnam. In response to Japan's aggressive acts, America and her allies had seized Japanese assets and blockaded Japan, preventing it from getting the oil that it needed and relied on. I shook my head left then right, thinking how America always managed to get involved in other countries' issues.

Anyway, next was a film clip of the Japanese bombing of Pearl Harbor in 1941. It was beyond horrible—thousands of Americans were killed, and our entire Pacific fleet was destroyed. The United States rebuilt its navy, then had a series of Pacific Ocean victories and land invasions from 1942 to 1945. Tens of thousands of American soldiers were killed to achieve these victories.

The documentary's narrator spoke over the clips, "To end the war, the Japanese homeland would have to be invaded. The death toll supposedly could have otherwise reached close to one million, as fanatical Japanese soldiers and citizens who were totally loyal to their supreme godlike leader, Emperor Hirohito, would never have given up. America had finally developed and then dropped the atomic bomb first on Hiroshima, and then on Nagasaki. Over one hundred thousand people were immediately vaporized, killed, and injured. The combination of these bombings and the advancing Russian army forced Japan to unconditionally surrender on September second, nineteen-forty-five, V-J Day, or Victory Over Japan Day."

The BBC documentary primarily focused on the war in the Pacific region and showed images of a group of eleven Japanese representatives arriving aboard the USS Missouri battleship in Tokyo Bay waters. Finally, images appeared as Japanese foreign minister Mamoru Shigemitsu was the first to sign the unconditional surrender agreements developed from the Potsdam Conference terms. Then Yoshijiro Umezu, Chief of the Army General Staff, signed the document. Countersigning was U.S. General of the Army Commander in the southwest Pacific and Supreme Commander for all Allied powers, Douglas MacArthur. Subsequently, Fleet Admiral for the United States Chester Nimitz and representatives from eight other allied countries signed. The Japanese emperor, and his countries highest-ranking ministers and generals, as well as its people were humiliated.

On that note, the documentary ended. It was a real eye opener, as the brutality of both countries hit me. That final blow to Japan was massive, killing as many as 120,000 people in forty-eight hours in two locations on August 6th and 9th in 1945. Hiroshima and Nagasaki were totally wiped out. And they say that these bombings forced Japan to finally accept unconditional surrender.

"Come on, tax man," Evelyn said, let's get back to present day. "You heard Ari, it's time to move your butt. I'm all set, you need to get organized and get the hell out of here."

"Thanks, you're right, Evelyn."

***

In about a fifteen-minute walk, we entered the city scene. I was convinced we were being watched.

"Evelyn, stay close. It's a crazy scene out here."

"Sure, of course."

We walked up Taksim Square. The crowds were still hanging out at 8:30 p.m. Too many people. We had to find our way to a more controlled area.

"This way," I said, ushering Evelyn in a direction. "Let's head down to that street."

As we took our next few steps, I felt two hands on my shoulders. I grabbed one hand, turned sharply, and flipped some guy to the ground. Evelyn was about to let loose a kick to his face when I heard a voice shout, "Stop!" and I saw it was Ari.

"Are you okay?" I asked. "Why the fuck would you scare me from behind like that?"

"That was a test, Stone, now I know what you and Evelyn are made of. Come on, my friends, let's eat."

"Ya know what, you're a crazy man, Ahrdeni. I was this close to kicking your face and now you want to eat." Evelyn remarked.

"Sure, why not," he answered back, laughing off the whole scene and dusting off his clothes. "In my world, you need to be cool and calm, take things nice and easy. *Naeem ve cal.*"

"What?" Evelyn asked.

"Oh, that means 'It's all pleasant,' or 'Nice and easy' in Hebrew," Ari replied.

"Give us a break, will you?" she asked, snapping a little. "We're in Turkey, stop throwing more languages at us. That's overload, okay?"

"Yes, sure, I can understand that," Ari replied.

A few people gathered around and asked if we were okay. I waved them off with a smile. We walked about two more blocks to the restaurant. On the way I spotted two guys eying us. When I stopped, they stopped, and then turned slightly. *Not very professional,* I thought, *unless they wanted to let us know we were being watched.*

"Come on," Ari said, "You have been followed since the moment you left the hotel. They want you to see them. If you were going to be attacked, that easily could have already taken place. We need to be in a more private spot, the streets are too dangerous and it's getting dark. I suggest we get off the streets and head into that restaurant."

I said out loud this time, "the Istanbul tension is always out there."

"Oh, how observant you are," Evelyn said sarcastically.

Ari turned to me with a smile and said, "That feeling comes with the territory. Shit happens in Istanbul every single day, but the idea is to survive."

I didn't bother to respond, although he somehow simplified things. He made sense out of the cloud that had hung over us the very moment we took our first step onto the soil of this ancient city.

We were ravenously hungry by now but at the same time, it was understandably hard to eat. Ari took over, sensing we were drained. Once a few starters were placed on our table, our appetites came alive as we took a few spoons of the hummus, tomato, and onion salad with warm pitas. The chicken shawarma was loaded with seasonings and the rice dishes were fabulous. All of us were indulging in the food, no doubt, paying little or no attention to our manners. All the while, we were in deep thought.

Evelyn, the expert at reading faces and making connections said, "Ari, I see your wheels are turning—what's up?"

"You gave me an opening, so here it is. This is the scenario. . . . Obviously, you cannot return to that hotel. I am now seen and linked to you both. We need a strategy." He said all this in a low and relaxed tone. I've been compromised, and all of us are now in the same boat."

"Ari, I'm very sorry." I acknowledged his concerns.

He held the palm of his hand out with his fingers pointed up then moved left to right and back to cut me off.

"It was my decision to hit the streets tonight to help you both. No question, you were in trouble. It's time to man up and move forward."

"You're quite a man," Evelyn added.

He took a long sip of beer and swished it in his mouth while thinking.

"I know the owner here," he said after a delayed swallow. "I brought you here because there is a trap door behind the kitchen that leads to a tunnel. We will end up on Muzik Street. See over there— those two guys who followed us just walked into the restaurant. They will be at a loss to find us after we go down under. But we need to get up now, one by one, to the bathroom. Evelyn, you first. It's toward the kitchen. Anyway, meet us inside by the large freezer next to the exit sign."

"Okay, I'm up and out of here now, guys," Evelyn said, getting up.

"Bob, now you," Ari said. "Those two assholes haven't seen us yet."

I followed Evelyn calmly toward the back through the kitchen doors, but I wanted to check on Ari. I slightly turned my head and used my side vision to look for him. He stood up and walked toward us. The double swinging kitchen doors opened as Ari walked in. Picking up his pace, he opened a dark wooden door off the kitchen floor next to the freezer. The chef and two busboys looked at us, the kitchen manager reprimanded the workers for pausing.

"Come on now, Bob, you step down first on that short ladder, then you can help Evelyn."

There was a single bulb hanging off a wire from the ceiling down below, just enough light for us to see last three steps of the ladder and the tunnel. I looked up and saw Ari give some guy a kiss on both cheeks and a hug before stepping down into the tunnel.

"Follow me," he said. "We will be up on the street again in no time."

"Okay, who was that guy back there?"

"He is the owner I mentioned and my friend of fifteen years," Ari replied. "This is probably the twelfth time I've used his tunnel to get out of harm's way, amazing, isn't it?"

"I'd say so," Evelyn replied.

"Okay, Ari, we're in your hands," I said.

"Good hands, Stone," he jokingly added as he held both his hands out.

Suddenly, there was yelling and screaming from the kitchen.

"Hurry, let's run," Ari said, in a firm but low voice tone.

Clearly something went wrong. There was a gunshot and then silence from up above. More noise and voices sounded, but it was less clear as we continued to run away.

"We'll be at street level soon," Ari said.

"Okay, great," I answered back nervously.

We ran harder, with Ari and Evelyn ahead of me.

"Ah look up," Ari said. "There it is—the exit plank, the door."

"The door to where, exactly?" I asked.

"We will end up in the backyard of an antique store on Muzik Street, about three blocks off Taksim Square," Ari replied.

"Okay, great," I said. "So, let's get the hell out of this dirty underground tunnel."

Ari hit the light switch on the side wall next to the dropdown ladder. He turned to smile, but we heard noises and voices from above—and his smile faded.

"This is real bad, we are in trouble, my friends. They must have wounded my friend back there and forced him to talk. We have no choice, let's just deal with it...I will go up, me first."

As Ari was about to push open the door above his head, the door was opened for him.

"Out, get out now," one of the men said. "Keep your hands high. No games or you're all dead."

Ari turned to me and whispered, "So sorry. We have to kill these guys immediately or they'll kill us."

Shouting came from above, "Out! Out now! Stop talking!" the guy yelled.

Ari started to head up as I reached for Evelyn.

"Evelyn, the pens, let's activate them now."

"Okay," she whispered.

"On the way up, we'll use the wood plank to tap our pens," I whispered into her ear. "Then click twice—you know the drill. If we screw up, everything we've worked for will be lost and millions will die. We cannot let this happen."

"It will be alright, I'm going up after Ari. I'll do something to throw them off guard."

"Are you sure?"

"I'm sure, that's my specialty," she replied.

"Come on, move it down there!" a guy yelled.

"Coming, what's the rush anyway?"

Evelyn took out her pen on the way up, then tapped it on the solid wood plank.

As her foot reached the top, some guy said, "Ooh, look what we have here, a very purty wuman."

I then heard Ari say, "Who are you guys? What do you want from us?"

"Shut up or this gun will be in your mouth. Hey you, get your American ass up here."

"Okay," I said, "I have a bad knee, give me a moment."

I took my first step up the ladder, activated my pen, and stepped up to the outside. There were three guys waiting at the top. One huge, heavy dude was wearing a burgundy bandana. The other two were more moderately built, with tattoos and beards—they were the underlings. The big one commanded us to keep our hands up high as guns were pointed at us. Their pistols with silencers revealed to me this was a prelude to being killed. This was it: three to six seconds and one way or the other, it will be over. I was waiting for some signal from Evelyn.

"Hey guys, let's work this out," Evelyn said. "We have four hundred million American dollars at our hotel. It's only two blocks down that way. We were going to deposit this money into a bank tomorrow. It's all yours, if you just let us go."

Her plea gave us another few seconds to regroup, as the three assailants hesitated and looked at one another uncertain of their next step.

Ari added, "The hotel is only two blocks down that way. You're all so close to half a million euro."

"Shut up, American pigs," yelled the big guy.

I noticed the other two men seemed interested in the money, waiting for their fat boss to make a decision. Almost simultaneously, Evelyn clicked her pen, letting out a laser shot while the big man pointed his pistol at Evelyn. She missed. Ari went into krav maga offense mode as he stepped in on the big man. He blocked the hijacker's gun arm, and seamlessly followed through with a surgical strike to his Adam's apple.

The man's hands involuntarily reached up to hold his windpipe, but it was too late. His face turned pale and he dropped to the ground. Ari finished him off, bending down to drive a hammer fist into his heart.

I wanted to just watch the show, but it was my turn. I pointed the pen at one of the other guys. I hit the top and a laser beam shot out of the pen like a guided missile. It entered his chest, knocking him down in a fraction of a second. The other man ran off. We knew he could not be allowed to escape. I ran after him for about fifty feet, shouting "Stop!" He turned to me with his pistol in hand. I had no choice. The next pen click shocked him with the Taser. He was jolted and thrown back ten feet, collapsing to the ground. Smoke was hovering just above his chest. I walked closer, to inspect his body, and he was done, burned, and sizzled. His fingers were shaking uncontrollably, and his arms and legs were giving off waves of involuntary twitches. It was horrible. I grabbed his weapon to put him out of his misery, looking around to make sure no passerby was close enough to see.

I heard a voice inside my head say, *Stone, can you hear me? Do you think you could kill to protect America?* How could I forget that day back in Langley, Virginia, at the command center when Ashton tried to hypnotize me and raised that question. I had no choice; the poor guy was suffering. Anyway, if he survived, he could not be allowed to report back to his superiors, so I pulled the trigger to end his misery. I turned back the other way to check on Evelyn. She was frozen, but trying to come out of it, as she tentatively walked toward me. I reached out and held her trembling hands.

"Thank you, Evelyn, you were amazing," Ari said.

"And you, Ari," she replied.

"Where did you pick up that move against a guy with a gun?" I asked.

"I was a commando in the Israeli Defense Force(IDF).That was twenty years ago, but you don't ever forget the moves that once saved your life. No big deal," he said with a smile that revealed his smoke-stained teeth.

"No big deal? Give me a break," I said.

"Of course, it's always scary, just joking with you," he said.

"Well, certainly, I was scared shitless," I admitted. "When Evelyn went into the money thing, at that moment I cleared my head just enough to observe the overall scene: how far away I was from the guy, the aim of his gun, and the position of everyone else."

Police sirens sounded, it seemed I wasn't as stealthy as I thought I was out on the street.

"Enough," Ari said. "We need to call it a night. We all stay together tonight. Let's check into a little bed and breakfast. There's one about five minutes down that way."

We followed Ari to the As Hotel Taksim. It was nothing to write home about, but it served its purpose. We took a double connecting room, then walked up to the second floor. After checking out the rooms and knowing we would be staying for sure, we settled in. We each took turns in the bathrooms. Ari took out a small flask of scotch, just enough for a healthy shot for the three of us.

"Let's call it a night," he said. "Tomorrow is a big day, starting with my friend at the bank."

"Absolutely," Evelyn and I said at the same time.

"I'm wiped out," Ari said.

"Yeah and I need a good breakfast before we head into that kind of action," Evelyn added.

"Me too, I'll be starving, but no more room service for me," I said.

CHAPTER **27**

After being unable to sleep for over two hours, I gave up and opened my eyes. I let my mind wander, playing my usual mind game of "What will I think of next?" whenever I couldn't sleep. I had gone to sleep anxious, and no doubt that was one of many reasons why I was restless. Then my mind wandered. I saw a table with six people and a waiter serving large plates of food. In each plate were pieces of chicken, meat, and fish with broccoli and carrots. I was observing each person to see what their first forkful was going to be. I focused on our freedom to choose, the ability to decide.

I then had a flashback. It was of my father representing an Asian client in court. The man had admitted to mugging an older woman and running off with her purse in broad daylight. Once a year, my father took on a case without a fee to help those in need. That was my father's choice. And the Asian guy—it was his choice to injure an old woman for a quick buck.

I needed to get some sleep, but it just was not happening. I sat up and took a deep breath, only to slowly drop back to the mattress and close my eyes. But my eyes popped open again as my mind shifted to that Friday five years ago in Manhattan when I walked into the flower store and gave Ammi my card, looking for business. I recalled the next meeting when I had made that life-changing decision. It was my choice to accept Ammi as a client, to compromise myself. It was a personal choice that changed the course of my life forever.

I dozed off with that thought and woke up in the morning thinking about the importance of making choices in life and how they have affected not only my life, but also my family and my friends. Who knows, maybe I even indirectly helped my clients to move their unreported cash into the hands of weapons dealers.

We all headed down for breakfast, and then walked to the bank. A huge sign read: "The International Bank of Turkey." The door was opened for us from the inside. We kept going in until Ari stopped us.

"You guys stay in the lobby until I come back to get you," he said. "I need to talk with the manager first."

"Okay, Ari," I said. "Give us the signal and we will join you."

Ten minutes or so went by before Evelyn tapped my knee, noticing Ari's signal first.

"Bob, it's time to join the party," she said.

"Ah, okay," I waived to Ari as he, in turn waved us in.

The intros began in the bank supervisor's office.

"Ismael Najeer," Ari began. "Please say hi to my American friends, Bob Savemoor and Evelyn Carver."

"Any friend of Ari's is a friend of mine," Ismael said. "So, hello, Bob and Evelyn."

Evelyn did her usual charming hand extension, coupled with that killer smile of hers. To show respect, I stood up and then turned to Ismael.

"*Merhaba,*" I said. I paused and added, "*Ben teşekkür ederim,* Mr. Najeer."

Ari looked at me with amazement. Ismael melted with my ability to say "Hello there" followed by "I thank you" in Turkish.

"Mr. Stone, we only have about fifteen minutes," Ismael said. "But I will extend to you extra time. How can I help you both today?" he asked in a low tone as he leaned in and moved his head over his desk toward me.

"Mr. Najeer, large blocks of money have been moving from New York to the Royal Bank of Toronto and from there, to the International Bank of Turkey at this branch. We are talking about four hundred million, maybe more. There is a sophisticated plot in progress against our homeland. It's our job to protect America and her allies. I need to know about this account here in your branch—the authorized signers, who requested the incoming transfer. If the money has already been transferred out of here, I must know where did the money move to? . . . Mr.

Najeer, I am worried that this flow of money is going to be used to acquire serious weapons, putting millions of people at risk."

Then Ari said, "Naj, we must determine who will be the seller and buyer of these weapons and what is the ultimate act of terrorism being planned."

"By the way," I said. "We already know that Omar Korbachi and another man named Hassam Al Boudeh Kandallah, are involved."

Okay, Bob, let me get to the point," Ismael requested.

Please continue, Mr. Najeer," I said.

Those two are global players in the arena of weapons deals. No one will talk about it, but—" Najeer paused to write down, *It is known that these two have a lock on the global market for germs and bacteria.* He ripped up his memo into about forty tiny pieces.

I noticed his hands became shaky, his lips were clenched, forcing twin lines between the top of his nose to the middle of his forehead. *He became quite a different man from ten minutes ago,* I thought. I could see that Ari had lost control of the conversation.

I backed off and asked, "Ari, I respect your judgement, what should we do next?"

My dear friend, Ismael," Ari said. "Can you show us the Korbachi account now right here in your office?"

Yes, but it must be fast. You know what I mean, Ari?"

Understood."

There was a two-second pause in which no one said a word. It seemed like two hours. Ismael pulled up the Korbachi account on his monitor. K&K Exports, LLC, popped open and the account number was a match from the Toronto bank's outgoing wire transfer information. I leaned forward, as did Evelyn. The money trail revealed one transfer for $200 million into this K&K Exports account. Then there were two outgoing transfers three days ago: $100 million went back to a Manhattan law firm's escrow account (Combs & Walker), and the other $100 million was wired out to the Bank of Japan.

I was in a daze. We were totally confused. Ari looked baffled. Evelyn was speechless.

"What the fuck? The Bank of Japan?" I exclaimed, losing my cool. "That New York City law firm is Laura's office! Let me see that, please."

I stood up, moving closer to the monitor.

Bank of Japan," I read. "Wait, Ari, may I—"

Sure, Stone, go ahead."

Mr. Najeer, please show us the original signature cards when this account was opened," I requested.

He hit two keys and there it was, Kandallah, Korbachi, and one more cosigner, Tomoyuki Togaki.

"Any idea who this Japanese authorized signer is?" I asked.

"No idea," Ismael said. "But his name was added on recently, not when the account was originally opened up."

"When?" I asked.

"This account was opened about ten years ago," Ismael replied. "TT was added only about eleven months ago."

"TT?" I asked.

"Oh, I mean Tomoyuki Togaki," said Ismael.

Evelyn kicked my leg behind the desk. I knew what she had in mind. *How could Ismael know this guy so well to call him by a nickname of TT?* Ari's face turned white, he picked up on Ismael's slipup.

"So, this one hundred mil moved to the Bank of Japan. What branch and to what account number?" I asked.

"I need to wrap this up, I have no further information," Ismael said very nervously.

"Come on, Naj," Ari said. "You and I have been close friends for years—help us, help save lives."

Ismael's forehead had beads of sweat dripping down onto his thick, black eyebrows and landing on his cheeks. His eyes were dilated—something was going on and it was weird. Something was definitely wrong here.

Look, there's a Bank of Japan branch down the street. Go there and check out account number BOJ-99111334-44. Now, this discussion is finished, my friends," Ismael rattled off that account number quickly before getting up and leaving the room abruptly.

Ari said, "That original fifteen-minute meeting became thirty-five minutes. It was time to go anyway."

Evelyn and I went to a different bank employee to open our new account for EB Partners, LLC. This was quick. It was absurd how easy it was to open an account with little or no documents as to the business name.

***

Soon after, we met back up with Ari just outside the bank near the front entrance. We walked after about six blocks and Ari took us to a quiet café with a small outside garden, a perfect spot to talk. The cool and calm Ari was noticeably affected by this new twist in the money trail.

The Bank of Japan," Ari mumbled as he shook his head in confusion.

It was clear that his friend, the trusted bank supervisor, was either more involved or knew much more. Turkish coffees were ordered. None of us had any concrete ideas and no desire to talk just yet. For me, I felt that undercurrent of danger again as it rose like a fog creeping in. How weird, since the weather was sunny with near perfect temperature. I had never been more afraid to pursue something, to follow through. My next step was not clear this time.

"Bob, I know that look," Evelyn said. "You're a dead giveaway when you get into your deep-thinking mode. So, I have an idea."

"Shoot. Let's hear it because, frankly, my brain is at a dead end," I said.

Ari shrugged his shoulders and flapped his hands in agreement. He was without a doubt deeply troubled by his friend Ismael.

"Clearly the key question was what he knew about the Japanese guy he referred to as TT, what was the nature of Japanese involvement in this scenario?" Evelyn started. "So, I will walk into the Bank of Japan and look for an employee sitting at one of those service desks. Hopefully, I'll connect with what I believe to be a kind and cooperative person."

"Oh, and how does that happen?" Ari asked.

"Evelyn has an amazing instinct for people and connecting the dots," I replied.

Ari looked up at me and tilted his head with doubt to seem like he was saying in code, *What a crock of shit.*

"Evelyn, keep going please," I said, ignoring Ari.

"Okay, Bob," she continued. "I'll tell the bank employee that a customer of mine has an account at the bank and intends to transfer two hundred million into my bank account, but the money must come from Tomoyuki Togaki's account. To avoid any issues, I wanted to be sure there was enough money in the account, without asking for specific balance info."

"It's beginning to sound interesting, but what's the end game here?" Ari asked.

"Yeah, Evelyn, I love the approach but what's next?" I asked.

"Honestly, I'm not sure," she replied. "But my gut is telling me to confide in the employee, or a supervisor if need be, about a very delicate situation. I may mention to them that I am with a special department of the U.S. Department of Homeland Security and we are aware of a plot to kill massive amounts of people. I may even mention World War Two and all the innocent people killed on the islands around Japan to end the war."

I became impatient and said, "Why the hell are you wasting our time with all this open-ended nonsense?"

She snapped back and replied, "It's my intuition. Being open-ended gives one room to talk, to maneuver maybe enough wiggle room to reveal some morsel of information in the flow of conversation. I'll then ask about recent payments coming out of the Togaki account." Evelyn countered and threw it back to us, "That's all we have guys, unless you two have another approach?"

Somehow her strategy fit nicely without all of us walking in and creating a scene.

"I'm good to go with this plan. Ari, what about you?"

"Yes, all we can do is to calmly go fishing and see what we catch, maybe a small bonito," he said forcing a smile.

"Speaking of fish, I'm starving," I said.

"Let's eat now, guys. I'm not walking into that bank hungry and cranky," Evelyn said.

"Agreed, Evelyn," I said. "Let's order now but eat light. You need to be alert for your Bank of Japan meeting."

"Agreed," she said.

Lunch was served fast. We kept it light, with only a few small starters of hummus, baba ghanoush, olives, and warmed pita. Perfect. We ate quietly in a working lunch without talking, just thinking and more thinking. It was tense.

"Don't worry, Bob," Evelyn reassured me. "I'll walk away with something—trust me," she said with confidence.

Once again, Evelyn was stepping up as needed. That was her calling card: in Toronto; at the JFK airport with the LT pen confrontation at security check-in, shooting the LT pen at the guys back in Taksim Square; and now.

"Hold on," I said. "Levine just sent me a text." *Stone, can we talk now?* I read it to Evelyn and Ari.

"That sounds urgent, Bob," Evelyn remarked.

"We'll find out faster than you can blink your—" I said as my cell phone rang.

"Hey, tax man," Levine said when I answered. "How's it going?"

"Not sure yet," I replied. "What's up, Levine?"

"Scott and Jaab were cleared for HPAT 21 service," Levine replied.

"That's it?" I asked. "You're not calling just for that, now are you?"

"Give me a moment," Levine said. "You sound nervous. Chill out."

"Listen, Levine," I said. "Istanbul is not exactly being in Sedona, Arizona, sitting in a hot tub—this place is tense. So, get to the real reason for your call. None of us have time for—"

"Understood, Stone," he said, cutting me off. "You better get yourself under control, though, I have never observed you sounding so wired. That's how fuckups happen, so please take it down a few notches."

"Okay, you're right," I said and shut up.

He then said, "You know what, I'll put Scott on the line."

There was a shuffle as Levine switched to speakerphone.

"Hello Bob, it's Scott."

"Hi, happy to hear you're now an HPAT 21 agent."

"Thanks," he replied. "I need to bring you up to date on money in motion. I just remembered and told Mr. Levine that there is another bank account where large amounts of money were transferred to. It's in the Netherlands, specifically Amsterdam. It's an offshore trust account that escapes taxation in Canada and the USA. The Amsterdam National Bank, NE—"

"Great piece of info," Levine said.

"Keep going, Scott," I said on edge.

"Okay," Scott continued. "My friend at the Netherlands-based bank contacted our homeland security office to inform us that close to three hundred mil was transferred out from an account in his branch to the Bank of Japan last week."

I could only think of one word and that was *shit*.

"Ari, your friend Ismael left out this one key fact," Scott said.

"It's possible Ismael could not have known about that," Ari retorted.

"Hold on and listen," Ari insisted. "As you know, Levine, earlier today we met the bank supervisor, Ismael Najeer, at the International Bank of Turkey. He told us the money went from his bank directly into an account at the Bank of Japan. There's also a location here in Istanbul. But he did leave out any info on that Amsterdam offshore trust account Scott just mentioned."

"I believe my dear friend Naj has turned. He's covering for people, hiding money transfers, and who knows what else. Maybe the poor guy had no choice?" Ari said, wiping his eyes with a crumpled-up napkin while slowly walking away from the table.

"Levine, can you look into a guy named Tomoyuki Togaki and check out this Ismael Najeer?"

"Of course, Stone," Levine said.

"Scott, excellent info," I said. "Please say hi to Jaab for me."

"Will do, Bob," Scott replied.

I heard Ari's phone get a text notification as he paced back, getting closer back to our table. Our quiet lunch was about to become crazy.

"We have a green light to meet Korbachi," Ari said. "Meeting is set for tonight. That's the good news, but we need to get on a flight to Bodrum in three hours. We meet Korbachi at eight o'clock at the Tower Rock City Bar."

"Where the hell is Bodrum?" Evelyn blurted out, standing up.

"It's the equivalent of Montauk in your Long Island area. It's a vacation resort area, about an hour or so flight from where we are now in Istanbul. It's actually a beautiful place, unfortunately not for playing spy games to save the world from terrorists."

"Okay, sounds sweet, Ari," Evelyn said. "But why Bodrum?"

"Simply because Korbachi is on vacation over there and because he's a prick who insisted we go to him."

"Maybe I should go shopping for a bathing suit," I said sarcastically. I was pissed.

"Bob, that gives Evelyn time to pull off her wild goose chase at the Bank of Japan," Ari said.

"You're right, Ari," Evelyn said. "I'm ready, guys. It's time to go fishing for some fresh sushi."

"Very cute, Evelyn," Ari said.

"Yeah, real cute guys," I said. "Let's pay the bill and get going."

The waiter came to collect payment. He looked so much like my client Darmush Khan that I looked at him three times before paying—a peculiar coincidence. It reminded me to check back with Levine about Darmush being held in the basement back in New York. It might be the time to press Darmush for critically important information.

I texted Levine after tipping the waiter. While we walked out, I was lagging behind while texting. I had to jog a little to catch up with Ari and Evelyn. We all walked over to the Bank of Japan, impossible to miss with its dark-stained wooden walkway, hanging slightly over a lily pond with brightly colored flowers and fish calmly moving around that occasionally broke through the surface looking for food.

"Wish me luck, guys," Evelyn said, walking toward the lily pond.

"Evelyn, wait," I said. "Let me go with you, I won't say anything more than a hello and then you take over."

"I can agree with that, Bob," commented Ari.

"Thanks, Ari" I said. "Evelyn, please?"

"Okay, okay," Evelyn caved. "Let's go already."

"Ari, what about you?" I asked.

"I'll go back to the café for a Turkish beer," Ari replied. "Come back to get me when you wrap it up. I need to be alone. I may even call Najeer to ask him to meet with me while you guys hit the Japan bank."

"Good idea, Ari," I said. "Maybe you can learn more from Ismael away from his bank," I suggested.

We shook hands. He gave us each a warm, double-handed shake. I took a good look at Ari as he walked away, his style, his confident walk, the star-shaped earring—his overall swagger was indicative of a man who has been around the block many times.

***

Evelyn's hair was up today and shaped into a bun for more of a business look, coupled with a high-neck dark navy-blue blouse and beige pants.

"Okay, Stone," Evelyn said confidently, "Let's get going."

"Sure, I'm following your lead—it's your show."

The revolving doors took us into the antique lobby area.

A greeter approached us and said, "*Kon'nichiwa,* hello. How can I help you?"

He was a well-dressed, thin Asian man with jet black hair combed over to one side and wearing a pin-striped power suit.

"We need to sit down with someone," Evelyn responded. "We have some service questions, please."

"Do you wish to open a new account?" asked the greeter.

"Well, that's a possibility," Evelyn answered. "But for now, we have a few simple questions first."

She took control and started walking over to a bank representative. I followed her toward the back end of the lobby. The greeter was a bit aggravated, trailing behind us and mumbling some Japanese under his breath. Sensing this, I touched Evelyn's shoulder and whispered to her.

"Slow down, let the guy go first."

The greeter very gracefully edged in front of Evelyn, turned, then smiled as if to say, *Thank you for respecting me.* He took us to the same desk that Evelyn was headed toward and said something to the representative in Japanese before leaving us.

"Hello, my American friends," said the bank representative. "I am Mrs. Tokata. What can I do for you?"

She was a very professional-looking woman who seemed to be about sixty years old. The time was right for Evelyn to step up and I had no doubt that she would do just that. I sat back to observe as everything began to unfold.

"I am Evelyn Carver and my associate here is Bob Savemoor," she paused as introductory handshakes ensued. "We are in the exporting business together. One of our most important customers has an account at this bank branch and is about to transfer a very large sum of money to our business account."

Just at that moment, a tiny red spider was walking across the desk. As I went to swipe it away, Mrs. Tokata stood up and very firmly said, "Please do not touch that spider. Let it be. You see, I value all forms of life."

This was an absolute dream come true for Evelyn's desired approach.

"So sorry," I said and put down my hand. "I understand."

Evelyn continued on, "Mrs. Tokata, I truly agree with you. Life is a precious thing."

Genius, I thought. And with that mutual common ground, the bonding process kicked in.

Evelyn resumed, "Basically, we are here to avoid any potential problems with a shortage of funds with one of our top customers. With permission and without specifics, we would like to know if your customer with account BOJ-99111334-44 has enough available funds to cover a two hundred million-dollar transfer?"

"That's not a typical question," Mrs. Tokata paused and looked up at Evelyn. "As you probably know, I cannot discuss specific balance information with you for reasons of privacy." She paused to click her computer mouse and typed away on her keyboard until the account hit the monitor. "It is a well-known account at this bank, but in general terms I can tell you this: Three days ago, there was enough money to cover that large transfer, but not at this time."

Evelyn took a full deep breath, exhaled slowly, and then looked at me. We both knew this was the moment of truth. Somehow, some-way, we had to know where this money went to. We needed Mrs. Tokata to help us. This was the opening Evelyn was referring to during lunch. Evelyn was going to bridge the discussion into the real issue of terrorism and I was fascinated to learn how.

"So, Mrs. Tokata," Evelyn started. "How is it you work here in Istanbul? Why not back in Japan, or anywhere else?" she asked.

She leaned back and then forward in the black leather swivel chair. I sensed Evelyn hit on something, noticing that Mrs. Tokata had difficulty expressing herself but still opened up to us.

"Most of my family and my grandparents were either killed or seriously deformed in nineteen-forty-five from your American atomic bombs," she said sadly. "I was born in nineteen-fifty-two, so now you now know my age. Two years later, my parents moved to Hiroshima during the start of the rebuilding since land was very cheap at the time. Growing up in Hiroshima during the postwar rebuilding phase was terrible. The national humiliation was huge. I saw my people ill and dying slowly from radiation poisoning. Because of all this, I grew up understanding and believing that life must be sacred. But the mental anguish, the depression and people dying from radiation years later, the bitterness and all the talk of vengeance one day from losing the war in such humiliation . . . it just never ended. I could not stay in Japan. I had to start a new life away from all of those self-destructive attitudes."

Evelyn was a genius, having used a brilliant and sincere approach. It was time for her to segue into our search for terrorists to prevent massive death and destruction and appeal to Mrs. Tokata's value for all life forms.

"Mrs. Tokata, I'm so sorry about your family and for what happened to your people," Evelyn said sincerely. "It's hard to understand why we humans have been so destructive toward one another throughout history. It's way before my time, but you know that Japan's military during the war was brutal. The key is to try to avoid this brutality in the future and the future is now." She had tears that were slowly streaming down her face.

Mrs. Tokata walked around her desk to embrace Evelyn. She returned to her desk and turned her back to us to cry privately, dipping her face into both her hands. This emotional breakthrough must have created a scene because another bank employee came over to Mrs. Tokata to see how she was doing.

She regained her composure and said, "I'm sorry, please excuse me for that. Is there anything else I can help you with at this point?"

If Evelyn didn't pop the question in the next three seconds, I was ready to start talking. I did a slow count of *one, two,* and as I hit *three* Evelyn leaned forward.

"Mrs. Tokata, we really appreciate all your help," Evelyn said. "Thank you for your time, information, and sharing your story with us. We are on the same page on many issues—especially on the matter of life and death. And now it's time to explain to you a few more things about us. Most importantly, we seriously need your help."

I could see that Mrs. Tokata suddenly looked anxious.

"My colleague and I are not in business together, but we do work together," Evelyn continued. "You see, we are with a special undercover crime unit of America's Internal Revenue Service linked to homeland security. It's called HPAT 21. I am sure you know that both our countries' banking systems and over one hundred other countries have cooperation arrangements that track and notify one another when there are large and unusual transfers of money around the world."

Evelyn led into that perfectly, giving away a small bit of information to appear open and to gain Mrs. Tokata's trust.

"Mrs. Tokata, we are aware of a very real terror threat," Evelyn said. "We have followed the money trail from New York, to Toronto, and now to Istanbul, which has led us to your bank in this branch. Millions have been moving around internationally over the past few weeks. We already know some of the players. We have reason to believe this money is intended to purchase deadly weapons. Why? To kill hundreds of millions of Americans, beginning with about three million in Manhattan, and eventually people from other nations will surely be at risk. We are here and it's the end of the line for us right now. We don't know where and when this mass killing will take place, but we must connect the dots immediately to prevent it. "We know you will help us if you can since you, your family, and your people experienced this massive loss of life and suffering in 1945, and the suffering and death continued on for so many years. Is there anything, anything you can tell us about this account? The authorized signers, or any minor thought that could lead to more important information? Most importantly, to whom did the last large transfer of funds from this account go to? It's life or death, Mrs. Tokata, and I know where you stand on that point."

It was time for Evelyn to stop talking. It was silent now. Watching and waiting for some response from Mrs. Tokata was almost painful.

"I am a very proper person with strong morals," Mrs. Tokata said. "You lied to me. How can I trust someone who begins with a lie? I suppose you could not find a way to be direct, but saving lives is the ultimate act of honor. This is your objective, is that correct?"

"Yes, completely," Evelyn replied. "This is what we do—we risk our lives to save others.

"I do not know how much I can help you," Mrs. Tokata said. "I am not a higher up in this bank, but I will try my best."

The little red spider now tip-toed its way across the desk again. This time, I didn't make a move as Mrs. Tokata gave me a watchful look, challenging me. She edged her rolling chair to the left and looked back at the account on her computer monitor. She motioned for us to lean in and look as if to speak was an admission of guilt. She scrolled down. The account profile popped up:

Bank account name: Committee to Rebuild Hiroshima
Authorized Signers: Kano Togaki, Founder
Tomoyuki Togaki, Treasurer
Konar Togaki, Vice President
Omar Korbachi, Secretary, dtd 1/1/2011
Date account opened: October 1, 1945

Evelyn resumed her questions. "Who are the first three signers?"

"Kano was one of the highest-ranking generals aboard the USS Missouri battleship during Japan's surrender. He was one of the original architects who designed and rebuilt Hiroshima," Mrs. Tokata replied. "There have been rumors for decades that Kano Togaki took bribes from construction companies during the first three years after the war ended. They became a very wealthy and influential family. Tomoyuki is their youngest son. He has been the mayor of Hiroshima for the last two years. He took over the account many years ago. In nineteen-eighty-nine, when our honorable Emperor Hirohito died, Kano Togaki fell apart, as they were very close. So, his grandson Konar, named to honor his great-grandfather, took over this account. When Kano became the mayor, the financial responsibility for this bank account went to Konar."

There was a brief silence.

"What else do you know about this Konar?" I asked. "Have you ever seen him or met with him?"

"He has been to this branch each month for the last nine months," Mrs. Tokata replied, checking the account records. "But never prior to nine months ago. He meets with our branch manager. I did talk with him about two months ago. He is a very high-strung twenty-eight-year-old with a nasty attitude."

"Thank you, Mrs. Tokata," I replied. "Oh, and who is this branch manager?"

"Ah, his name is Doman Kandallah," she answered.

Evelyn and I almost fell off our chairs with this sudden wakeup call that this Bank of Japan branch manager was obviously related to Hassam Al Boudeh Kandallah, from the Royal Bank of Toronto—the guy who we vividly remembered trying to kill his own bank's branch manager, Scott.

Evelyn shifted the conversation and said, "Can we please go over the last six months of transactions?"

Again, there was no vocal response. Only Mrs. Tokata's hands were in motion. She turned the monitor toward us again. It was easy to see various transfers totaling $300 million that came in from the Amsterdam National Bank's offshore trust account, the same account that Scott had just told us about on the phone. The money was wired into the account at the Bank of Japan. Finally, $285 million was moved three days ago from this Bank of Japan branch to an account named the Japan Payback Fund."

Evelyn responded, "Mrs. Tokata, where is this Japan Payback Fund account based?"

"I don't know, but let me scan this branch account listing," she replied.

The payback account came up on her monitor. It was an original account established right here nine months ago.

"What else can we see on this account?" Evelyn probed gently, sensing our time was running out.

"The authorized signer was only Konar Togaki," Mrs. Tokata replied. "Very unusual. You never see only one signer for not-for-profit accounts."

I was getting impatient and couldn't wait any longer.

"Please, let's go back to the three hundred million and then the two hundred eighty-five mil that went out," I asked hurriedly. "What happened to the other fifteen million?"

She scrolled and dropped down through the account's pages on her monitor and spoke.

"A wire transfer went out to Omar Korbachi for fifteen million dollars," Mrs. Tokata replied. "To where, though? Wait—ah, I see it. It went out to an account in his family name—actually, to an offshore trust account, the Korbachi Family Trust, based in Australia."

Two things then took place almost at the same time. Ari texted me, *Wrap it up, getting late. Must get to airport for flight to Bodrum!* Then a man approached me from behind and put a hand on my shoulder as he began to speak.

"I'm the bank manager," he said. "Is everything alright here?"

I carefully turned around and realized he was staring at Mrs. Tokata. I was caught way off guard, but I managed to say, "I want to compliment you on your professional banker here, Mrs. Tokata. We were discussing opening up personal and business accounts here, with possible transfers in for close to four hundred million euros."

"How nice," he said with a weird smile. "Well, I'm Mr. Kandallah, the manager here, and you are?"

"I'm Bob Savemoor and this is my partner, Evelyn Carver."

Evelyn did her usual appealing hello, always breaking the ice. And right now, the ice was thick.

"Tell me, Bob and Evelyn," he said. "It's quite unusual to start a new banking relationship with such large deposits. What are you looking to do?"

"To be perfectly honest with you, we are in the business of buying and selling weapons," I replied. "We have extremely wealthy backers. We are looking to make a substantial purchase if we find the right weapons. You see, our clients have very specific needs."

"Ah, I understand, Mr. Savemoor," he replied.

Evelyn supported my statements by saying, "Mr. Kandallah, Bob and I import and export specialty items, and one group of clients need very special and hard to find items. That's the expertise we bring to the table, our clients rely on us to gain access to their weapons of choice."

"Well," he said, "we cannot deal with such customers. We could never open an account for the purpose of buying and selling weapons." He abruptly turned his back on us and walked away.

"I understand, sir," Evelyn replied. "And of course, thank you again, Mrs. Tokata. You are truly an asset to this bank."

We sensed our time was up. We thanked Mrs. Tokata again as she handed Evelyn her business card. We left the bank lobby calmly, but inside we felt the urgency build.

CHAPTER 28

Wwe exited the Bank of Japan knowing that somehow, we needed to learn more about Konar Togaki, possibly even meet him. I texted Ari that we had just left, and he instantly replied, *Meet me where we had lunch and move it.*

We were back at the café in a short walk. Ari was not sitting in the outside area where we had lunch. Evelyn elbowed me.

"I know, I get it," I said cautiously.

We were set up. We had walked right into the enemy's hands. Suddenly, we were surrounded by about ten gunmen. Three approached us, one holding a pistol to my head while the other two handcuffed me and then Evelyn.

Another four guys were escorting Ari into an empty shop a few feet ahead of us, his face was bloodied, and his eyes were like slits from his face swelling up. His hands were tied behind his back. They pushed him to the ground, one guy holding his head back. The gunmen demanded our cell phones, searching our pockets placing them on a table.

Time was frozen. The henchmen kept us waiting, *but for what?* Then the unthinkable happened. The Bank of Japan's branch manager, Doman Kandallah, appeared holding the decapitated head of Ismael in his hand. I turned away only to see Evelyn throwing up.

Ari was distraught and yelled out, "Why, why?"

He was struck in the face by one of the gunmen, forcing his head to jerk back.

Doman started to speak. "I know all about you two," he said to me and Evelyn. "I know what you did in Toronto. My brother, Haas, told me you were spying at his bank in Toronto and that you took Scott McCann with you to America. You two work with the U.S. Department of Homeland Security. You are here to buy weapons, so you said."

I did not respond, so Doman approached Evelyn.

"You are a very pretty lady," he said to her. "Why would you waste your time here in Istanbul? No doubt you are also an American spy," he said with gritted teeth, spitting to the ground. He held up Ismael's head when Evelyn didn't reply. "Talk to me or the next head I will be holding will be your friend's."

Doman rotated his neck, looking over to me. I blinked my eyes rapidly and swallowed even though I had a terribly dry mouth. Evelyn still did not reply. Doman turned back to Evelyn and waited. There was a pause. Somehow, I had to defuse the situation. I had to say something, anything, to break the hostility.

"Okay, I'll talk, Mr. Kandallah," I said.

"Ah, so start talking," he said.

"I'm not sure where to start, but—" I spoke slowly, using each word as a little bridge to my next thought.

"Come on, don't waste my time," Doman said.

"Sorry, you are right," I said. "First, I want you to know that we are here to make peace and to stop what we anticipate will be a global disaster. We believe terrorists are planning to use weapons designed to kill or poison millions of innocent people. It is my job to follow money moving around the world that's suspected of terrorist-related activities. I was hoping that the truth would prevail. I do not work with the American FBI, CIA—not even the U.S. Department of Homeland Security."

"Then who do you work with, Savemoor?" Doman asked.

"Mr. Kandallah, I am an international businessman, importing and exporting, ya know? Evelyn is my partner and our business converts cash from various currencies in exchange for cutting-edge weapons. We have very demanding clients, but they understand it's first-come-first-serve. I also work with the American military establishment, the specifics of which I'd rather not disclose to you, at least not right now."

"Tell me more," Doman demanded.

"I can tell you that your colleague Omar Korbachi will be arrested and brought back to the United States in about one hour." *I lied.* "We know he is in Bodrum. It's too late in the game, his arrest cannot be stopped. This is inside information and people pay me lots of money to know these things."

I must've been on to something, as Doman looked shocked.

"May I keep talking?" I requested.

"Go ahead, but I do not care for any games," Doman replied.

"Games?" I repeated. "Let me tell you this: We were going to buy weapons from Korbachi tonight, but someone else who you may know, a young man, intercepted the sale," I paused for effect. "Oh yes, his name is Konar Togaki. He contacted my friend over there," I said, pointing to Ari. "You should know that Konar wanted to buy weapons behind the back of Korbachi. Actually, Konar told us that we did not need to bother with Korbachi and that Korbachi did not want to be disturbed while he was on vacation in Bodrum. Mr. Kandallah, do you know this Konar?"

Doman was furious, but he chose not to respond, so I kept talking, hoping to get more traction.

"I do have an idea that will allow all of us to walk away from this mess as winners," I proposed.

"What are you talking about?" Doman asked.

"First, let's be reasonable," I said. "Kindly have your men untie all of us? We want to help Mr. Ahrdeni over there and we could use some water and food. If you can show me you are willing to negotiate, I may be able to save you and your brother, Haas, from going to jail."

Doman laughed and said, "Do you think I am an idiot? Send me and my brother to jail—maybe I should kill you right now."

"Don't laugh, my friend," I said. "You know that Scott, the branch manager from the Royal Bank of Toronto, escaped with us and came back to America to testify against your brother. Don't you realize that your brother will be in jail very shortly? Oh, I forgot to mention—we had better make some fast decisions here. You see, my people know exactly where we are, and attack drones are on the way."

I kept my mouth shut. The next person to talk would be the loser. Doman made a hand motion and we were untied. Evelyn went to Ari and lifted him off the ground to a chair. Doman sat across a table directly opposite of me, his armed guards standing behind him.

"Drinks please?" I asked, testing my credibility.

"They're on the way," Doman replied.

"I want her and my other friend to be at this table, too," I said, pointing to Evelyn and Ari. "We work together. We all make decisions together."

Evelyn and Ari were brought to the table.

"I have a proposition for you, Mr. Kandallah," I continued. "It will be an offer you won't want to refuse."

"I'll be the judge of that," Doman said.

I sensed that I had rattled him when I mentioned his brother, and even more so after I mentioned that Konar wanted to deal with us directly.

"Go ahead, Savemoor," he pushed me to talk more.

"It's time for me to reveal my other hat now. I'm really an agent of a special unit linked to the U.S. Department of Homeland Security. My superiors know all about you here and your brother at the Royal Bank of Toronto. We all know about the money trail, how it started with your brother in Toronto and that it relates to your bank here in Istanbul. It's dirty money intended to buy weapons to kill millions in our homeland. We are your only means of avoiding a long jail sentence. We are your way out. You see, we can and will protect you and your brother."

"Look around you, Savemoor," Doman said. "You're an idiot."

His guards stood at attention, raising their weapons up to attack mode.

"Did you know, Mr. Kandallah, that we have a treaty with the Turkish government's Ministry of Finance against terrorists laundering money?" I told him this without really knowing if it was true. I threw it in for good measure.

Doman did not respond.

"Did you also know that you and your brother have been on the radar for months as you allowed money transfers between your banks? Your time as a free man is just as limited as your brother's in Toronto. Now, all I want is for you tell me why the money went from Toronto to Istanbul, then to your Bank of Japan branch, and finally, into the Japan Payback Fund, which we know is also at your bank. I must know the real meaning and purpose of this 'payback' account. We need to know exactly what weapons Konar bought from Korbachi and for what purpose. Go ahead, call your brother. Ask him if he knows where his branch manager, Scott McCann is. No one here is in a rush," I laughed, then said again, "Go, call your brother."

"Okay, just a minute," Doman grumbled, walking away. He dialed his cell phone and started to pace around with one hand over his other ear. His hands started moving around like a ground crewmember directing planes on tarmacs. He slammed his fist on the nearest wooden table, followed by yelling and nasty-sounding Turkish words. He walked back toward me very slowly as my cell phone began to ring from the table across the room.

"Expecting a call, Savemoor?" Doman asked.

"Absolutely, it is my supervisor checking in with me," I replied. "If I do not answer, it's a problem for you."

"Go ahead, answer your call," Doman granted.

I had no idea who could be calling me, but it was great timing. I was so thankful to pick up and hear Levine.

"Hello, Stone, your tracking devices have been stagnant for too long, so I thought to check on you. What's going on?"

"Oh, not much, just enjoying the weather in an outdoor café. Actually, we need your help now."

"Get to the point," Levine said.

I explained the situation to Levine, including the lies I had added. I asked for his permission to give the Kandallah brothers protection from being charged with accounts of terrorism and money laundering against the USA.

"What do we get in return?" Levine asked.

"We will get all the info we need about Konar's purchase of weapons from Korbachi, details about a linked trust, the Japan Payback

Fund, more info about Konar Togaki, and hopefully the date and location of the pending act of terror."

"Don't cave in so fast," Levine responded. "Tell him their freedom
is a fifty/fifty possibility and that it has to go up the chain of command.
Meantime, you guys are in harm's way right now."

"Absolutely," I replied. I started saying more things to Levine just
to reinforce what I had bluffed about to Doman. "So, the attack drones
will reach us in ten minutes?" I paused. "Korbachi will be arrested in
about one hour?" I paused again. "Really, Kandallah will be arrested at
his home in Toronto later today?" I paused a last time. "Okay, I understand."

"Let's talk," Doman interrupted. "Let us make a deal. I do not like
Konar. He is a crazy young man dwelling on something that happened
seventy years ago."

Levine was still on the phone and had heard everything.

"Go ahead," He instructed me. "Make the deal, but no hostages. All
of you must be able to leave within one hour. Let me talk to him," Levine snapped.

I handed my cell to Doman, nodding my head to talk. "Go ahead,
please. My boss is waiting to talk to you," I said, turning the speaker
phone on.

"*Merhaba,* hello," Doman said.

"This is Mr. Levine from the U.S. HPAT 21 IRS anti-terrorism unit.
Can you hear me clearly?"

"Yes," Doman replied.

"I have no time to play games and I am sure you, too, are very busy.
I will get right to the point, sir," Levine said and continued. "Everything
Agent Savemoor told you is correct. You'll need to inform Savemoor of
all the details he has asked of you immediately. Oh yes, and you will
also help save a million or two lives. Then I will protect you and your
brother from being brought to America and sentenced to extensive jail
time. Sorry, but your other friends, Korbachi and Togaki, are history. I
cannot help them at this point. There must not be any hostages, you
let everyone there go without another scratch on them. You have

forty-five minutes. And finally, if there's no callback from Savemoor in the next forty-five minutes, then you and your brother, ah the infamous Kandallah brothers, and all your dirty money will come to an end. Please confirm that you understand me."

Doman handed the phone to me, walked a few feet away, and then turned around.

"It's a deal, Savemoor."

I took the phone off speaker and Levine said to me, "Our drones will be overhead in three minutes, so tell the bastard that it's more like now or never."

"Okay," I said and hung up. "Mr. Kandallah, I was informed that our drones will be above us in about three minutes."

I was thinking that maybe Levine was fooling around with me or putting the pressure on Doman, but there they were moments later. A formation of three drones in a triangular pattern became visible outside about thirty feet up in the sky.

"You people speak the truth, I see," Doman said as he looked out the window. "So, let us begin the process. First, how can I be sure my brother and I will be immune from any criminal charges or money laundering issues and not be connected to any terrorist plots against America?"

"We are trying to save millions of people from being killed. You and your brother are much less important, believe me. But trust me on one point, if you guys ever play the money transfer game again, or even come close to any acts of terrorism, you will both be dead meat. We will be watching you until the day you die. So, it's time for you to start talking."

With that I shut my mouth until he responded.

"Okay, Savemoor," Doman agreed. "Let's get started."

***

I had no idea how much time passed in that empty shop as we listened and interrogated Doman. His resistance seemed to fade more into relief as he provided detail after detail, almost as though he was glad to have a way out of the mess he had gotten into with his brother.

"Konar is planning a huge take down," Doman explained. "His vengeance runs so deeply that he's completely gone over the edge. An attack is happening sooner than you Americans can think. He has access to the remaining stockpiles of biological warfare germs from World War Two and plans to disperse them on August sixth into your water supply, starting with the east coast in New York City. My brother and I have worked together in our banks to make the funds available and accessible as needed. And Konar also gets help from Korbachi as well, rewarding him handsomely for his weapon deals. That's all I can tell you right now." He was visibly shaken having to admit it all out loud.

"Hass and I have been stuck in this mess for far too long," Doman concluded sadly. "I don't even know how we got so wrapped up in these terrorist plans . . . maybe it's a lifetime of exposure to this deeply-rooted vengeance, which has become part of us—"

"Well we're here to help now," Evelyn reassured him with her usual charming and calming ways.

"We'll do everything we can to protect you and your brother," she added.

"You keep promising that, but how?" Doman demanded."

"That's what we need to figure out," I replied. "We need to regroup, people. Get a solid plan in place. Let's get some grub and refuel."

"I know just the place," Ari said. "It's not too far from here."

"I'll have my guards escort us," Doman replied.

We all headed out of the shop together. Things were seemingly headed in the right direction at last here in Turkey, but I still couldn't shake the feeling that something has gone awry or is about to unfold. *What is missing from this mess of puzzle pieces? The equation is out of balance. It still doesn't add up.*

All my fears were confirmed in the next instant as Doman collapsed out of nowhere in front of us. Chaos erupted as the crowded streets of people began screaming and running in all directions. Everything seemed to move in slow motion as I struggled to figure out what was going on. Then I saw Doman's guards drag his lifeless body under the shelter of a nearby store. He had bled out from several gunshots, his eyes already lifeless.

"The boss is down! Shot down by a sniper," one cried into his phone. "This must not get out! Protect the funds! Protect the mission! We've been compromised!"

"We were followed," the other said to us. "They know, and they won't stop at him. You're running out of time, Americans. I'm sorry, but we cannot help you—"

CHAPTER 29

There was so much to handle and figure out, that I became lost in a mental haze. My breathing still hadn't slowed down, even though Ari had found us a safe place to duck into. I was in shock and Evelyn and Ari seemed to be as well. It was quiet for a long time as we each caught our breath. As the smog slowly evaporated in my brain, it clicked back into focus. I was now ready to express my thoughts.

"We know for sure that Konar has been reaching out to Doman, so we need a connection to reach him," I said. "What about our friend over at the Bank of Japan, Mrs. Tokata? Maybe she can help us reach out to Konar? She can call him and say that Doman Kandallah has been away on business and she apologizes for him not returning Konar's texts and calls lately. She then sets up a meeting with Konar and Mr. Kandallah, only it'll be with us instead. When we all meet Konar, we will inform him that we're with HPAT 21 and that his friend Doman was killed. We can blame it on Korbachi and check his reaction. Then we let him talk and we go from that point."

I paced as more details flooded my thoughts. "Oh, and Ari, you should call Korbachi to call off any meeting you may have set up. Tell the bastard that we decided to do a deal direct with a guy named Konar. Let them question each other and hopefully fight over us."

After a few glances to check in with one another, we all agreed on the plan.

"I'm calling Mrs. Tokata now," Evelyn said. "I'd rather not wait until tomorrow to call. Maybe she's working late."

"It's only four-fourteen now, Evelyn," I said. "So, go ahead, give it a try right now!"

"Sure, Bob. She reached into her pocket to pull out Mrs. Tokata's business card. After three unanswered rings, she ended the call.

"Try again," I suggested. "Maybe she stepped away from her desk."

"Okay, why not? One more call," Evelyn replied. "This time I'll put it on speaker phone."

Again, there were three unanswered rings. Using hand motions instead of words, Ari signaled to be patient and not to hang up. Suddenly, a voice chimed in.

"Hello, this is Mrs. Tokata, Bank of Japan, Istanbul. May I help you?"

"Ah, yes," Evelyn replied. "Hello again, Mrs. Tokata. This is Evelyn Carver."

"So nice you called, Ms. Carver," Mrs. Tokata said.

"Thank you, Mrs. Tokata, I truly enjoyed our meeting earlier today. You are a very special woman and I admire you so much. If you have the time, I would like to meet with you right away. We need to talk . . . it's so important. How about one hour of your time, please?"

"It's getting a bit late, but it seems to be urgent from your voice. Okay, where to meet?"

"Thank you so much, Mrs. Tokata," Evelyn replied. "Your safety is of our utmost concern, so please be careful to ensure you are not being watched or followed. We can come to you wherever you think is safest?"

"I cannot talk much," Mrs. Tokata replied. "Yes, please come and look for me at Doremusic, a guitar concept store on Mis Sk. Street, you know, Music Street. Look for a large glass window with a poster of Lennon and Yoko."

"Okay, great, we'll meet you there shortly. Just wait for us."

"Us?" Mrs. Tokata repeated.

"Yes, I have to bring Mr. Savemoor and another colleague. We are all friends and want the same thing. It's called 'trying to save the world.'"

Seems like that phrase has become our new tagline, I thought to myself, not a bad one.

"I understand," Mrs. Tokata said.

Evelyn wrapped up saying, "Great, see you soon."

"That went smoothly," I remarked as she hung up.

"Yes, but I was a bit nervous," Evelyn commented. "Anyway, thank you, Bob."

Ari jumped up from the table and directed us.

"Okay, my colleagues, we do not have time to relax any longer here. Let's get moving."

***

We approached the square and walked to the Doremusic store. Mrs. Tokata was already there waiting.

She bowed her head slightly, then looked up and said, *"Kon'nichiwa."*

We all returned the hello.

"Please, follow me," Mrs. Tokata said, taking control and walking briskly into a narrow alleyway that led to another street.

We went with it, keeping up with her pace. I turned around several times to check that we were not being followed. She walked into another path, taking us away from the main Taksim Square area. The path led into a small public park with olive trees and assorted multicolored flowers. About one hundred feet off to the left was a cave covered with ivy on the outside with many flat and rough stones inside. We sat down on the flat rocks inside it. This was our conference room. The sun emitted just enough light to allow for decent vision. I noticed Evelyn was gathering her thoughts to talk.

"Mrs. Tokata, there is so much to tell you," Evelyn said. "Earlier we all met with Mr. Kandallah after we left the bank. We learned that he and his brother, who is the manager at the Royal Bank of Toronto, have been diverting huge sums of money for global terrorist acts together, along with Omar Korbachi. Korbachi apparently receives a generous commission for making weapons deals. Mr. Kandallah agreed to work with us in exchange for him and his brother's immunity from being prosecuted back in America. However, just after he agreed to work with us, a sniper killed him."

"Oh my God, Kandallah killed!" Mrs. Tokata exclaimed. "And I am somehow right in the middle of all this insanity. How can it be?"

"It's much more complicated, Mrs. Tokata," Evelyn replied.

"What do you mean?" she asked.

"We believe that Konar has plans to seek revenge against the United States for the atomic bombs dropped on Hiroshima and Nagasaki. He wants to honor his great-grandfather, Kano the mayor of Hiroshima, and Emperor Hirohito. In less than two weeks, on August sixth, we believe Konar will attempt to drop some form of biological or germ-based weapons into the New York City water supply and whatever else he may be strategizing to seek revenge."

Mrs. Tokata's hands were shaking as she cried out shouting, "No, no, not again!"

She collapsed to the ground. I caught her just before her head hit the cool, rough cave floor. After several deep breaths, she quickly regained her composure as she had in the bank.

"How can I help?" Mrs. Tokata asked. "This cannot be allowed, it cannot happen. This act of vengeance, this payback, would never have made the emperor proud. I know because my family, my father particularly, had a relationship with the emperor's family. He never wanted war with America. He was surrounded by aggressive generals who felt that we had to bomb Pearl Harbor to make a statement after America blockaded our country's oil. He wanted to negotiate, but as the discussions between our two countries began, the war-hungry generals took over. Konar has no idea what he is about to do. He is so wrong, and he must be stopped. Evelyn, what do you want from me? How can I help us all?"

"We are as shocked as you are," Evelyn responded. "And time is very much against us. We need you to call Konar. After Mr. Kandallah was killed, we recovered his cell phone. Konar has been calling and texting him. Call Konar to apologize for Mr. Kandallah being nonresponsive to his calls. Set up a meeting for tonight or tomorrow morning at the Bank of Japan. Tell him Mr. Kandallah will be there. Can you do this, Mrs. Tokata?"

"A simple phone call," Mrs. Tokata nodded. "I have had to deal with much more courageous acts in my life, of course."

"It's more than a simple call," Evelyn explained. "We need to meet him. You must relax Konar and tell him that you have new bank clients interested in imports and exports with Japan and a special focus on Hiroshima."

"Okay, I can say this, as well," Mrs. Tokata agreed.

Evelyn turned to me and I understood the implication. I showed Mrs. Tokata the cell phone we recovered from Kandallah.

"Here, take his phone," I said. "Do you know the passcode?"

"Yes," she replied. "It should be the same as the one he uses at the bank."

"Then let's get out of here so we can pick up some cell service," Evelyn said, taking the lead out as we followed. "Call Konar from Kandallah's cell. Tell Konar that Mr. Kandallah is talking with Korbachi and that he cannot call now but asked you to set up this important meeting."

Mrs. Tokata took the cell phone and dialed Konar's number while walking out of the cave entrance, trying to catch a cell signal. The call was brief, we listened in and then Mrs. Tokata hung up politely, smiling to us.

"It's all set," she said. "Tomorrow morning, nine-thirty at the bank. He's actually excited about the meeting."

I went over to Mrs. Tokata, placing my two hands on her small, extended hand reaching for a handshake. I bowed my head instead. She was touched by my gesture of gratitude.

"So now how about some food?" Evelyn asked. "Where should we stay tonight?"

Mrs. Tokata replied to Evelyn before Ari or I could think. "My little home is right across the park and down on the right," she said. "It will be tight, but please sleep at my place."

"No, let's keep it safe and simple," Ari spoke up.

"What does that mean, Ari?" I asked.

"We've already put Mrs. Tokata at risk and we don't know if we're being followed. Let's all stay somewhere secure tonight. I know the owner of a small nearby bed and breakfast. Come on, let's go," Ari prompted us.

Evelyn and I glanced to one another.

"Sure, let's go with that B and B idea," I said.

"Thank you, so much for your help," Evelyn said to Mrs. Tokata. "You're helping to save so many lives."

"It is my pleasure to help," Mrs. Tokata replied humbly.

***

The place had a rundown look, as if not a penny had been put into it for about ten years. Everywhere you could see large red letters on wooden rectangular signs saying, *"Hoşgeldiniz."* We went for two rooms, one for Evelyn and Mrs. Tokata, the other room for me and Ari.

"Let's rest up, shower, and then meet in two hours for dinner," I said to Evelyn. "We'll knock on your door."

"Good idea. Works for me, Bob," Evelyn responded in a sluggish tone.

We were all exhausted. Istanbul had been a draining place. It had only been a couple days, but I needed to get out of here already. I had a feeling that it was time to leave before our luck ran out.

We went to our respective, no frills, plain-looking rooms. I collapsed onto one of the beds while Ari contacted Korbachi to call off the meeting he had set up, since it would soon be eight o'clock within the hour. I was in a very weird state of mind, extremely tired but not sleepy. When I closed my eyes, they hurt more. I was overcharged as if I had consumed two cups of strong Turkish coffee. Once again, I played my usual mental mind game of "What will I think of next?" to let my thoughts wander. My mind reoriented itself to think about tomorrow morning's meeting with Konar: *What is our end game? What are our alternative plans B and C if the conversation falls apart? Who will take the lead in talking with Konar?*

I didn't think we had the time to be indirect and play games. Rather, the situation had become dire, with less than two weeks to prevent this catastrophic payback from taking place. We had much more to gain and less to lose by being direct with our Japanese "friend."

Something else was on my mind. I felt that there was a key file yet to be opened in my brain. Something very important, but the data could not yet be accessed from my internal hard drive. This feeling had been silently gnawing at me ever since we landed here. I needed to calm down, so I closed my eyelids in one last effort to relax.

Clearly, I was also trying to allow my mind to open in search of whatever it was that had been trying to surface. Somehow, my thought process drifted back to our first night at the hotel here in Istanbul. The special news report regarding the status of germ and bacterial weapons around the world replayed itself. Then my brain took me to the documentary I had watched that addressed the factors leading up to the outbreak of World War Two and Japan's surprise attack on America's naval fleet in Pearl Harbor. I was drained by all this thinking, but it allowed me to slip into a mild respite.

After about fifteen minutes, I noticed my breathing became irregular. My left shoulder that I was leaning on began to sweat through my tee-shirt. I woke up startled and immediately checked the time on my cell phone. It was 7:29 p.m. Those three digits somehow struck a chord in me. I looked again after a few seconds elapsed and it was now showing 7:31 p.m. Laying back down on the bed, I focused on the intricate spider web located in the right corner of the room's ceiling. My eyes were glued to the spider wrapping its glue-like strands around a mosquito that had flown right into its web. Somehow, this scene chilled my soul warning us not to fall into a trap. I was thinking of the three numbers 731, not 729, and not 730. I had to focus on this much more.

I stood up to check my flight number. I checked my passport numbers, but again nothing made sense regarding 731.

I was still at a loss as to what the number 731 could mean, but I absolutely knew that I had either read or heard something involving these three digits before. I took a frustrated deep breath. While exhaling, I noticed a postcard on the nightstand next to my bed with the word *merhaba* written on it. I didn't really understand why but my instincts were to break down this word into two syllables: *mer* and *haba.* I was onto something, but I just couldn't make the overall connection, so I decided to search for "731" on the internet. The first five or six references were meaningless. I went to the next page, and then the next and saw more nonsense. I was about to let it go, but I decided to click on one more page and there it was. I knew it had something to do with a war.

I spotted a reference regarding general facts about Unit 731 during World War Two. Now the word *merhaba* clicked as well; the word reminded me of Harbin. Yes, that was it! Harbin, Heilongjiang, in the Northeast Manchuria region of China. This was where the Japanese scientists, led by Lieutenant General Shirō Ishii, had conducted horrific bacterial tests and performed surgical procedures without anesthesia on Chinese prisoners in the Unit 731 complex in Harbin. At least three thousand men, women, and children were infected with various diseases under the Imperial Japanese Army in attempts to create germs as weapons in the war.

Searching for a deeper connection, I asked myself some questions. *What are the possibilities that Konar still has access to similar biological germ weapons? Maybe even to those specific bacteria from Unit seven-thirty-one? And could they still exist and be useful after so many years?* It was worth a shot, so I decided to call Levine about our progress and our meeting tomorrow morning with Konar. At the risk of looking ridiculous, I also asked Levine to look into Unit 731 and the possible existence of the biological weapons from that era. I told him Doman had eluded to this same thought before he was shot down.

"You have some hell of an imagination, Stone," Levine replied. "But in keeping with your name, I'll leave no stone unturned. I will get back to you ASAP on this."

"Okay thanks," I said, laughing at his pun. "Oh yes—get back to me on how Laura and Wendy are doing with the law firm, too."

"Will do," he agreed. "Tomorrow is a big day here. Laura and her office manager, Janet, have done a great job getting closer to the top partners of the law firm. The firm's escrow account will be seized in the morning. The FBI is going in to arrest all the partners shortly afterward. Your client Darmush Khan remains in our custody. He has refused to talk, but his time is running out. Unfortunately, he may learn the hard way what suffering really means unless he starts to help us—and I mean fast."

"Okay, Levine," I said. "Keep me in the loop."

CHAPTER **30**

grabbed a moment to reflect. Time goes fast when you're having fun . . . that's a lie. Things are becoming more challenging by the hour and we're not having any fun. *At least the food around here is great,* I thought. Levine would be in heaven. Ari finally woke up.

"Deep sleep, heh, Ari?" I asked.

"Oh yes," Ari replied. "I could sleep longer, but I'm more hungry than sleepy now."

"Then let's eat," I said, a bit impatiently.

"Okay, Stone," Ari agreed. "Let's get the ladies and we'll eat here in this place. The owner's wife is a great cook. Also, better not to wander the streets tonight."

"They'll serve us food?" I asked.

"They will, if I ask nicely," Ari replied.

"Perfect, Ari," I said. "I'll tell the ladies to get ready."

Out into the hallway, I approached their door with a *"Merhaba"* sign on it.

"Merhaba," I said jokingly, then knocked lightly.

Evelyn's voice returned a *"Merhaba"* back to me.

"Ten minutes to dinner," I called through the door. "Okay?"

"Okay, Stone," Evelyn replied.

Walking into my room, Ari gave me a judgmental gaze.

"What's up with you?" I asked.

"Stone, you appear to be nervous. I know you by now. It's something you can't hide. You should work on concealing that."

"Enough," I said. He had triggered my hot button. "Frankly, I am edgy. Let's discuss it all over some food. Maybe stuffing my face with comfort food will relax me."

"Sure, Stone," Ari said. "So, let's get Evelyn and Mrs. Tokata now."

304 • ERIC J. ENGELHARDT

We all made our way downstairs past the small lobby. Ari led us to a private door. He was about to knock when a guy appeared with disheveled dark hair, a mustache, and a welcoming smile.

"Ah ha, *merhaba arkadaş*," he greeted Ari as his friend. "Please come in, *chaver*," he said, using Ari's native language of Hebrew.

"Tumir, meet my new friends Bob, Evelyn, and Mrs. Tokata."

"Hello, Tumir," I said. "Nice to meet you and thanks for your warm welcome."

Evelyn did her patented graceful hand extension and Mrs. Tokata bowed slightly. A sweet lady walked in, smiled, and simply waved her hand to further prompt us to come in. We followed.

"Say hello to my wife, Ayse," Tumir said.

Ari hugged her, and we exchanged greetings of *"Merhaba."* Tumir brought out a bottle of Turkish red wine, Yakut, a dry, deep-flavored wine that was delicious. We were famished. The homemade food was the best we've had so far during our Istanbul campaign.

Now I was looking for the right moment to discuss our meeting with Konar in the morning. Ayse brought out small cups of Turkish coffee and a tray of freshly made baklava dripping with syrup. Ari launched a gaze at Tumir and suddenly we were left alone. *Amazing silent communication skills,* I thought to myself. Here was my opening.

"So, friends, what's the end game with the Konar meeting tomorrow morning?" I asked. "What's our approach going to be?"

Ari turned to Evelyn and said, "You've been our lady luck with your intuition, what are you thinking, Evelyn?"

Ari and I remained silent.

"Come on, guys," she flippantly replied. "I defer to Mrs. Tokata."

Mrs. Tokata began, "There is no time to waste. My whole life has been based upon the principles of honesty and respect for life. We meet with Konar, introduce yourselves as whatever—right, you said HPAT IRS tax agents—tell him Mr. Kandallah was killed yesterday and that Korbachi is in big trouble. We also inform him that you've learned of his plot to payback America. You make it clear to him that this is his final opportunity to stop his crazy plot. I, as a fellow person of Japanese descent and a survivor of the Hiroshima aftermath, will tell him that he has the power to choose. I will appeal to him not to use biological weapons of death."

Each of us looked at one another, remaining silent. Mrs. Tokata was right. My instincts rose up, bringing me to stand with my hands firmly placed on the table.

"I totally agree with you, Mrs. Tokata, but what if he denies his involvement, or he admits it, but is not willing to change his campaign of mass killings?"

"You're right. That is the real dilemma," Ari said.

"One more point I need to mention," I said.

I just had to bring it up, so I described my thoughts about Unit 731 from World War Two and my hypothesis as to Konar's possible use of those germs, if they still even exist in Harbin, China. Mrs. Tokata began to feel nauseous, leaving the table and running to the bathroom around the corner.

"Just to smoke him out, I'm going to mention to Konar that we know about those bacterial weapons from World War Two," I said. "His reaction will be telling."

We called it a night, immediately after Evelyn ran after Mrs. Tokata. Ari and I said *yi geceler* and *teşekkür ederim* to our hosts, thanking them for their hospitality.

Back in our room, I did a quick mental review of our meeting set for tomorrow morning. It occurred to me that this guy Konar might be cautious enough to bring bodyguards with him. If he is escorted with guards and things fall apart, we could be in a precarious situation. We were confronting a twisted evildoer face to face. After we went to our rooms, I checked to be sure I had my LT pen. I found it, then texted Evelyn to remind her to look for hers.

No worries Stone, I've got it, she replied.

I was now almost relaxed enough to sleep. Ari bent down and revealed a bottle of Arak.

"Very impressive," I said.

He went to the bathroom and returned with two glasses, then poured.

"Cheers, Bob Stone," he said, raising his glass. "Better yet, for the meeting tomorrow morning. We will need some good luck, so here's to life," he toasted.

I looked into his eyes, searching as I sensed negative vibes. Fear was in the air. I was troubled because Ari always seemed to have a positive outlook. He was a hard read, so I had no choice—I needed to ask him.

"Hey, Ari, what's on your mind?" I asked, then paused and waited.

"Either you are very perceptive, or I am a dead giveaway right now."

I said nothing and rechecked his eyes. His eyebrows moved closer together as two crooked lines formed on his forehead, a sure sign of stress.

"Look, Stone," he said. "I have a bad feeling about this meeting with Konar. We may be walking into a trap. I feel that we need to call it quits here in Istanbul."

"I agree with you, Ari, but we have to take the risk and confront Konar."

"Okay then. After the meeting, we'll take a taxi right to the airport. I'll head to Israel to inform Mossad of our findings while you guys will return to the States to do the same at HPAT 21."

"Agreed, Ari, so we'll all grab flights out of here tomorrow on standby. Hopefully, all will be well, and we can figure out how to keep Mrs. Tokata protected from danger at the bank."

"Good night, Stone."

"Good night, my friend," I replied.

***

Although I said good night, there was no way I could sleep. In my gut, I knew something wild was brewing. I took a deep breath, spanning over four seconds, and exhaled very slowly, counting to eight. Usually a few of these measured breathing exercises would take care of my stress. After the fourth one, I calmed down enough to take the edge off and checked my watch—it was 10:31 p.m., which reminded me of Unit 731. I would be forever haunted by those numbers 731. My next thought was that it was only 2:31 p.m. in New York.

I was troubled. Troubled enough to send Levine a text, *Hey, just checking in. Anything I should be aware of?*

Levine's quick reply came through. *All under control. Laura is under our protection and seemingly in good hands with Wendy* (a winking smiley face emoji followed).

I responded by saying, *Thanks, but what's the smiley about,* to which Levine replied: *Call it a night and good luck meeting with Konar—and do be careful!*

I simply responded, *Will do.*

It was now 10:48 p.m. and I dozed off. I received a text three minutes later, at 3:51 p.m. New York time from Levine and my heart sunk.

"Hey, Stone, "Ari mumbled. "What's going on?"

"I'll tell you in a moment," I replied. "Let me read these messages from Levine." I pulled up the text and read it out loud. "Mixed news. The FBI went into the law firm of Combs and Walker just before three p.m. New York time. The partners are in the process of being taken into custody. They are going to be charged with money laundering, tax fraud, and supporting terrorist activities against the homeland. The law firm's escrow and operating bank accounts are now frozen. All of this was supposed to be done tomorrow, but our beloved FBI did not coordinate with me, Levine added sarcastically.

"Levine says I was right about my suspicions regarding germ warfare, but he has not yet been able to confirm that they were the bacterial agents from World War Two. Konar was using Omar Korbachi's access to an empire of germ-based weapons. They effectively shut down Korbachi's tactics and learned he was behind Doman's assassination, hiring a sniper to kill him. But Konar is still out there. Levine says we may be sitting ducks for our meeting tomorrow morning. We can call it quits and get ourselves to the airport right now for a flight home or continue to pursue the mission. Levine reminded me to re-member that if we are captured, HPAT 21 cannot help us.

"Ari, this is a critical decision for us all. We need to talk with Evelyn and Mrs. Tokata. Now!"

Ari and I got up and went to talk with Evelyn and Mrs. Tokata. They were not sleeping, no doubt because of the long, nerve-racking day. After explaining the situation and how the imminent danger had just escalated to a much higher level, I suggested that we hold off on any decisions and just think for a few minutes while we were all together.

The silence was heavy, the eye contact was nonexistent. *Well, there goes our plan,* I thought, *and we need a new one fast.* We couldn't just leave Mrs. Tokata as a sitting duck while the rest of us retreated. I took a brief survey and saw everyone sitting and leaning forward. It was a very nervous time, knees were bobbing up and down while some of us were cracking our knuckles and others were covering their faces with hands. The tension level was rising.

Mrs. Tokata broke the stalemate at last and said, "When I think back to all that my family went through after the Hiroshima bombing, I will sacrifice my life if I need to, to prevent another horrible catastro-phe from happening in this crazy world. This cannot happen again."

Her words acted as a catalyst that triggered a sensation within me and launched me up out of my chair. I was in a zone, compelled not only to stay the course, but also to win this critical battle. I knew Konar was still a danger, an unpredictable wild card even if Korbachi wasn't selling him weapons. The possibility remained that the specimens of Unit 731 could still exist and end up in the wrong hands.

"I'm with Mrs. Tokata," I said clearly and firmly. I turned to Evelyn and said, "You can take a flight back to the States tonight. You do not have to remain here."

"I stand with Mrs. Tokata," Evelyn stated.

"Evelyn are you absolutely sure?" I asked.

"Yes, yes I am," Evelyn replied.

Ari rose up and said, "Terrorism against America is terrorism wait-ing to happen all over the world, so I am with you all."

We all reached out and held hands in solidarity.

"Okay then," I said, breaking the brief silence. "We need to be ready for anything. Konar's bodyguards, maybe Korbachi's snipers are still out there somewhere . . .whatever. We all could end up as hostages. These evildoers might need us for leverage—who the hell knows?"

Ari stood up to make a call. He went from one call to another, pacing in a circle. I lost my patience waiting for him to be done, so I stood up and asked, "What's up, Ari?"

His other hand outstretched and curled in the air so that his fingertips were altogether touching his thumb and shaking it as the Israeli gesture to tell me *"Rega,"* or "Wait a moment."

He finally got off his phone and spoke, "Don't ask how, but I made arrangements for three Mossad agents from the Israeli embassy to meet us at the Bank of Japan. Once the bank opens, two agents will enter shortly after us: a man with a white umbrella and a lady wearing a yellow hat. Another person will stand outside to observe. That will hopefully offer us some added protection."

"That's a huge break, Ari," I said.

I was so grateful that I went over to give him a hug. Evelyn and Mrs. Tokata embraced with relief. I held Mrs. Tokata's hand with my two hands and smiled, nothing had to be said.

Ari and I exited back to our room and called it a night. I suppose my nervous energy got the better of me. I started to organize the contents of my luggage. Ari shut the light on his side of the room and then stretched out on the bed. I noticed that he became a bit aggravated with me as I kept my light on. I laid my clothes and papers on the bed and then checked the luggage pockets. Finally, I shook the luggage bag upside down to remove the debris. The bottom piece flipped loose and onto the floor. Something was firmly strapped to the bottom. Taking a closer look, I spotted a small giftwrapped box. I thought, *What the heck is this? Must be a joke. Yeah, of course. Some stupid joke from Levine, Wendy, or maybe even from Ashton the psych dude.* I reached in, grabbed it, and took a closer look. I started to laugh, but then Ari threw a tissue box at me.

"Hey, come on, go to sleep," he grumbled.

"Okay, sorry, one more minute,"

He was right. I turned off the light and put my cell phone flashlight on lower brightness. Lying down, I unwrapped the box quietly. There was a small note taped to the bottom. *Hey Stone, just a little gift from me, Levine. Surprise, surprise. When your lips get dry, open this box.*

That crazy guy, never a dull moment. I opened the box and saw a cylindrical tube of lip balm with a handwritten memo on it, *See bottom.* Under the padding of the box was a tiny sheet of paper folded over. It read, *Just when the caterpillar thought his life was about to end, it became a butterfly.* I remembered seeing this quote somewhere, but I couldn't recall exactly where.

"What the heck?" I said out loud.

Ari snapped at me, "Go to sleep, my American friend. Enough already."

I ignored him. The other side was marked, *Instructions.* The following steps appeared: *Your weapon of last resort. Remove cap. Turn the bottom once to the left and aim carefully. Be strong. Never back down. Your buddy, Levine.*

CHAPTER 31

I dozed off right away and slept like a baby. The deep sleep rolled into the morning, which came upon me with sudden impact. I woke with energy, feeling as if I just drank two shots of espresso. I rose up out of bed as soon as my eyes opened. I touched Ari's shoulder to get him going and then sent Evelyn a text. I felt it was my time to take charge and to create momentum. In the bathroom while brushing my teeth, I took a careful look at myself in the mirror.

I was shocked at the large bags under my eyes and the crinkle in my forehead—all this in just a short time with HPAT 21. I was stunned. In the upper-left corner of the bathroom, I saw an insect trapped inside a spider web, but the spider was nowhere. Not much of a superstitious guy, it still caused me to pause. I knew in my gut that today could be a nightmare for us. It was time to hit the streets, time to face the enemy.

We all met in the hallway with near perfect timing. It was a humid, overcast day and a bit difficult to breathe. Fifteen minutes before the meeting, Ari suggested a quick Turkish coffee and a light bite at a café close to the Bank of Japan.

"Good idea, Ari," Evelyn said. "We can keep an eye on the bank and grab a bite."

Mrs. Tokata was quiet, somewhat withdrawn. It was time.

"Does anyone have anything to say at this time?" I asked.

"Stone, did you find the ChapStick weapon in your luggage?" Evelyn asked.

I grinned and responded, "Of course."

Ari then spoke, "My friends, this is not going to be a walk in the park. Anything is possible, so we have to be ready for the unexpected."

"Any suggestions, Ari?"

"Well, maybe each one of us should be linked to someone at the bank, set up the defense like in a basketball game."

"Smart," I replied.

Ari continued, "For example, I will be responsible for Konar's actions while Stone, you will deal with bodyguards if they appear. Evelyn, you can shield Mrs. Tokata and keep an eye out for other surprises and create a diversion as needed."

We all agreed, then Mrs. Tokata said, "I will be the voice of reason, keeping things calm."

I gave each person an added dose of eye contact, then stood up and said, "Alright, people, let's do it."

We left the café and walked toward the bank while evaluating the surroundings. I saw nothing unusual, no strangers hanging around. It was time for Mrs. Tokata to approach the entrance of the bank alone. Evelyn whispered into her ear, prompting Mrs. Tokata to move forward without us. We did a side step toward an adjacent building a few doors away from the Bank of Japan, watching and waiting. We noticed the Mossad agents taking position across the street, looking out for us just as Ari had mentioned. One of them moved to the opposite far side of the bank.

Mrs. Tokata walked toward the bank in a very calm manner, entering as though she would on any other day of work. Her demeanor was looking good. Some guy placed a sign on the window reading: "Bank Closed." We were now confused, and very concerned. After waiting ten minutes, we approached the bank's door and although the sign was still there, the door was unlocked. We entered the bank and sat in a waiting area. It was tense and then the shocker of the day appeared. Hassam Al Boudeh Kandallah, whom I remembered from the Royal Bank of Toronto, must have entered the lobby from the rear of the building.

"What the hell is he doing here?" I quietly mumbled out loud. "He'll be in huge trouble, between his brother and his link to Omar Korbachi. This could be a huge windfall for us if all goes well."

Two bodyguards accompanied him—more trouble. Kandallah approached Mrs. Tokata, whispering something close to her ear. She waved us over to her desk.

Totally caught off guard, I tried to think of how to counter this development.

"I'll leave the bodyguards to the Mossad agents," I whispered to Ari and Evelyn. "Instead, I'll start talking with Kandallah to divert his attention and control the flow of conversation. Ari, you focus on Konar, when and if he shows. Evelyn, keep an eye on Mrs. Tokata and the overall situation—oh, and we may need you to create a scene. I trust your instincts, Evelyn."

"Thanks, Stone," she whispered back. "I'll do my best."

We walked to the desk of Mrs. Tokata. This was the moment of truth.

"Composure is the name of the game, people," I whispered.

Just then a text came in from Wendy: *All Mossad backup found dead off Taksim Square. You're on your own. Be careful. FYI, your tracking devices are working well.*

I stole a moment to show this text to Ari. He had to know what just happened, his confident gait was interrupted as if a balloon had popped inside his gut. We continued to move forward. A third bodyguard appeared with an assault rifle. Kandallah began to close in on me, invading my space.

"You do get around, don't you, Stone?" he asked, almost nose to nose with me. "Last week you were at my bank in Toronto, and what a coincidence, now we meet again in the Istanbul branch of the Bank of Japan? I've had enough of you."

The three bodyguards approached.

"Get up now, all of you," Kandallah continued. "You too, Mrs. Tokata."

I was frozen, looking for any angle to create conversation. I had no choice—I had to initiate some discussion.

"Excuse me, Haas," I said using his first name only to put us on the same level, attempting to break the ice. "Don't you want to meet the one who gave the orders to kill your brother yesterday?" I paused and waited for his reply, while I seared my eyes into his eyes.

The pause was powerful. I waited, maintaining my lock on his eyes.

"What are you talking about?" he asked, as he edged in closer to my face.

"You mean you do not know that your brother was killed yesterday by a sniper just after he agreed to cooperate with our unit?"

"What unit, Stone?" Kandallah demanded. "What are you talking about?"

I was shocked he did not ask about his brother, so I assumed he already knew of his murder.

"We work in a special crime division with the IRS in America, a unit created to protect our homeland. You should know that we have unlimited power to arrest foreign and domestic terrorists who plot against the United States. Our job is to follow the funds. You know, money flowing to terrorists. . . . By the way, we always get the job done by proving tax evasion. Your brother gave us a gift, a ton of information, we now know everything, Kandallah. In exchange, our unit, HPAT 21, the CIA, and the FBI would have saved your ass and your brother's from going to prison."

His face went from a shade of Middle Eastern mocha to nearly white.

"Your brother is gone but you must know by now, Kandallah, that we have enough information to put you away for a long time," I said.

Kandallah smiled.

"Keep smiling," I said. "Come on, we know all about the global transactions you've had with Omar Korbachi matching weapons to buyers and sellers. We know how you diverted huge sums of money from your Royal Bank of Toronto to the International Bank of Turkey, and then to the Bank of Japan. You left a nice trail for us, Kandallah. I see you and your colleagues never took courses in creative accounting."

He was speechless at first and then said, "The hell with that crap! Who killed my brother? Mrs. Tokata, you have worked with my brother for years. Why didn't you call me and tell me?"

It was quiet. I was surprised that Haas finally asked for more info about his brother. The tension was building. Rage was all over Kandallah's face as his eyes twitched and his extended eyebrows shifted. I saw a lifetime of anger showing up with his distorted smile and twisted nose. He was going to be harder to break through than his brother, Doman.

Kandallah spoke to all of us next, "We have been watching you all closely today. We saw you walking to the bank together thirty minutes ago. We know all your names, we know you're in trouble here, you cannot escape Istanbul." Kandallah singled out Mrs. Tokata again as he turned to her and said, "Mrs. Tokata, you brought these Americans to my brother's bank. Now they threaten to arrest me? Why do you cooperate with them?"

Kandallah paused as if he was going to continue talking, but he suddenly reached behind his back and pulled out a pistol. Evelyn tried to lunge at him, but in four seconds it was all over. He took a step closer to Mrs. Tokata. While gritting his teeth, he squeezed the trigger. Her head and arm simultaneously dropped to the side, blood shooting from a hole in her left temple. Evelyn screamed, lost her composure and jerked back in horror.

"Who is next, you stupid Americans?!" Kandallah shouted.

Evelyn fell to the floor to caress Mrs. Tokata, her blood oozing all over. Evelyn's anger boiled over into a shout out at Kandallah. While she was on the floor bloodied up and holding Mrs. Tokata, Evelyn yelled at him.

"This kind lady did nothing!" Evelyn exclaimed. "You killed her for no reason. You are the idiot here. You should have saved that bullet for either Korbachi or Konar—one of them killed your brother! And they didn't do it with her help!"

"She's right," I said. "Ask Konar, he is supposed to be here now."

Ari spoke. "I know exactly what's happening here."

"What does that mean?" Kandallah asked, annoyed.

"How can you not know?" Ari asked.

I interrupted Ari and said, "Do you not know that Japanese extremists are diverting those funds from your Royal Bank of Toronto to buy germ weapons and kill millions of Americans as a payback for the bombs dropped on Hiroshima and Nagasaki in early August 1945? They are going to blame their acts of terrorism on Islamic extremists—your people. We are drawing in close to the anniversary date of this insanity. Mrs. Tokata lived in Hiroshima after the bombings and risked her life here to prevent Konar from carrying out his vendetta. We are here to confront Konar. Mrs. Tokata was going to talk with him, to plead with him to stop his insanity. This lady you just killed was loyal to your brother and only trying to help."

Kandallah was silent, trying to absorb the entire scenario. I sensed an opportunity to continue.

"Kandallah, please, let's be logical," I pleaded. "It's not too late for you. We know everything. We have your branch manager from Toronto, Scott, in our custody. He is ready, willing, and able to testify against you. Your brother is dead."

Then to slam it home, I lied. I convinced Kandallah that our special ops IRS unit arrested Korbachi the night before. For good measure, I let him know the truth about the law firm.

"By the way, as to the New York law firm into which you funnel money from around the world to purchase weapons . . . well, late last night, the firm's escrow accounts were frozen, the firm was shut down, and its partners were arrested. The game of money in motion is over for you. But we still need to save lives. Yes, American lives and millions from other countries in the process. You can help to avoid the inevitable worldwide condemnation of Islamic extremists. Our intelligence leads us to believe it is Konar's objective to poison the New York City water supply with those biological weapons hidden and stockpiled by the Japanese Unit 731.

I needed to get more personal with Kandallah—I began to talk again after a brief pause. "And what do you think happens next? Konar does not care about the collateral effects, the spillover around the world. He is a sick young man seeking vengeance for a war his country started over seventy years ago. But maybe, maybe you do care. Maybe you have a wife, a child, a reason to care, just a little for humanity."

It was time to keep my mouth shut. I thought I should win an award with that speech. Whatever happened now, I knew I gave it my best shot. Kandallah walked over to one of his guards, the one with the assault rifle. I was about to pee in my pants. They had a brief conversation ending with the guard bowing his head in acceptance of an order. Then the guard approached me.

"Mr. Kandallah wants to talk with you back there," he said, pointing.

As I rose up, the guard checked my body for weapons. I was directed to move forward. Ari rose up in a show of solidarity. The other guard pointed his gun at him.

"Sit down!" he shouted.

He almost whacked Ari in the head with the gun. I went to the back-office area of the bank with the guard. Kandallah approached me.

"Stone, listen carefully to me," Kandallah said. "This is what I can do, and it's all that I can do: I am leaving here in a matter of seconds. My helicopter is in the back. You will never see me again. My name and my identities as Hassam Al Boudeh Kandallah will cease to exist. I have been waiting for this inevitable day to come. My guards will stay here to help you. They have my orders to kill Konar—I just know it was him who killed my brother. Omar Korbachi would not have done that. He is a weapons middleman, a low life, and in it just for the money, not for any emotion. I am very sorry that I killed Mrs. Tokata. When my guards kill Konar, in my mind, we will all be even."

"But we need Konar to clarify all of his plans," I responded. "Don't kill him!"

"Konar is a dead man. You will find out all you need to know from Darmush Khan. I believe you may know him, tax man?"

I was shocked at his insinuation but wasn't given a chance to find out his connection to my client.

"My guards will escort you all out of here to the entrance behind me. Get your friends over here now."

The noise of helicopter blades spinning began, becoming louder and louder. I had no choice. Kandallah walked out the back and headed up the stairs to meet the helicopter on the rooftop. Evelyn and Ari were escorted to me by one of the guards. We walked out the rear exit feeling lucky to be alive. A helicopter with no markings rose higher to about one thousand feet up and spun away into a cloudy Istanbul sky.

We walked behind several retail stores for a few blocks, finally arriving at the main tourist area. Ambling into Taksim Square, we paused to collect our thoughts. With New York weighing heavily on my mind, I turned to Evelyn and Ari.

"Airport as agreed, right?" I said, breaking our silent walk. It was more of a statement confirming our next move than a question.

They both nodded in agreement. A taxi seemed to sense that we needed a ride and accelerated from two buildings away before jerking to a stop only a few inches away from my feet, forcing me to jump back. Swirls of street dust hovered around us. We rushed into the taxi to protect our eyes.

***

On the way to the airport, the date occurred to me, it was already August 1st. I also realized that the seventieth anniversary of America's bombing of Hiroshima was on August 6th and that the germ infestation could still occur within days. I had a dry heave caused by a convulsion somewhere between my stomach and my throat.

I mumbled to myself, "Time is not on our side—only five days left."

"Stone, what did you say?" Evelyn asked.

"Oh nothing," I replied. "Nothing."

Ari reset his eyes on me and I knew he saw my insecurity raise its ugly head. I had to say something.

"Hey, listen to me," I said to both. "Kandallah killing off Konar would not prevent his act of terrorism from happening. It's an act of vengeance so deep to honor Emperor Hirohito and Konar's great-grandfather, one of the highest-ranking generals who signed the Japanese surrender documents back in 1945. It will be carried out by Konar's evildoers and with even more conviction, especially when they find out their partner Doman Kandallah was killed, and his brother, Haas, has disappeared without a trace. Konar had a team in place. Let's not be naive."

"Of course, you are right, Stone," Evelyn replied.

Ari nodded his head in agreement. After a few more minutes of driving, I noticed that the driver was looking into the rearview mirror often, and then the sideview mirror, and then back and forth between the two.

"Hey, what's the problem?" I asked.

"Sorry, sir," the taxi driver replied. "Are you traveling with any friends?"

"What do you mean?" I responded.

"There is a car following us," he nervously replied.

A call came in from Levine.

"I see your heading to the airport," Levine said. "Are you guys okay? What happened with Konar—"

"Wait a moment, Levine," I said, cutting him off. "Keep driving faster," I directed the taxi driver. "Okay, Levine, here's the short version," I said. I had no patience to explain it all. "Kandallah showed up at the Bank of Japan, not Konar. We were being held at gunpoint by his bodyguards when I told him that his brother was killed by Konar. He took off, vowing to kill Konar in return. Kandallah left in a helicopter, but he told us that Darmush Khan knows everything and that he knew of my connection to him as a client."

"Okay, understood," Levine replied. "Stone, your hunch about Unit 731 from World War Two . . . well, you were right. Our ambassador to Japan, Avery Smith, found out that Konar obtained a permit to do Ebola research at the original site where the germ weapons were stored in Harbin, Manchuria. The bigger issue is that the canisters of germ weapons are missing. Smart thinking, real sharp, Stone . . . I need to call you back. I cannot say everything right now."

That was strange coming from Levine. I figured he'd spill the beans to me about some weird development right away. It wasn't like him to hold back.

Just then, Wendy texted me, *I set up three flights for you, Evelyn, and Ari. Delta Air leaving at 2:05 p.m. today. Ari is no longer stealth, he is* finito *in Istanbul. He has been reassigned to assist us at HPAT 21 in New York, at least until this act of terrorism is dealt with.* I replied, *Okay, understood,* just before my cell phone rang with a call from Levine.

"Hello, you can hear me?"

"Yes, Levine," I replied. "What's up? Should I be afraid of some crazy news?"

"Very perceptive, Stone," Levine replied. "I do have a problem over here. Last night, I believe my laptop was hacked. What we do at HPAT 21 most likely has been leaked. If it was a hack job, editorials will appear shortly in several national newspapers and then a congressional investigation may take place. I cannot communicate with you anymore. I don't know what other forms of communication have been compromised. Just get back here to Manhattan and go straight to the basement. There we can talk privately. This is a huge dilemma."

"Exactly what do you mean?" I asked.

"Come on," Levine said. "Don't play dumb now. All we have left is Darmush Khan. You said Kandallah knew about your connection to Darmush and that Darmush knows everything. A pending investigation may kick in. Do I have him tortured? Do I release him? Do I lie and say that he is not being held in America when we're holding him in Manhattan? Or do I lie with silence? I have to figure out the best approach."

"Understood," I said. "It's a mess. One last request since we cannot talk further? Check with Laura as to which buildings were purchased by either the Shirango Group, LLC, or the Narico Group LLC over the last twelve months. Then, check with the NYC Municipal Water Finance Authority to see if any part of the city's water supply pipelines, aqueducts, and tunnels flow under those buildings. If my hunch is correct, the buildings purchased through this foreign investment real estate group are linked to Konar and must be where the main water flows underneath. These buildings must be checked out and kept under maximum security. What we do not know is how those germ weapons will get into the homeland and then into Manhattan."

"Okay, understood," Levine said. "See you tomorrow about three p.m. New York time."

"Just another thought," I said. "Before you go on autopilot and bring in Dr. Sing to torture Darmush . . . try to talk with Darmush Khan first. Tell him that Hassam Kandallah from Toronto has disappeared and that his brother, Doman, was killed. Tell him the law firm is shut down and that Omar Korbachi was arrested and that we know everything, including Konar's plans. Try to offer him some break so he will talk with us?"

"HPAT 21 may be shut down in a few hours, Stone," Levine replied. "I don't know what authority I will have anymore. You know, things are about to be turned upside down now. I may need to lean on you for advice in the future. The tables have turned, Stone. You have become an invaluable asset for HPAT 21, especially for me."

"I can't handle too many compliments," I said jokingly. "Hey, we just got to the airport, see ya. You talk to Darmush. Tell him I said that it's over and that he needs to deal with reality. Save Dr. Singh as our last resort."

I terminated the call totally stunned and now the fate of millions may end up in a debate between people who believe in due process of law, which in theory is morally correct versus people who feel we need to do whatever it takes to save lives. And right now, we had no time to spare, *what a dilemma . . . what a nightmare.*

CHAPTER **32**

Whoever was following us to the airport had apparently called it off. Thankfully, nothing happened. We were cleared through security and boarded the aircraft. *Sloppy security,* I thought, as they didn't question me about my LT pen, nor the ChapStick weapon. They didn't bother to ask the right questions, either.

Evelyn, Ari, and I were totally exhausted. We ended up sitting a few seats away from one another. The aircraft lifted off without delay. *Finally,* I smiled and leaned back as Istanbul was history. Back to New York and the many issues still to be resolved under extreme time pressure. Getting out of Istanbul was such a tremendous relief. . . . The pilot began talking over the speakers.

"This is your pilot speaking. We are cruising at thirty-three thousand feet with calm weather. The seat belt sign is now off. Our ETA to John F. Kennedy International Airport in New York will be ten-forty-five Eastern time."

I inhaled deeply, followed by a delayed exhale while glancing at the flight movement on the TV screen in front of me. Right now, my single greatest question was what drink I was in the mood for. I hit the button to release the seat and lean back, my eyes glancing out the window. The wing gradually pointed up and the plane shifted sharply to the left. The flight pattern was altered. I flipped the channel from the movie to the flight information display screen, which indicated a drop in the altitude and a change in direction. I figured that I would take another peek in ten seconds, not panicking until it became a red flag that we weren't back on track. I double checked the flight pattern info screen again, and once again, no flight adjustments were visible. That was enough for me. I rose up to seek the attention of Ari and Evelyn, and then pointed to the screen with a shrug of my shoulders.

Trying to be positive, I assumed the pilot was maneuvering around a few storm clouds. I was looking for some logic to this, but the pilot just announced calm weather. I could not just sit here in denial. . . . I've learned never again to remain in denial. I knew in my gut that a situation was brewing. There was nervous activity among the flight attendants, two of them walking down the aisles, leaning in and asking each passenger something. Maybe they were taking drink orders, but I could not be sure. My attempt to read their lips was useless. The flight attendant on my side finally approached closer to me. I tried to read her lips as she talked to few more seated passengers. She was not smiling, and for sure, she was not taking drink orders. In fact, I saw a face filled with fear. Finally, I picked up on a word or two as her words became clearer the closer she was to my seat. The flight attendant was asking, "Are you—? Are you—? Are you whom I thought?"

Finally, she was standing adjacent to me. "Are you, Mr. Robert Stone?" she asked.

I looked up into her distressed eyes. I paused, and then replied, "Yes, I am Robert Stone. Why do you ask?"

"Please come with me, it's critical," she replied.

She was quite nervous. I had to control the moment.

"Look at me," I firmly said to her. "Listen to me: If something is wrong, I need a quick heads up. That's all I ask."

"Please," she replied. "I cannot talk too much. There are two men on board with knives."

"Okay, and exactly what is going on right now?" I demanded, remaining calm.

She took in a quick, nervous breath and replied, "They grabbed the copilot as he went to the bathroom, and then took a passenger too. They are forcing us to redirect the flight to Syria. One of the men told me when I found you, I needed to say, 'Omar Korbachi has a gift for you.' They also want me to say, 'It's your free vacation to Syria.' They told me that if you do not come to them up front, that if all of us do not cooperate, they would start killing passengers."

"That crazy bastard," I mumbled to myself. I had to calm her down. "See my two friends over there?" I asked. "We all work together with a special unit to protect the U.S. homeland. Listen to me, keep walking around the cabin and make believe you're still looking for me. I need time to get a fast plan going."

"Okay, Mr. Stone, bless you, bless you," she said with her tears in free fall.

"Take it easy, you'll scare the passengers," I said calmly.

"Okay, you're right," she replied. "I'll try. We train for this, but I've never experienced it."

"Come back to me in a few minutes," I said.

I walked to Evelyn to explain the situation and she, in turn, told Ari.

"Evelyn," I said. "I'll have no choice but to confront these guys in a few minutes."

I reached for the ChapStick weapon in my pocket, took it out and held it up to show it to her.

"Yeah, those dry lips are such a pain in the butt," she replied.

I smiled back and said, "Listen—give me exactly one minute to start walking, then follow me. I need to get back to my seat. You and Ari should be ready for a struggle. There is no way these guys are taking this plane to Syria. We're going to New York, and that's it—end of story."

"Alright, Bob," Evelyn replied. "Be careful."

I went back to my assigned seat, turned, and saw Ari give me a thumbs-up. My mind went back to the few hours of training at the HPAT 21 Langley Virginia Command Center with Claude. I remembered some of the kill-or-be-killed moves he had shown me.

That survival replay gave me a shot of adrenaline and kept my nervousness intact. The flight attendant waved me to the front of the plane near the cockpit area. I was in no hurry as I walked slowly to review anything and everything around me, checking out every possible detail. I stopped and waited for the flight attendant to see my pause so that she would be forced to approach me again. She turned and then walked toward me.

"What the heck are you doing?" she hissed. "They'll sense something, Mr. Stone, please."

"It's okay," I reassured her. "What's your name?"

"Stephanie Curtiss," she replied.

"Do you know how magicians work their tricks?" I asked her.

"Not really, why?" she responded, her hands shaking.

"Magic is based on the art of deception, Stephanie, and we must distract this guy. A second after you are close enough to the hijacker, you will slowly say, 'Here is Mr. Stone.' You will use your right two fingers but point to the left behind you. I will appear, coming in from the opposite side. It's not a great plan, but I need an edge, any slight advantage will do. Then, if possible, as I engage him, you grab the passenger he is holding and you both step away. Don't worry, my friends over there will be coming to help us. Where are the two hijackers now?"

"One guy has the copilot at knife point outside the bathroom on the left side upfront. The other guy is holding that passenger a few feet in front of the kitchen area, off to the right side. Right now, the only passengers who know what's going on are those in the first-class area."

Another flight attendant then tapped Stephanie's shoulder, motioning for us to move forward. I turned back and raised my hand to prompt Evelyn and Ari. They started to walk forward down the left aisle. I felt like a gladiator about to enter the Colosseum. After a final mental check, I realized that I could not use the LT pen, nor the Chap-Stick weapon, since either could cause damage to the airplane. No way, that would be a disaster. Now it was on me: my hands, my speed, and my brain. I turned back to Evelyn, pointing to my lips and then using my two hands to tell her not to use her weapons. She nodded.

I tapped Stephanie's shoulder and said, "You go three feet ahead of me."

She nodded. Evelyn and Ari were moving toward the bathroom area to free the copilot. I was glued to Stephanie. She walked just past the first-class curtains. This was it.

Stephanie told the assailant, "Okay, here he is, here is Mr. St"

I lunged forward before she finished saying my last name. There he was—a large bearded man over six feet tall holding a stiletto knife with one hand while his other elbow was wrapped around the neck of a whimpering young girl. I noticed his eyes veered off for a split second as Stephanie pointed to the opposite side as she introduced me. This went better than I imagined as he lost his focus for a moment. I launched a strong kick just below his right kneecap. As he buckled over, I whacked his knife hand. He was off balance enough now to enable the passenger to be freed up. Stephanie pulled her away as planned. She followed my instructions perfectly.

The attacker now had both hands free and he was back in control. He hit the right side of my head with the knife handle. I was stunned. *That was a gift,* I thought. He could have pierced my skull with that blade. Cornered in the kitchen area, I had no space to move which caused me to trip over some object on the floor. My forearm blocked his next attempt to land another blow. He pushed me using one hand with amazing force. My head hit a solid object behind me, maybe the lip of the counter top. I fell to the floor rendering me in a supine position on my back, looking for anything I could grab to protect myself. The attacker hovered over me. He yelled some phrase I couldn't understand and then plunged his knife downward. I tried to block his motion, but my reactions were too slow. A sharp pain rapidly unleashed inside my stomach and rose to my chest with radiating heat.

I was down and in serious trouble, heavily bleeding, and my eyes were shutting down. I was either passing out or dying. The last image I saw was Ari's arms wrapping tightly around the attacker's neck, putting him into a choke hold. They were both falling back away from me. I saw the knife fall to the floor and the attacker struggling to breathe. I had no idea what happened next.

***

328 • ERIC J. ENGELHARDT

I woke up feeling heavy and sluggish. My breathing was slow and the bandages covering the cuts on my stomach pain were uncomfortable. My eyes were open just enough to see a tube flowing out from my stomach area. Someone entered my room.

"Mr. Stone, can you hear me? Are you awake?" asked a feminine voice.

My throat was raw, I tried to respond, but my voice was dry and raspy.

"I'm your recovery nurse," she said. "You came out of surgery late last night. You're in a U.S. military hospital."

"Where . . . where are we?" I struggled to ask.

"You're a lucky man," replied the nurse. "You survived a jagged knife wound to your stomach. After the hijacking was prevented by all you brave people, the pilots were instructed to redirect the plane to land at Adana Sakirpasa Airport in Adana Turkey and you have been here at the Adana Hospital since late last night."

"How, I mean . . . where are my two friends?"

"I am sorry, sir, but your lady friend is in serious condition with upper chest knife wounds close to the heart. The other man, I believe his name is Mr. Arieh Korine—or was it Ari that he preferred—he is recovering from a head concussion. He should be fine, we're keeping the swelling under control."

Waking up to this news was overwhelming. My cell phone rang.

"Would you like your cell?" the nurse asked.

"Yes thanks. Let me have the phone, please," I replied.

"Hello, Stone," Levine said. "I heard you're alright, you're going to make it. We know exactly what happened on that airplane last night. Good news, HPAT 21 is alive and well again. Turns out there wasn't a breach of my laptop—false alarm. Back to your crazy flight last night: your tracking devices tipped us off that the airplane went off course, heading to Syria. It was a nightmare . . . we were going crazy back here in New York." He paused. "Stone, can you hear me? Are you there?"

I could not talk, as my throat was parched. I had no patience for this call.

"Levine, please talk slower," I requested. "I'm a bit groggy, I just woke up."

"Ah, okay, sorry," Levine apologized. "I understand how you feel, but you're going to want to turn on the TV. Watch any news channel—they're all carrying the story of last night's hijacking. By the way, just listen . . . I took your advice. I told Darmush Khan that the whole scheme was uncovered, and although I fed him fake news about Korbachi being arrested, I also mentioned that Kandallah disappeared. He broke down and told us everything, and I'm pleased to say it was without any torture. Now, let's hope Evelyn and Ari will be alright."

"Okay, I'll check out the news. Thanks for the call, Levine."

"You're going to smile when you hear the news on television, trust me," Levine insisted.

"Okay, I could use something to smile about," I replied just before hanging up. "Nurse. Excuse me. Nurse—"

She came back to the room saying, "Yes, are you alright?"

"Oh yes, I didn't mean to alarm you," I said apologetically. "I need to get the TV on. Can you hook me up with a news channel? Now please, it's important."

"Okay, here you go, Mr. Stone. Next time just buzz me with your call button," she said smiling and turned to look back as she left the room.

I must have been feeling a little better because my eyes focused on her with excitement as she left the room. I watched the news for a couple minutes, but nothing of interest was on. *Ah wait here's something—the BBC News—love that.*

"This is John Gardner in the BBC news room reporting with two key breaking stories. Several hours ago, a terrorist plot to poison the New York City water supply with bacterial weapons was prevented, thank goodness. The incident took place at two buildings in the well-known meatpacking district in New York City. Four men were arrested while unloading sixteen canisters off a truck. Each canister was marked with the number 731. No one yet knows the meaning of this number. It's too soon to make definite conclusions, but it's suspected by the authorities that the canisters contained bacteria to be dumped into Manhattan's main water supply.

He continued: "If suspicions are correct, over a million people, just in Manhattan for starters, would have been killed by deadly diseases as they spread into the other boroughs of the city and beyond, putting millions more at risk. The New York City Police Department has issued a warning that Manhattan's historical landmarks may have become targeted in a series of simultaneous attacks as the latest strategy in the world of terror. Stay tuned, there will be much more detail on this developing story."

A commercial break came on and all I could think was: *Thank God this insane act of terrorism was dealt with prior to the anniversary of the atomic bombing of Hiroshima, now only days away.* I was foggy on today's date, so I reached for the television remote, hoping the info button would display it. On the screen, the channel and time popped up, showing August 2, 2015. I had a scratchy feeling on the back of my neck, realizing there were only four more days until another act of terrorism would potentially transpire.

The BBC reporter returned. "Now for another breaking news story. . . . Last night a hijacking attempt took place during a flight from Istanbul's Atatürk Airport bound for New York's John F. Kennedy International Airport. The flight was taken over by two Islamic extremists and rerouted to Syria. Three passengers made the wrenching decision to confront the knife-wielding attackers. These brave good Samaritans sustained injuries while fighting off the hijackers. Shortly thereafter, the flight was redirected to an undisclosed airport nearby a hospital. The three heroes were: Robert Savemoor, an American who suffered lacerations on his stomach; Evelyn Carver, a Canadian who remains in guarded condition from knife wounds to the chest; and Ari Ahrdeni, an Israeli who was hospitalized with a concussion. A female passenger, who was initially taken hostage by the attackers, suffered trauma and a few bruises. She will be in the hospital for observation and will be released most likely tomorrow. Thanks to the heroic acts of these three passengers, no one else was injured. That's enough news for one day. This is John Gardner reporting for the BBC."

Levine was right, I did smile. At the same time, the reality of our unfinished business reminded me of the enormous challenge ahead. I rested for about an hour and Levine called me again.

"Stone, whatever it takes, you and Ari must get back to Manhattan immediately. You can continue to rest on the long flight. They will watch over Evelyn, it's a great hospital. You and Ari have medical clearance to board a flight out of Adana Airport in two hours."

"What?!" I exclaimed in disbelief. "Are you crazy, Levine? I'm not exactly Superman."

"I know, sorry, but another terrorism scheme may still be in the works for August sixth, according to our sources. It's serious, Stone."

"Sure of course, I'll push it," I said with perseverance. I thought about the same possibility myself."

"Go check on Ari and Evelyn and be ready to board your flight in two hours. See you tomorrow."

"Never a dull moment. Alright, Levine, see you then."

I buzzed the nurse and she came to my room right away. At my request, she helped me up and walked with me to Ari's room. Coincidentally, he was up already and walking to my room to check on me. Wendy had apparently already informed him that we were to take a flight in a few hours back to Manhattan. HPAT 21 really was in full swing again.

We were taken to Evelyn's room in the cardiac wing of the hospital, but we were not allowed to enter. I could see from the hallway looking in that Evelyn was in serious condition. I asked the nurse who accompanied us about Evelyn's prognosis.

"It's delicate, Mr. Stone. She's not breathing properly on her own yet. It's touch and go. Your friend Evelyn is in one of the best hospitals in the region, though, and she's in good hands. She'll have round-the-clock care and we'll do everything we can to get her back on her feet and home safely. Sorry, but that's all the information I can communicate to nonfamily members. And right now, I have discharge instructions to prepare you guys as best as I can under the circum-stances for your flight back to New York. Shall we get going back to your rooms? Get organized, and get some delicious Turkish food in your systems? You'll need to have your strength up to drive to the nearby local airport. So, let's get going, yes?"

"Yes, of course, and thank you," I replied. Ari nodded his head in agreement.

PART SIX

CHAPTER 33

We were escorted to the local airport and onto the jet by two guards. No doubt, Levine had set this up. He did have a thing for jets. The flight was a blur. I slept from the moment I boarded and sat down until we landed at JFK Airport in New York. I was awakened by a jolt caused by the jet landing gear hitting the ground hard and its noisy brakes screeching to a halt.

The guards escorted Ari and I off the jet. We were led to a special back door where we were checked in hurriedly and avoided the long lines required to reenter the country.

An HPAT 21 Jeep was waiting for us outside the terminal, with Jaab behind the wheel. I was surprised to see Wendy next to him in the passenger seat. Ari and I got in and made a dash to exit the airport, only to get wrapped up in the usual traffic approaching Manhattan. I have learned over the years just to accept it. But for right now, it was a welcome pause, allowing me extra time to think as I tried to struggle through the haze of my injury. The bandages were holding up well, but the pain meds dulled my thoughts a little. Still, I had to plan my discussions with everyone, since sooner than later we would be sitting around a room trying to figure out what we needed to do next. I decided to divert my thinking in order to lighten up.

"Tell me, Jaab, how have you been since I left you to go to Istanbul?"

"Well, as you know, I finished my training and assessment at the HPAT 21 Langley Virginia Command Center. I was then rushed back here to meet with you. I hear there are crazy things going down. I actually asked Levine if I could be the one to come get you guys."

"Thank you, it's good to see you again. You're absolutely right. There are troubling things about to happen here in Manhattan, so I'm sure over the next few days you will play an important part in helping all of us to defend the homeland."

Jaab's face was serious, his eyes blinked intermittently. Ari noticed, too, and gave me a knowing look of concern.

I stared at a tiny crack in the windshield, determined to focus and pull myself together.

"Wendy, I need a pen and paper," I requested.

"Sure thing," Wendy replied, handing me the items.

I needed to focus the old-fashioned way, by making a handwritten list. My thoughts were still jumbled, and I thought this might help. How could I ever forget the sixth-grade teacher who taught me how to write an essay? Ah yes, Mr. Novak, who once advised, "If you are frozen and cannot get started, pick up your pen and write down your name— write something, anything." And that's exactly what I did. My brain dumping starting random reminders and notes without much organization, but that wasn't important right now. I wrote:

- *Ask Laura if she ever made that list of all Manhattan properties the law firm's clients expressed an interest in buying or actually acquired.*
- *Ask Laura to review whatever she can recall hearing that night of the Ammi's daughter's wedding in April.*
- *Ask Levine what he found out about the inventory of Unit 731 germ canisters from the Japanese WWII archives.*
- *Ask if the Center for Disease Control and Prevention was notified and involved.*
- *Ask how many canisters were recovered from the attempted delivery in Manhattan the other day, which should have been six canisters altogether.*
- *Ask Ashton to be at the basement to hypnotize me, and possibly Laura, to uncover other remarks or details from the wedding that might uncover the whereabouts of Konar and Korbachi or more information on the historical landmarks about to be attacked.*

We were about to enter the Queens Midtown Tunnel, but we came to a complete stop with a sudden backup of traffic. I began to think about the possibilities. *Could an extremist group explode this tunnel, a famous church, Grand Central Station, the George Washington Bridge?* Unimaginable, but anything now could be a target of terrorists. My mind was wandering, racing for ideas, anything that might lead me to something logical. I closed my eyes and leaned back, seeking an answer. *Historical landmarks,* I began to rethink the possibilities of this plot. I recalled a miniseries on the History Channel: *The Men Who Built America.* I shook my head from side to side in frustration, sensing that I might have been locked on to something, but I could not connect the dots.

At last, the traffic started to flow, allowing us to make it through the tunnel. In ten more minutes, we hung a left onto St. Mark's Place and drove down to Avenue A. There it was: our destination, the brownstone building with the hidden door around the side, leading to the infamous basement.

Wendy led the way down the steps to the mini command center in the basement. She knocked on the door that was draped over by thick, old vines with fading leaves.

"Who's there?" someone from inside asked.

"How cute," Wendy commented. "HPAT 21's sophisticated code for—"

"It's okay, come in," came the reply.

Jaab looked at me, rolling his eyes. Ari stepped aside, letting me go first. Levine was the first to greet me with a hug, then leaned back to look me over.

"Not bad for a guy who has been through hell and back," he said. "Happy to see you, tax man."

"Same here, Levine."

Ari shook hands with Levine, saying, "Thanks so much for all your help along the way."

Wendy then guided Ari to another room to allow him to decompress and catch up on life with each other, I supposed, but didn't ask.

I was more focused on finding Laura and there she was, sitting down, so I walked over to sit beside her. I needed a way to break the ice, but it could not be forced.

"Hello, Laura," I said. "I'm glad to see you. You look great. Lost some weight, I see. Are you okay?"

"I'm as good as I can be, I guess," Laura replied. "I'm obviously out of a job since the law firm closed down—a blessing in disguise. I don't miss working with those sleazy bastards. I heard you were badly hurt in that flight from Istanbul to New York and that you guys foiled the hijackers. Bravo, I had no idea you were such a brave man."

"Yeah, I guess we did handle it all pretty well," I replied. "It was a scary scene, but each of us paid a price. We could've been killed. In fact, I was almost stabbed to death. But it's time to move on to more important things."

Levine approached us and jumped in, "Stone, let me bring you up to date."

"Hold on," I said. "Is Ashton here? Laura and I may need to be hypnotized."

"Are you crazy?" Laura exclaimed. "I have no intention of—"

"Please, Laura, if we can learn anything else from what we overheard at Ammi's wedding party for his daughter that night, then millions of people could be saved."

The room was silent. Levine touched my shoulder.

"I'll try again so calm down," he said. "Here is what we have learned in the past twenty-four hours: There were twenty-two germ canisters that were originally in Harbin, Manchuria, at the end of the war in 1945. The other day, only sixteen were recovered here in the city, leaving another six floating around. Not a good thing. Konar, the Japanese extremist seeking vengeance and honor, cannot be located. However, one good piece of news is that Omar Korbachi was arrested in Reykjavík, Iceland, yesterday by Interpol."

"Good stuff regarding Korbachi, Levine," I said. "Please go on."

"Yes, but the Kandallah brother from the Toronto bank is still missing and no one has a clue as to his whereabouts."

"What do we know about the possible historical landmarks being targeted for attacks?'"

"Perfect timing," Levine replied. "Are you ready to talk face to face with your very first undocumented foreign client who owned that flower shop in Manhattan?"

"What?" I responded. "What—what—?"

"You sound like some bird on the National Geographic Channel," Levine laughed. "Yeah, Ahmed, or Ammi as you know him. The biggest mistake of your career is tied up in that room over there. Remember the men who tried to kidnap Laura and take her to the mosque in Astoria, Queens? Ammi is linked to them and is the one who has been planning a series of explosions at several famous historical buildings in the city. Go ahead, talk with him."

"First, I want to be put under by Ashton. Is he coming here?" I asked.

"Yes, of course," Levine replied. "He is just a few minutes from here."

"Laura and I will meet with Ashton and maybe learn something else. Then I'll talk with Ammi."

"Your call, Stone, that's fine," Levine said and switched gears. "What kind of food do you all want? You must be hungry."

A joke surfaced from my brain, so I replied, "Nothing too 'extreme.'" I was referring to extremists with a dumb one-liner. It broke the tension around the room. "Actually, some Chinese would be nice, Levine. How about you, Laura?"

"Thanks for asking," she replied. "Yeah, I'll have anything, just no shrimp."

"Okay," I said. "Go for it, Levine, sounds good."

"Give it forty minutes," Levine replied. "Great food! Got to try the steamed dumplings."

"Whatever, I'll leave all the extras up to you," I said. "You're the same ol' Levine, our resident food lover."

There were eight knocks on the door to some sort of meaningless musical beat. I figured that was the psychologist, Ashton. The HPAT 21 clearance allowed the door to open. Ashton walked in calmly, took off his English checkered cap, and smiled at me.

"I see you're in one piece, Stone," he said with a grin.

"Barely, but yes," I replied.

"Bob Stone, the tax man," Ashton joked. "So, this time you asked me to be here when back in the Langley Virginia Command Center I think you pretty much despised me."

I paused before saying, "Let's not get personal here. I was under huge stress back then. Anyway, we do need your help, and fast. I cannot seem to remember everything from that crazy night of the wedding when I overheard so many horrible remarks about America and acts of terror. I was in a state of shock at that time. Maybe you can use your magic to retrieve something Laura and I suppressed or forgot—anything to help us prevent a disaster."

"Commendable," Ashton remarked. "Let's get started."

"I'm ready when you are," I said.

"I'll need you and one more person as a witness," Ashton said. "Laura should be the one to observe, to listen in. Who knows, your responses may trigger something for her to rethink as well."

"Laura, please join us into that quiet holding room down the hall," Levine suggested. "It has a comfortable reclining chair for Bob and a small couch for you."

We settled into the other room. There were no windows, but it had an ugly, worn-out green area rug in an attempt to give the room more warmth in this cold-looking basement.

"Okay, Stone," Ashton began. "Lean back and relax yourself in that chair. Take a few slow, deep breaths and exhale even slower."

I did as he instructed.

"Good, please repeat that again," Ashton said, his voice lowering and his tone becoming gentler.

He spoke so calmly with an overall demeanor that was relaxed and designed to relax me as well. It was working. This time I wanted to go under, no resistance and no fighting it.

"Bob," he said, "You are feeling good and completely at peace with yourself. You want to tell us what you heard at Ahmed's house after his daughter's wedding. Think, think, and relax. After you remember everything from that evening, you will wake up on my command. You will return to us feeling relieved, happy, and energized."

That was it. I was led into another zone, back to that April night.

***

Suddenly, I heard someone count from five down to one with a gentle command to wake up. I was a bit slow to come around, but I knew it was time to regain my senses.

"So, what did I say?" I asked. "Anything extra we didn't already know?"

"You kept saying, 'Kill the chickens in the pen' over and over," Levine replied. "The more you said it, the more upset you became."

Laura grabbed my arm and said, "Yes, yes, I remember that, too. As we left the party, we walked toward our car. Darmush said that to Ammi by the garage door. You turned around and I elbowed you not to allow them to know you heard anything. We looked at each other and tried to laugh it off as some stupid remark."

"Right, you're right, Laura," I said. "But what the hell did that mean?"

My mind was clear, and I started feeling energized despite my knife wound.

"Wait a moment," I said. "Laura, can you tell us which buildings the Shirango Group expressed an interest in over the past year? Other than the Empire State Building you mentioned before, that is. You must've learned more about their interests during your time at Combs and Walker."

"Sure, that's easy," Laura replied. "Let me see . . . they wanted to buy up some of New York's valued treasures, like the Woolworth Building, one of Manhattan's earliest skyscrapers, the Chrysler Building, Carnegie Hall, and several others."

"Any other locations?" I asked.

"You know what, there was a hush-hush indication of interest about seven months ago—" Laura trailed off.

"Come on, tell us more, Laura," Ashton prompted her. "It's safe to share information here. You're protected."

"This could be huge, please think it through," I gently suggested.

"Okay, yes," Laura continued. "I recall when Omar Korbachi, or 'Of Counsel' as the law firm referred to him, came up with this crazy idea to buy Penn Station. They actually tried to buy it from some trust, but the sale was blocked."

I couldn't help myself. I paced around the room, sat down again, closed my eyes, and stood up. I needed to stretch, so I reached my fingertips upward to touch the ceiling, and then let them drop to the floor. *Ah, what a great feeling.*

"Stone, what the hell are you up to?" Levine demanded irritably. "The world is falling apart, and you need to work out now? Come on."

"Oh my God, that's it," I shouted out, as it all clicked in. "The targets are going to be Penn Station, the Long Island Rail Road, the office buildings over it, the subways underground . . . places where thousands of people will be in harm's way."

I was blown away and thought, *What a perfect target.* I had always thought how poor the security was in the One Penn Plaza parking garage. I used to park there to see a few clients in the building. They never checked incoming cars for any weapons, bombs, nothing. They never even screened people for weapons and I don't recall ever seeing them check bags or backpacks. That always concerned me how they were so lax in such a busy location. So that was it.

"Kill the chickens in the pen," I said. "Penn Station. Those sick extremist maniacs. Now what other famous targets could be at risk?"

Just then, the Chinese food finally arrived. I was drained, tired, and famished, but more tired than hungry. I gave Laura a hug, surprising myself with such a natural manner as she smiled up at me.

"Long time, huh? Nice to break the ice, right?" I said.

"Yes, Bob, but it's too complicated for right now. Let's just eat," she replied.

"You're right, Laura," I replied.

We all moved into a more spacious room to enjoy the lunch. Before I could join them, I had to change the dressings on my stomach wounds. I could feel the pain throbbing and remembered the nurse's after-care instructions to prevent infection. I excused myself briefly, grabbing a kit out of my bag on my way to the bathroom. Levine had already updated Wendy and Ari about my Penn Station theory by the time I joined them to eat. I didn't think sleep would be on our agenda tonight, so I popped a couple more pain pills to keep me going. We had to figure out what other historical sites were about to be sabotaged.

I suddenly almost choked on a dumpling as I repeated the words, "The men who built America" to myself. *So, who were the men that built America?* I pondered.

While cracking open a fortune cookie, I said out loud, "Hey people, let's talk about the famous men who built up our country. Who were they?"

We were all embarrassed when Ari said, "Come on, my friends, let's start with Rockefeller."

"We all know about this guy. Good, Ari," Levine replied. "And that leads us to the Rockefeller Center. So, now we have Penn Station and possibly the Rockefeller Center."

Laura stood up and said, "Hey, Bob, come on, how many times have we seen concerts at Carnegie Hall?"

"Okay, so big deal, Carnegie Hall," I said. "Stupid me, shit, that's right. Carnegie Steel Company."

"And J. P. Morgan, who created U.S. Steel Corporation," Levine added.

"So, what do we have here guys?" I asked.

"We have precious historical landmarks possibly set up to be destroyed at any moment. We are most likely talking about Rockefeller Center, Carnegie Hall, and Penn Station," Frank confirmed as he stood just inside the room near the door.

"Well, well it's Frank Conway, our FBI guru," Levine said cutely.

I stood up to shake his hand.

"It's okay, Stone," Frank said. "No need to be so formal with me. I heard all about your Toronto and Istanbul adventures. Happy to see you're alive and well. Our colleagues at the FBI and at HPAT 21 thank you for your patriotism and bravery."

I felt a little inhibited, but I had to get a point across. "Let's not forget the Konar factor: There are six missing canisters of germ and bacterial weapons totally unaccounted for. How does that fit into this grand scenario?" I asked.

"Well, that is the missing link, isn't it?" Frank replied. "Clearly, the threat of poisoning the NYC water supply is still a reality."

"Yes, of course," I responded, thinking of another point. Levine and Frank leaned in, waiting for me to get it out. "There are two warehouses that the Narico Group expressed an interest in buying in Manhattan. But those deals fell through. Those two warehouses may have given them access to the water supply. Maybe it's a leap, but I wonder if any of these other historical locations have any water supply pipes or tunnels below the surface."

"Smart thought, Stone," Levine said. "Obviously not Penn Station, since there it's all subways. We must make a call into the NYC Municipal Water Finance Authority right now. Let's not make any assumptions here. Maybe, just maybe, there is some link to the water supply under Penn Plaza and those other historical sites."

"Maybe we're on to something," I said.

Frank took a look at me, paused, and said, "That just might be the last piece of the puzzle. I'll have my staff handle that one, right now."

Frank left the room to make some calls. It was already 4:45 p.m., so no doubt the folks over at the water district were about to call it a day. Meantime, Levine walked me to the interview room where Ammi was being held.

"Are you ready to go in there and level with your client Ammi?" Levine asked. "And I can say this, if he does not talk, we will call in Dr. Singh to make him talk."

"Sure," I answered. "I'm ready."

"Good luck, Stone," Levine muttered as he slowly walked away.

***

I gently pushed open the heavy metal door and was greeted with a disheveled Ammi. His hands and feet were chained to a heavy wooden chair. He looked up at me in shock.

"Bob Stone, my tax man," Ammi said. "Why are you here?"

"You were my client and we've gotten to know each other over the years. You and I have been through a long journey together, don't you agree? "I asked him.

He said nothing.

"Do you remember the first time I walked into your flower shop five years ago?" I asked.

"Yes," he replied.

"Do you remember that you asked me to come back the following week to help you with your tax problems?" I pressed.

"Yes, once again," he responded.

"I remember thinking that you were a foreign guy in a cash business in Manhattan with no checkbook, no records, no nothing," I ranted, launching into my next tirade. "And you asked me to clean up your unfiled tax returns. I knew in my heart that I was going down a bad road, but I chose to work with you for that large fee. I was hoping you would have said, 'No, too much money,' and I would have been ready to walk away from our deal. But you immediately agreed to my intentionally high fee of fifteen thousand dollars and you asked me to please help you. I compromised myself, my profession, and my values.

"You see, Ammi, I had a gut feeling you were somehow an evildoer just waiting for the right time to hurt us here in America, the same country that was so good to you and to your family over the years. You should know I found out only recently that the Internal Revenue

Service had been watching us: me as your tax preparer and you as the owner of a cash business diverting large sums of cash to terrorists.

"It's no secret any longer that these funds have been flowing to the Royal Bank in Toronto, to the Bank of Turkey and finally, to the Bank of Japan branch in Istanbul, Turkey. We know everything, Ammi. It's over. Kandallah has disappeared and is out of the picture. Omar Korbachi, the weapons dealer, was arrested yesterday. Want to hear more?" I asked without really seeking his reply. "The law firm Korbachi used as a vehicle to funnel money through was just closed down. It's over and done. So, Ammi, save yourself—and your family." I mentioned his family to see if I had hit a nerve.

One thing for sure, I recall how emotional he was at his daughter's wedding. Ammi's eyes dilated, and he immediately looked up.

"What do you mean, 'my family'?" he demanded.

That was it, the response I needed.

"Off the record, and sorry for what I am about to say, but if you do not help us—and I mean right now—we have plans to blow up your home and kill your entire family."

Tears rolled out of his eyes as he cried out, "No, no," he yelled. "This cannot be."

I stood up and walked slowly toward the door to make him think I was walking out of the room.

"Wait, please," Ammi pleaded. "I sent all my friends to your office, I put so much money into your hands," he cried out. "How can you do this to me?"

"You and your friends are disgusting human beings," I replied. "You came into our country to enjoy everything that we stand for, and then turn against us to force your own vision of how you think we should live and what we should believe in. You are free to believe in your ways, but leave us to believe in our chosen beliefs, whether they are Christian, Jewish, or whatever . . . Now, tell us right now, what buildings are your followers going to destroy? Why and when?"

He sat in silence for a moment. I walked over to him and stood over him, waiting another moment before I placed my hands on the sides of his head, squeezing in hard against his ears. I started to sweat with a rush of energy emerging within me.

"Tell me now or you will suffer from torture you could never imagine. You think we Americans are not able to do that?" I asked. Just then, the door opened. "Ah, here he is, our Dr. Singh."

The retired dentist walked in carrying his usual black bag filled with the tools of his trade. He placed the scrapers, pointy tools, and hooked metal probes on a metallic platter. I could see Ammi staring, sweating, and breathing heavily.

"Last chance to save yourself and your family, Ammi," I said. "Dr. Singh, can you show our friend here your first step?"

"Of course, Mr. Stone," Dr. Singh replied.

The doctor picked up one of the hooked instruments and moved it under Ammi's nose instead of his teeth as it was intended for. Before it even touched him, Ammi caved in.

"Stop, okay? Stop!" he screamed. "I will talk . . . just spare my family, please."

Levine came in and moved next to Ammi to tell Dr. Singh to stop and promised Ammi the torture would end. Dr. Singh wrapped up his tools and left the room, with Levine following him.

Levine came back in shortly after with Wendy and a voice recorder. Wendy gave Ammi a glass of water. We all waited for him to talk when he was ready. Three long minutes elapsed, the tension mounting.

Ammi started to repeat, "All praises be to Allah, the Almighty." He repeated this five times to himself, but just loud enough for us to hear. His eyes opened wide, his lips parted. "Islamic extremist brothers are going to wear explosive backpacks. They are going to start with smoke bombs and after that, four locations will be bombed."

"Tell us more," I said.

"They are going to destroy the buildings that stand today in the name of those men who built up America in its early days," he continued. "And they are Carnegie Hall for Andrew Carnegie and his steel company, Rockefeller Center, and George Washington's statue near Wall Street."

"You did not mention Penn Station," I interrupted.

"That is also going to happen, it is the grand prize for our Islamic extremist brothers," Ammi replied.

"But why?" I asked.

"Because Penn Station represents everything they envy and hate about America."

I said nothing in response, waiting for him to add more thoughts.

"Yes," Ammi replied. "All the people going into and out of Manhattan every day with their dreams and hopes to get ahead in the world, hopes that the terrorists feel they have no access to."

"I get it. So, when is all of this supposed to happen?" I asked.

He would not respond. A long minute elapsed, and he finally looked up at me.

"I have a question, Stone," he said.

"Yes, Ammi?"

"How do I know your government will not kill my family and what will do you with me?" he asked.

I turned to Levine and replied, "Just one moment."

We all left the room. This was a dilemma. Levine called Frank. They were on the phone together for about fifteen minutes.

"Stone, this is the deal—the only deal," Levine said. "Ammi will have to be in jail for the next three years, a reduced sentence from what could have been far longer. His entire family will be deported immediately back to Saudi Arabia. After serving his jail term, Ammi will return to his family. The only catch is that he must work for HPAT 21 and go undercover for us. Ya know, wear a wire and help us to catch his fellow extremists—maybe even Konar. If Ammi stays with HPAT 21, we may be able to reduce his jail term even lower."

"Seems like you are asking me to present this deal to Ammi, correct?" I asked.

"Stone, you have gotten so good at this. Yes, absolutely, it should come from you," Levine replied.

"All I can do is to try."

Levine handed me a document from Frank. It was a written confession and agreement for Ammi to assist us, to help save our homeland and our citizens from acts of terror. In return, his deal would be honored. Simple, in theory, actually. It was like any other business contract, Business Law 101: consideration given to another in exchange for a promised action, or in this case, for a promise not to participate in a future action. I thought of my father, the lawyer that I had always looked up to. How fitting a moment this was and he might even have been proud of me.

I looked up to Levine and assured him that I would do my best to get Ammi to sign off on this gift of a deal. Jaab walked through the front door of the basement. He had a large bag of food for himself, having missed out on the Chinese food. It gave me an idea.

"Levine, can you ask Jaab to hurry up and go out to the nearest Middle Eastern restaurant?" I requested. "I need him to bring back Turkish coffee, a plate of chicken kebabs with special rice, and a few baklavas for dessert. I have to warm up Ammi, make him feel attended to, cared about, like we'll have his back going forward."

"Okay," Levine agreed. "Good idea. Meantime while I catch up with Jaab, go back to Ammi. Give him a choice for either coffee or water. Let's relax the poor guy."

On his way in, Levine asked Wendy to join us as an additional witness. I had already begun asking Ammi how his daughter was enjoying married life. He seemed to appreciate that. After a few minutes, I sensed the barriers were coming down somewhat. I felt an opening to start the process. Internally, I also realized how much we had to do over the next forty-eight hours to make all this work. My attention returned to Ammi.

"Stone, why don't you start the discussion with Ammi?" Wendy suggested.

"Sure," I replied. "Yes, let's talk, Ammi. We have some good news for you. I know you will be pleased. You know, Ammi, I have never let you down with your tax issues, your business, and now with your life, as well. I want to help you again."

Jaab was about to walk in with the food but he came to a quick stop by the doorway. Wendy waved him into our room. Levine undid the hand cuffs. The food was spread out on the table used by Dr. Singh. Just the smell of the food was enough to break the ice. I set up a nice plate for Ammi and pushed it gently over to him.

"Relax now, Ammi, the worst is over," I said. "As long as you're going to help us. You eat, and I will read you the deal, your special gift from the American authorities."

It was a lot easier than I imagined. By the time he finished his plate and the baklava was shoved in front of him with the Turkish coffee, Ammi had agreed. He signed the papers. He also agreed to help us to locate and capture his Islamic extremist brothers. He seemed relieved and I sensed that he never really had the stomach for terrorism anyway. Perhaps in his mind it was his last chance to start a new life, a life without hatred. In my head, I felt terrible that I had to threaten his family. I never would have followed through with the threats against them, but he could not have known that for sure.

To tilt the odds in our favor, Ashton was asked to evaluate Ammi. Ashton requested that everyone leave the room except for me as a witness. Ammi went under in no time as Ashton performed his magic. While under, it was reinforced to him that his help was needed, that his past life as an Islamic extremist was terminated forever. Ashton told Ammi that his family would be safe, that he would be returned to his homeland eventually, emphasizing that this would only take place after he fulfilled his promise to help us find the evildoers. Ashton asked him if he understood what we needed him to do.

"Yes," Ammi replied.

Ashton asked him if we could count on his help.

Again, he responded, "Yes."

Ashton finished with a final command that when Ammi awoke he would never again seek to hurt or to kill anyone and that he would do everything in his power to save lives. Ammi responded, "Yes," and slowly woke up.

***

We all needed a break. As we exited the room, I suggested to Levine that I'd like to step outside with Ammi and walk around for a block or two. I wanted to test his sincerity to see if he would bolt.

"Let's bring Jaab with us outside and one of the HPAT 21 guards," I suggested.

"Go ahead, Stone. I'll go with you, too. I also need some fresh air," Levine agreed.

After about fifteen minutes, I realized that Ammi was going to be alright and we went back to the basement.

Frank greeted us in. "Guys, I need to get going," Frank said. "Levine, here is the voice-activated micro earpiece. You know the drill, just pop it deep inside his ear canal. This is our newest blue tooth earpiece and wiretap device linked directly to the U.S. Department of Homeland Security. It cannot be detected. And please, don't forget to snap the tracking device into the back of his neck."

"Goodbye for now, everyone," Frank blurted out, holding up his right hand with a V for victory.

"There are still unanswered questions to discuss," I said.

"What, Stone?" Wendy probed.

"Ammi, exactly when are these attacks going to happen?" I asked.

"All planned acts of terror are going to happen at the same time, at exactly 8:15 a.m. in Japan on the morning of August sixth," Ammi answered.

"I wonder why that specific time?" Levine asked.

"This I do not know, Mr. Levine," Ammi replied. "But it was set up by that Japanese extremist, Konar. He is a crazy one, believe me. I met him one time for just a few minutes. There was a horrible feeling this Konar revealed. He showed a true hatred beyond that of most people I have ever met in my life. It is hard for me to explain this."

"Try, Ammi," I replied. "Every detail is important."

"I witnessed Konar take a knife and slam it into his own left leg as he yelled and looked up. He laughed and shouted in Japanese before

352 • ERIC J. ENGELHARDT

dropping to his knees. There was no explained reason for this. The man is crazy," Ammi explained.

"I guess so. He's crazy, alright," I said. "One more confirmation that Konar's plans remain intact. That date was the exact time and day that America dropped the atomic bomb over Hiroshima."

"Ah, that's right," Levine said. "Now I remember. And this is the seventieth anniversary of that bombing."

"I see you're also a history lover, Levine," I said.

"Yes, but this is not the kind of history I could possibly appreciate," he replied.

Levine handed Wendy the surveillance items from Frank to install on Ammi's body. Ari headed over to help her. I hung around to keep Ammi comfortable. Somehow, I felt responsible for him. We had made enormous progress, but I sensed some lack of direction.

"So, guys," I said. "All this has been fun. Where do we go from here? What's the plan?"

Ammi shocked all of us as he responded, "Every night in our mosque, there is a gathering. After general discussions are finished and the members go home, about eight of us stay to discuss and to plan terrorism against America. I can go there tonight to try to see if any of the planned attacks I told you about have been changed."

We had no choice. It was time to let Ammi do what he was supposed to do. It was agreed, Ammi was to be released for now. The tracking device was securely in place on the back of his neck, hidden well by Wendy and Ari under his shirt collar. All systems were a go: the moment of truth had arrived as we led him out the door.

"Ammi, here is your HPAT 21 cell phone," I said. "Call us tonight at ten-thirty p.m. If you are with your brothers, call us as soon as you can without looking obvious. Maybe we will meet you later tonight to talk and regroup." I shook his hand while my eyes drilled into his eyes for confirmation.

"Stone, I see worry on your face," he said. "Do not worry, I am with you now."

He walked away, and the basement door was closed securely behind him. I sat down and collapsed onto the nearest chair. Laura approached me, putting her hands atop my shoulders.

"Choices, choices, huh, Bob? It's not easy," Laura said. "You could have just continued to be a boring tax man, but you wanted excitement in your life. You certainly got what you wished for, didn't you?"

I heard her, but there was nothing for me to say. I allowed her remark to melt away.

"Hold on, wait a minute," she said, suddenly looking troubled.

"Now what's up, Laura?" I asked.

"How did you meet Ammi? And why did you ever take him on as a client? What happened to your better judgment at that time?" she probed.

"Wow, if you are lawyering me, don't prejudge my past behavior, it's not so simple," I retorted.

"Come on, tell me. How did you connect with Ammi, an owner of a flower store, when at that time you had many doctors as clients?" she interrogated.

"In a nutshell, and if you can recall, I was fed up with those medical clients and due to my bad attitude, they began to leave my office. You were a rising star in the law firm. I felt insecure. I was afraid to break away into another career. So, I decided that I would look for more clients, any clients, who could help me to keep my financial end of our marriage on a level playing field. I wanted you to see that I, too, was doing well.

"When I went to buy you flowers in Ammi's store on one Friday, years ago in Manhattan, I flipped him my business card. He called me back a few days later asking me to return to his store to talk with him about some tax issues. When we met the following week, he told me that he had been in business for many years and had never filed personal or business tax returns. I was in a tough spot, at a crossroads. I sensed that he was way over his head in tax problems much more than a typical client with basic tax issues. In my gut, I felt he might even be a front for some underground activity. Whatever he might have been up to, I was in denial.

"But I really felt he was living in his own world, below the bottom line, if you know what I mean. Yet, I made my decision, I chose to work with him for all the reasons I mentioned, for the large fee he paid to me and fast forward, here I am. I have nothing more to say—"

Laura was fixated on my face and locked into my eyes as she said, "You took on a client because you felt threatened by my success?"

"Maybe you'll never understand that, but partially yes. I was also afraid to fail, so I needed a quick victory at the time, a new client to calm me down," I admitted.

"All you had to do was to talk it out with me, a little communication, Bob," she replied.

"You're right. I panicked, became impulsive, and now, I need to do my best going forward to make up for my past errors in judgment."

"I'm speechless. Let's just get some sleep," Laura curtly replied as she walked away.

I nodded my head in agreement and turned on my side for a brief interlude.

PART SEVEN

CHAPTER 34

The steamy, overcast August day in Manhattan turned into twilight. We were all escorted to a nearby Holiday Inn located in the Midtown area. Three HPAT 21 guards walked us to an elevator, then up to our adjoining rooms. I took a moment to step back and observe everyone present as all met up in the dining room in the deluxe suite. I thought to myself about the underlying world of terrorism and taxes that connected us altogether as I looked around the room at Levine, Ashton, Laura, Wendy, Ari, and Jaab. Missing were Scott McCann and Evelyn, who was always on my mind as she continued to recover from her wounds at the hospital in Adana, Turkey.

Ten minutes later, Greek food arrived. We didn't have time to waste going to dinner with barely enough time to eat. We were so much more nervous than hungry.

"Levine, I'm curious," I said. "We're all here except for Scott. Where is he?"

"A few days ago, I sent him to Reykjavík, Iceland. Scott uncovered that Omar Korbachi made large transfers from the offshore Korbachi Family Trust account based in Australia into a bank in Iceland. So, I sent him to follow the flow of funds and head off to the KRB Bank of Iceland. Scott's efforts led to Korbachi's arrest by INTERPOL. After that, I sent Scott to Hiroshima to check into Konar and the World War Two Unit 731 you uncovered, and whatever else he might learn. His first stop was the American Embassy and off to meet with the manager over at the headquarters of the Bank of Japan."

"When was the last time you heard from him?" I pondered.

"Yesterday," Levine replied. "He's doing alright. Time is tight and he's doing the best he can. I sent him there with another HPAT agent who speaks Japanese, to be his translator and guide. Scott should be texting me in one hour."

"Do you think it's getting late in the game?" I asked. "We still have not yet heard from Ammi."

I must have struck a nerve because as Levine gazed at me, he seemed to be looking right through me. He stood up to grab his cell phone off the table.

"Hello, Frank. We cannot wait any longer," Levine said. "Permission to go to Code WOP five-five-five—"

"What the hell is 'WOP'?"

"It stands for 'wall of protection.' We are sending National Guard troops, NYC police, and U.S. Marines to protect the city, including the George Washington Bridge, all other bridges, the Queens Midtown Tunnel, Penn Station, Grand Central Station, Carnegie Hall, Rockefeller Center, the Empire State building, and the statue of George Washington near Wall Street. They'll be watching for a possible attempt to dump bacteria into the water supply and/or to possibly blow up some of these landmarks."

I started to think about Konar and his great-grandfather, Kona, one of the highest-ranking Japanese generals, who surrendered on behalf of Emperor Hirohito in 1945. I thought of the power of the payback, the extent to which deep-seated revenge can drive people to commit unthinkable acts. I reflected, *Why not pick the brain of our resident psychologist, Ashton?* I walked over to Ashton and sat quietly for a moment. "I need your help with something."

"About. . . ?" he responded in one of his typical open-ended replies trained to get the other person to talk. The ultimate psychologist. "What's on your mind, Stone?"

I began, "Listen up. We are dealing with a young, extremist Japanese man, deformed from radiation. His family suffered horribly back in 1945 from the atomic bomb we dropped on Hiroshima. They continued to suffer for many years after."

"I'm sorry—how do you know he was deformed?" Ashton posed.

"Wendy showed me an FBI photo of Konar and it's not a pretty picture," I replied. "Konar feels it is his responsibility to carry out a vendetta to honor his great-grandfather, his country, and avenge the damage he and his family have suffered. What are we missing, Ashton? You are an experienced psychologist. Please talk to me about revenge. Does this all really drive a person to commit such horrifying acts against innocent people?"

He paused, looked at me, and then placed his hands on the sides of his face. Ashton was collecting his thoughts.

His head rose up as he said, "Stone, revenge is a human response to feeling slighted, taken advantage of, or cheated in some way. If a person who seeks revenge is also a controlling person, someone who needs social dominance and respect for traditions, those are the ones who seek out serious acts of vengeance."

I was taking it all in as Ashton continued.

"The triggers of revenge differ across cultures. Anger in individuals and shaming a large group of people may trigger acute revenge. Combine all of that with an angry individual who also represents a society that's been humiliated in such a horrific way, this may give birth to unimaginable acts of revenge. Think about this now, how does a person who has been physically and emotionally scarred, whose family, city, and country were destroyed as well . . . how does that person deal with it all? Would that person seek revenge on buildings, on another person, or to those individuals in charge who may have had a connection to the first act?"

"Well, I don't know, Ashton."

"It's deeply personal to the avenger," Ashton replied. "So, the potential acts of vengeance will be more emotional and much more personal."

"How do you think it all could affect Konar's retaliation?" I asked.

"I am a psychologist, not a historian, Stone," Ashton replied with a shrug.

360 • ERIC J. ENGELHARDT

The word *historian* launched my mind into a thought process. I knew I'd have to dig deep into some aspect of history. I felt the need to bounce this off Laura. She always had such a very sharp intuition.

"Laura, I need you for a moment," I began. "You and I love history, right?"

"Sure," Laura replied.

I paced around the room. Laura let me ramble on for a few minutes. I started to talk about the people who played major roles just before and after the bombing of Hiroshima.

"Why did we drop the bomb?" I asked out loud. "Yes, to end the war and to save potentially hundreds of millions of lives, as the Japanese would have continued to fight on for their Emperor within their homeland. Harry S. Truman was our thirty-third president at that time. He took over upon the death of our beloved Franklin D. Roosevelt and life went on. Hiroshima was rebuilt over the years, but the Japanese people remained ill and died over time from radiation sickness and cancer. Both sides were brutal to the other. Yet, the Japanese and the Americans moved forward in peace. The whole world moved ahead into a new age. New generations of young people emerged. Yet, we have this Konar, who feels the weight of revenge is on his back. So, what would make Konar's revenge extra sweet? What would even it all up in his twisted mind?"

"That's difficult to answer, Bob," Laura pondered. "But maybe not so difficult after all."

"Oh?" I replied, prompting her to say more. I grinned, realizing that I had just pulled an Ashton routine.

"If someone was deformed for the rest of his life, his family humiliated, and his ancestors destroyed by invaders, maybe the avenger would take it out on his counterpart, on the other side?"

"What does that mean?" I asked.

"This may sound crazy, this whole thing is nuts anyway, so here goes," Laura replied. "Is it possible that Konar would seek to destroy the life of his only contemporary enemy related to Truman? Let's do a quick search on President Truman's family, his children, and his great-grandchildren. Remember, I was heavy into legal research? For me, research is like a walk in the park, I love this stuff."

"Okay, okay, like a walk in the park," I said imitating her. I lost my focus.

"Calm down, buddie, just listen to your—err—wife, you knucklehead," Levine chuckled.

"Okay, Levine, now you're getting me in trouble," I snapped.

"Guys, give me a few minutes of quiet, please" Laura snapped.

Laura typed furiously on her laptop computer, researching Truman's family, his descendants, and so forth. She began reading out loud to us:

"President Truman's birthplace was in Lamar, Missouri. His only daughter, Margaret, married Elbert Clifton Daniel, Jr., and they had four sons, Clifton Truman, William, Harrison, and Thomas. Truman, who was vice president, took office in April 1945 after President Roosevelt died. Truman insisted on the immediate and unconditional surrender of Japan.

"Now check this out—on February fifth, twenty-thirteen, Charles, son of Clifton Truman, the great-grandson of Harry Truman, was an actor doing some tricks in an opera performance. His face mask caught fire while attempting a stunt during a dress rehearsal and he was seriously burned. He was taken to the hospital and diagnosed with only second-degree burns, no internal injuries.

That's an incredible story, but it just cannot be a coincidence. Do you think . . . ?"

"Come on, Laura, give it a break," I said. "Are you making a connection between that fire, Truman's great-grandson, and Konar?"

"How old is Konar?" she asked.

"I believe now he is about twenty-six," I replied. "How old was Truman's great-grandson at the time of the fire?"

"It says, age twenty-four. That was three years ago, putting Truman's great-grandson now at age twenty-seven."

"A near perfect match," Laura said. "So, it's starting to make much more sense now. Look here, it says that Truman's grandson, Clifton

Truman, went to Hiroshima on August fourth, twenty-twelve, to attend a wreath-laying ceremony at the Hiroshima Peace Memorial Park. When asked, he would not apologize to anyone for America's bombing of Hiroshima. Yet, he still became well known as the first member of the Truman family to honor the victims of this tragic event. The trip was sponsored by the Sadako Legacy, named after Sadako Sasaki, an atomic bomb victim, who died of leukemia at the age of twelve. Clifton later met with her seventy-one-year-old brother, Masahiro Sasaki, who had miraculously survived the bombing."

Levine jumped up from his chair and said, "Okay, I'm sold on this. This is one for the FBI. I'll update Frank on this theory. The FBI will immediately protect all Truman family members."

A call from Ammi came through on my cell phone. Levine nudged me to grab the call. I answered it on speaker phone.

"Hello, Ammi," I said, eagerly anticipating his information.

"Yes, hello, Stone," Ahmed said. "I must talk quick. It's Kandallah's Iranian followers, not ISIS—they will be attacking all bridges, tunnels, and other famous locations in Manhattan. They want a panic."

"When, Ammi? When?" I asked.

"I do not know that. But wait, wait . . . there's more to tell you. The Iranians want you Americans to believe—" The call dropped.

"What the hell just happened?!" I exclaimed.

"What's going on?" Levine asked.

"I don't really know. Is he in danger? Ammi might have been killed moments ago as he was trying to tell me something, apparently critical info.

"Damn it, that sounds ominous," Levine said. "The Iranians want America to believe . . . believe what? Seems like some sort of a deception going on, but what? What? I'll call the U.S. Department of Homeland Security. I'll also get on the direct line we have into the police chief. All hell is about to break loose, I can smell it after all my years dealing with acts of terror," he said, expressing his deepest fears.

"Absolutely," I answered in solidarity. I, too, revealed my fears expanding on Levine's remarks. "These terrorists are trying to pull off simultaneous attacks all over Manhattan. People, it's a war, a damn war zone. And yet, there is still a missing link, something Ammi was about to tell me within seconds, but he was either killed or forced to stop talking. Now is the time to dig deep, to fight the fight." My fist tightened. I was frustrated, and it led to a buildup of anger.

"Maybe it's time to begin an evacuation of Manhattan," Wendy suggested.

Ari, who had been quiet, replied, "Sure, but how do we evacuate millions in eight hours? No, it's time to go on the offensive. We have no choice."

"Right, I agree. We have no choice," Levine vehemently said as he reached for his cell.

Levine was on the phone for only ten minutes, but it seemed like hours.

"The president has been kept in the loop about these developments," Levine informed us. "He insists on informing the general public about a series of potential terror attacks in and around the city of New York. Now, it's up to the troops, marines, coast guard, and local police. The additional forces will be flowing into the city over the next few hours, with helicopters and gunships. Effective at eleven-forty-five p.m. tonight, all bridges and tunnels will be sealed off. Upon inspection, all cars and trucks will be seized or redirected back to the suburbs. A midnight curfew will be announced by the president in just a few minutes. We are getting closer and closer to martial law, it's scary."

"Meantime, we need to know more from Ammi and fast," I said. "Wendy, please check out his tracking device reports. Where he is right now? Is he on the move or whatever."

"Okay, Bob," Wendy said, pulling up the report on her laptop. "Right now, he is in the mosque located in Astoria, Queens. He did go home first and made a stop at a nearby 7/11 before going to the mosque. That's where he has been for the past three hours."

"Thanks for that, Wendy," Levine said shaking his head. "If he does not call back in fifteen minutes, we'll have no choice. We must take bold action."

"What does that mean, Levine?" I asked.

"It means we approach and maybe even attack the mosque, capture whoever we can, and get quick answers. I'll accept responsibility for this, I'll own this decision. It's time to get Scott on the line. He's your man, Stone, you call him."

I picked up my cell phone and dialed. "Hello, Scott?"

"Aye, Bob, is that you?" Scott replied.

"Put it on speaker," Levine commanded.

I pressed the button so that everyone could hear.

"Yes, Scott, this is Bob Stone," I replied. "We're all on the call with you. What's up? We are running on empty here. . . . Anything for us?"

"Yeah sure, let me start with a joke," Scott replied. "What's the most famous coffee in Afghanistan?"

"There's no time for this crap," I said.

"Okay," Scott said. "It's Osama Bin Latte."

"You're crazy, Scott," but I did manage to laugh.

"Sorry," Scott said with a chuckle. "Okay, this is all that I know here. The infamous Konar is in Hiroshima now. He will attend, as he does every year, the Hiroshima Peace Memorial Ceremony on August sixth. This year, Konar is the key speaker."

"What else? Keep going, Scott," Levine said.

"Sure," Scott continued. "I just found out that an American scientist signed a request to visit the site of Unit 731 four months ago. His name is Jason Cumberland. That's all I have. I suggest you guys check this Jason fella out immediately."

"I've got this one guys," Wendy said and then asked Laura to help her with research.

"Oh, my god. Here is something," Wendy said. "Jason Cumberland. Attended Stony Brook University in New York. Graduated twenty-eleven. He had a double major in chemistry and history. That's a weird combo. Worked for the Center for Disease Control and Prevention for three years. Terminated July thirty-first, twenty-fourteen, due to behavioral issues. Requested a U.S. government grant to start up a bio lab to study Ebola. Request was denied September twenty-fourth, twenty-fourteen."

"Currently self-employed," Laura added. "He works in a biosafety level three lab in Trenton, New Jersey."

"Really nice work," Levine said. "This is it, people. This is the moment of truth. It's when the tough get tougher or the weak bolt and crumble. Are we all together on this?"

I stood up immediately followed by everyone else who stood up. Each of us blurted out a yes.

"May I suggest that a special forces unit hit the mosque in Astoria, Queens?" Ari broached. "I sense that Ammi may have been discovered helping us, then captured or killed, merely by the tone of his voice. That dropped call at such a critical point with what he was about to tell you—you're right to be suspicious, Stone," Ari said.

"I hope you're wrong, Ari," Levine replied." Anyway, I'm in favor of hitting that mosque right away.?"

"I agree, Levine," I replied. "No more time to waste."

"What about the mad scientist in Trenton?" Wendy asked.

"I'll have Frank's FBI contacts pick up Jason Cumberland and coordinate with the CIA," Levine responded.

"One thing, Levine," I said. "I feel personally responsible for Ammi. I'm going with the unit to the mosque."

"Bob, you're crazy," Laura said.

"The whole world is crazy," I replied. "What's the difference?"

She looked at me and shrugged her shoulders, most likely in agreement.

Ari said, "I am no scientist, but if this guy is working with germs from that World War Two Unit 731 in a level-three lab, then it sounds damn serious. So, maybe those germ canisters were shipped to Trenton, New Jersey, first and then taken by truck into Manhattan the other day?"

"Good thought, Ari," I said. "Seems logical, but we won't have any answers until we find and arrest Cumberland."

"Of course," Levine replied. "But for now, we need to get Cumberland and simply find out where the remaining germ canisters are going to be dropped and when. That's all that matters now."

Levine called Frank to explain the Jason Cumberland situation. A SWAT team was sent out immediately to hunt him down. Then Levine contacted the New York police chief and asked him to deploy police forces and special ops' snipers around the mosque, in Astoria, Queens. This was to take place within one hour.

"Stone, you'll need to take a helicopter to get there in time," Ari yelled out. "I'm going with you."

"Okay, cowboys, you made it through Istanbul together, so go ahead," Levine replied. "The heliport is near the United Nations building at Forty-sixth Street and First Avenue. I'll instruct an HPAT 21 driver to escort you guys there. I'll call the heliport to have them fly you both to that mosque. Be careful, I've grown to like you guys," Levine said jokingly.

Wendy remotely clicked on the television. The president of the United States had just started a live appearance and was speaking.

"Good evening, my fellow Americans," the president began. "We do not have time to waste, so I will get to the point. We have been closely tracking terrorist threats over the past few weeks. The threat assessment appears to be quite serious. It is possible that some of our historical landmarks in New York City, specifically Manhattan, may be at risk in a series of attacks. I have also been advised that our water supply might be compromised. At this time, Police Chief John Krieger, Southeastern Director of the FBI Franklin Conway, and Director of the Department for Homeland Security Alan Jeffries have developed a strategy. All threat assessments and strategies have been coordinated and approved by New York's governor and mayor, who are with us right now."

The governor began to talk. "Thank you, Mr. President. Our beloved Manhattan, our people, and various landmarks including tunnels and bridges are all potentially at risk. Although we cannot be sure at this time, preliminary reports indicate that we are being targeted by extremist groups, most likely ISIS, in combination with other terror cells and groups. Our strategy is designed to minimize acts of terror and to maximize your personal safety. We are working together with the New York police force, the Coast Guard, and the National Guard to block all entry or exit to Manhattan. All cars approaching tunnels and bridges will be inspected, carefully evaluated, and redirected accordingly. Unfortunately, a city-wide curfew must be initiated, effective at eleven forty-five p.m. tonight."

Then the mayor walked to the podium to speak. "Please remain indoors until further notice following the curfew. With your cooperation and your prayers, Manhattan will be saved, and lives will be spared. Please cooperate and stay off the streets. As always, if you see something unusual, call the special hotline number on your screen. By all means, and until further notice, as a precautionary measure, please do not drink any tap water. Thank you."

The president concluded, "To all Americans, I say this: We are living in unusual times. We are in an era of unpredictable extremism leading to acts of terror beyond our imagination. It will be difficult, but we will prevail. We need to protect ourselves. We need to be more aggressive in tracking down terrorists, which means to a certain extent the invasion of our privacy. At the same time, we must avoid becoming a country moving closer to martial law. We must preserve our rights and privileges under the Constitution. Clearly, this is the dilemma of our democracy today. I say this, that we are on the right side of history. We will not only survive, we will defeat evil. Thank you. Good night and may God bless our great nation."

The president shook everyone's hands and then departed. Wendy shut off the television. To say it was depressing was an understatement. The whole scenario was beyond insane.

CHAPTER 35

Levine sparked us all into action. "Okay, it's time to move on," he commanded. "Stone, you and Ari go to the main lobby door. The guards are ready to escort you. . . . Here are your pistols and laser guns—one for each of you. Be careful. The objective is to find and secure Ammi, try to avoid killing innocent bystanders and of course, we need information, not dead bodies, okay?"

He stared into our eyes, searching for a reply.

I spoke up first, "Okay, sure," I answered in an insecure tone.

I checked my watch. It was just after midnight. My hands trembled. It was already August 4th, and since we were twelve hours behind Japan, it would be 8:15 p.m. our time when the Peace Bell rang in Hiroshima. There was just too much going on. I started to review everything that was in jeopardy, including the NYC water supply, historical landmarks, tunnels, and bridges. I thought about the mosque and recovering Ammi, the Truman family situation, the mad chemist, Jason Cumberland . . . and then I went back in time to Konar's great-grandfather, the 1945 bombings, trying to visualize what it may have been like in Hiroshima during aftermath of the massive explosions and radiation poisoning. Now the payback comes in the form of catastrophic acts of terror, with so many lives hanging in the balance.

I could not resolve in my mind why the Iranians' hateful plans and the Japanese pending acts of destruction were coming to a head at the same time. We had to keep going, we had to fight the good fight. If we lost this battle, it would only get worse. This was in reality, a war—a well-planned operation against the homeland. And it was starting right here and now, in our own backyard.

"Stone, I see you are in deep thought," Ari said. "Come on, get into the Jeep."

We arrived at Forty-sixth Street and First Avenue then were escorted to the United Nations building up to the roof level to board a NYC police helicopter. Up in the air quickly, we hovered over Manhattan and then looped toward the mosque in Astoria, Queens. As we approached what looked like a mosque from above, all lights over Manhattan behind us shut down completely. I was shocked and called Levine instantly.

"Hey what was that?" I asked him. "What just happened, Levine?"

"Not sure yet," Levine replied. "But it seems that the Islamic extremists penetrated Manhattan's electrical grid. It's a well-coordinated, smartly planned attack, Stone. You focus on Ammi and get your ass back as fast as you can."

The call ended. I searched through the darkness below, able to make out shadows and silhouettes of the skyscrapers and bridges in the distance.

I just couldn't believe what I saw in the night's sky: The George Washington Bridge exploded. Clouds of smoke filled the air as the bridge cascaded down into the dark waters below it. Ari placed his hand over my shoulder.

"Come on, Stone," he said. "I know it's devastating, but let's do what we can and move on."

I could not hold back the tears, yet I regained my composure. The helicopter slowed and hovered over a taller building. Our descent down to a rooftop near the mosque went smoother than I thought it might. The air was still on this August summer night but offered us an eerie calm away from the chaos happening in Manhattan.

Walking closer to the mosque, the building was surrounded by snipers, NYC police, and National Guard forces. A policeman at the edge of the perimeter waived us over, checked our U.S. Department of Homeland Security HPAT 21 security badges and granted us clearance to get closer. The Imam worship leader of the mosque came out to talk with the police. Ari and I introduced ourselves.

I took the lead and said, "We are here seeking peace and we need your help."

"I think that my people here need help as well," he proposed. "What do you want from us?"

"We understand," Ari said. "And what is your name?"

"This is my mosque," the Imam said. "These are my people. Most of them are peaceful, but a few are terribly extreme and unfortunately I cannot control them."

"Your name, please?" Ari insisted.

"I am Imam Adi Shirak-Aziz," he responded

"Imam Aziz, we are looking for Ahmed," I replied. "Is he here? Is he safe?"

"I am sorry," the Imam replied. "Ahmed was shot and killed by two extremists outside the mosque. It happened so fast. Ahmed was on his cell phone, he had the look of a guilty man on his face. I was at the doorway and witnessed his murder. Ahmed was a kind man. Earlier tonight, he told me that he wanted to prevent further violence, and that he wanted to stop acts of terror. He wanted to become a man of peace."

"Yes, I know," I replied somberly. "I was speaking with Ahmed on the phone when we got cutoff. I sensed he was in danger. However, I didn't know for sure if he had been killed."

"I had the same feeling. He hung up so quickly, I was sure that he was in danger," Ari said.

"Imam Aziz, please," I said. "We need your help. We are not here to place blame on anyone or on any group of people. You are a man of peace, so kindly tell us what you know. Did Ahmed tell you anything?"

"No, he did not," Imam Aziz replied. "Only that he was sorry that he had been helping the extremists and that he wanted to make up for his sins, his crimes against innocent people."

Ari intervened and shared some details to persuade the Imam. "Ahmed told us that all bridges, tunnels, and historical buildings around Manhattan would be attacked, but we are not sure by whom? Do you know anything about this? What time will these attacks take place and exactly where?"

"My friends, if I had the answers, I would surely tell you," Imam Aziz replied. "But I do not know these things."

Ari started to speak, paused, and then started again. "Excuse me, Imam, may we take a look inside the mosque?" he asked politely.

The Imam seemed taken by surprise by our request to go inside so he replied strangely, "There is nothing of value to you inside our sanctuary."

I lost my patience and time was running out. "Imam, the lives of millions may be on your hands unless you allow us inside the mosque," I urged. "And I mean now, right now."

"Of course, follow me," Imam Aziz agreed, and he walked toward the mosque.

I turned to one of the soldiers and nodded for him and two others to come inside the mosque with us. It was totally empty. I was enamored by the gold lining over the dome ceiling, the stained-glass designs on each door, and the simple prayer carpets laid out on the floor. The Imam paused midway into the mosque. We instinctively kept walking past him toward the stairs off to the right side of the room.

"Imam, where do these stairs lead?" Ari asked.

Ari and I looked at each other, waiting for an answer. The Imam quickly walked away, ignoring the question. His facial expression indicated that something was not right.

"Okay, let's get to the stairway," Ari said.

A police officer went with us as two others stood guard around the open areas inside the building. My instincts told me to pull out my laser gun, and to my surprise, Ari pulled a concealed pistol out of his inside coat pocket. As it turned out, the steps led down to what must have been a storage area of sorts.

When we came to the last step, I turned to my right and saw a man in shackles chained to the wall with a straw bag over his head. He was moaning, he was alive. I approached the man and pulled the bag off his head. It was Ammi, and he was in great pain.

"So, the Imam lied to us," I mumbled angrily under my breath.

The officer lifted Ammi up and carried him as we all walked back upstairs. As we exited, we saw Imam Aziz walking away. I ordered the officers accompanying us, "Hold that man for questioning, he's a person of interest."

Ari and I helped Ammi limp his way up the stairs and out of the mosque.

Levine texted me; the helicopter must leave immediately.

Although it was difficult to move quickly since Ammi was struggling to walk, we picked up our pace as best as we could. I actually carried Ammi half way back to the helicopter launch pad, just in time.

***

Up in the helicopter again, we approached Manhattan, which was happily a sea of lights. We landed on a rooftop helipad and were taken down to street level. An unmarked black HPAT 21 Jeep was waiting to take us back to the hotel with the others.

It was Jaab and Wendy who arrived first. Within minutes, we were back in our adjoining hotel rooms with everyone else. A doctor was there to examine Ammi. He was severely beaten, but no gunshot wounds were found. Although he needed to go to a hospital to be checked out further, that had to be delayed. We needed him with us, as new developments might continue to arise on this wild night. Levine's cell phone rang, leaving the call on speaker as he picked up.

"Hey it's Frank."

"Please tell us something good for a change," Levine requested.

"Copy that," Frank said. "Here we go. Jason Cumberland was captured at the bio lab. He had a remote bomb set up with his cell phone. The New York Municipal Water Authority provided us with excellent leads and we found out the bomb was hooked up to four of those Unit 731 germ canisters to the water supply lines under Penn Plaza. The other two missing canisters were going to be blown up under that statue of George Washington near Wall Street. Both locations have underground water supply tunnels. National Guard forces, our local bomb squad, and specialists from the Center for Disease Control and Prevention are already in both locations. It's under control."

With a smile as wide as the Grand Canyon, Levine jumped up and said, "That's huge, Frank!"

Relief swept through the room, as Laura and I hugged, while Ari and Wendy embraced, jumping up and down. Jaab came to shake my hand.

"We're not totally out of the woods yet," I emphasized.

"Of course, Stone," Levine said. "We still have all the famous historical Manhattan landmarks to protect."

It was now 3:35 p.m. and I had a hunch.

"Hey people, how can we find out the location of the USS Harry S. Truman aircraft carrier ship right now?"

"I'm not sure, but why do you ask, Stone?" Levine questioned. "Let me think about that. Laura, our resident researcher, what can you find out for us about the ship? Any articles? Can you do a few searches?"

Laura was like a child in a candy store, as she dove into her laptop. In less than six minutes, she spotted something and gasped.

"What is it?" I asked.

"I plugged in 'Peace Day in Hiroshima.' Here is an announcement that the USS Harry S. Truman is now in the Hiroshima Port Ujina Terminal to take part in the annual Japanese vigil, the Hiroshima Peace Memorial Ceremony. Every year at 8:15 a.m. a silent prayer takes place and the Peace Bell rings as a symbol of peace to honor the souls of those killed by the atomic bomb and to pray for eternal peace on earth. The announcement says that the USS Harry S. Truman will release fifty doves in solidarity with the citizens of Hiroshima, all at the same exact time."

"That's a beautiful gesture," Wendy said.

We all agreed. However, it was shocking to learn that the ship was docked so near to Hiroshima.

"Peace ceremony, my ass," Ari commented.

Levine paced around the room. I had this sick feeling engulf my head and stomach.

"What do you say, Stone?" Levine asked.

"I'll bet my life that Konar has planned some attack on the USS Harry S. Truman at eight-fifteen a.m. sharp, Japan time." Meaning, we need to figure this out before eight-fifteen p.m. tomorrow with the time difference."

Levine decided to call one of his contacts over at the U.S. Navy to have the captain of the ship double check for explosives on board. In fact, they needed to find out if anyone from Hiroshima had come on board in the last few days. Levine received a response to his request as his contact with the Navy called and he answered it on speaker phone.

"Ship docked in the port of Hiroshima three days ago," the contact said. "A dingy went ashore to Hiroshima Port Ujina Terminal to unload provisions and supplies. Yesterday, three representatives from Hiroshima's city council went aboard the USS Harry S. Truman with special foods and gifts for the captain and crew."

"Get the names of those three who went aboard the ship," I whispered to Levine. "Better yet, ask your contact, if Konar was among any of those three who came aboard and signed in?"

Levine requested the information.

His contact answered, "Yes, Konar did sign in."

"Does anyone recall if Konar left the group, perhaps to the bathroom or whatever?" Levine asked.

"Konar and his two representatives requested a tour of the ship," the contact replied. "They appreciated the tour, then lunch was served with the captain. It was noticed that Konar went to the bathroom two times during their short visit on the ship—a bit unusual for such a young man."

"That's it, that's it!" Levine exclaimed. "Emergency—check the ship's bathroom and other areas for explosives. Repeat, possible bomb or explosive device on board."

"Roger that, we'll do a full check aboard right now."

Just then, the police chief, John Krieger immediately called Levine's cell and he kept it on speaker.

"What's up, sir?" Levine asked.

"You already know the George Washington Bridge is history," Krieger said. "All other bridges and tunnels are now secure. We are left to deal with the Manhattan buildings and historical landmarks, which are not yet under control. We'll keep you in the loop."

"Guys, things are finally looking better," Levine said. "But it is now August fifth and it's four-fifteen p.m. It's getting much too close for comfort.

Another call came in, this time from the captain of the USS Harry S. Truman. We all anxiously listened in.

"You were correct," the captain said, "Thanks for the tip. Sure enough, a huge explosive device was found in the bathroom just off the lunch room. This bomb was more than enough to sink the ship. We're okay now. You guys at HPAT 21 saved over three thousand lives, you are truly the best. Thank you again."

My mind began working overtime. I once again revisited the wedding night of Ammi's daughter. Ashton had helped me to remember the phrase that Laura and I overheard while walking to the car, "Kill the chickens in the pen." Previously, I did not trust my instincts, but now I was convinced that the "pen" had to be Penn Station. So many solid reasons pointed back to it. Ammi had mentioned before the symbolic meaning it had to the Islamic extremists. And the germ canisters had been recovered from the water supply below it. Not to mention that it was possibly the busiest location with little or no security in the One Penn Plaza parking garage.

I was one thousand percent sure that Penn Station was at serious risk. I knew that it was a prime target. I had another flashback as I remembered the room in Ammi's house after the wedding. I recalled the large picture of King Salman of Saudi Arabia hanging on the wall. As I thought of it now, I wondered who the hell we were fighting and who the real enemy could be. Were we fighting the Iranians, the Saudis, ISIS, or maybe another splinter group trying to compete in their world of terrorism? Could the same terrorists from 9/11 be at it again?

I expressed my concerns over Penn Station to my team, focusing on my suspicions that the Saudis were trying to pull off another 9/11. Levine immediately responded by contacting Police Chief Krieger again. I suggested that the police should search all vehicles parked at the One Penn Plaza parking garage immediately. Krieger dispatched K9 police units to sniff out the explosives. My watch showed that it was now 4:55 p.m. I'd have to deal with the issue of who was the real enemy later.

Right now, it was a waiting game. We had done everything in our power to prevent a disaster. So far, we were lucky. But time was against us, especially if an explosion was about to take place during the early morning commute when thousands of people would be traveling to work.

CHAPTER 36

Finally, Levine received a text at 6:05 p.m. from Krieger, reading it out loud for us. "Penn Station is all clear, no explosives found."

"What about the parking lot?" I asked in disbelief.

"What does he mean, 'Didn't think about checking that,' . . . is he stupid?" Levine yelled as he texted a reply.

Levine sighed as he read Krieger's reply, "He wants clearance to search the Penn Plaza parking lot."

Levine called Krieger yet again at the risk of telling the police chief what to do, but he made the call anyway to double check.

"Hey Krieger, it's Levine again. A few of our men here want clearance to inspect the Penn Plaza parking garage. They seem to have a hunch. Can you set that up and fast?"

Levine paused as he listened. He soon nodded to us, indicating Krieger had confirmed.

We were pacing and pacing as the minutes passed without a return call from Krieger. It was 6:18 p.m. The silence was deafening—no more calls, no texts, nothing. Beads of sweat were accumulating and spilling over my eyebrows. Ari, the cool and calm one, was walking in circles, squatting in between walking. Wendy and Laura were holding hands. Jaab suddenly stood up, about to speak. He was interrupted as a call came in on Levine's cell at last.

Levine listened, then spoke, "Okay, great Krieger, it's a go!"

"Listen to me, please," Jaab interrupted assertively. "I have been around cars my whole life. I've been driving a taxi for the past twenty years. I cannot explain it, but I have a sense of when a car is out of place, looks a bit weird or suspect. I am requesting to go there to help with the search. Mr. Levine . . . please allow me to go."

Levine nodded his head in approval.

"Don't forget there is still a curfew out there. I'll set it up for all of you," Levine said. "Stone, you should go with him. You're the one who pieced all the details together. Maybe you could be useful at the scene if you're up for it."

"I'll go with Jaab," I replied. "After all, I brought him here from Toronto—it's my duty to be with him. Anyway, this Penn Plaza parking lot is my hunch, my baby. I am convinced the parking garage, once exploded, will collapse into Penn Station—the real target. We cannot allow it to be blown away, it just cannot happen."

"Okay boys, your escorts will drive you both over to the One Penn Plaza parking lot in two minutes," Levine said. "After you've searched through the various floors of the parking lot, you will be escorted outside to street level. At that point, survey the parked cars outside. With the police and the bomb squad already in place, you'll have plenty of backup."

Wendy turned on the television just before Jaab and I left as a news alert appeared.

"The siege on our city continues from last night," the reporter began. "I'm so sorry to report that Carnegie Hall has just been attacked. An unidentified car parked outside exploded with such great force that this treasured New York City landmark crumbled within moments of the blast. Thanks to the mandatory city-wide curfew, no one was injured."

We shut the door behind us as we left in an HPAT 21 Jeep. On the car ride to Penn Station, I checked my watch yet again. It was now 6:58 p.m. Levine texted me and I read it aloud to Jaab: "A specialist from the NYC bomb squad will meet you at the One Penn Plaza parking garage."

"Okay sure, Levine", I texted back.

The rest of our ride was filled with enormous pressure and silence.

***

We pulled into the lot at exactly 7:15 p.m. not really knowing how to begin.

"There are multiple floors," I said to Jaab. "How the hell are we going to do this?"

"Let's drive quickly to each level," Jaab replied. "Give me a few minutes on each floor, depending on what we see."

"Okay, let's go."

Jaab steered the Jeep down to the lower levels first.

"These assholes love to blow up foundations to crumble buildings, so go all the way down to the bottom."

Jaab did not respond, he was too focused on the cars around us.

"We'll work our way back up," I suggested.

Just then, the bomb squad approached us. I explained our strategy, so they followed along with us. We drove in slow circles through the lower parking levels. Jaab had no comments yet, but he appeared discouraged.

"Keep going," I encouraged him calmly.

"See that?" Jaab said, pointing. "Check out that gray car over there in the corner."

"Why, Jaab, what's up?"

"I don't know," Jaab replied. "It's that gray 2012 Toyota Camry."

The bomb squad moved closer with the K9 unit just ahead of them. The dogs showed no reactions.

"Nothing," Jaab shook his head.

"Okay, let's keep going," I said. But after two more minutes, I lost patience. "Times up on this level, Jaab." I said, looking at the Jeep's clock.

"Okay," He replied, driving up one level.

We were still driving in slow circles, creeping along at five miles per hour. Jaab suddenly jammed on the breaks to stop the car. He jumped out like a dog on a scent.

"What are you looking at now?" I asked, stepping out of the Jeep.

"This car is a Honda Civic and has a sticker on it," Jaab replied.

382 • ERIC J. ENGELHARDT

"I see a pattern to what you've been doing. You're looking at Japanese cars. Do you really think they would be so stupid?" I asked.

"I have no idea," he replied, brushing me off.

There was no reaction from the bomb squad dogs as they searched around the vehicle's perimeter.

"Come on, Jaab," I said. "Let's go. We have one more level and we still need time to go outside."

"Okay, sorry."

Finally, we were back to the main level of the parking garage. There were only four parked cars.

Jaab was in deep focus as he once again pointed, "See those four cars, one car is parked about two feet further back than the other three."

He got out to take a closer look. It was now 7:48 p.m. and the pressure in my head was beyond the maximum.

I instructed Jaab; "You walk left to check out those two cars and the one car you feel is parked too far back from the others. I'll go right to take a look at these two. He went left, and I walked around to the right to inspect the cars. The first vehicle was a black Volvo SUV.

Jaab yelled out, "Bob, here, here, please."

It was another Honda Civic, year 2011. The car had a sticker on the rear window of some nonsense about peace and bells. I took a closer look and connected the dots. I remembered that at the Hiroshima Peace Memorial Ceremony they always rang the Peace Bell as a symbol of love and remembrance. There were too many coincidences, this *had* to be it.

"Jaab, amazing work. This has to be, this better be the one," I said nervously.

I shouted to the bomb specialists, "Hey, over here, now, now."

"No worries," Jaab reassured. "That is definitely the vehicle this time."

"Bring the dogs to that car, fast," I shouted out.

The bomb squad dogs went crazy with nonstop barking, forcefully lunging toward the car. The dogs' teeth were grinding tightly together at the car's trunk. That had to be it. The bomb squad unit took over first, waiving us all away. Our job was done here. The car was disarmed in a matter of minutes. It was now 8:03 p.m.

I collapsed to the ground onto my stomach, crying and kissing the dirty parking lot floor. I rolled over onto my back, stretched my arms and legs out, yelling and laughing and screaming again. Jaab collapsed down next to me. Now both on our backs, we shook hands in the air, exhaling deeply in relief, gazing at the ceiling in disbelief that we were victorious. My cell phone beeped with a call from Levine as I answered it on speaker.

"Congratulations… both the Penn Plaza parking garage and Penn Station are all clear. It's eight-ten p.m. and there's a special report on the BBC right now that I want you guys to hear. Something is happening. Listen up, here it is."

"Good morning. This is John Gardner reporting from Hiroshima for the BBC. I've been covering the annual Hiroshima Peace Memorial Ceremony for the last few years. It's an annual tradition, a very special day of remembrance. Every year at exactly eight-fifteen a.m., the Peace Bell rings to reflect on this horrific date, when the United States of America dropped the first atomic bomb at this moment on August sixth, nineteen-forty-five, on Hiroshima. The ceremony is intended to allow reflection and prayer for the lost souls who perished on that day.

"However, today's honoree, Konar Togaki is nowhere to be found. As a descendant of one of the highest-ranking generals of the Imperial Japanese Army who surrendered bringing World War Two to an end, Konar, as he is known, was going to speak here this morning about peace and forgiveness.

"Hushed suspicions were spreading frantically as the crowd began to grow uneasy on what was supposed to be a peaceful day."

I was in shock Konar was a no show. *That Konar is a lot smarter than we gave him credit for,* I thought. Levine said nothing and Jaab's celebrating had ceased as he lay still, no doubt in shock as well.

"I have a theory," I said. "Konar must have been informed that his scheme was falling apart. But that had to be yesterday with the time difference between Japan and New York. Must have been that Jason Cumberland who had tipped off Konar before being captured by the FBI."

"Makes sense, Stone," Levine remarked. "Damn it, bad break for us!"

"What do you mean?"

"We have snipers in place ready to take Konar down," Levine replied. "It would have looked like some crazy person in the local audience killed him."

We could hear John Gardner begin to speak again.

"In another twist, an American aircraft carrier, the USS Harry S. Truman, made a special trip to honor the day. This is especially fitting, as it was the order of the then American President, Harry S. Truman, to drop the bomb. The USS Harry S. Truman arrived to Hiroshima's Port Ujina Terminal a few days ago. While the ceremony was performed, and the Peace Bell rang at eight-fifteen a.m., fifty doves were simultaneously released under orders from the ship's captain. Minutes later, an explosion in the captain's quarters ripped through the ship. Over three hundred sailors and crew members were injured, resulting in five deaths. The captain and his fellow officers remain alive. The ship is unable to return since extensive repairs are needed.

"Back in the States, the great-grandson of former President Harry S. Truman, Wesley Truman, has been reported missing for days, according to a filed official missing person's report. The FBI is investigating this series of unfortunate events to determine if there are possible links to acts of terrorism."

The BBC anchor offered one final note. "The American Secretary of State wrapped up his appearance before Congress. He continues to push, on behalf of the president, for expanding the nuclear deal with Iran, recently agreed to on July 14, 2015."

Levine came back on the line again and screamed, "Did you hear all that?"

"Yes, I did, and I feel like throwing up," I replied as a call beeped through. "Hey Levine, Laura just called me. I need to go. Talk later."

"Hey, Bob, are you alright?" Laura asked after I had switched over.

"Am I alright, you ask? I'm not really sure. What's up over there?"

"Listen to this," Laura explained. "The partners of the law firm who were arrested and promised reduced jail sentences from the U.S. Department of Justice . . . they of course lost their law licenses. Anyway, in exchange, they told the FBI everything they knew. The foreign investors in The Shirango Group, LLC were the Iranians whose objective was to destroy the bridges, monuments, and other historical landmarks in Manhattan and in the process to blame these acts of terror on another regime. As to the Narico Group, those investors were all from Japan and they did, in fact, purchase those two buildings in the meat packing district in Manhattan. The purchase of these properties was done internally through the law firm's escrow account on a hush hush approach. It's crazy how interconnected everything is . . . Bob, are you there?"

"Yes, thanks. You've been great, thanks so much Laura," I replied and hung up.

I took a deep breath and rose to my feet, dusting off my shirt and pants. I wondered where Kandallah could be hiding now and under which new alias he was using. I thought of Konar, who was unaccounted for, knowing full well that he would resurface down the road with another evil plan. And I was also curious about Evelyn's recovery. My cell phone rang again.

"Hello, Stone here," I was joking, as it was the ring tone set up for Levine.

"Let's have lunch together. We need to talk."

"Come on, Levine, give me a break, I'm wiped out."

"It's beyond important, Stone."

"Well, give me a hint. What's it about?"

"Okay, I just received a report from the Banco de México's supervisor at its headquarters in Mexico City. Yesterday, five hundred million was transferred from a nonprofit account in that branch to a bank in

Reykjavík, Iceland, the same bank where Scott tracked down Korbachi's recent transfers. Stone, this new case has your name on it. Better brush up on your Spanish."

"Levine, I need to go back to the hotel, take a shower, chill out, and then I'll break bread with you. I hope all our comrades can meet us at this great Mexican restaurant called La Esquina. How fitting, Mexican food . . . really authentic, you'll love it."

"You're beginning to sound like me, Stone, perfect idea, see you there, *amigo.*"

"Oh, Levine, when do I head out for Mexico City?" I asked.

"Wendy booked you and your team on a flight from JFK to Mexico City International Airport. You leave tomorrow night," he replied.

"Team, what team?"

"You're going with Ari, Scott, and Jaab," Levine answered. "Oh, I have to tell you, the president called me twenty minutes ago. He congratulated our department for saving the lives of millions of New Yorkers and fellow Americans."

"Better call the president back and tell him to be careful about which countries and regimes he chooses to make deals with—I mean nuclear deals," I said sarcastically.

"I hear you, tax man, loud and clear," Levine sniped.

***

I drove back to the hotel with Jaab, dozing off in the passenger seat from utter exhaustion as my stomach wound begged me to rest. Upon arriving and escorted up by an HPAT 21 guard, we found Laura in the living room with Wendy. We all greeted one another near the doorway with embraces of relief.

Yet, I couldn't shake the feeling that there are still a few missing pieces in this puzzle. *I cannot yet put it all together. . . . I feel something has gone awry.*

"What are you thinking about Bob?" Laura asked.

"I need to gather my thoughts, but thanks Laura. You know, it's time to change the subject. Enough is enough, right?" I suggested. "Obviously you're done with that law firm and out of a job. Where do you go from here? What are you going to do next?" I asked her.

"Now that's a great question," she replied. "You're right, Bob. Let's stop thinking for a few moments about evil acts designed to destroy humanity. Ya know, ever since this journey started to unravel, I've wondered to what extent other law firms engage in the unethical use of their escrow accounts to conceal questionable activities. So, to answer your question, I've decided to investigate this further, write an article about my findings, and submit it to the American Bar Association. One thing we both have learned from this experience is that life is a journey. Who knows, just maybe my research will take me to places in the legal community that I could never have imagined."

"Yeah, and possibly get you killed. By the way, you should think about doing your legal research on the misuse of law firm escrow accounts for HPAT 21. We need all the help we can get."

She gave me a searing look of displeasure and turned her head away, then looked back again at me out of the corner of her eye. I knew I had planted a seed.

"How about this—just maybe I can become a legal analyst for some network news program covering legal issues," she replied.

"Wow, you were always amazing at turning a lemon into lemonade," I said. "I wish you all the best, Laura." I gave her a warm hug, whispering into her ear, "Keep HPAT 21 in mind."

Levine entered the room with an air of accomplishment.

"Lunch for everyone at twelve-thirty sharp," he announced. "Stone's picking the place this time."

"Hey, let's go for a walk, do some shopping, anything. We've been in this hotel far too long," Wendy suggested.

"I agree," Laura replied. "Let's go."

The rest of us stayed behind. It was time for a much-needed break, some rest, a shower, and time to chill.

***

As the steamy hot water engulfed my body in the shower, the pieces of the puzzle came together. Our leaders wanted a nuclear deal with Iran and right under our nose, the Iranians attack America in secrecy, insulated under the Shirango Group entity. We know how the Iranians operate; they delegate their missions to other groups to carry out their objectives.

I wondered, *Could it be possible that their game plan was to have America blame another country, maybe even ISIS, for the attacks in Manhattan?* This might not have made sense, as I recalled reading that the Iranians had supported ISIS to weaken Iraq, which would be in Iran's best interests. Whatever it was, I smelled a diversion.

I had to talk with Ari. He would have a better handle on this subject, being our Middle East expert. I dried off, got dressed, and saw him in the other room.

"Hey, Ari, we need to review this whole mess. You are our Middle East guru. What's the end result of this episode?" I asked.

"What do you mean," Ari asked.

"Why all the secrecy with the investor groups and these entities created as a buffer? Who were the Iranians trying to set up? That's the way they work, isn't it?"

"Absolutely, let's get Levine in on this.

"Not a bad idea."

Ari and I found Levine in another room wrapping up a phone call.

"What's up guys?" he asked after hanging up.

"I'm trying to resolve something. There must have been a few terrorists who were captured. Where are they from?" I queried.

"That is a critical question," Levine answered. "The FBI and the U.S. Department of Homeland Security are looking into this as we speak."

"Hold on," Ari said. "Let me interrupt you guys. I was informed by Israeli Mossad intelligence that the Iranians were trying to deceive America. I found this out while you and Jaab were hunting down the bomb together. I was going to tell you this during lunch."

"What does that mean, 'deceive America'?" Levine inquired.

"The Iranians wanted America to believe that the historical buildings in Manhattan were attacked by the Saudis," Ari responded.

I had to speak up. "Isn't this a perfect scheme? After all, the pilots who smashed into the World Trade Center on 9/11 were all Saudis. This would justify the idea that the Saudis were doing a repeat performance of invading the homeland once again. The Iranians wanted to instigate America to do their dirty work by triggering us to retaliate against Saudi Arabia."

Levine confirmed, "Sure, this would leave Iran as the most dominant force in the Middle East...that's the Iranians for you, stealth evildoers, delegating their acts of terror around the globe to other players. Thank you for this priceless information, Ari. I'll reach out to my contacts to inform them immediately."

"Thanks for taking this into consideration, Levine," I said. "There is more that needs to be mentioned. The attempted bacterial attack by Konar and his Japanese extremists, that's a more simplistic scenario. They had one mission: to kill as many Americans as was possible, starting in Manhattan. A mission based upon honor and revenge. Unfortunately, Konar is still unaccounted for, and he'll resurface someday. A scary thought."

"Agreed," Levine replied. "We need to stay on our toes and track him down. We'll talk more at lunch."

Levine and Ari walked outside, and I sat down in the cushy chair next to the window overlooking the city streets. I was still dwelling on the discussion regarding the Saudis and Iranians. My mind shifted to Evelyn's progress in the hospital. Levine had to be reminded to look out for her. I would check with him after lunch. I had a momentary need to escape the insane events of the past twenty-four hours.

I clicked on the television and searched for some harmless news. I settled on something about a warm weather pattern approaching the Northeast. *Of course, it's August, so what's new,* I thought. A special news report interrupted the weather.

"The president of the United States is calling for a thorough investigation into the acts of terror in New York. He will ask Congress to consider a vote for a formal declaration of war against the country or group who supported and harbored the perpetrators. The president wishes to normalize America's relations with Iran. As an added incentive, once the expanded nuclear deal is agreed upon, all previously frozen Iranian assets will be released."

The news put me on edge. How could our leadership be so naïve to even consider a deal with Iran, a country who seeks to destroy America and Israel? My nervous energy led me to begin organizing my clothes for Mexico City. I quickly lost patience and felt like I needed to do something more valid. I had a need to pray, realizing how lucky we were, *this time*. A tremendous urge to walk around Manhattan emerged. It was clear that I had to embrace the city streets, the people, and the buildings we just saved from disaster. As I slipped on my sneakers, I noticed the inside label, *Hecho en Mexico.* I laughed, thinking....*what an appropriate coincidence.*

I took a long walk downtown and I stumbled upon one of the oldest synagogues in Manhattan. There it was, the Museum at Eldridge Street, a restored historic synagogue. I looked up, then down, admiring the stained-glass windows and archways, the spires above, and the elegance of the structure that had been renovated to stay intact. Yet, an invisible barrier prevented me from entering. I wasn't up to it, so I walked away slowly, taking a few steps backward to show respect, my head bowed. I was disgusted with the evil in this screwed up world.

I looked up to the sky and asked, "How can this be? Why has this insanity been going on throughout history?"

A text came in from Levine, interrupting my frustrations. *Stone, come on, we're all waiting.*

Yes, I'll be right there. Just practicing my Spanish. . . . Un minuto.

He replied with a smiley face.

I walked faster, picking up my pace, now jogging toward the restaurant. On the way, I began testing my memory of Spanish words. I was gearing up for our next HPAT 21 assignment to follow the money trail around the globe. Although I was in New York, I began the shift into a Mexico City state of mind.

I had a sense that I was being followed, so I stopped jogging and turned around, only to see hundreds of people moving about, while impatient drivers were loudly honking their car horns in the congested city streets. I began walking cautiously, taking a few steps back ped-dling toward the restaurant. I spotted a bearded individual who took a sudden side step into the entranceway of a dollar store just as I caught his eye. Although I was unnerved by the thought of being watched, I reversed my walking to a normal pace, while trying to shrug off my paranoia with the logic that the man was likely an HPAT 21 guard.

I entered the restaurant and spotted our table in an intimate back room. As I got closer to the table, I was shocked and pleased to see Evelyn seated there with our entire HPAT 21 unit. She seemed weak yet in good spirits with her usual amazing smile. I made it just in time to join the toast, each holding a shot glass filled with tequila. I noticed the bottle and it was good stuff, Anejo Reposado, not just any tequila, it was aged tequila.

"Go ahead, Stone, you make the toast," Levine suggested.

The server passed me a shot glass. I paused, seizing the moment to dwell on just how dangerous our world had become. I made eye con-tact with each person at the table, Levine, Frank, Randy, Laura, Wendy, Ari, Ashton, Jaab, and Scott, who I was also surprised and happy to see again. My shot glass was filled up to the rim, so I held up my glass care-fully.

"Cheers, my friends, to life—and now let us pray for a safer world."

All the shot glasses rose in the air. I walked around the table clicking each and every person's glass. I toasted from my heart.

An image of my father appeared, who I knew would have been so proud of his son, who rediscovered the way, the *right* way, this time. Yes, I had risen from the depths down under, from a world where the code of honor, ethics, and goodwill was breached, from below the bot-tom line.

I was just about to sit down in my seat, yet I decided to remain standing for a few more precious seconds to soak up the feeling of this special moment. I chose to repeat the same toast in Spanish. The words somehow came to me and I said, *"a un mundo seguro."*

The room became silent, a pin drop probably could've been heard. The other patrons turned to me, stood up to join our toast with their drinks in hand raised high. One man began by thanking me in his native language, "gracias buen hombre."

Then, in unison, every person in the room, several from countries around the world, cheered and repeated once again,

"a un mundo seguro."

It was a beautiful scene, words spoken in one language, possibly not understood by all, the meaning however was clear enough; a simple wish, all together for a safer world and for peace on earth.

The End

Author's Notes

The following were historical facts used in this story:

Pg 46:
The Patriot Act: This was an Act of Congress signed into law on October 26, 2001 after the events of 9/11. The author added a fictional addendum to this law which authorized the IRS to form a secret unit called HPAT 21 to protect the Homeland. (HPAT 21- Homeland Protection Anti -Terror; add 9+11+01 = 21). This was the basis for dedicating the novel to the events of nine eleven.

Pg 68:
International Data Exchange Service (IDES): This is a real department in the United States Treasury which cooperates with over one hundred fifty countries to track the flow of funds in connection with terrorist activities.

Pg 69:
In 1861, President Abraham Lincoln signed the Revenue Act which established the first Federal Income Tax to help pay for the Civil War. Lincoln and Congress agreed to impose a tax of 3 percent tax on annual incomes over $800.

Pg 302:
Unit 731: The Japanese conducted lethal human biological experiments using diseases on about 7,000 prisoners of war in this covert unit located in the northeast city of Pingfang, Harbin-China. The purpose was to develop bacterial weapons for use during World War 11. Thousands of people died from these experiments.

See Next Page – About The Author

ABOUT THE AUTHOR

Eric J. Engelhardt is a certified public accountant, tax advisor, and a seasoned public speaker with a career spanning over thirty years. Eric has a penchant for history, specifically the American Revolution, the Civil War, and World War II. One of his hobbies is to collect old magazines. Eric feels that each periodical represents a snapshot back into history. *Below the Bottom Line* is his debut novel. He lives on Long Island in New York with his wife and family.

■■■

Eric is available to speak at seminars and book events. Go to: ericjengelhardt.com or call Eric directly at 631 495-4929

Follow Eric's upcoming events and updates about his soon to be released book two in the "Bob Stone Thriller Series."

Made in the USA
Middletown, DE
06 November 2019